TEXACO

Also by
PATRICK CHAMOISEAU

Creole Folktales

TEXACO

PATRICK CHAMOISEAU

TRANSLATED FROM THE FRENCH AND CREOLE BY
ROSE-MYRIAM RÉJOUIS AND VAL VINOKUROV

PANTHEON BOOKS
NEW YORK

Chamoiseau, Patrick.
[Texaco, English]
Texaco / Patrick Chamoiseau : translated from the French
and Creole by Rose-Myriam Réjouis and Val Vinokurov.
p.   cm.
ISBN 0-679-43235-3
I. Réjouis, Rose-Myriam.   II. Vinokurov, Val.
III. Title.
PQ3949.2.C45T4913   1997
843—dc20   96-26976

Random House Web Address:
http://www(uscp).randomhouse.com/

Book design by Julie Duquet

Printed in the United States of America
First American Edition
2   4   6   8   9   7   5   3   1

What will the scribe recall, who through herself already tells of the stern destiny of all these women forever condemned to pregnancies, who, in order to foresee the day's weather and figure out what labors to take on, are expert at deciphering the prophecies of the wind, of dusk, or of the misty halo which sometimes seems to ooze out of the moon; these women who, while fighting—as much as men—to survive, made what is known as a fatherland, and whom calendars reduce to a few noisy holidays, to a vainglory after which streets are named?

HECTOR BIANCIOTTI

The city was the sanctuary of the word, of the gesture and the geste,* of struggle.

You, game . . . are nothing but a city-blackman: that's where you have to speak from! . . .

ÉDOUARD GLISSANT

CONTENTS

TRANSLATORS' NOTE

In the original, the author's French translation usually follows any Creole sentence: wherever the author's translation diverges substantially from the meaning of the Creole, we have included our own footnoted version. We distinguish our footnotes from the author's by the use of brackets. Also, please note that an asterisk signifies the first appearance of a glossary item in the text.

T E X A C O

Milestones in Our Attempts to Conquer the City

To escape the night of slavery and colonialism, Martinique's black slaves and mulattoes will, one generation after the other, abandon the plantations, the fields, and the hills, to throw themselves into the conquest of the cities (which in Creole they call "*l'En-ville*").[1] These multiple assaults will end with the fractious creation of the district of Texaco and the ominous reign of a boundless city.

The Age of Longhouses and Ajoupas

At that time Caribs, Arawaks, French colonists, and the first African slaves lived in longhouses and shelters (called ajoupas) made from branches and leaves. Caribs and Arawaks are exterminated as slave sugar plantations appear and cities grow.

3000 B.C.E. to 1492	Galibis, Arawaks, Caribs occupy the Caribbean islands.
1502	Christopher Columbus arrives in Martinique.
1635	France definitively takes possession of Martinique and erects a fort, around which the city of Saint-Pierre will be built.
1667	Construction of Fort-Royal, which will bring about a second city: Fort-de-France. *Our great squatter districts will cluster around it. At this point the site of the future Texaco Quarter is but thickets and mangrove.*
1680	Mass importation of black African slaves.

---

[1][Translators' note: Literally, "the In-city." Hereafter rendered as a proper noun, "City," as in "New York." See author's footnote on page 386.]

THE AGE OF STRAW

Once the slave plantations fall apart, marking the beginning of the reign of large central factories, sugarcane straw covers Martinican hutches.

18— *Probable time of birth of Esternome Laborieux, the papa of Texaco's founder-to-be; he is a slave on a plantation near the city of Saint-Pierre.*

18— *Probable time of birth of Idoménée Carmélite Lapidaille, the mama of Texaco's founder-to-be; she is a slave on a plantation near the city of Fort-de-France.*

1848 *April 27:* Abolition of slavery decreed in the French colonies.
May 22: Slave rebellion in the city of Saint-Pierre forces Martinique's governor to decree the Abolition before the arrival of the official decision.

1853 The former slaves refuse to work in the fields and leave to settle in the highlands. Replacement is required for them: arrival of the first East Indian workers (coolies) into Martinique, to be followed by Africans (congos) and Chinese, and later (1875) Syrio-Lebanese merchants (syrians).

1902 *May 8:* Mount Pelée erupts, destroying the town of Saint-Pierre. More than 30,000 deaths.
Mass exodus toward Fort-de-France, where the first squatter districts appear.

THE AGE OF CRATE WOOD

When the precarious reign of the large sugar factories rises atop the ruins of the plantation system, hutches stand on crate debris.

19— *Probable time of Marie-Sophie Laborieux's birth; it is she who will found Texaco.*

1914   *August 3*: Germany declares war on France. Caribbean con-
                scripts are dispatched to the front: Somme, Verdun, Darda-
                nelles . . .

1928   *Probable year of the death of Idoménée Carmélite Lapidaille, the*
                mama.

1930   *Probable year of the death of Esternome Laborieux, the papa.*

1938   *Establishment of the oil company on the future site of the Texaco*
                Quarter.

1939   *September 3*: France declares war on Germany.
                September 19: Arrival of Admiral Georges Robert in Martinique,
                where he will enforce Vichy's repressive measures.
                Aimé Césaire publishes *Le Cahier d'un Retour au pays natal*
                (Notebook of a Return to the Native Land), the grand poetic
                roar of Negritude.

1940   *June 16*: France capitulates.
                June 18: General de Gaulle calls on the Résistance, a call which
                Martinicans hear. Martinique, under blockade, is starving.

THE AGE OF ASBESTOS[1]

As the sugar economy collapses, hutches are wrapped in asbestos.

1945   Aimé Césaire is elected mayor of Fort-de-France.

1946   *March 19*: Law establishing Martinique as a French province
                (département).

1950   *Marie-Sophie Laborieux's first settlement on the future site of*
                Texaco, and her first police expulsion.

---

[1][We use *asbestos* to designate what the author calls *fibrociment,* a cement mixed with asbestos.]

1959   *December 20–23:* Riots in Fort-de-France.
                  New waves of rural exodus to Fort-de-France. The site of Texaco
                  is invaded.

THE AGE OF CONCRETE

As the fall of economic production inaugurates the reign of the city, glorious con-
crete transforms shacks into villas.

1964   De Gaulle's trip to Martinique.

1980–83   *A road called Pénétrante West joins the neighborhood of Texaco*
                  to Fort-de-France. Messianic arrival of the urban planner in Tex-
                  aco. Beginning of the rehabilitation.

1985   *Meeting of Marie-Sophie Laborieux with the Word Scratcher, the*
                  one who makes books.

1989   *Death of Marie-Sophie Laborieux, who was "the Source."*

THE ANNUNCIATION

(in which the urban planner who comes to raze

the insalubrious Texaco Quarter instead

finds himself in a Creole circus and

faces a matadora's* word)

Ti-Cirique's Epistle to the Shamefaced
Word Scratcher: "At the task of writing,
more than a few might have seen my noble
pencil pointing to the Olympus of feeling with
many an elegant line, as suits a worthy gentleman; many might have seen me, *Universal
Man,* rise above the oxygen in the horizons, ex-
alting the depths of man's raison d'être, the
why of death, of love, and of God, in a French
more French than that of the French, but not at
all like you do it, you small pea lost in the pod
of the monkeying of your Creolity or in Texaco's decrepit asbestos walls. Forgive me,
Oiseau de Cham,* but you lack Humanism—
and especially grandeur."
Reply of the Pitiful One: Dear master, literature in a place that breathes is to be taken in
alive . . .

U pon his entrance into Texaco, the Christ was hit by a stone—an
aggression that surprised no one. In those days, truth be said, we
were all nervous: a road called Pénétrante West had joined our

Quarter to the center of City. That is why the ever-so-well-to-do from the depths of their cars had discovered our piled-up hutches which they said were insalubrious—and such a spectacle seemed to them contrary to the public order.

But, if they stared at us, we certainly stared back. It was a battle of eyes between us and City, another battle in a very ancient war. And in that war a cease-fire had just been broken, for the construction of that road could only bring a police crackdown to make us clear off; and we waited for that assault every minute of every day, and amid this nervousness the Christ made his appearance.

Iréné, the shark catcher, saw him first. Then Sonore, the câpresse,* hair whitened by something other than age, saw him come. But only when Marie-Clémence, whose tongue, it is true, is televised news, appeared was everyone brought up to speed. Looking at him, one thought of one of those agents from the modernizing city council which destroyed poor quarters to civilize them into stacks of projects, or of one of those bailiffs from the old dirt-poor days who would enjoin us to disappear. That's probably why he was hit by the stone and lost that bit of blood which slid along his cheek. So who threw the stone? The answers to this question were so abundant that the real truth forever slipped through our fingers. Every leap year on Sunday evenings, we'd suspect the most terrible of Texaco's inhabitants: one nicknamed Julot the Mangy, who fears nothing but the return of his dead mama on earth. But, as soon as that cruel unbaptized mother who had scorched his childhood was six feet under, Julot had taken the precaution of securing her coffin beneath the seven invincible knots of a hanged man's rope. Feeling confident because of that precaution, he braved death, took God for one of his rummies, never bowed to fate. When chance sent him to us, to Texaco, he protected us from City villains and became a Boss whose benevolence covered only those who looked up at his balls—I mean: only his vassals. At each police onslaught, you could see him in the front row under a hail of billy clubs. All this to say that he was always ready with stone, acid, or blade, and on his own initiative, to welcome undesirable guests in a most brutal way.

But let's not lose the thread here—let's go back to the story stitch by stitch, and if possible one stitch before the other. We'll start with Iréné . . .

THE CHRIST'S COMING ACCORDING TO IRÉNÉ

On that day, the shark catcher, my man Iréné, you know, had gotten up in the darkness, as the harvesting of these monsters required. Getting early to the sea, to the place where his Styrofoam floats signaled his bait, saved him from having to come home with nothing but the gnawed-up cartilage of hooked sharks. Having gulped down his coffee, he would stand up in the clean pre-dawn wind, then scrutinize his dreams which revealed the day's catch. He would call out to me from his doorstep the fish he would hook that day and confirm it on his return. That morning, his dreams were not prophetic. They held only the random ravings induced by Neisson rum. Three-quarters of the hour the sea gives up nothing for the bait. So Iréné went on his way without any swagger, already pondering where to dirty his secondhand mason's trowel after the fishing. He brought the oars, the fuel can, and the motor from his lean-to, dumped all of that in a wheelbarrow, and went up the Pénétrante toward his plastic gum-tree canoe, subsidized by our regional council development experts.

Along his way, he saw the Christ. The latter was just walking, nose in the wind, dazed, scrutinizing our shacks and their assault on the timorous cliffs. There was some repugnance in his stride. The stiffness in his bones spoke of his confusion. Iréné understood in a heartbeat: this strange visitor was coming to question the usefulness of our insalubrious existence. So Iréné looked at him as if he were a bag of flies dressed up as a man. The Christ did not see him or pretended not to and continued down the Pénétrante into Texaco.

. . .

Iréné rejoined his canoe where his crew awaited him: a dreadlocked waif, blindfolded by dark glasses, lost in the yellow phosphorescence of a navy oilskin. It was Joseph Granfer. They went about their shark business without Iréné even mentioning his deplorable meeting.

They didn't have to do much thinking before finding their line today. With Joseph balancing the canoe with his oar, Iréné grasped the horsehair thread with the irresistible power of his twenty-five years of making the same movements. My man Joseph is not tall like one of those Harlem basketball players, but he's not tiny either like those born under a low moon. He is thick like that, you know, arms toned by the weight of sharks, strong neck, thin legs, skin the peanut color of impassive chabins.* So he pulled-pulled with regular movements which coiled the horsehair line behind him. Without consulting each other, they were about to pull in hooks that looked silly with their untouched bait, but when the line began to resist, they were certain of a catch. Since Iréné remained somber, however, Joseph thought he was just bringing up one of those black sharks with satanic pupils that no Christian would wish to eat. When the line pulled, Iréné held it tight. When it got loose, he brought it back quick. He adjusted his strength to the resistance so as not to tear apart whatever was coming from the abyss.

Suddenly the line became loose-loose. Then as he was mulling, a twelve-year-old memory warned him of danger. Swift, he wound his line around one of the planks of the wharf and told Joseph to hold on. A tremendous quake jolted the world. The horsehair whistled like a crystal. The canoe began to glide faster than water off a duck's back. Joseph, astonished, held it back with the oars. This lasted a few seconds and then everything came to a standstill like an alizé* which suddenly dies.

Iréné began to haul in the thing with all his might, cautious centimeter by cautious centimeter. For four hours he yielded none of the hundred-and-twenty-meter thread. He became still at times, and the line, ready to break, sawed at his iron palms. He then murmured to the invisible enemy, It's me, you know me, Iréné Stanislas, child of Epiphanie of Morne* Etoile, and of Jackot, jabot-wearing mulatto dandy . . . The line then got loose. Iréné brought it back with the greatest care. He punctuated each bit won with a *yes* breathed out in effort and exultation. Soon the whiteness of the line heralded the fishhooks. Joseph left his oars to go harpoon a light-colored shark, then another, which had already drowned and whose gut had spilled, then a third with its jaws still moving, then a fourth. He almost passed out cold when the blue of the sky seemed to recede before the immeasurable mass. On its back, crucified on the last fishhook, the thing looked upon him with all the meanness in the world in its so small eyes.

If he could have, Joseph would have cried out, but the monster's pupils, though half submerged, had sucked out all of his soul. Above the left side of the canoe, he was crossing himself in a hurry like a Catholic about to dearly depart, his fingers tapering off at the end all confused. Behind him, Iréné was still bringing in the line when he noticed the inexplicable frenzy of his crew's right hand. Then our shark catcher, without even bending down to confirm his intuition, with an imperceptible gesture, that's how fast he was, and yes, with great calm, cut the line.

The sea opened before a departing strength, and then, exploding in concentric circles, its wake pushed the canoe toward some far corner of the earth. Joseph, freed from the charm, placed his Tonton Macoute shades on his nose and began to mill with his oars in the direction of dry land (full throttle).

Iréné was sitting in the back like a pope, using each side of the canoe for an armrest, a warrior's beatitude etched on his face, all the more easy to imagine since he wore that expression among us for a long time after that. When Joseph, reassured by the proximity of the cliffs of Case-Pilote, put down the oars to question him about the distressing encounter, Iréné answered pompously: My son, in the days to come you're going to have a really beautiful fight, in this harbor here there's a mean shark that'd eat us good . . . Saying that, he was trembling the way I tremble in anticipation of the fight I'll have to put up.

They sold the four sharks in a drip-drop: Iréné was going round with them on his wheelbarrow, absentminded as if he were already in the future battle which would pit him, like me, against some awful kind of shark. Joseph hailed the vendors, dealt out the slices, weighed them, and cashed in. Back home, this brought us the small joy of paying back four debts and of buying half a bag of cement to coat our façade. All of these things made my fisherman Iréné the first to suspect that the man he ran into this morning coming through Texaco did not grow out of a seed of misfortune as we so readily believed, nor was he the sign of a bad season. Nought but a battle. My great battle.

But, without getting all in a huff, let's see it through Sonore's eyes.

The Christ's coming according to Sonore

Annette Bonamitan, born Sonore, was Julia Etoilus's daughter. Her papa, a lay blackman,[1] holder of an incomprehensible certificate and a teacher's position in the commune* of Marigot, destroyed his career in some French World War I trench where none of us had sent him. I could tell the love story (in Cinemascope) between the instructed layman and the lady Etoilus who was ignorant even of the blank spaces between the twenty-six letters of the alphabet, but a detour would be risky.

---

[1][Chamoiseau uses the French word *nègre* (negro) in the Creole sense of "man." This is why we invent "blackman" to translate a word which is specific to the Creole lexicon, albeit not unrelated to the genealogy of "(my) nigger" as used in contemporary African American slang.]

.   .   .

Be that as it may, whatever it may be, their passion fathered our Annette who, one Saturday, married a ne'er-do-well called Jojo Bonamitan, though it would have been saner to swallow a toad that day.
There again, a detour would have been edifying (a casino dog, who
dissipated his life in an inferno of double-six, who got married every
nine months in different towns and under different names, so that
no one knew whether his real name was actually Jojo Bonamitan,
and who probably loaded his dice with lead or fixed his cards since
he'd always win money soon-spent, and who, avid for excitement,
went to play baccarat with a dirty zombie in a church with lightning
for its sole congregant, and who, as was his wont, cheated without
ever thinking that his adversary was the acme of vices, so that he
was certain of victory until his winning ten of diamonds turned into
a four of spades when it came time to show his hand, and so on until
Bonamitan bet his last underwear, his signet ring with the cross on it,
the blood of his left leg, then the memory of his baptism, the loss of
which transformed him into rotting flesh which the garbage collectors threw into the sea, having mistaken it for a dead rat . . .) but it's
not for me to say.

In any case, no death certificate ever came up (except maybe with
the barracudas who ate that filth). Unsure whether she was a widow,
or even whose widow she might be, Annette Bonamitan blared the
loudspeakers of thirteen sorrows from her chest. Thus she was heard
until her memory harvested some forget-a-little. Right away the
blackmen nicknamed her Sonore. That little name brought her back
to the surname of the lay blackman. Lord, all that stuff will be the
death of me . . .

But let's tackle the tragedy: the ne'er-do-well crapshooter (helped,
without his knowledge, by some shoulders-to-cry-on who took advantage) had left her some seven children whose insolence the
whitening of their mama's hair attested to day by day. Sonore always

tried to savor life before the little creatures got up in the morning. The sun was sending off the first of its rays to her open window. That filled the câpresse with a hypnotic optimism from which she drew strength for the daytime. Besides the calamity of impossible children, Sonore was facing the calamity of not having worked for a stretch of time which the ANPE* had lost track of in their calendars. The latter had been placed in the care of Parisian bureaus for a special study the results of which had been awaited for three years, ten months, two weeks, fourteen days, plus hours the distressing number of which would be tedious to mention here. Fighting back in her own way, she left her rented place at Terres-Sainville once it became probable that Bonamitan would no longer contribute to it. Like us, she had come to fence off a piece of land and erect a house in the shade of the Texaco oil company. At dawn she went into City for the maid's jobs in the compassionate hotels. She would reappear at the end of the afternoon to grill peanuts or sauté some corn flakes to sell to movie watchers later.

Ti-Cirique (a Haitian man of letters who peeled books, just settled in one of the Quarter's hutches) had composed two thousand and seven hundred employment applications addressed to the mayor of Fort-de-France. Knowing the mayor to be a poet and littérateur, Ti-Cirique had displayed a strategy which, although vain, nonetheless had extreme finesse. Sonore's life didn't appear too noble to him, so within each application our scribe had scattered sediments of a miserableness copied right out of Victor Hugo. Sonore's children, not really fit to be presented, in his opinion—and neither was their number, for that matter—he transformed into three fatherless angels poisoned daily by the milk of an unemployed breast. And finally he had peppered this delicate misery with chosen citations: For Roland is pious and Oliver is wise *(author unknown)*, Sorrow rides pillion and gallops toward him *(Boileau)*, Pain that keeps silent grows *(Racine)*, My heart, weary of hope, will at last no longer with its wishes importune fate *(Lamartine)*, The voice of time sounds sad for the abandoned heart *(De Vigny)*, Oh never insult a woman who falls *(Victor Hugo)*, Oh woe, woe, time is eating my life *(Baudelaire)* . . . We now knew about these because on her doorstep, with more wonder than conviction, Sonore often mumbled episodes xeroxed from this new life.

The city council had answered only with regrets. The social worker had only advised her about maneuvers for more welfare. As for the ANPE reception clerk, she gave her news about the calendars, then without any pretext went to seek cover behind the file cabinets. Sonore stood up to them as best she could, yielding only her eyes' youth, her hair's black color, and some invisible tears attested to only by the unusual hushes of her terrible children. (Better miserable than dead . . .)

Now, some time ago, Ti-Cirique had gotten an idea. He appeared at Sonore's window as if riding the clarity of the sun, his bald forehead electrified, his book-worn glasses on his nose. The Haitian had written one of his usual letters, embroidered this time with the following quotations: Indeed which of the two is the deeper, the more impenetrable: the ocean or the human heart?—Goodness, your name is man.—If I could but look through these angelic pages upon the face of the one who's reading me . . . Each accompanied by a little number which sent you back three pages, end-of-letter, for the name of the author: *Isidore Ducasse comte de Lautréamont*—some illuminatus[1] about whom the mayor had written in his youth.

The letter flew away like a last hope. The night before the Christ's coming and sooner than usual, Sonore received an answer from the city council in a letter which she found impossible to open. She put it on the table, a corner of it under the pot of flowers. She went out.

---

[1] Ti-Cirique calls "illumination" a chaotic multiplication of visions. Next to Lautréamont, Rimbaud, according to him, would weigh light as a school brat.

She came back. She held it to decode what was impossible to decode with her fingers and put it back a little heavier and denser. The white rectangle stamped with *City of Fort-de-France* sucked up all the house's hustle. Hearing their mama holler when they came near it incited the children to hover round. Their roughhousing ceased within inches of the tablecloth, then began again further off. The smaller ones would stop just short of it, with tears in their eyes to ward off the thing. Others took the deepest breath and threw themselves as if into the void with the sole goal of touching it. Sonore herself kept watch, came and went, dusted a piece of the table, filled the umpteenth glass of cool water for her bunch of hibiscus.

Sonore's sleep was a nightmare of letters with yellow beaks which fell upon her eyes, eyes bulging with fear. In it the mailman was a witch wearing clogs and other such atrocities. She ran out of bed to hope for the sun by her window. It came—it was magical: the whitened, revitalized câpresse stood ready to turn the world upside down. She crossed herself upon seeing my shark catcher Iréné fly on the bridge with his stuff: people in Texaco didn't think it very Christian for a fisherman to be so interested in sharks. Then, just like that, without any fateful rumbling, she caught a glimpse of the Christ. A bony silhouette—examining the ravine dozing under the bridge, our stilted houses in the slimy mangrove swamp, the old company's last trucks, then the cliffs—climbed by our leggy houses.

Sonore saw him as vanguard of a police crackdown and felt her anger rise. She was already spitting up thirteen curses when her eyes fell on the letter. In the same breath, she caught it, opened it, unfolded it, and was about to give sound to her sorrows on her doorstep when she read it in one blip-of-a-glance, *Dear Madame Bonamitan, In reply to your letter dated July twelfth 1980, it gives us great pleasure to inform you that you will be granted a position in the office which the urban services of the said city council will establish. We would appreciate if you would present yourself to the bu-*

reau of personnel as soon as possible to fill out your employment forms. Sincerely . . . Sonore remained open-mouthed with the curses now dying on her lips. Her fist raised with rage fell back down like a soft vine. In the fog of her joy, she had seen the Christ flinch from that first stone. It weighed heavily upon her, for she had understood on reading the letter that he was not inaugurating any kind of Egyptian plagues for us.

But no speeding on slippery roads: here's what Marie-Clémence has to say about it.

THE CHRIST'S COMING ACCORDING TO MARIE-CLÉMENCE

The truth is, Marie-Clémence had detected the Christ before everyone. And if one should pay heed to her words, before he even came she knew he was coming. It wasn't any sort of oracle, just nosiness, that made Marie-Clémence now able to tie everything together in her vicious memory. She was able to look at the world with great astonishment and see what no one else saw. She could decipher the murkiest eye and link a quivering lip to a broken heart. She could catalog all life's struggles shaking through the Quarter, for the benefit of the whole wide world. Through her, we learned for example that a bright and early morning departure with a small suitcase and eyes too downcast announced the shipwreck of a Catholic love on the abortionist's table. In other words, with her in our Quarter of Texaco, a life without witnesses, like life downtown, was a difficult wish. All was known of all. Miseries shouldered miseries. Commiseration intervened to fight despair and no one lived in the anxiety of extreme loneliness.

Ti-Cirique had declared one day that according to the Illustrated Larousse Dictionary, we were—in French—a communauté. Well, in this community, the chocolate wafer of communion was Marie-

Clémence. If her tongue was something else (it went on and on even on holidays) her way of being, of saying hello, and of asking you about everything had an exquisite sweetness. Without any meanness, in the most natural way, she exposed the intimacy of lives to the sentinel of curiosity. No one wishing to be more exposed than anyone else, everyone fed Marie-Clémence with the choicest morsels of the lives of others. The equilibrium being thus respected, she became our beneficial glue, dispensing just enough bitterness to make life passionate.

This mulatto woman, in the days of yesteryear, was doubtless a fiendish beauty. In the hour of the Christ, she seemed a featherless fallen angel. She wore her straw-colored hair in a braid down her back. Old age refusing to wrinkle her extra-thin skin, the color of damp straw, had conferred upon her a texture of eternity. Her translucent fingers lengthened into many gold rings. In the sun her eyes took on the shade of Creole sugarcane glazed by dryness. And her lips, ah, pink, still full despite the folds of time, reflected the unsettling backroom of her youth—true mirrors of true felicities. These lips (if one was to believe Carolina Danta, the devout church-roach who lived with us) put the final touches on her legend as an angel exiled from the sky as a result of sins committed with her mouth.

Such rumor remained, of course, pure supposition: inexhaustible about others, Marie-Clémence was mute about herself, as if her life had only begun in the shade of Texaco's trunks. When she washed up among us to build the Quarter, she was already wearing the mantle of an angelic old age and of her strange legend, but she was a bit silent and absent. It wasn't until our Quarter defied the oil béké,* City, and the police that, just as in her youth, life would astonish her once again.

So, coming out bright and early to empty her tub, she glimpsed our Christ when that fisherman of mine, Iréné, was still waking up. At that moment of truth her fantasy begins: seeing the bony silhouette, she affirms finding herself in the situation of the prophet John the Baptist, who in the River Jordan saw the son of the Good News appear. The truth is that Texaco's Christ was not yet Christ. He was coming there in the name of the city council to *renovate Texaco*. In his scientific language that really meant: to *raze* it. Furthermore, Marie-Clémence was probably busier cleaning out her tub than taking hold of this vision of a make-believe silhouette attended by a dove (she's really going too far with the dove—since nobody's ever seen one in these parts). And it's even less probable that the fellow was crowned by the usual lightning which accompanies all events of world salvation. Letting her tell her story out of respect for her age, we still praised the exaltation of her melancholic brain at the arrival of the one who—from having heard me out and without any hallelujahs—would become our Savior.

THE CHRIST'S ENCOUNTER WITH THE OLD BLACKMAN OF THE DOUM

In fact, Marie-Clémence had felt that an event of great importance would take place before our nine lives were up. Looking for the first signs, she had concentrated on Iréné's procession behind his cart, then on Sonore's shutters hoping for the sun. Her formidable intuition was soon arrested by an unfamiliar walking silhouette. She thought best to sound the alar-r-r-u-mm. Now one must know that Marie-Clémence could work wonders. In no time she could scuttle around to sixteen households. She could make the thirty-three coolie winds going through the partitions pregnant with messages. She could release silent tocsins into deep dreams, hang whispers to shutters, make her tongue echo in keyholes, transform a room's quiet into buzzing bees. Thus, she scudded back up the ravine, door to door, up to the waterfall which plowed the cliff, then cried havoc in Upper Texaco. She said: Fire! Fire!—A sure way of announcing life's burns.

• • •

That alarm provoked what they called in the hills one exquisite kettle of fish. Though thirty-two nightmares were fortunately shattered, twelve sweet dreams were aborted under anxiety's needle. Some children shed untimely tears. The men became stiff and silent. Some women howled, coarser ones became torches of Creole insults. Our first impulse was to leave our homes, then return to them and proceed with the measures learned from multiple police raids: wrap anything fragile, hide the money in our deepest pockets, swaddle our papers in blankets, spread the children into all of the houses since the police might hesitate to break into an innocent home . . . But it suddenly became clear that the police were not there. The air was not heavy with the catastrophic agitation of booted panting, threats, and orders. Only the silence of the insignificant dawn and somewhere on the bridge the squealing (an eternal instant) of the Christ hit by the stone.

All descended upon the struck-down body. Preoccupied with distributing the children among all the houses, I had stayed in the haven of the hills, but I've heard the story so often that I sometimes doubt my own absence when I start telling it. All Texaco gathered around the body and the stone. There was anxiety. Believing the fellow to be murdered, the killer-quarter pictured itself wiped off the map by an upcoming police reprisal. The men[1] remained indecisive in a reverie. On the other hand, women[2] proposed to scald the body, to bag it, to toss the bag in some anonymous old gasoline drum, and to drown the whole thing in a seventh wave by the coasts of Mexico. To that

---

[1]Fishermen who were late, jobbers at work, the port's longshoremen, muscles working in sheds and stores, dreamers from nowhere whose only identity was the label of their favorite rum, exiled Caribbeans, fallen mulattoes, travelers who led in Texaco one of their seven lives with a concubine and a rosary string of children, and two or three more characters I will come to later in more detail . . .

[2]Bigmouths with rings in their ears, blackwomen red like the Vert-Pré soils from endless fights, creatures living only for pregnancies and children peeking out of every sleeve, wrinkled damsels with somber looks, matadoras with long lashes whose full figures tortured the seams of shrunken cloth, plus I imagine there must have been smiling and anxious persons wearing curlpapers about whom I am sure to find a way to give more details . . .

picture, the children who were there added all sorts of cruelties natural to them. That's where things stood when the Christ sighed. Carolina Danta provoked a panic when at that moment she fled shouting: *Oy! Dear! his soul's back* . . . (Rockbottom luck . . .)

Not that much soul returned. The moaning body remained dazed. The audience scattered into bushes of hutches. Marie-Clémence and Sonore were the only ones still haunting the end of the bridge. The man who had been stoned seemed a bit more frightening to them. Sonore was the first to suppose that the accursed stone thrower was our Julot the Mangy and suggested bringing the wounded one to the old medicine man in the Quarter. Since that was the only way to escape the danger of having to call the police, everyone agreed.

How to lift the injured one was the question everyone was asking when O-oh! Julot the Mangy, innocence himself, suddenly appeared. His house was down Lower Texaco behind Sonore's. His insistence on raising an ingenuous eyebrow convinced Marie-Clémence of his guilt. The minute the Christ had appeared in his field of vision, Julot must have thrown the stone that any of us would have thrown if we had been as mean as he. And in light of the upcoming reprisals, he affected that naïve air any of us would have taken. With feigned thoughtfulness, Marie-Clémence and Sonore told him what he knew better than they. A finger gravely on his mustache,[1] our man pretended to learn the news for the first time. Finally he got an idea that wasn't his, to bring the injured fellow to the black medicine man who lived all the way down in the Quarter in a place covered with impenetrable vegetation, full of magical shades and smells, a place we call the Doum.

---

[1] He was a tall fellow, ye big, no thicker than a sigh, a skeletal face with icy eyes—his skin wore the ever-changing shades of a thousand scars, some of which were self-inflicted, others were from his mother's hand and the rest from some definitely deceased audacious souls—and to crown it all, his voice, high like a girl's breath in a broken flute, was his only relic of a child mummified in a body which was turning bad. Ah Julot, dear, what an abyss you were!

The Doum was a world out of this world, a place of sap and of dead life, where mute birds flew around flowers that opened at night. There we could hear the sighs of the she-devils in the hollows of acacia trees about whom sleepwalking children dreamed. They would throw night-butterflies blind from the sun at the children. For those reasons, no one ever went there. We'd never stray past these rocks by the river where the laundry was done. Today the river isn't the same, it's muddy and is no longer used by anyone for anything and the she-devils seem to have disappeared.

Thus, our future Christ was carried like a clump of rabbit grass on our Boss's back. Julot ahead, the women behind, they crossed a fenced space where a smell of stale oil permeated the soul. Texaco, the oil company which used to occupy that space and which had given its name to it, had left aeons ago. It had picked up its barrels, carted off its reservoirs, taken apart its tankers' sucking pipes, and left. Its tank trucks sometimes parked there, to keep one foot on the dear property. Around that abandoned space are our hutches, our very own Texaco, a company in the business of survival.

Julot approached the Doum and called out for the old man from a reasonable distance, *Papa Totone ho! . . .* The medicine man suddenly appeared wearing an air of sweet stupidity which fooled no one. He was round like a happy papaya, of medium height, and his gestures were impeccable. Anyone who could see, saw Papa Totone move with perfect economy. He wore his mud-black screwpine hat, a hemstitched jersey, American shorts, and a pair of sandals the syrians had put on sale after the hurricane. The medicine man did not inquire about what services were being requested. Looking like he was living out a storybook plot, with a careless hand he brushed the wounded forehead of the Christ (who then awoke) before muttering: *Take him to our Marie-Sophie . . .* Which they did without delay.

That's why the Christ was brought to me, Marie-Sophie Laborieux, ancestor and founder of this Quarter, a woman of an age I will keep to myself, not from vanity (I am too old for that) but because I know only too well that my memory no longer attends to certain details.

THE CHRIST'S ENCOUNTER WITH MYSELF

I saw this whole crew coming after I had taken care of the distribution of the kids among the houses in Upper Texaco, which wasn't much but it was enough to provoke some weakness in my body. Sad is the condition of the plant faded by the tricks of time, not lacking in water or sun, not wanting a desire to live, but struck by the irreversible and growing distance between each fiber of its being and the living fibers of the world. Weakness was becoming my condition. I had begun to understand the kinds of things that tormented my poor papa, Esternome, taken aback by that intimate twilight. When we spoke of such things, I did not understand and that was just fine: the spirit fascinated too early by the coming mystery of death is not a clear spirit. Texaco, my work, our Quarter, our field of battle and resistance summed up my interest in the world. There we kept up the fight to be part of City, a century-old battle. And this battle was the beginning of a final confrontation in which the stakes were either life as we knew it or our definitive defeat.

In discovering the Christ (age increases sight's judgment) I got the feeling he was one of the riders of our apocalypse, the angel of destruction from the modernizing city council. The council had been waging an open war, for a few years now, against the insalubrity of a few quarters. Morne Pichevin was one of them. It had been bulldozed and its population scattered into the holes of projects. It was Texaco's turn now. Despite our ancestral custom of survival, I had the feeling that this time no escape was possible.

For that reason I trembled upon seeing the coming of the angel of destruction. Julot made him sit at my table and I offered him some old rum. Not really knowing what to do, I asked the others to leave us alone. An unforgettable moment. The Scourge and I remained silent, he sailing in a mist sweetened by my rum, I distraught like a moray in a trap's jaw. But being a matadora, I had gone through too much to remain thus.

The Scourge was tall, lean, but not dry, with somber eyes full of a melancholic pain, and a dark and very thin skin. Nothing in him pointed to a suspender-wearing ne'er-do-well or a mad bulldog without a leash. His way of sitting on a chair indicated a good-mannered boy. And most of all, I didn't feel in him the inflexibility of stiff certainties. He was a fellow of questions. There was yet a chance.

Age on my side, I asked him about his mama and his papa. He replied the way you answer grown-ups. Interrogating him again, I found out that this angel of doom whom I would make our Christ was preparing an urban planning thesis at the Institut de Géographie at the Paris Fourth District campus, under the direction of Professor Paul Claval, that for now he worked in the urban services bureau created by the modernizing city council that wanted him to rationalize space, and conquer the pockets of insalubrity which were a crown of thorns around it. I also learned that, having arrived in the middle of things, he had witnessed the first destructions of the Quarter, justified in the name of insalubrity, and didn't know what to think of them. When the Pénétrante West was to be built, he had, without knowing why, asked to supervise the access and evaluation operations, and to look after the last details. It had been decided to open an office among us in order to coordinate the expulsions and the relocations (I didn't know yet that it would create a temporary job for Sonore). The angel of destruction had come that morning to familiarize himself with the setting for his future exploits.

—But what's the use of visiting something you're going to raze?

He hadn't known what to answer and had concentrated on emptying his glass. So I took a real deep breath: I had suddenly understood that it was I, around this table with this poor old rum, with my word for my only weapon, who had to wage—at my age—the decisive battle for Texaco's survival.

—Little fellow, permit me to tell you Texaco's story . . . That's probably how, Oiseau de Cham, I began to tell him the story of our Quarter and of our conquest of City, to speak in the name of us all, pleading our cause, telling my life . . .
And if it didn't happen like that, that doesn't matter . . .

THE SERMON OF
MARIE-SOPHIE LABORIEUX

(not on the mount,

but over some dark rum)

BOOK ONE

AROUND SAINT-PIERRE

(in which the slave Esternome,

having embarked on the conquest of City,

brings back nothing but the horror of a barbecued love)

The Age of Straw
1823(?)–1902

S ay what you will, do what you will, life is not to be measured by the ell of its sorrows. For that reason, I, Marie-Sophie Laborieux, despite the river my eyes have shed, have always looked at the world in a good light. But how many wretched ones around me have choked the life out of their bodies?

Coolies would hang themselves on the acacia branches of the plantations they burned down. Young blackmen would let themselves die from their crumpled hearts. Chinese would flee the country, panicked, flailing as if drowning. Good God! How many have left the world through the gaping hole of some madness?

But I never had these bad thoughts. With so many rags to launder in misery's rivers, I've never had time for melancholy. What's more, in the few moments life has left me, I learned to let my heart gallop on the saddle of intense feelings, to live life, as they say, to let her be. And note if you please that neither laughter nor smiles have ever tired the skin of my lips.

But what saved me was to know early on that City was there. City, with its brand new chances and sugarcane-less and béké-less destinies for sale. City, the place where toes aren't the color of mud. City that fascinated us all.

. . .

To be a part of it, I chose to act. And like the local youths say about politics around here: I chose battle over tears. We've shed tears, we can fight too.

The sap of the plant becomes clear only once the roots have revealed their secret. To understand Texaco and our fathers' rush toward City, we'll have to go far, deep down my own family tree, for what I know of collective memory is only what I know of my own. Besides, my memory is only faithful when it tells the history of my old flesh.

When I was born, my papa and mama were just returned from the chains. A time in their lives no one has heard them regret. Sure they spoke about it, but neither to me nor to anyone else. They whispered it to each other kssu kssu kssu. I sometimes heard them laughing over it, but deep down it really ate up their silence, turning it into shudders. I could have just forgotten about those days. Mama, to avoid my questions, pretended she was wrestling with my hair she was braiding. She would drag the comb back like a farmer plowing rocky ground who, surely you understand, does not have time to chitchat. Papa was more evasive. At my questions he slipped away smoother than a cool September wind. He would suddenly remember yams to pull out of the little puddles he had everywhere. I, patient to a fault, learned of the path that had brought them to the conquest of the towns, from an inch of recollection here, a quarter of a word there, a tender outpouring in which their tongues would snare themselves. That of course wasn't the same as knowing everything.

Let's begin with my bit of memory, starting with my papa's arrival on earth.

GRANDPAPA OF THE DUNGEON

My papa's papa made poisons. Not as an occupation, but to fight slavery on the plantations. I am not going to reinvent a History lesson you've already learned; the old men of the Doum reveal stories beneath History most essential for understanding us, stories no book speaks of. So among those who cleared the land to plant the Béké's cane or coffee, ruled men of strength who knew what none should know, did what could not be done. Their heads were full of the forgotten wonders: the First Land, the Great Land, its tongue, its gods . . . That knowledge bound them to other demands without distinguishing them from the rest. They hauled a load of common pain on their shoulders. They took care of the yaws * but left alone the sweet languidness that carried the dead to the First Land. That way they thwarted the unjust prosperity of these plantations in the heat of pain. The men of strength would say *No children born in chains,* and the women would only open withered wombs to the suns of life. They would say *No harvest,* and rats would begin gnawing on the roots, winds would devastate and dryness would burn the cane, rain would turn everything to mud all the way up to the hills. They would say *No strength to slavery,* and the ox livers would turn to rot, so would those of mules and horses. The dead animals would block the mills all around and obstruct the delivery of bagasse, starving the flame of the sugarworks' seven boilers.

> In the South, Marie-Sophie, limestone yields me mortar.
> By the sea, I roast shells and polypary, the Carib way, to
> make the mama of all cement.
>
> NOTEBOOK NO. 4 OF MARIE-SOPHIE LABORIEUX.
> PAGE 9. 1965. SCHŒLCHER LIBRARY.

If any one animal died, the Béké would pounce, whiter than his own linen, and order an autopsy. Anxiety crept up his face as the blade cut into the belly's roundness. Fear shook him as the liver would glide out, rotted by the Invincible. So he'd bellow: *Poison!* . . . and his manager, overseers, accountants, vets would join him: *Poison!* . . . *Poison!* . . . Then came the harangue: Despite all the good I do you, there is meanness in some of you. The threat: The guilty party is going to live through one peppery hell . . . ! Finally in retaliation, no cocomerlo* for two or three weeks, reduced salt cod rations, men locked in the barn, deprived of the women now shoved into the bagasse sheds.

Later, to frighten poisoners, the békés invented the dungeon. I still tremble each time I see one in those landscapes that I don't forget. Their stone is still the gray of bottomless sadness. Those presumed guilty never came out of the dungeon except maybe for labor beyond all fatigue, with legs, neck, and soul chained. Allow me not to go into details about the dungeon, Marie-Sophie, because you see those things are not to be described. Lest we ease the burden of those who built them.

Such horrors were useless of course. What can anyone do against the power of men of strength? Beasts still fell one by one, not a woman gave birth, and plantations shuddered. Like so many others, my papa's papa died in one of those dungeons. They say he was one of those men from Guinea,* all somber, all mute, with big sad eyes, and hair coming out of his ears. He did everything well, the harvesting, the weeding. He took care of his garden one movement at a time. Only one strange thing: he never laughed, but he smiled to the birds. And if anyone begged a word with him (for there was something special about him), he'd turn around and leave his doorstep with an inaudible Low Mass on his lips. Some believed he was mumbling powerful formulas that could tame loas.* People believed it even more readily because one day the fellow had succeeded in curing a long-one's[1] bite. It happened in the fields. All had clearly seen the

---

[1][The Creole *bête-longue* (literally, "long-animal" or "long-beast"), given here as "long-one," is a general word for snake, used in order to avoid pronouncing that dread word.]

beast's tongue at his neck. All had seen the vein rise beneath his
burnt skin. They all thought he was dead when he rolled on the
grass, rolled around here, rolled around there, tearing a leaf here,
scratching some bark there, chewing this and that root, bellow-
ing some blurry song in an unknown tongue. Carried back to
his house on a mule's back, he spent four days there, disdainful of
the matron-healer sent by the Béké. No one thought he'd live: a
snake bite means a funeral. But he, beg your pardon, nevertheless
reappeared in the light of rest-day to visit a star-apple tree that
twenty blackbirds were madly shaking. Some scales remained on
his slightly stiff neck, but his health had been perfect ever since. He
was only to lose it (or let go of it) in the shadowy eternity of the
dungeon.

The Béké had found out about his astonishing recovery. He came
himself to visit him, entering the house, slapping him on the shoulder. The slave owner wanted to know if the miracle worker could
protect his livestock from the twelve poisons or reveal the source of
this scourge. My papa's papa breathed the only thing that ever came
of his silences: his inaudible Low Mass. Saying it, he pointed to
blackbirds and other blackbirds, blackbirds and other blackbirds,
and his unbound movements seemed gestures of the powerful kind.
The Béké, who thought he heard a witch's song, got him thrown in
the dungeon. That thing had just been built but had already calmly
and cruelly destroyed two congos suspected of poisoning. My papa's
papa remained silent there, admitted to nothing, said nothing of the
poison, not even when the Béké got one of the most ferocious torturers of blackmen[1] from the city to come and unleash all the resource-
fulness of his pliers on him, to braise his blood, peel his skin, shatter
his nails and some very sensitive bones, only to leave vanquished by
this human wreck more mute than the dungeon itself.

---

[1]Wanted by the law for acts none too praiseworthy, he was living in a hole of the military
prison in the company of others condemned to death, who, like him, until the final blow were
allowed a favorite occupation.

. . .

My papa's papa began to speak again in the full silence of night. From the dungeons flew sighs that the oldest trees hung on their branches. Then in an audible voice, he made his anguished Low Mass blow apart his dark hole. All listened and bowed with pity, for the impossible mute Low Mass had been only one long question. Until the end of his life the man had wondered how birds could be and how they could fly.

GRANDMAMA LAUNDRESS

My papa knew the man from the dungeon to be his papa the day they pulled his remains covered with whitish fungus out of a foul-smelling hole. The Béké had it put on a pile of wood which he set on fire himself. An abbot from City intoned thirteen verses in solemn Latin. We had all been summoned around this pyre, my papa used to tell me. On our knees, our hands clasped like in the Gospel, we lowered our heads. At my side, my dear mama was crying. Her pained heart strangling the breath in her breast. I, not understanding anything, ventured an anxious crab eye on her sorrow. So she put my head down and said: *Prédié ba papa'w ich mwen,* Pray for your papa, my son . . . My papa played his role beautifully, even shedding, so he admitted without false pride, the most real tears of his life. Together they went back home—she shaken and he eyeing her as if he'd just discovered her.

She was a red blackwoman. She had escaped the sugarcane horrors by working in the Big Hutch. Blankets, tablecloths, underpants, holland were hers to launder in the river. The rest of her time she had to sew the slaves' blouses, weed the garden with the help of a cripple, lend a hand at the henhouse, and also took upon herself the etcetera of a list of things to do. That life was still preferable to a life in the fields. A bad fall had gotten her out of those. Her hip having left the veterinarian (something of a novice) speechless, my papa's mama limped. Each step required the assistance of her torso, turning about like a skiff fighting a wave. To get her ill luck off his land, the Béké made her a maid, then promoted her to laundress when the old woman who held that position got lost in the waters. Later, the Lady of the Big Hutch (an ex-strumpet from the Salpétrière who walked not with her legs but with her whole body), having taken an interest in her, entrusted her with her secret lingerie. Dresses made of cotton clouds, blouses made of wonders, lace mantillas which seemed like steam. The Lady had a childish laugh. The naïveté in her eyes protected her from this horrible plantation. She floated in an unreal innocence contracted during a trip to the islands when her schooner was shipwrecked, despite the fact that the wreck had caused more fright than harm. Since then she moved like the clouds and filled the world with perfume and flowers. To my papa's mama she offered needles, a pair of scissors, a thing to measure the cloth with. Hoping one day to make a seamstress out of her, she encouraged her with escalins,* a piece of scarf, and even an old wide-brimmed capeline Grandmama wore on feast-days.

She met the man who was to die in the dungeon in the full light of laundry-day. He had jumped out of an allamanda bush, eyes arrested as usual by a flock of blackbirds fidgeting in the alizé. They say he blew her a few words then came back the following day, then another, then a whole day, careless of the overseer's eye. *Kouman ou pa an travay,* So how is it that you don't work? asked Grandmama all astonished. *Man ka bat an djoumbak la,* I haven't left work, he would answer opening his eyelids wide around his eyes. And when Grandmama asked around, no one had ever seen him leave his post or sabotage his cutting. The overseer who accounted for the number of slaves at work never fell upon his missing backside. Yet the fellow stayed with her in the depths of the ravine where the clothes got washed. And how he could do such a thing was a real nice mystery.

• • •

The fellow was not so somber, nor that silent, nor even so naturally absent. His lips weighed not a word. They spoke of joy like the hummingbird's wings. He plunged into simple talk about water, catching crayfish, about what the small lapia fish drinking the basin's water might be thinking. He taught her how to replace the Béké's soap with foaming creepers so she could barter with the soap she saved. He showed her how to perfume the shirts with the essence of some seed curled up under pale leaves or whiten dull cloth with opaline sap. But he especially revealed to her the pleasure of the memory of an impossible land which is, he whispered, Africa. If he gave her his distaste for the sea, he taught her his sacred wonder before the smallest shiver that ran through nature. Since then she became obsessed with evoking for the world that beauty available to whoever would look. Such a philosophy brought her the misfortune of spending her miserable old age lying in the weeds, eyes vulnerable to the anthills which she always found beautiful. The little beasts chewed her eyelids until, giving in to sleep, they fell. She had to keep them open with her fingers in order to take care of the day's tasks. When her hands were too busy to keep them up, they shut helplessly and she would stagger back into the Big Hutch like a sleepwalker. But that sadness was really for later, for during the lifetime of the man dying in the dungeon, she knew some kind of happiness: a taste of living by that laughter I inherited.

> By the river, volcanic sand is already good sand. But the seaside sand is heavy with salt and and riddled with iron. So I used to leave it to the rain's pleasure until it was the right color. Sometimes I mashed the bagasse ash and the gluing mud into the lime and the sand. What a job, my girl . . .
>
> NOTEBOOK NO. 4 OF MARIE-SOPHIE LABORIEUX.
> PAGE 18. 1965. SCHŒLCHER LIBRARY.

So she began to wait for him, for a growing need for his tutelage crept inside her. It happened one day that (since no one's got forever)

fifteen shivers grew on her neck from his touch, a wheelbarrow of
sweet caresses ran down her belly. Soon she felt her hips widen, her
face fill with light and her breasts with milk. The news of this pregnancy was a misfortune for the man who was to die in the dungeon.
It hardened him like the logwood, made him rough like a cliff by the
sea. Bitter as a lump of salt, he almost insulted her before shouting,
No children born in chains! . . . which by the way shows that no
man, if he is a man, is really any good.

He wanted to make her swallow some foul tea. Yet on another day
he wished to feel her belly. On yet another day, he jumped out of the
allamanda, with magic gestures and a very ancient song. They say
she felt her belly plunge into a wet season and melt into that most intimate crimson shower. She shed tears worthy of that word, set her
fury upon him, with her belly in her hands. He remained speechless,
stunned by so much rage and so much love. When he disappeared
(his eyes, I suppose, darkened with mercy), she felt her belly forget
the wet season for a sweeter season of sunny waters.

The Béké danced with joy around her belly. He had her fed milk
from the Britannia cow, salted turtle, Irish red meat, and slices of
cheese. He forbade her the river and the slave quarters where pregnancy never reached full term. On the porch he put out a pallet
which she left only to help in the garden and to sew in the house. She
spent long hours on the sewing bench the Lady had put in front of a
window. From there she overlooked the fields, the pasture, the small
coffee shrubs, the timber standing to be carpentered, the mill, the
sugar buildings, the rum distillery, the slave quarters, and the small
straw hutch used as a hospital. The wind carried smells of bagasse to
her. The horizon stretched the hill's blues into greens.

When craving pulled her to the ledge, she would catch a glimpse of
the man dying in the dungeon. He was staring at her from too far
away to humanly see her, but he still stared, as if his eyes were special. A mute and no doubt emotional shock emanated from his sil-

houette. She mistrusted him, however, and feared the long-distance dispatch of an evil which would wreck her belly. One night she left her pallet, carrying a big knife, and crept toward his cell, thinking of cutting his throat. I envision the colors of her pain dressing her in the scales of the murderous snake. In the deserted place, a smell of roots rushed at her, giving her the dizzies. She was thus unable to watch out for that night-butterfly flying near her navel. Her return to the Big Hutch was like that of a ghost. She was barely aware of who was standing at her side—sometimes the man dying in the dungeon, sometimes the butterfly—and all the time she'd hear a throaty breath murmur by her side, Killing him, killing him is just what I don't wish to do . . .

Of this strange expedition, she brought back a diffuse conviction: the man dying in the dungeon tolerated his baby. So everything went well: she had a pregnancy like a fern in the rain. Breaking ten years of obscure resistance, my papa was the first slave to be born on that plantation. He emerged onto the veranda of the Big Hutch in the middle of a cold wet wind. He took twenty-six hours to come out, following waters that had made him lose his way. Shown the way out, he said he had some slight difficulty turning but that the matron succeeded in grasping him by the neck (it's lucky for in those ill days, thousands of blackwomen died of a baby who'd turn back round and refuse to come out on the easy pretext that the times outside were not so good).

> From the Caribs I learned the roofing technique while taking advantage of the land around me. Reeds. Mountain palm trees. Palmettos. They taught us about the tiles made of plants and the schooner moorings made of mibi vines. Craft is good memory.
>
> NOTEBOOK NO. 4 OF MARIE-SOPHIE LABORIEUX.
> PAGE 15. 1965. SCHŒLCHER LIBRARY.

The conquest of the Big Hutch

My papa lived like the houseboy of the Big Hutch. He was first a breastsucker. Then a disastrous needle-and-thread mess maker. When his muscles could lift a dozen ants, the Lady gave him his job. He was a flea hunter, a fan handler in the hot season, a louvered shutter cleaner, a shutter closer. He was a roach crusher, a rat trapper, a guard against the visiting snakes of the outbuildings. He was his mama's laundry basket carrier, peeler in the kitchen, weeder in the garden, plucker of thirty birds at feast-day dawn, dishwasher, houseplant carer, blanket shaker, and mattress beater. He was a keyhole oiler under the senile authority of that old plantation locksmith blackman. He was also expert in occupations rewarded by nobody. He was a spy of the domestic fornications, intruder on the crippled gardener's nap, someone who looked at the Lady's translucent breasts when he filled her morning basin, teller of silly tales which of course no kind of history keeps track of. When a bit older, he became courier between the first and upper floors, the garden and the kitchen, the fields and the Big Hutch, and other nearby plantations. But of all this mess, the job of exploring the majestic things in the Big Hutch was the only thing that caught his interest.

It was a long building made from immortelle, surrounded by thorny lemon trees, sweet grass, and orchids. Coolness curled up on its fragile tiles into which the sun's rays plunged without heat. Trapped by its louvered shutters, its partitions, the winds went through it all around. A covered porch, ringed by rain jars, filtered in the exhalations of the sugar and the garden's flowers. In full daylight, a half-light filled the inside, bringing out the mahogany redness of the furniture's massive shapes. He became fascinated by a marble sideboard which looked like a person, by beds with columns undulating under mosquito nets. A diffuse magic of the mooring of the beams and the planks. He wondered what kind of strength could have erected this, combined these scents, domesticated these winds, these balmy shadows, and these lights. This admiration reached its height in the forgotten attic where a geometry of girders tied the knot of the Big Hutch. This view of the frame probably determined the course of his life, his destiny, and finally mine. But since the future doesn't walk around naked, he only heard the music once the violin already took up playing.

The Big Hutch rose in the center of the outbuildings, sheds, and straw huts. From it poured the fields, gardens, the coffee-sown lands climbing the slope of trees (with precious wood). It dominated the whole, seemed to inhale all. The oxen's exhaustion, the slaves' despair, the cane's beauty, the mills' soft hiss, this mud, these smells, the rotten bagasse existed in order to feed its magnificent airs of power. The men, catching sight of it from every nook and cranny of work, acquired the furtive looks that we would come to have at the Cities or their cathedrals. The manager and the chiefs walked with increasing nobility upon approaching its steps, their injurious throats became oily smooth, and they took their hats off under the porch. The Béké himself didn't get so much respect. In the fields, cut out of the distant façade, his silhouette seemed frail or feeble—but, by the Big Hutch, on its doorstep, he was invincible.

My papa noticed all of that without really understanding much. He became arrogant toward the cane blacks as any house servant would. To be dismissed to the fields, outside humanity, became a permanent fear for him, the worst of all possible punishments. With incredulous sadness he admitted to having been a real houseboy. His ambition rose to kitchen disputes for leftovers, to the proud wearing of the Béké's timeworn scarf. He schemed to receive the gift of a piece of Polish cloth or to make himself loved by a pest born of the Lady. He fought to announce a guest, or mail from France. He knew how to sigh at the sight of a bailiff or express the joy of the household during the constabulary's noisy arrests. How it could even be possible to survive the ruses that Br'er Rabbit teaches in his tales, he never understood. For him, unforgivably and whatever the circumstances, conquering the Big Hutch this way was like dying. But he only learned that on the outside—in an hour still far away from when he took stock of his life.

A sharp turn of fate changed his life. Delayed ships from town created a shortage in barrels of salt cod, salted beef, and dry beans which were the staple foods. The Béké had never thought of scratching the ground to make a vegetable garden. He then saw his own pantry get thin. The slaves, used to sagging bellies, brought back from invisible gardens enough to stand on their legs. What's more, they were able to grab the river's crayfish, make the lapia fish drunk with a bark juice, trap the flesh of migrating prey. And though it wasn't enough for a feast of first communion, this averted the famine for the Béké and his servants on top of hectares of cane and coffee.

An extraordinary thing, the soft-bellied Béké picked up his musket from the English days. Flanked by my papa, he began to go down toward the promising woods, hunting ground for the passing ortolan or teal, and fell right upon a maroon of a bad sort, covered with the yaws, his leg eaten by mastiffs, a scab-covered back still recovering from the work of a whip, and a spirit drowning in hatred. Erupting from behind a thorny tree, the demented slave caught the Béké by the throat. As sure as I am speaking to you, he shoved an unhealthy bayonet into him and pounded him with a hundred-year-old rage like he would beat conch meat to be grilled tender. My papa (he couldn't tell why but I have the feeling it was without regret) seized the musket and fired Boom! . . . The maroon looked at him with the most painful surprise. Then he collapsed so dead that one might have suspected him of being in a hurry to leave this life.

Not daring to mount the horse, my papa carried the Béké on his back until he reached the plantation. The manager turned up, a gun in his fist, and sounded the alarm bell. The field work stopped chip-chop. The dogs howled like on a full moon. An influx of traveling folks and of colonists from around the plantation gathered. Papa was believed to be guilty; they were letting down the rope around his neck when, coming out of a stupor, the Béké exonerated him.

> In the days before the lumber laws, I used to cut down bit-terwood trees and a load of Cyprus laurel which I cut up with a splitsaw and a handsaw. These trees can be cut into thin strips with a hatchet or a straight knife. Today, to sculpt the shingles, the young carpenters have to get the Oualaba tree from Cayenne for whom no one has a feel. My own shingles, Marie-Sophie, discouraged the winds, even fifteen years down the road.
>
> NOTEBOOK NO. 5 OF MARIE-SOPHIE LABORIEUX.
> PAGE 22. 1965. SCHŒLCHER LIBRARY.

The wounded Béké endured many days of fever in the upper reaches of the Big Hutch. During his illness he was visited by some doctor who smoked a pipe and constantly spat on his cart horses. Plantation life adjusted itself to the doctor's rhythm. His presence brought work to a halt; only the sugar boilers went on smoking. His departures freed all from anxiety the minute the Lady floated back from the porch and disappeared inside into the shadows. She welcomed him on the veranda and brought him to the bedrooms. He dressed his patient's wounds, sucked out the pus, filled him with white powders dissolved in water. Then coming back to sit with the Lady on the veranda rocking chairs, in my papa's presence who served the drinks, he prattled on about slave medicine.

He had invented the anti-scurvy punch, an abomination made of a white wine, horseradish roots, barbane, cochlearia cress picked before dawn. For him leprosy was not red sores followed by degenerative yaws, but a nuisance to be treated with applications of mercury. To the astonished Lady of the Big Hutch, he argued that hanging was no remedy for raging dementia, that scabies was not a venereal disease, and that mating melancholic earth eaters could save them. He tackled elephantiasis with vitriol oil but remained sensitive to Bertin's idea of adding gum to the treacle's nutmeg paste. For the stomach ache that made one olive-green and unable to do much of anything, he went on prescribing, lavish in detail, a fermentation of rusty nails, coarse ammonia salts, monkey's-hand, neckweed, ginger, seven lemons mixed with common honey. He took care of tetanus with vinegar potions and sweating procured by a roaring fire. As for syphilis, his great enemy (source of his royal confidence), he was experimenting with bloodletting at the neck coupled with a terrifying dilution of mercury. His results led him to think that the powder of Ailhaud, the surgeon from Aix, was, forgive the expression, complete crap. And if the Lady ever complained of languidness, he would mention before his departure the stimulating effect of cinnamon taught him by some old slave imbecile.

> With their words, they would say: *l'esclavage,* slavery. But we would only hear: *l'estravaille,* travail. When they found out and began to say *Lestravaille,* to speak closer to us, we'd already cut the word down to *travail,* the idea of plain toil . . . ha ha ha, Sophie, the word cut across like a weapon . . .
>
> NOTEBOOK NO. 2 OF MARIE-SOPHIE LABORIEUX.
> PAGE 9. 1965. SCHŒLCHER LIBRARY.

The cured Béké summoned his manager and asked for news of the plantation. They decided to start a blessed vegetable garden on the fallow hill; the Béké asked for my papa. Lost in the middle of the four posts of his bed, he stared at him for a long time. I've often tried to imagine that fellow. Papa, who claimed to know neither his name nor his history, refused to describe him to me, probably fearing he would come back to haunt his old age. But I like to think that his lip was thin, and that he had the dull eyes of those big cats who no longer walk man's earth. And I am sure I'm right because today the young békés in import-export have that same lip, the same eyes, and are moved more easily by a number than by the most beautiful poem. At the end of his silence, the Béké said to my papa that he was going to *emancipate* him, a word which at the moment meant nothing to him. Of all of the Béké's explanation, he remembers (for eternity) only this rag of a sentence: *you will be free to do or not to do what you want and to go wherever you so desire* . . . And on the list of his furniture, livestock, and slaves, the Béké had inscribed beside his name: *Libre de savane.*

The easiest way to free a slave was to give him savanna * freedom. You declared him free without any act of notary, tax, or mandatory food pension. He issued a sheet of paper which my papa kept all of his life and that I was able to read one day, blurred with pity. The Béké had written there: *I give and bequeath to the one named Esternome who has saved my life, savanna freedom, food and drink for as long as I live. I pray that my wife, my sons, my manager, and this letter's reader, whatever his rank might be, not trouble him or exact any service from him.* Instead of signing it, he had stamped it with a cross.

> Sophie, my Marie, my Sunday absinthe, would you believe that the Béké would greet new slaves with gunpowder monkeying, fire, sparks, with bizarre gestures and prayers? Thus in the prison of our terribterror we all believed him to hold the Power.
>
> NOTEBOOK NO. 3 OF MARIE-SOPHIE LABORIEUX.
> PAGE 16. 1965. SCHŒLCHER LIBRARY.

It took my Esternome[1] some time to understand that he was no longer in chains. That he could work or spend his day belly up in the

---

[1] He was certain that this was his name only when the Béké so designated him. What is a name, Marie-Sophie, what is a name?

sun. That he could show up at the ration call, dance the calenda at baptisms, stay in his quarter or take off. At each discovery of his new freedom, he suspected a trap put there by the Béké, until little by little he took in all of it. His old mama took pride in it. She had become housekeeper-seamstress. No longer in charge of the dirty laundry to be washed in the river, she took care of the cleaning of many of the upstairs rooms. In the afternoon, raveled in her threads, she sewed the field blouses. The blackworkers offered her jewelry made of scales. They wanted her to ensure the particular elegance of their Sunday pète-bombe* hats. Some of them spent their waking moments thinking up an outfit for the trips they'd take to City at holiday time. They would secretly bring back swatches of madras, velvet squares, crumbs of lace, waterfalls of colorful cloth whose crash elaborated a raiment of distinction. My Esternome's mama would realize it for them, while mixing some of her own taste into some of the designs for the Lady's clothes. But behind the clever seamstress was a woman giving herself up to daydreams.

She would be caught, needle in the air, listening to the harmonies of a throaty mandolin. The shrews smelled sentimental luggage. They imagined that she was in love with a chimera, an unfaithful bird, a troublemaking wind. Esternome my papa noticed it from afar and saw it close up on Sundays when they roasted game birds by the river. Though he had had to leave the Big Hutch, he remained on the plantation, leading a life according to his heart, hunting, fishing, drifting down roads, tracks, paths. During his first savanna freedom days, he had tried to catch sight of maroons, those initiated into freedom. It was useless. Maroons lived but had no shadows. They seemed to have deserted this earthly world. So my Esternome went, turned, exhibited his paper to the gendarmes at the smallest Who goes there? of a suspicious béké. He dared neither leave nor really stay. Strange baggage, the plantation had become for him a kind of haven.

THE MENTOH AND THE CARPENTER

Of course the bad times continued there: blackmen at the end of their rope, the whips, the endless labor in the mud of harvests. The poisoning of animals was as usual contrary to the running of the mills. The Béké got meaner and meaner. His dungeon functioned in all its atrocity. One day he imprisoned the silently muttering blackman who had cured himself of a snake bite without any help. During that man's endungeoning the plantation awoke under the gray down of a bird flapping its distraught wings in the mushy air of its sky. But no one cared. The down settled everywhere, enhancing the landscape with the color of a full moon. It must have also covered the lungs (for everyone sneezed) and lined their dreams with feathers (for some dreamt of yellow-beaked humans flying in hurricanes). My papa Esternome too heard the last silent Low Mass of the man stuck in that dungeon's throat. Witnessing the burning of the remains, those of his own papa, he decided[1] to flee this worthless plantation, to abandon these fields, never to see cane, and to obtain his old mama's freedom—(oh Mama darlin', my unknown intimate, oh Grandmama, your laugh is all I have of you! your old age was an abyss under broken eyelids . . .)

For my Esternome, his savior, the Béké would accept the old seamstress's freedom in exchange for some money. But finding this money meant leaving, and leaving was not as simple as setting down one's chair to attack a meal. The békés had reduced this earth to a frightful circus whose laws they guarded. For that reason, the idea of leaving whistled an old tune of misery for my Esternome. So rather than action, he chose calculation—and was still calculating (a true characteristic of my papa is this calculating, calculating, calculating before lifting a finger or moving a muscle) when a rustle hisshissed

---

[1]Decide . . . I use the word decide because Papa said decide, but I believe he was rather taken by a kind of horror which uprooted him and made him prone to the slightest passing wind. That's what I believe.

behind him. He was in the back of the plantation, in a part where the earth rolled itself up before plunging into a hill under a knot of thickets. That's where his eyeballs came to rest, simply and calmly, on what anyone initiated to it would have liked to see: a Mentoh.

Forgive me for the detail, but to understand anything you must know that with the men of strength (History calls them necromancers, conjurers, sorcerers) sometimes Strength *itself* would show, and its name was The Mentoh.

How could I disbelieve that he had seen a dazzling blackman then, thick like a silk-cotton tree, wearing a hazy beard, and, why not, on some winged mule? If he took some pleasure in leaving me with such illusions, my Esternome reminded me all the same that to judge a manchineel by its fruits is to die from poison, and that by the same token, to look down upon the juice yam's muddy face is to miss the pleasure of that meal. These words of his, applied thick over my schooling, would offer me material for profound meditation upon the philosophies of the habit and the monk. But I, who was already letting life go its course, held on to the vision of the wondrous Mentoh until the later offering of the good truth.

His Mentoh was an old blackman of earth, neither very strong nor very tall, a round rigid head set over a box turtle's crumpled neck. One of the first to disembark here, he had used up his youth to clear the plantation, and the manager made use of his old age for ox guarding, mule guidance, keeping an eye on the pasture, and twenty-and-twelve occupations that didn't tax the muscles much. The Béké never had any trouble with him. And he never had to deal with the Béké or the manager, nor any overseer, nor anyone else. He was smooth and discreet like a quiet draft. A Mentoh, so they say, has never suffered from the whip or the dungeon; by the time of the chains and the rod they were entirely forgotten; they never suffered anyone's envy. And that (if anything) was the mark of a Mentoh.

They lived among humans without any noise or smell, in invisible ways. Today still, few people suspect their existence. Yet only the Good Lord knows how we could ever have done without them.

What my Esternome meant by Mentoh, my heart found hard to admit. It's still difficult for me to imagine *the* slave Power on a plantation; *the* Power looking after oxes' legs in a grass full of long-ones, *the* Power waking by a bell, going to bed at the designated time, receiving the Sunday morning mass and free Sunday afternoons in order to roll the ka-drum,* dance like snakes , eat up salt cod in a stale peppery oil. To this my Esternome replied that a Mentoh never was a slave. You could, Marie-Sophie, wear chains on your feet but imagine good game flying over your head. And more than one so-called free blackman carried under his hair the massive chains of the miserable congos. If there were maroons in the hills, so too there were maroons in the middle of the plantation itself, so much so that I met the Mentoh at an hour when he should have been looking after I don't know what, so while he wasn't at his task still he was seen there which is why no one noticed his absence. Because he was not absent, you understand . . . my papa would say. Free in the midst of misfortune, Papa continued murmuring (in a tone so strange it seemed he couldn't believe himself), the Mentoh preserved what remained of our humanity. He was the fuel for a fight without heroes and whose heat can only be measured today by the cruelties conceived by the békés in order to cripple it. One more thing my papa added: when a béké held a Mentoh among his men, whether he wished it or not, take it with salt or without, with oil or with vinegar, mass or no mass, whether he was nice or mean, whether his land was good or barren, whether he was from a good family or not, in the near future or further down the roads of time, you hear me, Marie-Sophie, that béké was ruined.

Sometimes, agitated like a juvenile under the weight of his three times thirty years, my Esternome would ask me:

Marie-Sophie, please forgive, but . . . *what is freedom?*
While I answered he listened avidly, looking real happy,
then his eyes would drown with pity. And then I, losing
my nice airs, would realize that age didn't mean so much.
One day, probably in the season of his coming death, he
whispered: Sophie, bamboo flower, crutch of my old age,
raindrop on my thirsty tongue. Oh Marie, my sweet
madou* syrup, *one must not answer all questions . . .*

NOTEBOOK NO. 6 OF MARIE-SOPHIE LABORIEUX.
PAGE 30. 1965. SCHŒLCHER LIBRARY.

Esternome saw this remnant of humanity appear all the sudden just
when his desire to leave was turning into a plan. The fellow, smiling
like a village idiot clueless duh-duh-um under a ripe avocado, asked
him: *Ou sé ich misié Pol?* Ar'ya Mister Pol's child? (Pol, the man
who died in the dungeon after probably poisoning seven oxen, nine
mules, three horses, after drying up productive wombs and afflicting
the Béké's cane plants with a hundred rats, vermin, searing rain, and
five merciless winds). My papa had, of course, no desire to speak to
such an insignificant being. He was turning on his heels when the fellow grabbed his wrist with the strength of a new mill, almost crushing my Esternome's arm. Heat shot through his body.

Since then, my Esternome became a believer in devilries. The winds,
the light, the blades of shadows were for him sanctuaries of invisible
powers. Reality seemed to him too simple a blindness and was to be
tackled with care and suspicion. As for truth, he would only grant
it in a cautious plural. The old man's eyes were imprinted with an
immemorial authority, capable, this I swear, of hypnotizing any
chicken hawk or uncoiling a curled-up long-one. And he repeated:
uncoiling a curled-up long-one—a sure sign for him of what he
called the Power. So he who had nothing on a snake sat back down
ffllap, respectful, attentive, before the old blackman who had become light as husks again.

. . .

The man spoke to him in a Creole different from the Béké's, not in the words but in the sounds and the speed. The Béké spoke the tongue, the Mentoh kneaded it. My Esternome pretended to no longer recall the terms of that way of speech. His imprecise memory still retained the fact that the dungeon man, his own papa, followed that fellow, that he got some of his strength from him. Anyway, that speech, this much is sure, breathed into his heart the desire to leave. It also established the Mentoh at the beginning of our nettlesome conquest of the country. To take (the Mentoh would have made himself understood with words too slippery for conscious recollection— here I suspect my Esternome rebuilt his memories a bit so as to appease his stories' need for contraband), to take with the utmost urgency what the békés had not yet taken: the hills, the Southern drylands, the misty heights, the depths and the ravines, and then besiege those places that they created, those places in which no one could foresee our ability to unravel their History into our thousand stories. *Et c'était quoi ces côtés-là?* And what places were they? I asked my papa. A bit soused, he gave me a dirty look as if considering whether I deserved his revelation, then in a most careful French murmured twice, once for the ear, the other straight for the heart: *L'En-ville fout',* City, goddammit: *Saint-Pierre et Fort-Royal* . . .

Of course, despite having made up his mind, my Esternome, being his old self, didn't jump onto the roads right away. He needed a push, some real sort of takeoff, like a swagger rocking his body, and with destiny being how it is, this he got by way of heavenly discharge: a hurricane. A matter of water and of wind, familiar to everyone but in these parts it carries more wind and water than usual. It was the month of the digging, for the cane planting, and so all were pulling out the crazy weeds. First a fine drizzle-drizzle wouldn't go away, dazing the work, forcing men to look out for its precipitty moods, to figure out how many longer workdays it would cost them later. Then the rain began to show its bad temper, and a

perennial waterfall poured from the sky until it thickened into an orchestra of winds and patient trumpets filling with nine blow-me-
downs. This inaugurated the Béké's ruin which was to reach its
finale in the Abolition days.

The fields became marshland. The shingles, the tiles, the straw of the
buildings and huts flew away to make a house for the clouds. And it
was one fat you-mama, if one can forgive the expression, that you
discovered in the submarine clarity of the dawns (the Mentoh's
house, to which no one ever paid any attention except my Esternome who since that meeting studied the fellow, was the only one
left standing). The Béké, his steward, his managers, his overseers,
and his favorite slaves surveyed the disaster, eyebrows adrift in consternation. It didn't take them two centuries to decide what to do.
Blip-blip, made no difference whether slaves were of the fields or of
the Big Hutch, boiler operators or herders, whether they had balls or
breasts, had their wisdom teeth or were still suckling, all were soon
saddled with a task. The Béké even forgot that my father was a freeman and made him sweat in the cane-crushing unit where the mill
screams. That was lucky for him, because there he met the man who
was going to heave him along into the wind of the great roads, down
to the village and then to his first town.

> I have seen those secret societies of congos, Ibos, Bam-
> baras, who during the public feasts walked in processions
> of discipline and fine cloth. Wood cutlasses. Pointed hats.
> They had a king, queen, flags, and ceremonies—and per-
> haps didn't have no great magic knowledge.
>
> NOTEBOOK NO. 4 OF MARIE-SOPHIE LABORIEUX.
> PAGE 20. 1965. SCHŒLCHER LIBRARY.

The fateful man was a white master carpenter. He answered to the
name of Théodorus and something else after that, but the blacks
called him Sweetmeat, so much did he like to enjoy the warm tender-

nesses of some ho-hot blackgirl on the plantations. He paid for these services and claimed he was more ingenious there than in the wooden asceticisms of a frame. Sweetmeat had disembarked the day following the hurricane accompanied by two free blackmen who were his apprentices. Hands shaking his head, hearing of the destruction of the roofs of the mill, the small sugar works, and the Big Hutch,[1] he estimated this beyond-catastrophe to exceed his powers *oooh what rotten luck etcetera . . .* —such preliminaries were directed to curtail in advance any discussion of his fees. Once the deal was concluded, he and his help began to work along with my Esternome. Fate being fate, the latter had been assigned to Sweetmeat's work group.

The work lasted a couple of weeks: cutting the standing timber, carving planks out of it, as well as girders, joists, putting the dried wood in reserve for just-in-case, climbing up the buildings and putting their frames back on their feet. My Esternome, always shrewd when need be, sharpened his eyes, cleared his ears, and let himself be initiated into the layout of the wall frames, the skeleton of edifices, their roof's calabash. He became concerned with the secrets of resisting earthquakes and the lunacies of the wind—all these things are standard, for beyond that, it's no longer in the carpenter's hands, you follow me, but up to chance and prayers, said Théodorus clearing his name.

The fellow it seems knew his craft well. During his sailings in the brand new world as they used to say, he had been a navy carpenter, then he worked on a Dutch island following a shipwreck, and-then was a buccaneer, and-then a militiaman God knows where, and-then the ruined owner of a little farm in some hole in Guadeloupe, and-then sailor on some God-knows-what floating thing in the Mexican

---

[1]As for the blacks, through the night they had covered their hutches with thicket grass for lack of the more efficient cane straw.

Gulf. One day he disembarked in the city of Saint-Pierre (once again fresh from a shipwreck, shoulder wounded, a red shock of hair on his head, eyes yellowed by the cannibal fever of those who have had to make a meal of their mate's cadaver in order to survive) where he took up his craft again. Master artisans being rare in this country, contracts piled up before him. Soon he was able to make time for his orgies again and even found time, on the days of abstinence his tired body imposed on him, to philosophize about the colonial idea.

It was with such a man that my Esternome discovered the craft that was to become his: the art of tying beams without putting in a single nail, the art of the equilibrium of masses and the balancing of weights, the art of calculating the right slopes, the art of shingles and tiles held together by copper. Théodorus Sweetmeat would add his Norman knowledge to the teachings offered by the African huts and Caribbean longhouses. Bit by bit, his science of buildings grew more particular, attuned to the ways of the wind and the earth in this country of novelties. Evenings he retired to one of the overseers' quarters, with wheat bread, some modest Bordeaux wine, and dry sausages from Alsace. At the head of his pallet he kept a bark beer which the Caribs called mabi,* whose virtues helped him to ride out some charmed blackgirl. He would be heard laboring all night, with pauses in which he'd down one of his gallons, bellow tunes from his country, cry like a child about exile's rigors, then bawl out according to the moment *Death to slavery!* or *Viva slavery!*—or for an encore: *In making mulattoes I condemn slavery! . . .* No one knew where he found the strength to wake up before the hummingbird, climb his ladders and girders, keep his balance handling his long handsaw, head upside down. His acrobatics straightened out smashed roofs and foundations. When he went back on the roads, my Esternome wished to follow him. The fellow accepted with simplicity since he paid his help with only symbolic remuneration, your true salary is this science I'm extending to you, Zounds! blasted savages . . . !

THE DESCENT INTO CITY

Thus, my papa took to the road in Théodorus Sweetmeat's dust. He had announced the news to the old seamstress at a Sunday meal by the river. He had promised her he'd be back in no time with the money for her freedom. The old woman, eyelids mushy, told him to follow his heart's desire, for in libertyland her plant, wilted a long time ago, wouldn't give her any more fibers. Finally, her voice almost filling with tears, she ordered him, *Ich mwen souplé pa pouézoné pon moune.* My son, above all don't you poison anyone . . . My Esternome who had no taste for such kinds of joys gave her his word with great cinematics.

> "Descendants of mixed blood[1] able to prove at least one hundred years and a day of freedom, whose great-grand-father, a legitimate son of a black father and mother or of colored people freeborn or affranchi,* has taken for legitimate wife a woman who was at minimum a free mulatto, and whose grandfather has wed in freedom a mistive,[2] and whose father has wed a quadroon, will be—because of the excellence of the blood—said to be themselves white."
>
> *A fantastic reading by Théodorus while bloated with cheap wine, standing on a table in a bar, in order to underscore the wonders of the age.*
> NOTEBOOK NO. 5 OF MARIE-SOPHIE LABORIEUX.
> PAGE 31. 1965. SCHŒLCHER LIBRARY.

During the following weeks, the little band marched marched marched, repaired four indigo workshops, marched marched, fixed up two coffee plantations, marched marched, and an etcetera of warehouses, barns, or slave quarters. Théodorus ahead, his two

---

[1][The French *sang-mêlé* refers to the offspring of a white man and a mulatto woman. The Code Noir of 1685 placed no restrictions upon inheritance of property by a mixed-blood, born legitimate or not.]

[2][An eighteenth-century French word for someone of mixed race, according to Raphaël Confiant.]

helpers behind, my papa in the middle, they charged up the muddy
hills, the sliding ravines, climbed the heaps of fallen red earth and
the bedlam of fallen trees. My Esternome who had never left the
area of his plantation discovered the country: a land never flat,
standing in virgin greenery, filled with birdsongs and the hissing of
long-ones. The latter filled the silences with anguish and pushed life
away. Except for the proud solitary plantations that fed themselves
out of their own navels, the country was deserted. By the sea, in the
havens, the culs-de-sac, the inmost depths of coves, at the meeting of
the rivers and the four roads, the governors and parish priests had
planted market towns, through which sugar, coffee, tobacco, or raw
cocoa left for the European markets. There under the parish cross
lived small shipowners, petty merchants, servicemen, and civil servants. The first market town my Esternome saw had suffered from
the hurricane and was spreading the sweat of a few blackmen
around its wounds. It was a geometry of low houses with shutters
and balconies, with a quay for travelers in a melancholy harbor
where ferries left heavy with sugar. Its two-three streets were
crowded with slaves that were needed in the port or some shop. You
could meet busy mulattoes strapped up in dark suits, whites anxious
at being away from their ledgers for a day, who pronounced numbers with a strange accent. Between the market towns and the plantations, the church had strewn a few chapels. They were at the
center of the houses of the chabines and free blacks who cultivated a
thin slope or the aridity of rocky ground. My papa looked at all of
this with the faith of the innocent. Sweetmeat and the others just
went on their way, eyes indifferent.

Théodorus's helpers were affranchis. They had been freed before a
notary for somewhat murky reasons about which they were none
too loquacious. Reasons like, say, snitching on the sabotage plot of
some slaves who were building an infernal canal in the Carbet hills.
One was named Zara, the other Jean-Raphaël. They sweated, working for themselves in masonry, carpentry, locksmithing. That knowledge came from the master craftsmen to whom they had been

apprenticed. After the hurricanes or earthquakes, Théodorus hired them for what he himself called *the great tour of the slave-owning savages*. Zara and Jean-Raphaël had sometimes attempted independent runs with their tools on a small donkey, but the plantation owners wanted to deal only with the white master artisans. My Esternome worked and marched without fatigue like a moth to the light. The idea of going down into City simply took him over. He was shaken from that trance when the maroons surprise-attacked them without any bells. After the bad weather, they plagued the roads, waiting for the chance cart of provisions destined for the békés. They were dilettantes in anything likely to assist their wild freedom. Zara did the strong-jaw thing behind a handsaw wielded like a saber. The head of the maroons with the blow of a cutlass made him fit for funerary carpentry. Théodorus, chest slashed, stood cold, discolored like a three-week-old sweet potato. My papa, he hid behind Jean-Raphaël who was carefully selling the maroons a string of words meant to save his life: that back home in Saint-Pierre, he had taken in thirty-dozen and seven maroons, that he wasn't a maroon himself for health reasons, that he lived in such a place, by such a place, at such a height, where they were welcome to stay should they be on the run . . . —this babbling nine-speed appeased the thieves. There were six of them, skinny like stringy tamarinds sucked dry, bitter with swellings, mouths crowded by three African tongues held together with Creole. Blip, blip, blip they carried off the provisions, the tools they needed, Théodorus's guns, and gallons of cheap wine and Carib beer. My Esternome saw them take-and-disappear like they never really existed. He was to see them again in a not so distant future, in Saint-Pierre, joyful among the flames of Abolition.

OSÉLIA'S CREAM

They carried Zara's body across a donkey. Sensing the touch of the dead on its hair, mixed in with its usual load, the animal was faltering. Théodorus had lost the desire to sing or even to drag himself[1] toward the freed blacks' huts. Numerous all about the edges of City, their straw stuck out from behind the thickets. Upon their entrance into Saint-Pierre, night had fallen and thickened. Esternome my papa opened his eyes wide as if he had landed in another country. First: the blind shadows of one low house after another, now getting taller and taller, then a bridge over a furrowsome stream, then all of a sudden a sparkling of the sea despite the dark sky cut up by façades taller than Big Hutches. The donkeys moved along on rocky ground, swaying like blackgirls on high heels. With Théodorus leading, the company went back up a large street which snaked between walls of stone, lit up by small streetlights receding further and further until all was dark. After rounding a curve, the street took narrow paths, crumbling into the sea, forcing them to hang on to the sides. *Ah, the pissied streets, the pissied streets,* Théodorus warbled, suddenly wide awake. And my Esternome understood why right away: from all around rose the laughter of women in heat, of clarinet pleasures and brass emotions, hollering, agonies following strong drink, a bacchanal leaking from behind some poorly closed shutters. Hatted (or hatless) shadows went up-down-and-all-around, looking as if they were living it up. After going down some slippery half-smashed steps, the company came out onto a large square before the clumpy harbor, a dark thicket of masts. Théodorus hollered like someone getting his throat cut, *Sergeant! Sergeant! the maroons, the maroons . . .* Something moved, a light went on, doors creaked open on the hollow of a façade. It was a militia house. In a room crammed with logbooks, under the beam of a smelly lamp, they spent the rest of the night relating the aggression they had suffered and describing the maroons. My Esternome had to identify himself and explain why the scribbling which proclaimed his freedom had not been scratched by a notary, and lacked the governor's or any other administrative wax, you understand, Mr. Théodorus, for

---

[1]He was in fact waiting for the smile of an available blackgirl above salt-sack breasts.

the slightest thing these idiot planters throw these freemen onto our turf. And what is a freeman, Mr. Théodorus—the gendarme fulminated pronouncing the tongue of France in a way my Esternome had never thought possible—but a crank, a drifter, a liar, a dancer, with his wits about him only when he's rolling dice and carrying on with daughters-of-joy and who, what's worse, gives refuge to maroons . . . Théodorus who didn't give a damn softly acquiesced: No question about it, sergeant, planters are savages . . .

In that blasted town of Saint-Pierre, my papa's first carpentry job, if a little simple truth be told, was Zara's coffin. The gendarmes pretended to go on patrol and left the body on their hands. Slaves pounced from the shops, from the islands of homes, on their lopsided way to water-carrying chores. The least public fountain became a place of battle, of jittery vessels, splashing, washing, of giddy pleasures bouncing off the blackgirls' locks. Théodorus disappeared in the mist, looking for, he said, some bonesetter. Jean-Raphaël looked after my Esternome, in the time it took to go around the bay, recross the bridge in the direction of a part of City made of hut straw. There, yellow blackids, blackwomen with baskets, blackmen with downcast eyes, bustled about with bamboo keepnets, casting nets, ropes, floats, pitchforks. They seemed to venerate all these things useful for their survival off fishing or off the steep soil that holds the hills in place.

The late Zara had lived in that quarter. In his house they found a blackwoman sleeping, very cross at having to unlatch the door on her dreams. She received the body of her man with a frightened mouth open round like a full moon. Then without further ado, she let forth the soul-eating screams of a butchered heart. My Esternome cried. Jean-Raphaël cried. Children, women, and grown-fellows cried all around her. Devastatingly calm, the blackwoman was now stroking her man's face (or rather whatever bits the knife had left of it) and sighing her melody. This lasted two centuries of time. An antique kafir who'd seen worse than this (judging by the rate of her wrinkles) took matters between her claws, helped the unhappy woman up, cleaned the remains, adjusted the bits and pieces under strips of cloth, disguised the whole thing in Sunday linen, then said to Jean-Raphaël: *I té za métè bwa'y opadèhiè kay la.*[1] That meant that at least he wasn't foolish enough to forget the planks for his own coffin, so's he wouldn't be put in the earth in a guano bag.

Esternome my papa and Jean-Raphaël set to work on it on the doorstep of the house. The curiosity of a band of blackids surrounded them. Measure the body. Saw the white wood planks down to the right length. Assemble and nail them, adjust the cover. Fix upon it a West Indian cedar cross. If the Lord was a brave fellow, Jean-Raphaël kept repeating, he would allow carpenters to build their own coffins . . .

Memory has its little gardens: it doesn't just grow like scurvy grass. My questions about Zara's burial, about the priest's coming, if there had been a wake or even in which hole of Mouillage Zara was put, were never answered by my Esternome. His sole memory of that time was sweeter, more bitter, more shocking too: Zara's home became his, right along with Zara's woman.

He first slept there in a corner, on a guest pallet. Sensitive to his devotion, the woman had not wanted to leave him to drifting. She had offered to shelter his sleep until he found permanent refuge. My Esternome would see her come home in the morning. In a mulatto clarinet player's casino, she spent entire nights pouring out tafia,* serving cod fritters, pampering the customers. That brought in enough to buy a massive collier-chou* bead by bead and ells of madras out of which a needle handler in the quarter put together

[1][He had already put his wood behind the house.]

beautiful dresses or têtes calendées.* Her name was Osélia (later he
learned that her mulatto clients, officers, marines called her Osélia-
tin-o'-syrup or Osélia-hot-pepper, it all depended, and for talents not
very evangelical). She was a thick-haired câpresse. A gleam of mischievous impurity boiled in her eyes. She'd shed seven stages of love-
liness to blossom into a beauty. Her mouth could force any man to
pass out under the table. Which my papa Esternome did. One day he
said to her (while she was still offering him the benevolence reserved
for a passing visitor): Ma'am Osélia, please, life is what it is, you
have to know how to grasp her. Me, I know how to work and I am
not lazy. With your departed Zara's tools, I could comb City and
bring back food. Why not sip life together-together, what do you
say? To which Osélia answered, without any sugarcoating, as if to
instruct him right away about the harshness of the times: If you
wish, dear boy . . . but only until I meet my mulatto or my white
man.

Zara had done things well. His frame was solid enough to hold up a
tile roof. He had tied it with snakevines. His poles were made from a
fat agouti tree. His girders were made of an eternal wood called
mastic-bully tree. His cover came from palm tree leaves, reeds, and
cane, and his partitions were a wise braiding of white camasey and
trimmed wild sage. In a corner, on a few raised planks, a bag of perfumed grass served as his mattress. Benches, canaris,* bottles, tools
complemented that array. Not large, it was a good shelter from the
rain and a roof over one's sleep, because at that time life was outside
during the day. All of the hutches around were built on the same
model and were sometimes just plain replicas if Zara had had a hand
in it. They housed yellow blackmen, fallen mulatto girls (God knows
what from) and black oldtimers, shifty fellows, and a trail of kids
hanging on to mothers fighting invisible misfortunes one-on-one. All
were free, affranchis one way or another, legally or illegally. The
darker ones ceaselessly exhibited their titles of freedom. Those who
didn't have one had to follow the gendarmes back onto their original

plantation where the béké would confirm their statement, or not. Esternome my papa went through that a dozen times until Abolition
put an end to it. His béké barely welcomed him, confirmed whatever
was wanted, and left mumbling. Since the hurricane, his plantation
seemed ever at the mercy of a bad wind's high-waist dance. During
one of his visits, my Esternome found his mother lost in the abandon
of the garden. Lying in the grasses, she was scrutinizing the same red
ants that had already chewed up her eyelids so much. A young mulatto girl had replaced her as the dressmaker. Since then, taking tiny
steps she emptied the chamber pots, carried pot after pot by the
hour. Then, sitting idle, she celebrated the world by observing the
cockchafers, the wood-horse bugs, the potato bugs, the blue fleas,
the flowers, the skin of the hot-pepper plant, the small rough-hewn
stones like pearls, the bits of clay, the waterdrops, the markings on
the tree lizards, a bird's bones under a rosebush, earthworms thrice
knotted without once breaking, and of course, the ants of destiny,
fatal to her eyes. Her hands, too busy guiding her eyes, were now
useless. In the declining plantation she was left to her own misery.
She dragged her insomnia under the veranda, cleaned herself under
a gutter, and would relieve herself in the back of the garden with
the ants which, tired of the taste of her skin, couldn't care less about
her.

Osélia would come home at dawn. She went to bed, slipping into a
moonless sleep. She emerged from it in the afternoon to eat a bite,
do her laundry by the river, straighten her evening gown. Late in the
day she combed her hair for a long while, got dressed, rubbed some
good-smell on herself, and left for work. My Esternome followed
Osélia's life with a painful gaze. During the day he'd roam Saint-
Pierre offering his services as carpenter-locksmith-handyman-
cleaner. He came home at the edge of the afternoon in order to cook
some sweet greens and watch for Osélia's waking. At her every
shiver, he'd lie down on her. The first time he had the audacity to do
that, Osélia took him in her arms, wrapped her legs around him, and

undulated like a mibi vine under a rush of snakes. With her teeth, made for that, she chewed his ear, neck, lips, and nose. Her fingers dipped his every backbone in a cauldron of three shivers. She became a starving bird pecking at his skin, pecking his sweet juice, pecking a bit of his blood and the rest of his soul. On the so-sweet crest of pleasure, he wished to scream sigh cry breathe die. He felt himself carried like a shipwreck at the pace of a greatly feverish and burdened mule. His balls were exploding. When he fell soft again like a canoe after a wave, she fished him out of the water of lassitude and brought him back in a shower. Each time she would catch his sauce in the bustle of her hands, then would restore it on his body like the laws of a tide. Soon he was a smell of algae and armpits covered with a mother-of-pearl which she dissipated with her tongue. When she straddled him, shaking like a frigate, that was altogether another story. Alas, I never learned it. My papa Esternome hadn't done school. In his pumpkin he only had carpentry methods at his disposal and nothing of the fifty-dozen pages of the dictionary useful to make a sketch of what happened.

THE LIBERTIED AND THE AFFRANCHIS

Probably because it resembled her night job too closely, Osélia did this to him only once. Afterward, she only supplied an immobile, somewhat sleepy snatch, though open wide to allow him a solitary pleasure. This disheartened my Esternome terribly, a languor more terrible than a broken heart, which he dissipated in the cocomerlo of the freemen taverns. This was a foul time, he usually groused, but by the words escaping him little by little, I found out that in reality he had sunk into the dark voluptuous turmoil of wanderings. Most of the mulattoes and black affranchis had parked themselves in town. They were fleeing the plantation fields which were hostile to any seed other than the Béké's. City on the other hand was open to the winds of the world. A place for new flights. To speak of City at that time was to speak of Saint-Pierre. There you met the Dutch, Portuguese, Espanish, or English sailors, titillated travelers, learned abbots here to write chronicles, servicemen, whites from France, new products, wines, new machines, harmless ideas. Saint-Pierre was a beautiful horizon for those who knew how to do it but also for those without talent. She offered herself to anyone who tried to dream life rather than live it, who stayed cool instead of sweating. A number of black affranchis[1] and mulattoes of talent practiced their art without too many problems. The women were matrons, cooks, laundresses, seamstresses, linen maids, and vendors of etcetera. The men, barrel makers, carpenters, blacksmiths, locksmiths, cart drivers, bakers, masons . . . The big-time mulattoes kept stores, businesses, and workshops crammed with slaves. Some of these mulattoes were just back from the reserves where they had been drum beaters or flesh beaters on the front lines. Others, of a special category, standing stiff-necked in crackly jabots, frequented the casinos only in the shade of moonless nights. They were all forever coming back from a wonderful stay in the sweet land of France where the slave creature was becoming human again. A weak-hearted béké had taken them there. In the ports of Nantes, of Le Havre or Bordeaux, they had been able to learn strange know-hows (wig making, silversmithing, clockmaking), acquired some feel for accounting, unraveled the skeins of law, reading, and writing. Sometimes they became lawyers or got positions wearing top hats. Many freemen activated their brains with the oil of cunning. They erected themselves as keepers of dives, kneaded the clarinet, the violin, the horn, became card and

[1]Free because they had saved some plantation from a fire, saved a white-skinned child from drowning, grabbed a snake from an old béké lady's garter before the poisonous lick, because they had fought against the maroon slaves' assaults, the pirates' onslaughts, battled the Anglish, the Espanish, had spent their life in unwavering devotion, nursed the children of the Big Hutch, birthed a long litter of brats into slavery, had been meaner to the fieldhands than if they had been the owners, or then, more simply, had, thanks to a fortunate turn of events, mastered a profession which had rendered them indispensable and had been able to rent themselves out, stack up cosmopolitan coins and had been able, one bright and early morning, to buy themselves. Others got this freedom by being born of the free, from having married a freeman, or from having come into the world with skin so light that it had anguished békés who beheld them in the slave fields or in black quarters. There were a thousand and seven hundred and fifty twelve thirteen ways, of which all slaves dreamed in their quarters. The governors who read the consequences in the city police reports had nightmares.

dice doctors. Around them, feminine warmth offered the cooing joy of the world's oldest profession.

Right in between the slaves and these mean miserly toads was a final category. Given to begging, they strayed in distress, slept in the depths of the woods, under huts, ate crayfish without even a dash of salt. They completed their struggling in jail, or, in order to pay fines, found themselves working next to slaves rolling rum casks, loading their backs with impossible barrels, and draining the merchandise under the noses of the customs officers. The same ones also practiced maroon coastal fishing until one day, finding their calling in it, they turned it into a job and went off on the open sea to trap the white fish. Often, thanks to a crew reduced by yellow fever, two-three would leave as sailors into the vertigo of the wide world, see other skies, breathe other winds. They came back disoriented with truths, more confused than washed-up zombies. Sons of the world but outside it all, half transparent, they floated about in town, stiff, hard, without a past. He had so little desire to run into one of them, that my Esternome would rather cross paths with one of the privateers' oblique detours.

> Marie-Sophie, Phiso Rima, my little breeze in the heat, between City's freemen and the great maroon blacks there was nothing similar except perhaps for a way of being in freedom without having chosen the real direction of the path, its north or its south. Oh sweetie, true liberty may just be to have more intelligence than the stone that rolls down the path it has been set on . . . *but to be "free," what is that?* In town or in the country that was the sole question . . .
>
> NOTEBOOK NO. 7 OF MARIE-SOPHIE LABORIEUX. PAGE 3. 1965. SCHŒLCHER LIBRARY.

This was the world my Esternome navigated, surrounded by an ocean of industrious mulattoes, guava-békés,* and france-whites.*

Békés and france-whites went around in carriages, dined on dinner on the top floors of restaurants, and paraded on the steps of the theater or the cathedral whose creamy white stone broke up the shadows. They endured in the districts of Fonds Coré, around the Fort and the Ex Voto parish where all kinds of religious affairs flourished. They babbled in lodges and private clubs. You could see them sipping the falling day under the tamarinds of Bertin Square. One saw them savor the melody of the orchestras around Agnès Fountain. They opened the holes of their noses to medicinal iodines or gazed in open-eyed wonder at the tritons spitting mountain waters. Esternome would get up before the sun in order to get to the botanical garden. In Duel Alley, surrounded by fellows in black, they saluted, exchanged rifles, and fired on each other until someone's brain flew out. Other times, they fought with immense rapiers manipulated more or less well, which disemboweled, gashed, or mutilated an eye, a finger, or a tendon. They were evacuated on a stretcher, their honor cleared from who knows what. Their sinister duels gave a strange pleasure to the affranchis rotting in their disdainful shadows. When they left orphans, the Sisters of the Délivrande, whose mercy was confined to the white-skinned, took them under their wings with touching solemnity. Sent to the Saint-Joseph-de-Cluny boarding school, their girls came out only for the Fort's church services, a Pentecost day by the Roxelane, a steamer ride into the faraways of Fort-de-France, or to the family Big Hutch of a plantation in the hills. They were fascinating . . .

In their shadow, manipulating law, word, and grievances, swarmed the big-time mulattoes who dressed like them, walked like them, ate and moved their behinds like them, hated them, and who eyed their place in the houses made of precious wood or cut stones. The mulattoes waged politics. They grabbed the available positions in the administration while, unwarned by prophecy or prediction, békés and france-whites had seen them crop up, the heart overtaken by a foul surprise. The mulattoes raised their heads, grabbed the word. They organized circles, committees, associations. They besieged the masonic lodges. Strengthened by their growing number and their white halves, they swiped anything that seemed like opportunity, denounced the oppression despite the banishments they might suffer. It was even said that during one of the cockaded lurches of the Revolution in France, a governor had kissed one of them in a sign of friendship. Since then, the mulattoes had stored up still more pride. The earth had a hard time carrying them. They venerated the books brought back from France by schooners. They gathered in studious pomp to read the newspapers, comment upon them, write lines in pretty-pretty French too tortured for even the planters' patience. Their brats learned their ABC's with strange abbots or old mulattoes back from a journey waving the golden fleece of a somewhat insolent science. Against the béké ferocity, they erected France's generous eternity, Oh goodly mother lost in the horizon and filling our hearts. Boy! these fellows were quite extraordinary . . .

My Esternome learned to label each person according to his degree of whiteness or unfortunate darkness. He learned to brush the waves of his oiled hair with the hope that one day in that honey year they would wave on his forehead. Each and every one dreamt of whitening themselves: the békés looked for blue-blooded France-flesh able to dissolve their past as common freebooters; the mulattoes eyed those more mulatto than themselves or even some fallen béké; and lastly the black affranchis, like my dear Esternome . . . These lived as if they had insuperable zombies to civilize under their resplendent rags and descendants to humanize with a ray of whiteness. That didn't stop them, all the same, in the depths of their being, from hating that white skin, the mulattoes' bearing, that tongue, that City, and the rest of all these wonders. My Esternome would tell me all about this and then later the opposite of everything. One side was worth its reverse and two sides were often one side. And when he got all confused he murmured, embarrassed: Blind-ups, mix-ups, little Sophie—last cup of my days, nothing was clear back then. He never imagined for a second that any of these phenomena would go on beyond his death, and even more so when his hollow bones were no longer good enough to be of service as horns.

Marie-Sophie, don't believe it, sure it was about color but it was also about manners and nice airs. With manners and bearing they saw you as a mulatto, so that mulattoes were sometimes completely dark. But without the manners or the bearing, a mulatto of skin (same thing or worse goes for the white man) remained who he was. It's complicated but here's the real thread: the best bearing was a skin without slavery's color. And what color was slavery's skin? What color? Not mine in any case . . . LONG LIVE SWEET-MAMA FRANCE!

NOTEBOOK NO. 5 OF MARIE-SOPHIE LABORIEUX.
PAGE 7. 1965. SCHŒLCHER LIBRARY.

A WOMAN'S BLOW

He lived like Osélia, sleeping in the morning, scrambling up a few jobs in the afternoon. Forgetting his project of buying his mother's freedom, he dissipated all of his money in two-three cabarets (avoiding the one in which Osélia performed) drinking filthy wines, ringing a bell for a clarinet player who blew out a mishmash of music picked up in the port. He bawled, played, lost, tried to rob drunk sailors, solicited those creatures who worked standing up without letting anyone suck on their cinnamon mouths. He found out about Théodorus's runabouts in these places. The master carpenter died next to him, crashing into bottles, howling *These maroon bastards stabbed me with a poisoned blade* . . . Théodorus had never recovered from his wound. He had gone from fever to fever, then from various skin spots to dead skin. He'd emerge from comatose deliriums to celebrate the coming alongside of a Norman crew, and salute the remains of dawn inside the skirts of a quarter of blackwomen whom he infected without his knowledge. Because in fact our man was rotted from one end to the other with syphilis. He expired at the end of a pathetic frenzy of ballads. The room emptied swish! The innkeeper barred his shutters. He was a politicized mulatto, jolly fellow but a newspaper reader, worshipper of another mulatto named Bissette exiled by the békés after the publication of a red-skinned little book. After midnight, the politicized mulatto (though he was extremely white-skinned, he was nicknamed Chabin because his heart was negro) would turn down the lamp's oily flame, lock the door, ask for quiet-now, and carry his wrinkled lampoon around the tables like it was a holy wafer. It was an unsigned pamphlet of about thirty-two pages printed in Paris. The politicized mulatto never droned out anything else but the title: *"Regarding the situation of free colored people in the French Antilles."* For him, this text of Genesis contained terrible things feared by the planters, the france-whites, the kings, the servicemen, and the rest of the world. The voice of mulattoes rose in it for the very first time, demanding equality with the whites, singing universal liberty. Since then, from deep down the galleys, from under the hangings, or in the midst of chains, in the English isles or the heights of good France's tribunals, it hadn't ever stopped. What is it, the politicized mulatto would lecture, is it paper or History marching? He wanted to hear *It's History marching,* which everyone replied, except for that delirious Théodorus who just before his last delirium bellowed: *What history, but what history? Where's the blackman in all of that?* He meant "the slave," Esternome explained to me, because in those bad days both words carried the same luggage. The politicized mulatto didn't have the time to answer him. Wracked by syphilis, Sweetmeat began to sing some madness or other. He collapsed breaking four tables, dead and already decomposing, with the lampoon which he had succeeded in grabbing crumpled in one hand.

After everyone split, Esternome found himself all alone rolling out the body of the old worker in an empty barrel in order to throw it down the rocks of the Roxelane, from which the gendarmes scraped him off at dawn without any questions and did little besides sounding a useless tocsin to warn of cholera or yellow fever or one of the other familiar now-forgotten atrocities of the time, until an informed blackman appeased this public health turmoil by diagnosing clap which received a standing ovation, so sweet was it to their ears after the earlier scare.

In that long-ago time, thick-livered and potbellied, Esternome my papa became skinny as a salt cod. Tafia reddened his lips, rusted his stomach and the edges of his brains. That's probably what saved him from syphilis because, ow-ow-ow shit, the little critters that jumped onto his stick must have gotten burnt upon contact with the alcohol in his blood. Doing fewer and fewer odd jobs, he smuggled tax-free guildive rum which numbed the nightclubs, he pillaged Carib tombs for very bizarre stones with three tips and three powers solicited by the abbots. He tried to make himself the pimp of a newly freed damsel who threw him back into his mother's womb the minute she figured out how things worked in this world. Then, more humanely, he became a professional weeper, when one bad-bright-morning, Osélia left on a steamship of the Americas with a pale-water-eyed white she had picked up. The lady-in-love emptied the house while he slept, and took off after scrawling on the door with coal a *Pa moli* (Hold yourself together) which only the glowing cloud later to broil up City was to erase in a-one-and-a-two. The worst was that beneath that mean good-bye the blackwoman vagabond hadn't even signed.

He wept, you know, in the way weeping makes a mess of you in the deepest despairs. We have to set aside his desire to drown in the Latouche River. Forget his desperate swims around the big ships (the passengers threw him the small change destined for the begging piccaninnies). Let's simply say that this woman's blow must have done him some good: he recovered none too badly. The love tears drained him of his tafia sauces. Sorrow's fasting dried up his drifting. Jean-

Raphaël pulled him out of the slumber of cemeteries by coming to
offer him a building job. Not wanting to let in anyone who could
swipe the deal away from him, Jean-Raphaël (my papa used to say:
An-Afarel, and that's how I'll say it too) came one day to hire this
gentle Esternome who'd been out of his sight for aeons. He found
him in ashes, gray like a chien-fer,* sitting in front of the door under
an inscription which he was threatening with his fist, howling *O isa-
lop ou sé té pé siyen,* You bitch you could at least have signed . . .

BUILDING CITY

It was thus with An-Afarel that my Esternome turned around to come
back to the norms of existence. He spent his new life perched on a
building frame at the height of the pigeons. He was sawing rotten
beams, replacing dowels, readjusting tiles, and tumbling down barely
hanging on. He was sweating carrying tools, strings, planes, measuring this, cutting that, eating yam squares in a hot-peppered sauce
without tafia. At that rhythm he regained his muscles, a clear head,
and discovered from up high (he had never really seen it) the town
that the Mentor had sent him to conquer: a string of red roofs facing
the bay peopled with boats going from Coré's depths to Thurin's cove,
then rising in tiers on the hills of standing timber whose conquest the
city was never to complete. Uncounted red, ocher, age-and-bird-
poop-blackened tiles were cracking under the sun like parched land.
The Bon-Port Cathedral's twin towers, the tip of the Chamber of
Commerce clock, gabled skylights, bits of façade, frameless windows,
louvered shutters active as eyelids. Everywhere the green of an old
tree between the cracks of stone and wood, haughty crosses, arch-
ways, pale silhouettes in the shade of a dwelling, the slow swaying of
God-knows-what tied to the clouds' going away, a bit of the theater's
majesty, the fuming torch of the Guérin factory, all of this vibrating
with subterranean rumors (merchants, carts, horses cloppity-clop
with each step). A mule-drawn tramway's slow-regular screeching
sighed over all of that like a clarinet. Esternome my papa was not a

poet (of the chimerical kind who is moved by words handled like mirrors and by pain), but in this bric-à-brac he could see a kind of power. He understood that here the misery of the great plantations ended. All of that lonely blood, the godless pain, all the work-like-an-ox against the floods of the wet season[1] or against the fire's clutching around carême,* ended up here in boucauts,* barrels, packages, to follow the sea routes inside a cargohold after the magical unction of some fat accounting books. He also understood (though with confusion: Esternome did not have brainy clarity) that the plantation's wealth had created this town by passing through quickly, feeding with the crumbs left in its track thousands who knew nothing of the field slaves and couldn't give a damn.

The thing went to his head. He became worried at seeing it closer and closer. He got into the habit, between the tasks that An-Afarel, now his boss, entrusted him, of taking his ball-and-chain onto the roof where he'd look around, feel things, not because he was poetry-stricken as I've already explained, but because he was beginning to examine the turns he had taken in his life (but this time, the story would turn out otherwise). The town was of a long-ago time, solid, thick. It offered very little room for its streets, except Rue Victor Hugo which strolled large and proud. The town was yellow, gray, frothy, wet in its shades, it chuckled with the subterraneous water of the hills. In the north the town was fresher. By the Fort it spread into a vertigo of alleys and steps tumbling toward the sea. The middle of the town swarmed with deal makers, the longshoremen at the anchorage plagued by the heat of the wind-swallowing hills. There the smell of a rum refinery, here the steam of a smelting works, on this side the hammering cadence of black barrel-music makers. In the

---

[1] In fact, a good season for my Esternome as for all plantation blacks. Rainy season: season of rest, of pauses, and of jokes about the anxious béké who cursed the weather. After a hurricane: a time of freedom. For the City blacks it's another season. One must know times aren't the same for everyone here. That's why my Esternome used to say that this country is like an anthill blown to pieces, but the hoax is on whoever failed to realize that underneath all that strangeness was a people that would confound all dictionaries.

south the high cathedral touched the mulattoes' factory with its blessed shade. Esternome my papa was happy about Rue Monte-au-Ciel, not for what its name suggested but for its thousand steps climbing the hill from the seafoam. He also liked it for its central aqueduct from which clear water confidently rushed toward the sea. That street was cool because its façades blocked a good deal of the sun. The Rue de la Madeleine led to the convent of the Sisters of the Délivrande. A tall-and-low convent, massive, with a roof pierced by two skylights and a crossed turret guarding orphaned girls. There the girls learned obedience and the arts of charm. My Esternome contemplated them, lost in their black long-sleeve—despite the heat—merino dresses. They wore joyless hats. Their hair was always braided with a mourning ribbon. He went to watch the laundresses from the Roxelane's bridge. They spent the day beating linen, then hanging it while babbling like drunk birds. They only stopped to grill a bit of cod on logwood embers before crumbling it in the oiled avocado. Left hanging here and there, the white sheets shivered like angels' wings fallen in the heart of the bright spell. All of them were fatherly women, slaves or free, whose feet and hands were wrinkled by water. Sometimes—but very rarely, because man is oblivious—these babblers brought him news of his old mother, my grand-mother-sweet-mama. Then he slowly turned onto the Morestin Bridge, contemplating the river more or less clean depending on the day. Despite the barrier of a small wall, that Roxelane River seemed to have the patience to eat away at the town and change it into one of those round stones that let the current have her way. He also spoke to me of Rue Bouillé: tied to the chest of a slave donkey, a tram screeched out its heyday there. The donkey didn't have a shot at becoming affranchi one day, Esternome thought. Unless of course (he added to himself) if death wanted it. But at that time, even death, he used to sigh ironically, was on the békés' side.

Oh my sweet Marie-Sophie, imagine the main street, its scattered stores like seeds, its tinplate canopies so useful in the rain. There a clump of vendors was yelping *get 'em here, get 'em here.* They were selling all that blackmen, whether free blacks or chained dogs, could make, grow, pick, steal. One had to sell right and left to make it in this life. So picture that.

NOTEBOOK NO. 3 OF MARIE-SOPHIE LABORIEUX.
PAGE 1. 1965. SCHŒLCHER LIBRARY.

But Esternome my papa[1] understood that they (these black vendors, blackwomen with baskets, those in the port, those who babbled at the Roxelane by the celestial linens, who played music in the casino and danced all night, who smuggled the smuggling or who, like An-Afarel, made their work into a kind of sacred cult) had but few opportunities. City was the province of store-békés and boat-owning france-békés. The mulattoes (the truth is my Esternome said "mila-toes" so that's how you're going to take it) fought hard in order to widen the crack they had made. But it was already clear, despite their great speeches and the tap on the shoulder, that, like fireflies, they only made enough light for themselves.

What did he do? Work. Esternome my papa worked, worked, gathering his money without addition or subtraction. And, if you will, one can say he built the city in its expansion. Since need dictates law, he became a real Greek in the mason business. He learned to paste the stones with lime or friable stone mortar. He learned to make the basalt rise, to carve out dacite, and even to shape himself ghostly pumices. He learned to fill his mortar with ashes from the bagasse which bound better than all the strong glues put together. The békés and france-whites always wanted to build houses like the ones in their original province, wanted thick walls that would hold in the coolness. The big-time mulattoes reproduced these models. But on the construction sites, my papa Esternome witnessed how the spirit of the blackworkers undid and reinvented the dwelling. So, easy-

---

[1] How did he confide this to me? With a lump of sorrow in the bottom of his throat? With an eyelid blinking with panic over a repressed tear? With a song with nothing-to-say but pain? How did he confide this to me?

here, easy-there, Saint-Pierre moving "this way and that way." "In a special aesthetic," I think he wanted to say.

SHOELESS BLACKMAN

Sundays saw the land slaves come down. Road passes in their pockets, they'd come to sell things from their gardens at the Mouillage market. With baskets, yams, fingers of plantains, dasheens, sweat peas, featherweight hens, and scrawny pigs, they were strangling the port. The men had put on their whitened linen, undershirts, and striped pants with fat silver buttons or buttons decorated with little colored stones. A more or less tired hat shielded their eyes. On their napes thus bared, tiers of madras scarf or of beautiful yellow-red cloth piled up. The women sported their jeweled trinkets, rings, necklaces, bracelets of shell, tortoiseshell, conch pearls. White undershirt and long cotton cloth rose on one side. Their hair was wrapped around a madras calendé* whose ends looked like wild cabbage leaves. Around their neck, waist, wrists, ankles, multicolored ribbons shivered in the wind of the pier, looking like lianas laden with long, impatient flowers.

Free blackmen and after-mass milatoes joined that scene, so did a few france-whites, and a bunch of white laborers, amateurs of black-girls. Esternome always left his hutch a little sad when he was going there. He felt that the blacks at that market were closer to him. Yet, Sunday after Sunday, he was distancing himself from them without even understanding how. Their hawking, their ways of speaking with war cries and a milling of gestures, their generous sweat, their parading about in their singular beautiful linen, their imperial Creole, rich, tortuous, swift, or otherwise murmured in the depths of the throat with motionless lips, threw my Esternome back into the free blackmen's world, into the shadow of the milatoes. The land slaves (or big blackmen) were silent upon seeing him come busting in with his City freeman's ways: feet in shining shoes, belly tucked in a jabot, head caught in a wide-brim hat found one night at the bottom of the casino (unless he'd snatched it up in one of those attics where he was replacing tiles), fists closed to hide the wear on his gloves. Before him, their demeanor changed. They became the blackmen békés think they know, sly bushmen, eyes cast low, real gentle-and-sweet. The land slaves (or slaves in chains) hated the Free. They also envied them, eyeing their jewels. And they imitated them so much that without the prohibition against wearing shoes, more than one slave in his Sunday attire promenading after mass would have been taken for a free blackman.

The sale of their produce allowed land slaves (or blackmen-like-dogs) to hope to gain back their freedom. But it really just allowed them to acquire signs of elegance. Along the waves, they plucked the poultry, sliced up the scrawny pigs. My papa Esternome got his meat from a fellow named Bonbon. Thick like a mango tree, with a good sense of humor, Bonbon sang a joie de vivre almost insane for the dolor of the times. Each month, he brought back a frail pig fed in the secret ravines of the tall Prêcheur woods. He also found some in the heights of the Soufrière when he participated—money is money—in hunting maroons.[1] For a scrap of lace or of anything else, Bonbon offered a piece of his meat in a plantain leaf. He would weigh it arm out-stretched, one eye winking, with a happy grunt. Esternome my papa would go back to his house with that cooked meat. He would dip it in brine, and would return to savor it among those who resembled him so much, at least in origin. That contact enhanced his worth in his own eyes. For the land blacks, he was, if not a somebody, at least more than he thought of himself deep down in his heart.

Late in the afternoon, the effervescence gone, the land slaves (or the no-good blacks) would wander in City's streets, eyeing the stony façades like they didn't believe it. They watched out for the play of shutters, behind which antique béké women insulted them to death.

---

[1]The mulatto owners of subsistence gardens organized these hunts against the fleeing blacks who pillaged them.

They spent their money on vendors' sweets, confectioneries, butter rolls. They filled the shops which remained open to attract business. They rushed into them like a fly-on-syrup, buying here, winning there, oh that's beautiful, give me . . . Finally, they won their way into joints that accepted them for the duration of a drink, for a shuffle of cards, a roll of dice. Some of them, vicious in such games, foully ruined those who hoped to ruin them.

In the marketplace, others stood like holy images, watching for the fur trappers, suppliers of trinkets. My papa Esternome saw them fight over the color of a fabric, or stare without moving, backs to the sea, at City's presence. Tall City. Massive City. City from whose memory they were excluded. For them City remained impenetrable. Smooth. Waxed. What to read in this wrought iron, these painted wood shutters, these enormous cut stones? These parks, these gardens, of which all these city people seemed to master the secrets? Bonbon once said to him, and he was right, that City was a Big Hutch. The Big Hutch of all Big Hutches. Same mystery. Same power. This made Esternome my papa a tad bit sick.

In fact in the slaves' market he was looking for help. He was watching them, following their gestures and weighing their silences with that in mind. He looked for a special kind of firmness in their back, a special magic in their forehead. Their presence was strong under the sun of the great square where the whole town came for the spectacle. The gendarmes patrolled their baskets, with distrust on their face. Yet here were no warriors in conquest but rather simple wanderers at the bottom of the wall where one picked up crumbs. City fascinated them. They seemed to eye this phenomenon as if it were impregnable and the free blackmen strutting about never succeeded in dissuading them. Esternome my papa would say to Bonbon: *Ou pé pran'y! Fok nou pran'y, sé la tij manyok-la yé*[1] . . . ! (You can have it,

---

[1][You can take it! We've got to take it, that's where the manioc lies.]

you've got to take it, the time is now . . .) but the mirthful blackman didn't seem to hear. My Esternome, who looked for so long, was later surprised to see them, when the time came to grab Abolition from the governor's hands, charge like floodwater, in waves of knives, foams of anger, immolating this City with furious demands.

Sunday afternoon became a rite for him. The land slaves had accepted him in the end. They had understood that Esternome was not forgetful of his chained roots. He helped the old women carry their baskets with their stiff necks, took part in chasing after pigs and hens, spoke freely on the virtues of a plantain-mahoe rope when the goat gets excited. At times my Esternome would give them coffin planks (greatest treasures in life), let them have for not-too-much smaller ones which were verrry smooth, entrusted them with tins that trapped crabs and walking prey. He nailed a few much-needed wood panels to their barren hutches. All was beautiful. All was joy. My Esternome only understood in his old age (at the soft hour when age turns the eye inside) the meaning of these frivolities. With necklaces and jewels, ribbons and hats, they were erecting in their soul the little chapels which would at the right time stir up the fervor of their short-lived rebellions.

Oh, Marie-Sophie, the old fellow would mutterputter, the land slaves were marching toward freedom by paths more unkind than those the maroons took. More unkind, I tell you: for their battle held the risk of being thrown in the deepest of ditches where, without resistance, you took whatever you had coming. The maroons would break from the confrontation, but the land slaves would remain in formation, standing over mud as best they could, a bit like those waterlilies of the blind marshland, you had to hold on, hold on, and moor the bottom of your heart in the sand of deep freedom, without noble gestures, just like a dry seed arrives on the beautiful alluvial lands riding the rain. Do you understand? my old blackman worried.

. . .

I don't know if I ever understood, but my Esternome (the rest of his life would illustrate it) had noticed this: between the heights of exile where the békés lived and the milatoes rushed to change their destiny, the land slaves had chosen the land. The land to survive on. The land to feed themselves with. The land to understand, and to inhabit. When the békés were brewing hectares of cane to export, well, sitting by their canaris, they were counting their yams. When the milatoes were howling about rights, uncovering principles, and looking out for ways to sail to France, they were untying the leaves, deciphering the roots, spying on the last of the Caribs fighting the sea. That is why they, who lived the memory of this place, knew before everyone else that the lumpish mountain overlooking Saint-Pierre was in reality a raging bull.

But my papa Esternome did not know that History, accelerated by the milatoes, was going to lift everyone from the moorage of the earth. That, transformed into mad prey, we would all fly at the full desire to become French. So much so, that when during the week he would find Jean-Raphaël in a tavern sitting with small-time milatoes, workers, or prosperous shopkeepers, and would see them dream of 1789, of the apparitions of the Republic in that great land of France, when he would listen to them read, in a religious voice, *Le Courrier des Colonies* where someone named Bissette denounced the planters, would hear them name Victor Schœlcher in a rite of invocation, and finally, right before raising a bowl of wine, suddenly exclaim: *The Monarchy is condemned, Liberty is coming! Liberty is coming! . . . It will come from the great traditions of France!*—he, my Esternome, would get up, yes, would declare in a vacillating French and in a silence which in the end became rarer and rarer: No, gentlemen and Directeurs, freedom will come from the land slaves, from the conquest of that land . . . Then all, him included, would plunge into their wine which they drank like the békés, into their music from all over the world, and into this way of dancing like the france-whites, holding hands, on a drumbeat but without a drum of course.

In fact, Sophie my Marie, I who received it know that Freedom is not given, must not be given. Liberty awarded does not liberate your soul . . .

Notebook no. 5 of Marie-Sophie Laborieux.
Page 20. 1965. Schœlcher Library.

Sweet Ninon so sweet

It's strange but of that Abolition period, my papa Esternome could only clearly remember his Sundays with the blackslaves. One day, suddenly-vlam, when I wasn't even asking him anything, he admitted that among them he was looking for a Mentoh. He was seaching in each of them for a certain way of eyeing this City the way a man of Power or the Power itself would. A back straightened in a different way. Authority glowing under a weary eyelid. In their songs he looked for something very old, etched with certitude. He questioned Bonbon, Kawa, Solinie, Misérah . . . , asked to be shown the man of words or the one who cured the long-one's deaf bites. He asked them if the plantation was well, if it rained poison there, if precious horses died open-eyed. But they knew nothing. The Pécoul plantation, or another called Perinelle where most of them came from, was doing great without any of the stories you're talking about. My Esternome thus believed that the Mentohs never came down to City (about which he was wrong, but he never found out otherwise).

But if Sundays remained so clear in his pumpkin, it wasn't only for this reason. It was for many other things, the first of which was named Ninon (a woman) and a second: Liberty (which was I don't know what). In his great age, *Liberty* and *Ninon* would whirl so much in his oblong head that he would often halt in the middle of the road, in the middle of the market town, in the middle of Mass, in the middle of sleep, in the middle of a joke, around a glass of punch, to scream *Oh tchoué mwen ba mwen libèté mwen, tchoué mwen mé ba mwen Ninon mwen an,* Kill me but leave me my freedom, kill me but leave me my Ninon! . . . and it wasn't always easy to figure out which of the two he was really worried about.

So he lived the beginning of his second love right in the middle of the Sunday blackmarket when an ocean liner brought to the wharf a crazy béké who claimed to be a Directeur. The crowd gathered there recognized the fellow as he went on: one named Husson. The latter declared in the surrounding consternation or joy that on February 24 of that year 1848 (the only calendar date my Esternome would ever remember in all of his life, having quickly gone back to his way of telling time by such and such hurricane) a revolution of barricades three times a day had been followed by an unbelievable string of celebrations. This revolution had toppled, he said, the Monarchy of a certain Louis-Philippe. Husson also said (and that provoked a wind blowing tearful hysteria through the Saint-Pierre streets, hotels, orphanage cells, plantation verandas, dark business offices, and its thousand shops) that the slaves' freedom had been decreed in an implicit way; that each and every one, universally, except for the womenfolk, could attain the joys of electoral votes. The news began to fly and pick up speed. The blackslaves began to hurl pigs, hens, baskets in the air, to stomp on yams, to dance like Zulus, happily hugging each other. Bertin Square was also invaded by milatoes, free blacks, red békés coming and going on horses drowning in the crowd. Some musicians took out clarinets and violins, reeds and brass, military drums appeared under throbbing big blackmen, fat fingers managed to cajole out seven valiant heartbeats. A strange carnival, in truth: Fat Monday's joy mingled with Ash Wednesday's tears. A large crowd took the Newsbringer into City's West Indian cedar living rooms. The streets belonged to the rumors of freedom, of eternal France, of metropolitan generosity, and splashing over all of that were gunshots, broken glasses, sick joys before which gendarmes and servicemen remained speechless, Calm down, nothing's been confirmed, nothing's official, stupid monkeys . . .

But the official thing for my Esternome of a papa was this slavegirl he held in his arms and whom he wouldn't let go of. The wind of great joy had blown her his way. His lips had found hers, he kissed her smack, she kissed him, they were still kissing each other screaming *Pa ni mèt ankô!* There are no more Masters! . . . Their fingers laced like frames. Their hearts held to each other like masonry. He was happy about her. She was happy about him. They ran together across the square like children, asking questions here and asking questions there, listening to the milatoes who went on long tirades with feverish circles around them, poking fun at the old békés fleeing madly in carriages. My Esternome was trying to explain to his blackgirl strange words like Monarchy, Revolution, Ephemeral Royalty, the Dynasty of Orleans, Bourbon, Electoral Reform, Girondins, Marseillaise, Emancipation, Provisional Government . . . She opened eyes full of tenderness while, for example, he was sagely revealing that in a Republic everyone was crowned king and that Revolution was just as if, instead of flowing down, the Roxelane changed its course for the crater's hole of water. And she, more intelligent maybe, would begin to run around even more, vibrant with true felicity. My Esternome followed her, held her back, caressed her neck, glued himself to her hips, his body already burning to feel her sweat, the firmness of her thighs, the sacrificial dance of her tipped-up bottom, oh here's to you, and here's to me ah la la . . .

When the shadows rose until they caught up with the sun, he took her back to her plantation, located on the Prêcheur highlands. She took the big steps of one used to wide stairs. He, on the other hand, was breathing heavily by her side, keeping up with difficulty in order to hold her hand which he only let go when the sweat choked his fingers. They walked along smells of logwood which rose like trees, and along a deep darkness inhabited by a waterfall. She underlined for him the scent of the cinnamon, the climbing vanilla, the blue breadfruit that a possum was breaking, the allspice, the comellina grass dying softly under their steps, the cush-cush yam in its big leaves losing all savagery under the sweet cover of night.

In the plantation hutches, they found the same fever, carried by the winds. The lights of the upper floors of the Big Hutch were illuminating some tricky moments. Horses and carriages remained attached in front of the veranda. Exclamations jumped out of the open windows. These worried the fearful slaves, gladdened others. A bunch of torches shook the shadows of the slave hutches. The news was commented on, learnedly explained, or danced, in small groups. My papa Esternome took refuge in Ninon's hutch. The latter would have much preferred taking him to the gatherings so as to exhibit his smarts regarding the events. But only one thing was on his mind, to hold her, to squeeze her, to peel her body, brush against her hair, to suck on her tongue and try to disappear into her like a fisherman from Anse Azérot in the whirling night of an alley leading to Miquelon. He lived through a night with her according to the laws of his desires and the program of his anchored heart. He left her well before the call of the overseer who handled the conch like one blows on a trumpet.

THE MEAN CHABIN

In those days, Jean-Raphaël saw a foggy Esternome. They were working up a sweat repairing some stairs which had caused the death of an antique milato lady. The family had wanted to reduce the danger of these killer steps. In tears the family had pulled chairs around the stairs and sat, like at a wake, attending the repairs in silence full of pain, between two Irish lamps. My Esternome and Jean-Raphaël had to whisper and submit to a grief not really felt. The latter, his breath shorter than a hen's piss because of his night life, revealed, in vain, the echoes of the latest news. When he explained to

him that on March 4, Victor Schœlcher had convinced Arago
to abandon all transitional measures concerning the abolition of
slavery, and that the latter had published a decree saying, among
other things, that *No French land can hold slaves*—my Esternome
dumbly grumbled, Oh kill me now but give me Ninon . . . That's
why I've always thought love to be a disease. To live in times like
these and still only think of so material a thing as a blackgirl is for
me a sign of brain damage from sipping too much rum near screeching violins.

And each night, while in the now-studious town coteries spread
news faster than the ships, my Esternome tracked down his slavegirl
through the woods. He walked hips swaying. On his way there, he
threw his shoes in a guano bag, keeping on only the poor rags of underwear. He soon plunged into a kind of unconsciousness that swallowed the kilometers, the hill-climbing, the ravine-crossing, the
slope-stumbling in the moonlight. Forgetting about the snakes, forgetting about the zombies, he was going straight ahead, full sail. His
eyes, I can tell you, only saw Ninon's face—a beautiful face I suppose with eyes glittering like childhood's water, eyebrows curving
thickly like strange umbrellas, a mouth for smiling, lips more bluish
than the skin, and large voracious teeth. He crossed through the
slaves' hutches which were calmer than usual. Only mute hopes
verging on the maddest aspirations ruled there now. Sitting by the
side of her hutch, Ninon cheated the wait by tying up her hair or by
roasting a few coffee beans. Her mother, an old African who cut her
Creole with the Bambara tongue, picked out my Esternome with a
cold metallic look. Though he was still a few yards away, she would
disappear in the shade of another hutch. Right before his arrival, he
would stop at a nearby spring he knew about where he would, eaten
by impatience, take a bath, rub himself with soap, splash on some
good-smell, put on his wide-brim hat, his white shirt and pants, his
shining shoes, put up his collar, and bounding with elegance appear
before the amazed eyes of his ever so sweet sweet lady.

> Oh Sophie, darlin', you say "History" but that means
> nothing. So many lives, so many destinies, so many tracks
> go into the making of our unique path. You dare say His-
> tory, but I say histories, *stories*. The one you take for the
> master stem of our manioc is but one stem among many
> others . . .
>
> NOTEBOOK NO. 6 OF MARIE-SOPHIE LABORIEUX.
> PAGE 18. 1965. SCHŒLCHER LIBRARY.

But Ninon, drunk from the smell of impending freedom and the fascinating ways of this shoed blackman, had a swinging heart. On one
hand, my papa Esternome and on the other, a red-haired chabin,
mean as a bee-eater, who often and truly lost his head in one mother
of a rage. My Esternome discovered the matter abruptly. One
evening. Ninon on the doorstep of her hutch. By her side, not the
impossible African mother but the roaring fellow. And while every
man in his right mind was discussing béké Husson's declaration regarding freedom, which will come if you keep patience, and which
he had proclaimed in Creole to the slaves from everywhere who
were now his new "friends," my crazy Esternome, my moronic carpenter, was fighting a slave chabin, hissing hotter than a long-one.
While well-balanced people were celebrating the news that Fort-
Royal was once again Fort-de-France, were howling about the nom-
ination of Saint-Pierre's new town council, composed of békés yes,
but also of a mulatto called Pory-Papy and of an oh-la-la blackman
called Cordier, both of whom Husson had embraced, my demented
dingo was crossing the ravines to address the issue of his many advantages over a nutty chabin with an enlightened blackwoman who
no doubt scoffed at such excessive sentiment.

If the chabin was no handyman, he knew how to build a hutch, clear
ground for a garden, scrape the coastline when the fish formed a
shoal, turn over the turtles he sniffed out on the pre-dawn beach, sell
them by the slice, keep their shells for another slave to carve jewelry

from. This made Esternome who was my papa regret the annunciad of freedom without which he had more to offer than the chabin. Alas! the latter too would soon be free to wear shoes and an interesting collar.

He painfully learned about another of the chabin's advantages. He had arrived on the plantation in the middle of the night, later than usual, when he fell upon one Ninon groaning like a pig on the Saturday before Christmas. On top of her, the chabin seemed to be having fits inside her gourd. At first Papa thought he was killing her, so much does pleasure resemble pain, then he understood that the fellow ground the manioc* of her flesh like a master. So, forgive me for going into it, but he picked a fight with him, trying all night to snatch the snatch, then went back to his City framing, destroyed in great shame like a donkey caught in the brambles. Ninon wanted neither to choose nor lose him. She walked him back halfway and up against an Indian reed took the time to wrap herself around his neck, to seize his waist between the jaws of her thighs, and from the pelvis milled him up one of those joys that warm the cockles of the heart, which led, lead, and will always lead men's spirits until the end of time oh let that mill keep grinding . . .

Ninon's plantation soon became as lifeless as someone after a bout of falling sickness. The blackmen began to wait up for freedom. They spent more time invoking it than responding to the overseer's fretful orders. The latter no longer dared (and he was right) raise his beefy whip. The Beauty therefore had free time during the day. My Esternome forgot about his City carpentry in order to grow some roots in the plantation's dingy slave hutches. Fearing to leave too much room to the chabin with whom he often fought, my papa became Ninon's shadow. He followed her down to the river. He followed her here. He followed her there. But when she left for duties in the cane fields he would remain on the step of her hutch, worried nonetheless, despite his folly, of falling back into the puddle he'd crawled out of. So he would busy himself with some odd carpentry job, putting in a door back, fixing a small lock, reinforcing a frame on this side, adjusting a patch of straw or sometimes replacing it. The chabin was now used to his presence. Maybe he no longer had enough energy to feed his red rages. Both had agreed to share Ninon's shadow. Let's just say that there was a house shadow (my Esternome) and a field shadow (the mean chabin). At night all cats are gray and both roamed around Ninon's hutch, one watching the other, neutralizing the one which tried to enter. Soon the shadows built huts on port and starboard of the coveted hutch. They stood there like watchdogs while the Beauty, flattered, threaded, strung up beautiful dreams. Sometimes the chabin dog broke his watch and put on an air of indifference. Sometimes my Esternome-dog left for City, seeming to say he wasn't coming back. The malicious Ninon hung on to whoever was the faithful one until the other reappeared, sicker than a chien-fer.

Coming back from City, my Esternome brought back rumors and news for the land slaves. He also brought them the rumors about the news. And he strung all of that together like Job-seeds on Milanese thread. Saint-Pierre's township, and Pory-Papy most especially, had canceled all surveillance of the canoes by which the slaves left daily for the English isles. City's council had also wiped out of existence the sinister company of the Hunters of Martinique who tracked down the maroons with cruelty. He announced to them (who were all sitting around him like around a storyteller) the arrival of the *S.S. Packet* by the end of April. That boat carried freedom in the pockets of a commissary of the beautiful Republic. With things becoming more manifest, Ninon decided to leave with him for Saint-Pierre, like many other slaves from the area. The overseer watched them leave without even cursing out their mothers, without even raising his voice, without even mumbling squat.

In the shade of Bertin Square they awaited the aforementioned boat. *Le Packet* only unloaded a sickly crew, a few servicemen, then the

news that the abolitionist Schœlcher was named Under-Secretary of
the Navy and of the Colonies. On hearing this, Ninon danced along
with everyone else. My Esternome, he was waiting for the mad
chabin who was roaming around, each eye like an anthill. In the
evening he tried to persuade her to move into his City hutch, because
slavery is already dead anyhow even though freedom has not yet
been declared, and no one is going to come get you. But Ninon absolutely wanted to go back. The commissary of the Republic, she explained to him, on the next *Packet* of May 10, is going to bring
freedom and he is going to distribute all of the lands, you understand, divide all of the lands between all of us, so I want to be there
to get what's mine . . . She left, with the chabin serving as her
guardian angel. My Esternome wasn't able to make up his mind to
stay in City. He followed her, babbling that land was useless if you
weren't béké, that everything was in City, it was in City that one
should catch happiness.

On the plantation the long wait was using up the slaves' patience.
They cried out over any little thing. Fought between themselves,
brought aggressive ka-drums near the Big Hutch. They cursed the
overseer the minute he pointed his yellow nose outside. They sipped
the night. They danced the day away. They sang their desires,
moaned their anguish. Despite the absence of a man of Power, they
implored the gates' spirits to let them go through. At dawn, during
the holy week, the Béké (all pink, all skin and bones, with a voice of
a blackgirl) came to lecture them, exhort them to get back to work,
and finally insult them *Into your mama's snatch* . . . My Esternome
saw them, despite that, turn down the appeals of the overseer behind
his conch trumpet.

To turn up the heat, the Béké hired a dozen flat-broke free blackmen
from Saint-Pierre. He promised each a senator's salary. They arrived
early, and in a careful line behind the overseer slipped toward the
urgent tasks. The mad chabin, always on the lookout, saw them in
time. He rounded up the hutches with muddy insults, which the land

slaves, once ejected from their dreams, took up in bold print. The free blackmen still advanced despite their being in a pickle. Then, excuse my Esternome who was my papa, bare chest, in underwear, feet in the wind, threw a brutal kind of French at them. Frightened, the part-time maroons took flight much to the Béké's great despair. That morning the land slaves carried my Esternome in triumph up to Ninon's quarters. And dizzy with vertigo, the Beauty fell in his arms. When the chabin showed up, a bit flushed, she told him for real, *He's my man from now on.* The same day, the mad chabin left the plantation. He was never seen again around Saint-Pierre and up till the infernal fume's great sweep, only at Easter or in mid-carême like the song moans.

My Esternome's French sentence had been: If whichever of you cut the cane, us consequently, in the name of the Republic and of universal suffrage, we are going to cut you the citizen way . . . Which, one must admit, went down well . . .

THE WORD OF THE MENTOHS

Wait, hope, wait, hope, such was Ninon's life and therefore that of my Esternome. Some crazy people talked nonsense. Rumors ran through the bushes. They snaked through the canes, climbed the slave hutches, crossed the Big Hutches. They even went as far as the pumpkin seeds. And people's eyes. And people's heads. One ran there to see Freedom, and came back here, it was over there, no, here it goes down below. Though people ran around looking, only counter-alizés arrived. The maroons left the heights in order to roam nearer City's lights. They no longer robbed passers-by but asked the thirty-twelve questions. Each one responding lalala lilili, sending them into a coal tar of confusion. The maroons looked at the land slaves with round eyes, envious of their knowledge of the events. Already free, proud, they still felt like the margin of the general movement. Yet, there they were, with an array of weapons ready to weed

out all of white humanity. When rumors that the békés were gathering shotguns reached the maroons, they began sharpening their
blades against the wind. When people told them freedom was be-
lated by a conspiracy of the whites, they became enraged, and we
even more, groaned my Esternome.

He too had finally taken that deranged waiting upon his shoulders.
He walked Ninon and others to Saint-Pierre to welcome the boat of
freedom a thousand times. A thousand times they climbed back up,
distraught, some even crying nia nia nia with fear and vexation. My
Esternome would take the opportunity when there to get informa-
tion from his milato friends and Jean-Raphaël. The latter were apparently maneuvering like mad, meeting after meeting. They were
digging canals which would divert a bit of this surging History their
way. But (*saki pa bon pou zwa pa pé bon pou kanna,* food not fit for
geese is not fit for ducks) at least they had begun to understand that
freedom was indivisible, that theirs was tied to that of the land
slaves and all the other wretches.

On Ninon's plantation the Béké and the overseer had disappeared.
You could see them emerge sometimes. Peeking about sloppily. Disappearing along the cane-strangling thickets. The Big Hutch was all
closed tight, as if with nails. On their own, the house slaves spent
days on the veranda counting flies. All of them persisted in not mixing with the land slaves. They seemed not even to hear the insults the
latter swung at them. Sometimes they were so crushed by boredom
that they went down to the fields. One could see them awkwardly
trying to take care of things. On some nights, accompanied by a sub-
dued ka-drum, they kept watch around dishes of ground yam. At
other times they got drunk on strange tales where brown witches
confront blond fairies in a land of four seasons. My papa Esternome
participated in this plantation life. Despite the general listlessness, he
found in it the ways of his childhood he had taken care to forget
during his time in City. The days were going by like this. The wait-

ing. The hoping. The syrup honey of Ninon's sweet flesh. One day, Esternome who was my papa finally saw with his own eyeballs, and so perfectly that he'd never forget the details, those he had so strongly wished to see.

It took place one night. Like in the tales. But on a more sober one than in the tales; that night was not bright. Men and women had spent a blessed day full of disappointments and scared pursuits. In the wide alley of the slave hutches, they prattled to death about the miseries of the world. Ninon and my papa Esternome were sitting in front of their hutch with the addlebrained African mama. The latter was telling extraordinary things about a voyage in the hold of a slaver. During each one of her silences, my Esternome murmured incredulously, Forgive me dear-Mama, but such amount of cruelty appears to me not exactly possible. So, the old lady, a bit cuckoo, would multiply the details. She mobilized the resources of her language, built with all of the other tongues she had rubbed up against, to do that. Busy, stirring roasting coffee, Ninon discreetly laughed at Esternome's fright. A-ah! . . . a silence strangled all of the words ventilating the hutches. The thickness of the silence made my Esternome expect to see militia, gendarmes, marines, some béké with official papers. Well, nothing of the sort. He only saw four old blackmen carrying sculpted clubs, handled like divining rods. Their pace was that of those who have come very far and aren't there yet. They advanced crowned by the reverence which their old age inspired, turning their heads right, turning their heads left, bowing in order to greet the most insignificant person in their path. One of them towered high like a coconut tree carefree of big winds. His screwpine hat gave away only a goatee. Two of the others were of the same height, walked at the same pace, together raised their hats of grass braided according to Carib science. The last one was small and round with a neck . . . well blow me down! . . . my Esternome jumped up: there was his Mentoh.

. . .

The four of them wore the field slave's coarse blouse. Their pants
ran out around the calf. Small light pouches swung at their sides.
They crossed the wide alley of hutches in the crowd's general stupe-
faction, until they reached the ravine into which they descended
after a hesitant pause. Everyone began to run down there, my Esternome at the very front, like at cod ration distribution. They were
then seen playing in the river like kids. They were splashing each
other and chuckling like young girls. Then they went back up, gaz-
ing at those who were watching them. Their eyes were full of tenderness, full of sweetness, but also full of ancient and imperious things.
One felt like calling them Papa. My Esternome placed himself in the
path of his Mentoh and when he walked by whispered Papa ho . . .
Without even looking at him, the old man affectionately crumpled
the leaf of his ear. There was total silence. And they, reflecting shadows or moonlight, seemed to go their way without disturbing the
wind. Their presence filled the universe.

I've always thought that my Esternome was just telling me a folktale. I had to wait a long time, until my arrival in the Quarter of Texaco, to learn that that's what a Mentoh was, and more than that,
assuredly more than that. The four old men, it was clear, were four
Mentohs. Four Powers. Simple, insignificant-looking fellows, yet
seeing them nevertheless left the living speechless. Back in the alley
they turned around setting their penetrating eyes on the world. This
lasted no time. Then one of them walked through the gathering once
again in the direction of a round hut, all made of straw, where an
old Ibo woman vegetated, more often forgotten than remembered.
Only a few old women, not as old as she, fed her once in a while.
The ancestor hadn't gotten up in seven quarters of a century. She put
her bald bird's head out of the hut. There hadn't been a knock on
her door for a long time. The Mentoh spoke to her in a tongue without this-means-that, either inaudible, or pretty badly pronounced,
but in any case deferential. You'd think they had both sold their
Christian dictionaries, since she answered in the same manner and in

a voice which had not been of this world for many years now. The Mentoh made a brief speech, sweetly bowing, and joined the others. All left with smiles and greetings at each step, hen cackles which must have been laughter. They vanished. Suddenly released, the world's noise covered up the teeniest trace of their steps here.

All remained clustered in front of the old woman's round hut. Two-three little rascals had followed the apparitions. These soon came back, yelping all at once and each in his own way that they had disappeared. Only the old woman could explain now. Some voices hailed her, *Man Ibo ho, Man Ibo, sa tala té yé,* Ma Ibo, say, good God! what was that all about? All stood at a good distance from her door, as if on the edge of a hex. When her silhouette shook under the rotten arch, the assembly stepped back. She looked at us with a blind-one's eyes, said my Esternome, always ecstatic at this evocation. Then she uttered in a voice none would have suspected so strong:
—Mentoh!

She repeated again Mentoh, Mentoh, Mentoh, pointing with her claw at the place where the latter had disappeared. Then she howled a command (unless it was an entreaty, it depends on your ear): *Yo di zot libèté pa ponm kannel an bout branch! Fok zot désann raché'y, raché'y raché'y!* . . . (Liberty is not a sugar apple at the end of the branch, you'll have to wrench it out . . .)

Then she went back into her hutch, like a turtle scared of lightning. From the depths of her lair, you could hear her grumbling something about the delta of the Niger River. Some lingered in front of her stack of straw, so rotten it had turned into a kind of wax. Then, all strayed into the customs of the night, commenting upon the event and the Word brought here. Not everyone had understood the Word, but all had grasped it as if by going behind the words. The Word, assuredly, had reached a different part in everyone, preyed on everyone's mind, and everyone deep down felt liberated. Thus, City's invasion, with wars, fires, as if by the orders of General Mangin hidden in the scurvy grass, was to be achieved by a human tide. That human tide was to burst from everywhere, rise in one go, as if the four messengers had reminded, in every corner of that misery, that freedom is to be taken and not to be offered—not ever to be given.

NINON'S ILLUSION

What served as a pretext for the invasion was one fellow. Slave fellow. He was seen going down at the wee hour of the humming of the pippiree bird. He was led by gendarmes. He was being brought to jail following no-one-knew-which matter of drum, insults, or assault on the manager of a neighboring field. A few yards behind him, the blackmen of his plantation (maybe of the Duchamps plantation) followed them screaming: *Météo nou la jol tou!* . . . *Mété nou Mack-auline tou,* Jail us too . . . Jail us too . . . Followed by my Esternome, Ninon involved herself in the affair. Their whole plantation did the same. With each step closer to Saint-Pierre, the gendarmes threw frequent glances over their shoulders. They discovered they were being followed by a growing crowd, thicker every second. In City's streets the shadowing turned into a procession of hatred. Maroons, free blackmen, slaves, small- and big-time milatoes found themselves in the flood rushing onto the stone tiles of the central jail. Sharpened sticks. Big iron bars. Conch shells. Knives rusted like shipwrecks. Bayonets stolen from God knows where. Pitchforks. Caribbean clubs. Dried jaws of bad-mother swordfish. Fists plainly enraged. Speeches in a long-winded French that some milatoes, perched atop shoulders, unfurled like flags. An etcetera of words full of disrespect for the mothers of all Creation. There it went. Here it flew back. Turning-circling. All crashed on the walls of the jail.

Suddenly Pory-Papy, the most popular councilman, came out. An invisible horse seemed to hoist him above the riot. He was a cold mulatto. His eyes revealed that in him there was no desire to joke nor any taste for Saturday nights around three-dice. Invested with local authority, he went into the jail and reappeared right there and then with the fellow the gendarmes had cuffed. Pory-Papy freed him, then raising his hands, declared in his lawyer voice:

—I empathize with your apprehension. The inquest reveals neither infraction nor offense: slavery having been legally abolished. I have therefore freed this man . . .

All hell broke loose! The crowd carried Pory-Papy. He was kissed. He was declared the Father of Liberty. The crowd ran across City, through the port, between the barrels and boucauts of sugar, insulting the békés, cursing the france-whites, dancing, howling, Papy Papy Papyyyy . . .

Soon the crowd was circling around nothing. The shopkeepers, businessmen, shipowners lowered their shutters, took in their stalls, brought in their anchors. City was drowning in a foul carnival. The garrison's fifty fellows and some gendarmes had been posted at a few special points. They looked on the situation with great anxiety. We circled around them like beasts on short leashes. Pory-Papy reappeared once more and led us out of City, my Esternome said to me. He walked in front of us. He appeased our cries. You'd think he was the magician fellow of the tales, who led a pack of rats out of a village with the sound of a reed. My Esternome no longer recognized his Ninon. The Sweetie was now all claws. He had seen her throw stones, take apart shutters, unhook canopies, knock down flower pots from the béké women's windows. He had seen her make every white that crossed her path say yes I'm a friend of Liberty. Now, part of her, subjugated by Pory-Papy, followed him out of City, but the rest of her body still wanted to scrape up some destruction.

On the Prêcheur road where Pory-Papy had abandoned them, the horde saw a rising dam of sailors, gendarmes, and other servicemen.

Oblivious of patience, the latter fired ba ba boom at the first stone thrown at them. Blood. Blood. Shattered bones. Pierced heads. Brains scattered all around. My Esternome got very scared for Ninon. She had torn her blouse and offered to the armed men a generous chest. She was busy screaming: *Tchoué mwen! Tchoué mwen*, Kill me! . . . He had time to jump on her. He nailed her to the ground with his weight. He was able to drag her, despite herself, up to the first houses of Saint-Pierre's City.

There the carnival degenerated into a riot without a mama. In each one of our souls, Sophie-Marie, funeral guitars strummed dringding. It was clear: there was a conspiracy by the whites to cut the hocks of our Freedom. We all cried out: They're going to kill us one after the other, cut off our members, deform the women and all the innocent kids, strangle the old like pigeons, oh good God, they have already killed Pory-Papy, they have already killed Pory-Papy . . . ! To these stunned minds, City itself had suddenly become the jaws of the trap.

Each street was now a demijohn. You went round and round in there without being able to leave it. The walls had moved closer as if to choke off all rage. The dead ends had multiplied. Each window seemed like a jaw. The stairs now fell in slippery slopes. Behind each shutter, a béké was aiming at us, a béké was plotting, a béké was loading bullets, through cracks of the louvered shutters. We seemed to see them everywhere. The canopies would fall on our terror-stricken heads. That imaginary fright lasted thus until the first shadows of dawn. Then a massacre, just as imaginary, took over.

The békés began to shoot us. Either that or one of them fired. A scream followed. Then blood. Or a smell of blood. At that point all became ablaze. We spilled all the kerosene, liquor, fuel oil in our path. It was a night from hell. My papa Esternome never recalled the details. He was protecting Ninon from bullets which, he would say only to deny it a few seconds later, were raining from everywhere. At times, drunk from the bloodshed, he would break, set fire to, hit white silhouettes. At other times, broken with fear, he held his Ninon under his wings and, curled up in a corner, watched the melting of the crazy landslide. Some milatoes tried to ease the hysteria, to protect such or such a house, No, no, he's a good guy, he doesn't deserve that. Their Creole suddenly functioning anew like abracadabra in the blind heat of the slave tide. That violence was put out in the middle of the night, no one knows down which sewer it tumbled.

This time, Ninon had not wanted to return to her plantation. She spent a shivering night in my dear Esternome's City hutch. They slept there for a long time, sleeping through that piece of history, for, the next day, around two in the afternoon, while they were dreaming still under the deaf fear of reprisals, the governor came from Fort-de-France to let all know that the freedom desired was, without further ado, decreed. The end of May was therefore as beautiful as a nine rolled in a serbi game. Slavery, or travail-ery, was abolished, oh Marie-So.

> Marie-Phie, my lump of barley sugar, in Creole we know how to say slavery, or the chains or the whip, but none of our words or our riddles can say Abolition. Do you know why, huh? . . .
>
> NOTEBOOK NO. 6 OF MARIE-SOPHIE LABORIEUX.
> PAGE 19. 1965. SCHŒLCHER LIBRARY.

In those days Ninon thought the world fit in her hand. Some just God, she thought, would harvest our miseries and then divide human existence into parcels of happiness, this is yours, that's your land, that's your home. Everyone would get his three boucauts of luck, and keep the coiny change of joy. My Esternome, who'd been free already, had not known these wonders. Eyelids half-closed, he coughed incredulously: sweet Ninon dear, freedom is not as simple as pulling out a chair by a plate of yams . . . Like all of the land slaves, Ninon didn't get it. She would get up very early to hail the sun of a world renewed. She wore clothes washed the night before for the imposing presence of the day, then went into City like a bee buzzes into the depth of a flower.

There were a bunch of them wandering in the middle of Saint-Pierre. In the still port, in the dead markets, more words were exchanged than fruits and vegetables. They furrowed City, shaking laurels or little flags of the so-good mother France. They peered into blind shops, inspected the ruin where a cluster of whites had been set ablaze. To see the békés come out of their distant shelters amused them. The old masters now ventured into City with less than confident airs. Some of them kept wretched downcast eyes on a new skiff. Others eyed the insolent mobs. Carrying freedom is the only load that straightens the back. The blacks flew, light like yellow butterflies. Reflexes of angst only came back to them around the militia which went up and around without really knowing what to do. Having no papers to ask for, no affranchi to check, and nothing to say to those fellows in rags who were once maroons.

The békés and the france-whites were moving out trunks. They were carrying all they had toward small boats leaving the country. Others mobilized heavy cane carts under their wrapped-up wealth and trudged for Fort-de-France. Children, young ladies, babies, and black mammies came out into the sun eyelids blinking. With baskets, boxes, suitcases, canteens, scarves, everyone was pouring toward some strange haven or another. Thus, City was left to the wandering blacks and the babbling milatoes who were petitioning the governor. The gendarmes paced up and down City as if the field of vengeance was yet to be taken.

Sophie, I don't know what you call "Revolution," but you can celebrate that May day. We possess the memory of

that day while so many of our other memories have been
erased, while we have no trace of so many of our loads of
anger! . . . Besides, it's better to have that than not to have
it. It's better to have done it. And besides, Sophie, call it
what you wish and do with it what you want. History is
not worth much more.

NOTEBOOK NO. 4 OF MARIE-SOPHIE LABORIEUX.
PAGE 24. 1965. SCHŒLCHER LIBRARY.

Esternome my papa had left Ninon to her city parading. Suddenly
worried about his old mother, forgetful Esternome went to the hills.
He crossed paths cluttered by moving wheelbarrows, exulting fellows offering up their broken chains, like frenzied messengers. He
ran into wounded people who were being carried in the flour-sack
cloth of bamboo stretchers. The country throbbed in desolation. The
plantations echoed with raiding slaves. Here and there: some fields
were ablaze, fences toppled, oxen wandering, still mills, a Big Hutch
with gates agape, ruined, or ill-closed. Some fellows came and went
with big bags full of their booty. Some scandal-loving blackwomen
rolled down the trails to settle scores. Something that was untied
now curled up and lurched about itself.

At times my Esternome crossed places beautiful with silence. There,
enormous trees swallowed up eternities and unleashed their lianas
against the wind's maneuvers. Surprised at finding them all intact despite the big upheaval, my Esternome always stopped before them,
listening to their bark, the shiver in their leaves, the milky budding
of their still-green fruit, the impatience of the unruly young trees
around them. It all seemed out of this world. And my Esternome
would just cry out: *Wô Ninon tan fè tan, tan lésé tan*[1] . . . , a bit of
despair which a milato with a goose quill would have thought to
translate as: Oh, Ninon dear, life hasn't really changed . . .

---

[1][Oh Ninon, time makes time, time leaves time alone . . .]

. . .

As to not having brought her, he regretted that. She would have faced her childish exultation with the indifference of these trees towering above the thickets. If only they'd moved too, if only they'd moved too, my Esternome kept repeating without knowing why while clutching the soil to ward off disillusionment.

At other times, around a hill a bit removed from the path, behind God's back, he would stub his toe against the straw hutch of someone who'd retired into the mystery of the woods. It was either an antique maroon or a freeman or some foreign and nocturnal old lady. My Esternome called out ho ho ho. When the hutch's resident came surprised with a welcoming nod, he would cry out with false joy *Tout neg lib aprézan!* We're all free now . . . The resident responded to that incredible news the way one responds to incredible news, that is with Thank-you-sir, good-day-sir, *Mèsi, misié-é-à pita-misié, Misié-mèsi-é-à pita* . . . And they would disappear into life again. Turned mineral, their lives rolled out no carpet for the blinding dice of fate.

He found his old plantation throbbing under the embers. The Big Hutch had been spared, but was open to the four winds. The slave quarters sheltered only a few invalids deep in meditation about the times. On the veranda he discovered some old house slaves, dreamily awaiting a push. They did not recognize the old slave given savanna freedom. His City blackman clothing, held like a flag away from the dirt, made them anxious. It took some time before they finally recognized him.

Once they recognized him, they told him how things had gone downhill since that hurricane. The sunny days had been either too few or too dry. The rains had been too early, too sparse, or too strong, or futile. The tilling was delayed. They would have to catch up at night until the overseer forgot all about it. The mill would get derailed, choking on one piece or another, and then God knows what else. The boilers coughed one after the other. The oxen, more than ever, begged for poison. In the eddies of this drowning the master became ferocious. It was work and punishment, work and punishment without even bothering to distinguish land slaves from house slaves or from fellows living in straw huts. His wealth slid through his fingers little by little. So did his overseers. Fewer friends visited. The logwood trees were just beginning to devour the soil when two-three bands of God-knows-what-kind of blackmen fell upon the plantation. Taking in their wake a bunch of unhappy slaves, they defied the Big Hutch with torches and knives. The Béké and his faithful, such as my grandmother-mama-darlin', mother with the drooping eyelids of my dear Esternome, led a great battle, with rage and courage, until the Béké howled the name of his mother under the burn of a horrible blow. The final cry of his life.

They had found my grandmother by the side of the Lady. Dead without wounds. Her heart had simply let go of life and sunk lower, lower than the eyelids, far below our fates.

My Esternome was shown a mound covered with cabouya weed. Some good soul had adorned it with shells and a cross made from lianas now unraveling. He searched the plantation, picked up tools, in three days cut down an old mahogany tree. In the tree's red heart he cut out planks shivering with sap and nailed them into a lovely coffin. In it he threw the oozing bag from down his mother's hole. He mimed, with the house people, some kind of funeral. All wanted the same done for their sons daughters brothers buried with-no-bell-a-tolling in guano sacks. The mahogany and my dad's genius supplied twelve coffins and a half—the half was without a cover and had to be closed with braids of balsam.

As he was returning to City and to Ninon, leaving the survivors waiting for a new start, it seemed to him that the woods had run up arrogance over the disheveled Big Hutch. He took three steps in front of him, three steps to the side, then ran back to the plantation deaf with rage. To these fuddled ones, he called out: *Fouté li kan en vil, pa menyen tè ankô, fouté li kan an vil,*[1] Leave for City, don't touch the land for anyone again, leave for City . . . With a happy heart he turned home toward Ninon without knowing whether the others, dumbstruck by freedom, had really heard him. Nor did he know whether, since their being forced from harbor, they could even try to understand him . . .

> It should be said that the red coffins shot up roots; and one could see several agony-trees, branches contorted with pain, rise on the backside of the years. Looking at them brought back memories one didn't have. It stiffened in you like a sad muffled drumbeat. And these trees, Marie-So, were no longer mahogany . . . a damn story by Father Grégoire, but who's going to make a book about that?
>
> NOTEBOOK NO. 4 OF MARIE-SOPHIE LABORIEUX.
> PAGE 11. 1965. SCHŒLCHER LIBRARY.

HEADWORK AND TROUBLES

In those days my papa Esternome was all full of love for his Ninon. It was all sugary coconut hearts in honey sauce. He found her by the house, filled with a two-pronged anxiety. The first was about his absence. The second, about everything else. Ninon had difficulty expressing it. Bitter békés predicted misery: the bosses in France would invalidate the Abolition. No blackman believed them but everyone was still worried. Those who roamed around Saint-Pierre, looking like blackbirds in the middle of mango season, brewed beneath the same anxiety. To reassure Ninon, my Esternome took her to see a few of his milato friends. The latter guffawed: *The Republic is no*

---

[1] [Literally, "Get the fuck out to City, don't ever touch land again, get the fuck out to City."]

mazurka, everything is irrevocable, the representative is coming soon to see to the details . . . but nothing brought her any peace. In the street the news was catching like burning stubble in the cane, in all directions and even back to the same point: Waiting, waiting, waiting for the Representative of the Republic who would soon be here, but who was arriving to say Good-Lord-Jesus-Mary what? . . .

To help her wait, he taught her to behold City's beauties. In the garden with the strange plants, a bit forgotten, he made her see Caracas roses and Guyane lilies, he made her sit under a shelter in the shape of a parasol where the sound of a waterfall turned to foam. He made her gaze at the tramway restored after the events. In the depths of dark shops he showed her strange objects from other countries. The least storefront window held unexpected treasures. Carafes made of misty porcelain at a cloth salesman's. Pans with guaiac handles at an angelical haberdasher's. Portuguese lace inside a jewelry store. Silver spoons. Intricate bottles made of thin and whistling glass. Where a witch was filtering aromas, he found Judean balm, double-rose water, raw mint water, templar water, epicurean water which smelled like marjoram, and maiden water. Proud, he would point to the bits of arches he had replaced at the bottom of the façades. He showed her the balcony guardrail he had replaced and on which, forgetful of him, some dreamy mulatto girls rested elbows and sighs. Through louvered shutters he pointed out to her portraits of ancestors slashed with light, paintings with dead hues, the bluish pitchers of evening ablutions, the marble of a dresser whose sole use was as an armrest for an old person. He showed her pedestal tables with lion's feet, lamps made of copper and gold-laced glass, walls of books sculpted in earthy leather. He made her listen to the distant piano sounds coming from deep courtyards, catch a glimpse of the peculiar flowers on some dining room tile. She saw in a backyard, near a basin made of bricks, somnambulent black mammies sleep-rocking suckling angels. He drew her attention to the freshest hues of each of the tiles he had just put in. He showed her the blessed play of light and shadow on the Seamen's Virgin on top of Morne d'Orange.

Since it was the season, he took her to the mouth of the Roxelane where the sea came to suck on fresh water. They went there at night, camping right there, under lit shelters, among other water enthusiasts, drinking, singing, telling jokes. While he held her fingers, *Oh Ninon I am happy about your existence*, they waited for the wonderful return of the titiri fish. Magnetized by the moon, thousands of minnows deserted the ocean to wriggle up the river. Scintillating waves of them shook the fresh water or washed up on the sand. The other campers raked about with buckets, bags, nets, basins, sheets, or other things. The night was but phosphorescent lightning, milky glow, sparks. The silver commas spurted out of all the containers, jumped around ankles, glued frenzied mirrors everywhere. These living lights enchanted Ninon. You could seize and free them in a luminous broth.

The enchantment fell away blap. The waves were dark and quiet again until the next onslaught which was even briefer. Not very inspired, my Esternome would say, *Ninon, you see, you go up the river of my life at titiri-speed*. The Sweetie would laugh. I would have also laughed, sure . . .

On the same spot, among the round stones, the group threw the miraculous catch into a pot. Salt. Tomatoes. Garlic. Onions. Hot peppers. Ancient cooks for the békés added exotic spices to the broth, with learned airs. And everyone ate some from each canari, going from fire to fire to douse the meal with a good bowl of tafia.

On the other nights my Esternome and his Ninon didn't go out. It wasn't a good idea yet to show one's blackness in the clear moonlight. Clumps of gendarmes patrolled the city. At home he'd sing her tunes from the dungeon times, ask her riddles, cook up wonders for her. He described the wood as a living fabric which grafted the sun to the earth. He told her of immortal trees growing out of dried-out stumps. Then without thinking about it, or rather while pretending not to, he touched her fingers, followed some vein, reached the shoulders, and aroused a shiver. Still talking he closed in on the stinging smell of her braided hair, then put his head on her chest, breathed in her breasts, retraced her belly. He muttered silly things which went well with the shivers running through him. He suffocated. Slower than him, she began to get goose bumps and drown in the fine oil pouring from her deep fold. That is life, meowed my Esternome, that's all there is and nothing else, to live the showers of one's passion. Though sinking into pleasure, the Sweetie still had boughs of anxiety in her head that the vicious lover's tool never succeeded in sawing. But he persisted.

But he persisted, offering her hour after hour (in the lifeless port where blackmen expected the Representative's sail) golden palm-worms which a big old vendor sold in grape leaves. She began to see him as some kind of discoverer, to take his hand, often you know, to speak like children speak, from the freshness of their soul. For fun, she would slip her face against his neck, letting the spasms of her joy explode on his feverish skin and they would stay like that, outside the world, looking at History going by, oblivious oxen at pasture.

The frigate nonetheless came one day. Long. Streamlined. Powerful. She drained thousands of people onto the piers. Ahead of everyone, officials spoke of papers that had been unsealed. When the boat drifted in the harbor, they attended to their errand on postal canoes. The world fell still. A stunned silence in the air which the Sweetie (escaping the anxiety which mortified their hearts) used to sing a sweet word to my dear Esternome. He, floored, began to reply with a bunch of silly shit. They ignored the rolling drums, the fits of blackwomen hollering *Ba nou'y fout!* Give it to us, already!. . . . and who gestured in the air to catch fate. A canoe was advancing in fits

and starts under the flag of France. The Republic's Representative, standing at the bow, was approaching the coast like a conquistador. Ninon and my Esternome, for all their kissing, participated in the crowd's movements which the waves restrained. On the quay, the shoving was throwing people into the water. The fever to catch a glimpse of the canoe coming alongside, to see the Representative's first step so as to gauge from his bearing whether he was bringing freedom or misfortune, was strong. And once he could be seen better, the crowd became delirious. The békés began to tattle, the milatoes to fill the first rows, and the blackmen to dance yes just as Ninon was dancing, hanging to his neck, drunk with anticipation. The Republic's fellow was a native son, someone from here, small, with oiled hair. People recognized him and were already shouting his name: *Ti-Perrinon, Ti-Perrinon, Ti-Perrinon,* which Ninon translated as He's a blackman, see . . . Checking for himself, Esternome my papa softly corrected her:
—He's a milato . . .

My Esternome began to live with a heart heavy for his Ninon. It's not as if he saw clear through these times, but it seemed to him that the Sweetie (and lots like her) mistook life for a bowl of mashed arrowroot. In the early days of the confirmation of freedom he danced with her, drank-this and sang-that. They danced even more when the town council opened fat registers to compile a census of the land slaves and give them civil status. After a century in line, my Esternome and his Ninon parked for two seconds before a three-eyed secretary. With one ink stroke, this personage ejected them out of the savanna life for an official existence under the patronymics of Ninon Cléopâtre and Esternome Laborieux (because the exasperated secretary with the quill had found him laborious in his thinking of a name). Then he began to wait with her, like the others (though he had no liquor in him), for someone to come slice the plantation for the right number of blackmen. But the wait was getting to the Beauty . . .

. . .

Already, on the plantation, more than one impatient blackman pronounced himself land divider. Armed with mahoe ropes they paced
up and down the fields covered with the velvet of budding canes,
measured the land up to the hills then up to the Big Hutch. Their rigorous allotments still left it a respectful parcel. Each Redistributor
then took care of the contentious apportionment, *Mi ta'w, mi ta
mwen, mi ta'w, mi ta mwen.*[1] The recipients squabbled. My land
isn't flat enough. There are always long-ones there. There I'm too far
away from the road, citizen, citizen. The word of interest was citizen. How are you, citizen? . . . Well, hello, citizen . . . Excuse me,
citizen . . . Hey, citizen . . . , citizen in all flavors, with oil and with
hot pepper. Hens, cats, pigs (only dogs remained dogs) became also,
thanks to that dream, perfect citizens.

Flanked by his lady citizen, his children citizens, his overseer citizen,
and two-three blackmen folding beneath a load of tin trunks (these
latter were reminded that this was no place for a citizen), the citizen
béké, returning from God knows where, spoke of going back to
work. We all got up to tell him, Marie-So, something like: *The land
belongs to the good Lord. If you get some, we too want some . . .*
Béké became strange. He slipped into the Big Hutch which he
opened shutter after shutter. No one saw him again for about a
week. His shadow sometimes roamed behind louvered shutters from
which you could see the fields. The simple reopening of the Big
Hutch sent languishment among the house slaves. They were hearing it live again, hearing it slam its doors, neigh with its horses. Its
tall light was once again stooping our shadows into familiar positions. One time, without looking at anyone, not even to those
watching him, Béké, followed by the overseer, left to gauge the field.
They went over, they went under, they felt up the growing plants,
checked the canals, measured the mad weeds fed by abandonment.
Then citizen béké rode into City on a raging horse.

---

[1] [That's yours, that's mine, that's yours, that's mine.]

• • •

He came back to the house with an assistant-adjoint-penpusher from the town council or from God knows where. The nameless penpusher stuck to a very good French, yes, with sentences truly beautiful. Everyone remained speechless. Citizen béké left with the nameless penpusher. They were seen again on the veranda clinking madeira over some joyous thing. When my Esternome questioned those around, he realized that no one, and Ninon least of all, had understood the pretty French. So with them gathered around a rock, he explained (making himself look for words despite himself, because he wanted to live life with Ninon, not these stories) that the fellow had said: *A citizen's first duty is to respect the laws of the Republic.* That the fellow had said: *In the laws of the Republic one has the right to possess what one possesses.* That the fellow had said: *If freedom is a beautiful thing, it is no bacchanalia.* And that the fellow had finally said: *The earth indeed belongs to the good Lord, but the fields belong to the békés and the owners.*

It took Ninon and the others two hours to understand. They were smiling. Everyone was especially concerned with making the others think he had gotten it all. Resigned, bitter, my Esternome had gone to bed. But, little by very little, his word took root. The blackmen suddenly burst out of their still hutches. Rushing to the veranda where the citizen béké and what's-his-name were still sipping on the balustrade, they hollered a bit harshly, *Alé koké manman zot!*[1] . . . Blackmen are ill-bred.

This scene took place almost everywhere, in the distant plantations of the hills, at the very doors of Saint-Pierre or Fort-de-France. The officials, with Perrinon at the head, and lines of mulattoes, came to necklace the illusion of sharing the land. All spoke of Work, Work, Work, go back to Work on your plantations. Each time they met Perrinon, the few delegations of organized blackmen were offered

---

[1] [Go fuck your mother! . . .]

nothing but the word Work. It was first seen as one of the Republic's formulas. Then they finally understood that the fellow was just talking about work and would not hear of anything else. An-Afarel (whom my papa Esternome had gone to find, accompanied by Ninon and a plantation crew) confirmed it to them. They had come into the city to look for Law, in hopes of bringing their citizen béké to reason. But An-Afarel dispelled that first illusion, sang the Work tune, offered them liquor in a glass streaked with gold, and explained that there were two ways of working for the béké. The salary way where he pays you one franc or two francs for each task, depending on what you have agreed to. Or the cooperative way, where you share with him the fruit of the season, after he's taken out his expenses. The cooperative, An-Afarel, explained,[1] is much safer because you don't deal with numbers, there are no funds, and if salaries were to be given to everyone, they could only be honored by distributing pieces of paper with numbers on them as is already happening in that Guadeloupean folly. Then he left them to their new perplexity and disappeared in the direction of city hall.

The crew, with Ninon and my Esternome, found City packed with wandering blacks. The squares were oozing with impotent old folks, people with the yaws, leprosy, tuberculosis, coughing, spitting, with blackwomen older than Lucifer's baptism. Happy to be rid of them, the békés had left them there. These addled wretches would then wash up in City, the heart of the supposed happiness freedom had brought. The port was going about some of its business once again. Sugar reserves, released from the high hills, were once again flocking about. With its milatoes meddling in election matters, its oldtime free blacks back in their routine, City was up and going again without even creaking. The streets offered little room for those blacks from the hills.

---

[1]He was wearing a new frock coat with silver buttons and a lace jabot as fine as bamboo mist, for he was going around to public places to create electoral lists matching the registry books of the new civil state, because surely you understand how important elections are. The pro-slave hydra must not grow another head.

• • •

They walked around Savanna Park, yawned on the sidewalks, drank the fountain water, followed the massive arrival of Puerto Rican oxen, shadowed the shuddering trams step by step. Not knowing what to live on or eat, they nevertheless failed to claim the least odd job. It's damn true that freedom is anything that you want, citizen, but it's not work.

Back at the plantation, they gave citizen béké a hard time within the framework of a cooperative. As head of the crew, my papa Esternome negotiated the harvest sharing on the model: two thirds for you, one third for us. Where's this guy from? quavered the Béké who had never paid attention to him. Then seeing that my Esternome was a moderator, Béké calmed down. He must have thought that in those no-good days there was no use trying to understand. So everyone went back to work under the cooperative. Not anxious to return to the mud, my Esternome used his talent fixing up the surrounding houses. For a little while, let's say a wee bit of one season, ancestral noises echoed on the plantation. Then came the ups and downs of the farming (the shares didn't look too promising) and the boredom of the hated movements under the honey cane,

> . . . even if the overseer no longer had a whip, he stood in just the same old way. Citizen béké despite his citizenship came by at the same time and on the same horse, gauged the work with the same eyes. The sweat, Marie-Sophie, had that same old taste, the snakes hissed just the same, and the heat hadn't changed either . . .
>
> NOTEBOOK NO. 4 OF MARIE-SOPHIE LABORIEUX.
> PAGE 12. 1965. SCHŒLCHER LIBRARY.

they exacted a salary negotiated with thirty-two strikes,

> Ah, the exhilaration of the strike! It was like applying hot pepper to the Béké's wounds! It would break the routine

of that life for a few days, a return, for the space of a moment, to the exultation of the first taste of illusion. Oh the
drunkenness . . . that was living.

NOTEBOOK NO. 4 OF MARIE-SOPHIE LABORIEUX.
PAGE 24. 1965. SCHŒLCHER LIBRARY.

then they got tired of the salary and only went to the fields when
they felt like it, on such a day here, on a such a day there. The citizen
of the Big Hutch was losing hair over it. My Esternome often had to
go explain to him under the veranda that he shouldn't count on us
for today, citizen, we'll see about tomorrow . . .

Time went by like that, exactly like that. Ninon was becoming list-
less. Something had gone out in the flame of her eyes. My Esternome
knew that landslides crumbled deep inside her. He would say to her,
Ninon, it's going to be all right. And she replied, *It's OK, Ternome,
it's all right . . .*

One day An-Afarel arrived mounted on a new horse. Like a true
General Mangin, he was mustering up folks in the countryside in
view of the coming elections. This was new. Exciting. Universal. The
citizens listened to him from their hutches with touching attention.
A few days later, he was able to cart them off like a yam harvest. All
of this was about dropping their paper ballots into rabbit boxes. On
the road, An-Afarel explained to them that in order to cut the rising
heads of the pro-slavery hydra, strong tools were to be enlisted. The
names of these tools being: Bis-se-tte, Po-ry-Pa-py, Vic-tor-Schœl-
cher, whichever you wanted as long as it was one of those three. And
all repeated in a song of joy Bisèt Powy-Papy, Cheulchê . . . And
they danced more than anyone when these axes were elected to God
knows what.

My papa Esternome, now turned citizen, handled his saw, hammer,
and trowels. Each morning, while Ninon was out empty-hearted to

the tasks of the cooperative or of the wage work, he went looking for ruins to restore. If the countryside offered nothing, he went into City where An-Afarel found him a job. (An-Afarel was now breezing like wind all over the place. A boss of political commerce, he only had time to tell you the news—You understand, Esternome, the elections are annulled, we have to do it all over . . . Then he went back to his numerous committees where erudite milatoes faced planters.) The burnt ruins provided opportunities to make money. The shop owners' workshops, the wind-battered windows, the louvered shutters broken by no-good blacks, the disjointed steps, the balcony rails defeated by the sun, assured him daily francs or daily marked papers when it was banknotes. Otherwise, my Esternome was paid in cloth, old clothes, old watches, or some other happy toy for an honest couple: a silver goblet or a bottle with a crooked neck.

In hard times there were always the streets to repave (the night of the uprising, the blacks had ripped up everything), for which a starving crowd offered their talents. Others, hundreds of them, wandered in the calabash of wild freedom. Back from the salaried or cooperative ventures, they were fleeing the countryside to moor their hopes in City's enigma. But what kind of fields were these, they asked? It seems that here it's always harvest time, regardless of the season? Under which moon do you spread the manure? . . . But my Esternome calmed their ardor: Beware citizens, City has no breadfruit season . . . But them blind possums insisted on singing: *This is out of a dream without mud . . .*

> Texaco. There I see cathedrals of shafts, arcades of scrap iron, pipes carrying poor dreams. A non-city of soil and of gas. The town, Fort-de-France, reproduces itself and spreads out here in a novel way. We have to understand this future, knotted like a poem before our illiterate eyes. We have to understand that this Creole town has been

dreamt—I mean engendered—by its plantations, our plantations, by every Big Hutch of our hills.

THE URBAN PLANNER'S NOTES TO THE WORD SCRATCHER.
FILE NO. 7. SHEET XII.
1987. SCHŒLCHER LIBRARY.

As for Ninon, she was losing her footing. The light in her eyes wavered. She looked like the oil flame of a candle ring in the wind. She had found her cane bearings again, her mechanical movements to fend off their blades, her rags rolled up to the round of her shoulder, the old hat which pitilessly grated her temples under the heated sun. This badly watered life was hurling her every day down the bottom of the cliffs of her heart of hearts for good. My Esternome would make sure to be there when she came back home. She would come back like a withered flower. Month after month. Ninon was alighting from the world. She was beginning to look like the old African, her mother, no point in talking more about her. Soon she looked at what he brought her back (a glossy turtle shell, a small steel knife, some yellow scarves that she loved so much, a clear eau de cologne) with indifference. It made him so sick; he thought he could see her slow descent into an echoless depth.

To complicate matters, her African mother died beneath one night (the night before, she had give Ninon a carving made of guaiac that she was always kneading as she sucked all evening on her pipe). In the open day, on her pallet they found the young body of a blackwoman surprisingly wrinkled. Those who discovered the body saw, intertwined like in a basket, the innocence of morning and the unspeakable bitterness one finds in today's flophouses. That day no one answered the call to work. Mute before this lamentable miracle, the company dared not touch it. The overseer himself burst into the hutch on impatient heels. But he stood caught like a mussel during a bright spell, high and dry like those flowers in the dry season on the Vauclin Road.

. . .

After sunset, around the bats' hour, Ninon pulled a rustling, half-embroidered heavy cloth out of a casket. The African mother all her life (along with the cane, the coffee, the sucking of pipes, and caring for Ninon) had threaded it with thousands of twigs of violet wood with yellow reflections. That geometry transformed the cloth into a moiré that was disturbing to say the least. Everyone, even those who were only full of tafia, understood that it was her funeral veil and not one of those tablecloths the békés exhibit on communion day. There was no wake, just music rasping from sticks being rubbed against the partitions of the hut. Very few gathered to remember her. Though the whole day my Esternome had sounded a funeral note,

> *Ma Pipe the African is dead,*
> *I call you for her ceremony,*
> *Come one come all,*
> *you've got no feet*
> *ride on a horse,*
> *you've got no horse*
> *come on a mule,*
> *you've got no mule*
> *come on an ass,*
> *you've got no ass*
> *come, don't let the sweat*
> *soil your goodwill*
> *and your good deed.*
> *Ma Pipe the African is dead*
> *goddamn it,*
> *whoever hears me*
> *will spread the word . . .*

She was quickly buried. Even wrapped in its strange cloth, the little body thwarted fervor: it wasn't from here, never had been, it came from a great rumor still unknown to us and it was carried like a rock broken off from the moon following a crime.

The death of the African woman marked a new era. My citizen Esternome remembered that well. He narrated that death tirelessly, vaguely anxious and excited. The strange corpse was brought in a little procession up to the market town of Prêcheur so that a missionary could see it. She was buried in I don't know what. The funerary gathering drifted to Prêcheur, hoping to get lucky. Ninon remained by the grave. The only thing that now attested that her mother was from Africa was this fresh mound of earth decorated with calabashes. That enormous country about which none knew squat. The African herself had only evoked a cargohold, as if she had been born in it, as if her memories stopped throbbing there. Ninon didn't know that though she honored her mother's memory she would forget Africa. All that would remain would be the woman, her flesh, her tenderness, the sucking noises she made with her pipe, her insane immobility, but nothing of the Other Country. Not even the word of a name.

Going by there in his old age, my Esternome saw a strange kind of tree on this grave. Bespectacled scientists were stationed there for endless surveys. The tree was not from here. It had never been seen. On the other hand some congos here under contract had no difficulty identifying it. They replanted its branches throughout the country, wherever work took them. Above Saint-Pierre's remains, my citizen has always told me that there exists a tree of that kind, a massive survivor of the volcano, spread like the spirit of a man who still owns his memories. I've never gone there to see it myself, because you know, Chamoiseau, these stories about trees don't interest me. If I tell you this it's because you insist, in my appeal to the Christ on behalf of Texaco, I, Marie-Sophie Laborieux, was a little neater and the only reason I spoke was because I really had to, but if these things are to be written, I would have noted different glories than those you're scribbling.

• • •

So Ninon stood stock-still by the grave. A few steps away, my citizen patiently waited for her despite the heat Prêcheur bears. He understood she could be tarrying seven quarters of a century. With her mother, Ninon had buried a part of herself. She now lived on the edge of thirteen graves, in a great cemetery. So as the saying goes—if your mother won't give suck, try your father—my Esternome decided to make a turn in their lives.

Before this necessary turning point, he plunged as usual into a calculation as long as an old woman's tit but this time not so sterile. After a thousand detours his thoughts brought him back to the Mentor's words. The man had spoken of taking City. My citizen had tried without finding the right door. He was now wondering if that door truly existed for him, or for Ninon, or for others of his kind. City, already old, had put shutters with locks and bolted doors on each of its opportunities. In City, time went by too fast. He went otherwise. Only the mulattoes, already prepared, knew what ladder to climb, and through which vices to rifle in order to stumble on virtue.

Around him there was nothing clear to understand. Perrinon had been gone for a while, others had come. Today, one called Gueydon ruled ruthlessly, taking his orders from one Napoleon called the Third. Freedom had gotten itself a contract, a bankbook, and a passport. Any contract with a béké for more than a year made you a man worthy of honors. Contracts of less than a year made you vulnerable to the patrols checking your passport. To work by the job or by the day (taking it easy) was asking for it. Where do you live, what do you do the rest of the time, parasite of the Republic!? . . . The others, the stargazers, the stubborn blacks like Ninon who insisted on carrying their dreams wherever they took their shadows, they were called vagabonds, were arrested, condemned to some sort of slavery said to be disciplinary. They were made to do forced labor for the public good, meaning the colonial one. And that, my citizen narrated, that's how the beautiful Gueydon Fountain was built, that you can see above the Levassor Canal when you go down toward Texaco. Those who built it in the workshops of discipline were the black dreamers, forever dreaming, terrible dreamers. For them, the only good chains, whether they were the Republic's or Napoleon's, were broken chains, cast off in the streets of City. And neither the gendarmes, nor their notebooks, nor even the income tax that hit all of us, forcing you to find a way to pay it, have conquered our dreams. That's why my citizen has always called that fountain *Liberty Fountain*.

Besides, a bit nutty in his old age, it amused him to rechristen everything, re-creating the country according to his memory and to what he knew (or imagined) of the stories we lived underneath the History of governors, empresses, békés, and finally of the mulattoes who more than once succeeded in altering its course. Not to do that was like floating in the wind. And he no longer wanted any of that. He didn't want to be a wreck either, going crazy in the disciplinary pens. He didn't want to use himself up in City underneath soulless odd jobs and live in the wind of days without yesterday and tomorrow. He absolutely didn't want to join those who drooled in new flophouses, vanquished by old age and falling sickness and who were fed without honor or respect. What then: when Ninon asked herself *Ki léta nou jôdi?*[1] What's going to become of us? . . . the answer jumped blip in his head.

Along with City, the Mentoh had mentioned the hills the békés and mulattoes had not yet besieged. My Esternome said to her: *Ninon, dear, no rushing, the bamboo flowers every seventy years. It doesn't look around to see what the hibiscus is doing.* That was his way of saying that at nineteen years of age, free in the big bang of history, he chose marooning. And holding Ninon, almost kissing her, pointing to the greening Prêcheur heights, he murmured: *Oh sweet, we've got to leave freedom to go frolicking into life . . .*

---

[1] [What state are we in today?]

. . .

As usual, he needed a push. Destiny sent him some kind of fever that turned its victims all yellow. This flung City into the commotion of the military hospital. Békés and france-whites stifled each other in a room where doctors came and went. Onto the ground's sawdust, each spread liver pieces here, some gall there. They were cared for with powders, bloodletting, scalpels. On the steps, City blacks begged into this medicine-hospital with plantain-colored eyes. Every skin dripped green sweat. All life, even if unharmed, was hindered. The thing had come to the port with some crew, had infected City, contaminated the asphyxiated hutches in all its recesses. With Ninon hit by the first sweats, my Esternome wished to bring her to the hospital steps and beg for some powders. But the trip being risky, he resigned himself to the land slaves' know-how: lemon rubs, blessed-jatropha teas, infusions of monkey's-hand and male bois-lait bark. As for him, all day he ate plump star-apples, as enjoined. His fear of losing Ninon in the feverish heat went against his calculations but matured his plans. Fevers, cousins of the long-one (so he had heard), wriggled barely above ground. High land was therefore healthier. They thus took the path to the hills as soon as Ninon felt better.

My citizen was a bit anxious about the ease with which Ninon left her bitter freedom for the new country. Up there, the békés did not have a claw in the soil. Because their cane was only profitable on lands where their plow worked with ease, they had settled by the sea, on the good ashes of the North, the center's alluvial flows, and on some Southern plateaus. They had only (my citizen thought wrongly) tackled the hills up to the coffee's height. In any case, he would say to Ninon, who, bundle on back, went along like a semi-zombie (he, a knife in his hand, carried his toolbox, a bag of provisions, and blessed plants, his head caught in a new screwpine hat), up there the land will be ours, two innocents in paradise, and life will make tall yams grow in our garden. They had left early, at the time the overseer came to sound his "workers." My Esternome had called out your-mama to him as he went by and then woke up Ninon. They had climbed the backs of the first hills. They had rested in the shades of springs, by thick moss and serene bamboos.

> Sophie, it was like leaving their stories to go and live our own. But their stories went on, and ours was just taking another curve. Think of curves. The Caribs took a curve. The mulattoes went down a curve of their own. The békés went on one, and all of us shook with the History that the boats from France unloaded in Saint-Pierre day after day.
>
> NOTEBOOK NO. 4 OF MARIE-SOPHIE LABORIEUX.
> PAGE 27. 1965. SCHŒLCHER LIBRARY.

> In what I tell you, there's the almost-true, the sometimes-true, and the half-true. That's what telling a life is like, braiding all of that like one plaits the white Indies currant's hair to make a hut. And the true-true comes out of that braid. And Sophie, you can't be scared of lying if you want to know everything . . .
>
> NOTEBOOK NO. 1 OF MARIE-SOPHIE LABORIEUX.
> PAGE 3. 1965. SCHŒLCHER LIBRARY.

They had crossed waters so mighty they looked like solid glass. Plants rising from these waters joined them to the sun. Taken aback by some holes, they tripped and stumbled beneath big leaves that held the cany smell of sap cemeteries. They would rise out of it by nets of land which lifted harsh vegetation to the sun. Clouds ripped by the mountain or by the Pointe des Pitons floated above them. What they went through there (my father only found out in the free lands) a lot of other fellows had also gone through. They were in the North, others in the South or still in the middle of the country. To divulge such a mysterious odyssey, my Esternome often used the term *noutéka, noutéka, noutéka*. It was a kind of magical *we*. He loaded it with the meaning of one fate for many, invented the *we* that would prey on his mind in his last years. But I am not going to recite yet this Noutéka of the Hills. My season is ending and I've already lent the valiant days of my life to my notebooks, writing down a bit of what he used to tell me. This took me a time I gave to it without counting. Why? Because without understanding it I knew this: our Texaco was budding in all of that . . .

THE NOUTÉKA OF THE HILLS

Noutéka . . .

We felt like we were going against the winds. These guarded their domain. At each outlet above a ravine, it swept us away before it cleaned the landscape. Purer. More savage. Without any other smell besides that of the water cane. But especially colder . . . *(illegible)*

Silence. Not a bird taking shade under a bush or flying in the light alizé creates disorder. *(illegible)*

We went on. The hills were not that empty, as it turned out. An antique life rose here and there, though it became sparser as we climbed up. Ruins of ancient Big Hutches. Chapel floors. Canals of dead stone. The bones of a wheel sticking out of a river. Cocoa trees mummifying the shadow of a plantation. Etcetera coffee trees, tobacco plants . . . Here more than one colonist had lost his share: that was legible.

Noutéka . . .

We ran into some old whites stationed by folly. Engaged men freed of their contracts, they had climbed up here in the days of the Marquis d'Antin, when Carib men still ran about the land. They watched us go by without surprise, hands on their chassepot rifles from buccaneer times. Sometimes they took us for maroons. They would then greet us. But it wasn't about marooning for us, Marie-Sophie, it was about *going*. It wasn't refusing, but *doing,* each back fully carrying its load, but that's a Father Grégoire story . . . *(illegible)*

These old whites made us pick up the pace. Their presence told us we weren't far enough away. And definitely not high enough.

Noutéka . . .

We ran into békés' blackwomen. They had gotten a flank of hill, a ridge of land, early on. And they were living on it with their trail of mulattoes, their explosion of chabins, outside of the world, outside of time. Bowed over the earth as if over their fate which they were trying to decipher in the crooked roots that gave them eats.

While going by we would cry out that Liberty had come. Their sons, beings with yellow hair which the wind disheveled, kept their mouth shut and didn't understand squat. Only the old mother bothered to blink, peering out of her solitude. The old one, up from a century-old sleep, would make three little signs in our direction. But signs of what exactly? Signs that said neither hello nor adieu.

At other times, the béké's blackwoman ran away, refusing our existence and refusing any existence other than that traced by her desire: to be the mother of mulattoes who by marrying each other will end up becoming all white and possess life . . . *(illegible)*

. . .

We ran into maroons. Their hutches blended into the ferns. They were somber, also absent from the world, different. They had, as time passed, remained in the spirit of the country from before. Seeing them come out was strange. They carried loincloths, lances, bows. They exhibited all kinds of bracelets sculpted in bamboo, with chickenhawk feathers, had rings in their ears and ash on their faces. They came out, not to say hello, but so we'd know that this place was taken, that we should beat the bush a little further.

To them too we would call out: Freedom's here, freedom's here. They looked at us without the least curiosity and disappeared swooosshh. It was like saying: This freedom business it goes back awhile. In these rebels of the early days, there was not the least bit of feeling for us. Not a friendly gleam. From them we could only expect contempt. So more than one of us would shout back with rage: *Yo pa ba nou'y fout'! Sé nou ki pran'y.*[1] They didn't give to us, we took it . . . Thank God, that piece of history was ours . . .

We ran into some mulattoes' gardens. They were cultivating things in the highlands through slave stewards. The latter didn't know they were free yet. They went about their masters' land like dogs on a short leash. They never wanted to follow us, as if already trapped in the habit of being dead before their funeral.

When the falling day painted threats and the rising day its valiant glorias, up there, it was good to keep quiet. The night carried noises (bwa-kabritt,* frogs, crickets) that

---

[1] [They didn't give the damn thing to us! We're the ones who took it.]

would die around four in the morning. Then the yellow-bellies chirped until it got silent as a church marinating in the hot sauce of midday.[1]

Noutéka . . .

We found black affranchis: they had not joined the nearby market towns or City. They welcomed us, pointed out spots for us. Among them sometimes were shipwrecked whites who spoke Polish or another motherless tongue. We also found guava-mulattoes, obscure békés here on earth to harmonize the world with their mad love for a puzzling blackwoman. In the torments of this cloudy earth, all had spread *the Trails*. They had dug narrow paths on the ridges, had drawn with their heels, wherever they'd gone, the geography of another country. Our quarters would find their niche exactly at the crossing of these first traces.

They showed us what békés called standing timber. The békés, we learned, had gone through the country with a fine-tooth comb. Even up to the furthest reaches of the birds' flights they had swept everything up, laid a greedy hand. From time to time, they'd barge in savagely, dislodge the occupant, undo the straw hutches. Sometimes, tolerating these hovels, they reminded those they spared that this land without anyone was not the good Lord's.

---

[1]Lè fin-bout la jounen téka bay koulè goj, lè jou téka lévé gloria toudouvan, an môn falé ou té pé la. Lannuit téka chayé an latrilè bruitaj (kabribwa, grounouy, kritjèt) tonbé kanyan koté ka tred maten. Epi, fal jôn té ka sonnen bek yo, jis lè pa té rété piès bri, kontel an fon légliz lè soley la ka bat. (*Other version, on page 7 of notebook no. 2.*) [The very end of the day colored the gorges, the day sang gloria all the way ahead; on the hills, you had to keep quiet. Night brought a trail of noises (bwa-kabritt, frog, cricket) falling only around four in the morning. And then yellowbellies sounded with their beaks, until you heard nothing else, as quiet as a too-hot church.]

. . .

Noutéka . . .

We learned not to settle too high up—*cold front,* where our hutch walls made of wooden knots could not withstand the wind—*water front,* where our little knits didn't cover us enough—*rare air front,* where we would have to eat some other way to be able to stand on our feet. The tall ferns marked where the climbing should end.

Noutéka . . .

Too high, the land was badly chabinous, that is ill-tempered, nervous, unfaithful, betraying the hutches and the crops. Carrying on its old affair with the rain, it would suddenly elope, ruining lives, tools, and gardens in its wake.

How many hutches we buried before we understood. Pain shook the Médaille.

We saw the wild pigs that the Spanish had let loose in the country a long ago time, running around.

Noutéka . . .

We moved in on the high country's dented backs and the peaked heads. That was building the country (not the mulattoes' country, not the békés' country, not the coolies', not the congos': the country of the blacks of the land). That was building the country by Quarters, Quarter by Quarter, towering over the market towns and City's lights.

Frangipanis with yellow and red flowers perfume the oldest miseries . . . *(illegible)*

To say *Quarter* is to say: blacks who came out of freedom and entered life through this side of the land. Plantation meant: Big Hutch, service buildings, bound-up land, and blacks. *Quarter* meant: sun, wind, only God's eye watching, soil on the slide, and blacks who had finally broken free. But, careful! Marie-Sophie: here I'm telling you about the *Quarters up there*, neighborhoods of the ridges, of the hills, of the clouds. The *Quarters down there*, by the canefields, meant the same thing as plantation. That's where the békés stuck their workers.

We learned that here the ground was richer than below, newer, still flitty, not yet milked by etcetera harvests. And we learned to find the right slope.

The difficult thing was to survive without having to go back down. We grew what békés call secondary crops and we call food crops. Near the food crops you have to plant medicine plants, which bring luck and disarm zombies. Growing them all tangled up with each other never tires the soil. That's Creole gardening.

Work again, always work: weeded soil is no garden yet.

Mark the borders of your plot with crushed glass; plant some ruddy immortelle on top.

First, plant the providence of the breadfruit tree. Reduce oil shortage by planting avocado. Mind the shade and the watering. Watch for the moon: the moon which rises makes all things rise with her, the moon which goes down flattens everything. Plant on an empty stomach and the tree will bear no fruit. Plant on a full stomach, the tree will be generous. Put up barriers against salt winds. Where the soil shivers plant thickets with roots like claws: sweat pea, local pear, rose-apple, orange trees. From far away this seems all due to chance; in reality, Marie-Sophie, it is fate's beckoning. You've got to read the landscape.

The silk-cotton tree yields its shade soon enough and even yields cotton good to guard your ears from useless words . . .

Noutéka . . .

We learned to put down our hutches on terrace platforms dug out of the vertical slope, to knit them to the bone of a rock if a rock was around. To seal them with soil. To use the sloping parts for the hutch's entrance. The hutch's other half leans on two stilts which go deep down in the earth looking for the back of the land.

Furrow, furrow, furrow in a straight line.

We avoided valleys too deep: life there is wet and dark. But the valleys that are open to the sun offer a maternal, fertile soil, lavish with calm river water. Water from the valleys carries the promise of irrigation for the splitting thirsts of the dry season. Like God's carafes.

We learned to settle behind the backs of the hills: they rip apart clouds and force them to rise. This makes for a warmer and drier nest.

Noutéka . . .

Think hard about where to put up your hutch. The rest comes easy.

. . .

The terrace is built with a helping hand. All aboard, no one below, tafia, maracas, and drumsticks. Two fellows at the end of a rope break the land. They dig horizontally, throw the soil down below. Around the cleared space, hold on to the wounded soil with a pile of big rocks, and there plant trees that grow without thinking. On that terrace set down your hutch.

Everywhere, around the clusters of hutches, the thirstless green of our breadfruit trees. The sign of a very long freedom.

To grow on the land made horizontal. No slope is to be feared: the machete and the pitchfork were our only tools. Light to carry. Light to work with. We went from one terrace to another. Soon the tiles of gardens appeared on the steepest slope. Gardens of green tenacity, gardens of tilled soil, living on sandy ashes, colored with ocher tufa. Furrow, son, furrow on . . .

We carried our products on the heads of our women, the shoulders of our men, on the back of our donkeys. The Trails were therefore something other than the colonial roads: they led, without any trumpet, to where your heart desired. Later, when there were schools, with the changing weather, we had to tell the mayors to cement over these Trails for us, to reduce their sliding slopes, their sharp angles, their abrupt descent. Later we had to connect the Trails with roads going to the factory. But the Trails still remained something other.

Noutéka . . .

. . .

Roads uncover solitude and suggest other lives. They bring you up to City. They sweep all of the hutches along in an anonymous dance and destroy the Quarters. A road is good neither too early nor too late. If you get it right, consider yourself lucky.

We learned to love solitude. Not like that of the just-off-the-boat coolie living in a daze. At the pippiree bird's song, one should be able to hail one's brother to the right of your garden, one's sister on the left. To be too alone in the hills was to offer one's spine to the zombie's dirty hands. Helping each other was the law, a helping hand to do what was possible, working together for the immediate needs: in the hills, solitude must fight isolation. Many of the first colonists failed in their adventure because they did not know that. Solitude is a relative of freedom. Isolation is snake food . . . *(illegible)*

The family grows. The child finds the strength to work in the garden. Then he goes further on to look for his own plot. The gardens were further and further away from the hutches until they were no longer in the Quarters. That's why. Otherwise, hutches and gardens went together.

The Creole Quarter exists with geography's permission. That's why places are called Valley-this, Mount-that, Ravine-this, Ravine-that . . . It's the land's shape which names the group of people.

Shaken land gives rise to small hutches glued to each other on each side of the Trail, which follows a stable ridge. The gardens hold on to the slopes, and the valleys are left to the waterfalls. Shaken earth means a tight Quarter, in the shape of a belt, dictated by the place.

. . .

Plant your coconut tree with three fistfuls of salt. Angola pea won't give you no trouble . . . *(illegible)*

When the relief is soft, the hutches take flight. The Quarters touch each other and mix. When the soil's bone leaps off a cliff, hutches shoot up from its tip following the edges. The Quarter is a string.

Noutéka . . .

The Creole Quarter obeys its land, but also its grass from which it takes straw. And also its woods out of which it builds its hutches. And also the colors of its earth from which all its masonry comes. The Creole Quarter is like a native flower.

The Creole Quarter is people who get along. From one to the other, one hand washes the other, two fingers smash lice. *Helping out* is the way things go. That's even how a Quarter calls. So I don't need to tell you . . .

A pitchfork. That's all. And the land, if you can get there, will be your neighbor, and a most fertile one too. Just a pitchfork . . . *(illegible)*

> NOTEBOOKS NOS. 3, 4, AND 5
> OF MARIE-SOPHIE LABORIEUX.
> 1965. SCHŒLCHER LIBRARY.

DOCTOR OF HUTCHES

My Esternome and his Ninon settled somewhere on the hill, just like one settles in new country. His spirit seemed struck, that's the word, with possibilities. Around him, no Big Hutch, no one to cut the wind in his sails, no cane rustling over suffering. The world was yet to be made, and he would tell his Ninon, *The world has yet to be planted.* He felt himself glisten like sea under moon. Valiantly, he set to work. And this valiance he kept until the hour of his misfortune.

His first hutch was made of bamboo. Bamboo partitions. Bamboo roof. Braids of coconut straw to stop the waters. Guarding against humid winds, the straw covered the whole hut with an old woman's hair. Depending on his moods my Esternome erected other kinds of hutches. The most beautiful one was a nest of wild sage picked from the driest areas. He was lucky because up there his profession was a blessing. All the blackmen that moved up into the hills called on Esternome, Doctor of Hutches, for help, agive me a hand at such a time please. So much did he help everyone that he and Ninon never lacked anything, neither plants for the garden nor medicine leaves. On one terrace after another, my doctor built hutches made of turtleshell tree for others, hutches made of ravine, low-wall, drumstick, and of course of logwood trees. He built hutches easy to move if the ground changed too much, and hutches that held tight to the cliff heads. When there wasn't too much wood, he finished the hutch with an oily mud mixed with little leaves that he kneaded with his heel to the cadence of drums. In other places he'd smear onto the walls a coating of his own making (limestone-shells-sand and ox caca). Oh Marie-Sophie, the hutches covered with earth stay coolest. To stop the sun, I would add another layer of white earth to the façades and protect them by lengthening the roof's edges, and they would last a decade.

During these evocations, ardent vanity flowed in my Esternome. To see him thus, master of the hills, he who knew nothing of the earth, made Ninon happy, and maybe even a little proud. That of course wouldn't prevent the misfortune to come; but for the moment, my Esternome was wallowing in his "*I.*" I this. I that. I built the hutch with bitterwood to discourage the hungry termites' teeth. For poles,

I used West Indian cashew, Marie-Sophie, or the simaruba which astounded the birds, or even the mastic-bully tree, the bulletwood tree, cabbage-bark tree, the tall ferns, the rat-bean tree, or even the locust tree. What do you know of these woods, Marie-So? My know-it-all, what do you know about the breadfruit tree, mammee-apple tree, or dried pearwood? What do you know, Ma'am-o'-Science, of the laurels' perfumes, of the prickly ash and the river tree? *I know. I. I. I.*

For hutch floors or for walls exposed to rain, I used dead rocks, rocks that had rolled into ravines, detached from the soil. Or I surprised everyone with light pumice, insulator from misfortune, easy to cut (you can find it all over Pelée's sides). My emergency straw came from the foxtail, the vetiver, the Indian plantain. I patched up all of the holes with mountain palm and martabane. My hutches didn't lose their hair in the wind, my roofs rose smoothly, high as a man's shoulders. I knew the right slope on which straw would resist best. I. I. I.

The women went down far to pick cane leaves. Twenty dried leaves make one head of straw. Fifty heads of straw will cover a normal hutch. I tied those heads in a special way, with siguine, mibi lianas, or mahoe string. First I would secure a few to seal the rooftop. With scurvy grass, placed roots in the air so it might dry on the spot, I filled in the roof's holes. The women would throw me very damp heads of straw and I would tie them in a line my hands buried in the straw. Then I would go down, down, until I had covered the roof with a rustling hat. Then I would become a hair stylist: cut the bangs by the door or blocking windows, and comb the hutch well so it might mock time. I. I. I.

> Do you realize what it means, So-Marie? To be able at one point in one's life to say: I . . . Fate's thunders, what do you make of that?
>
> NOTEBOOK NO. 5 OF MARIE-SOPHIE LABORIEUX.
> PAGE 29. 1965. SCHŒLCHER LIBRARY.

But straw never lasts long enough. It all had to be done over every two-three years. That's why I was glad when corrugated tin came along. Oh, the strength of a roof made of corrugated tin kept cool with some grass! I. I. I. For pigpens and outdoor kitchens, I put together tiles made of eternal bamboo. I. I. I. I straightened the tips of my poles in the fire before coating them with mud, except when the wood oozed with stubborn sap. I. I. I. My windows slid shut, so did my doors, and I garnished the entrance with a flat stone. I. I. I.

For Ninon, I outdid myself: a beautiful room, two beautiful bedrooms wrapped in downy light. In each bedroom, a bed on locust tree feet safe from the long-ones. I. I. I. I made her a mattress of coconut fibers, a chest of cypress mixed with vetiver which forever perfumes, its bottom covered with mahogany, and the linen (City linen or nice funeral linen) would come out of it as innocent as morning dew. I. I. I.

FACTORY CHARMS

As for Ninon, she was no burden. My Esternome was astonished to discover that his woman possessed a vast know-how. A knowledge of the land and of survival. Without it, they would have been lost in these motherless heights. Right away, to chase off mosquitoes, she smoked the hutch surroundings with castor oil seeds. She braided brooms with screwpine which made the earth inside the hutch shine. She planted around the hutch some of these plants which perfume, which feed, which heal, and which knock out all kinds of zombies.

Once their hutch was finished and the years went by and my Esternome, once all the hutches were built, grew a potbelly, he had to initiate himself into Ninon's know-how, to live according to the seasons given by the earth.

In the months of May and June: prepare, she said, for the rainy heat which will shake the ground. Plant, it's time to plant. Saint John's Eve is a good day for that. My Esternome followed her step by step. With her, he learned to attach a bamboo support to the plantain trees, to tie the climbing plants threatened by the rains. To pick the mangoes, cucumbers, chayote squash, or yams with a good hand. Pick and sell at the crossroads or at the entrance of the market towns.

July. Finish the planting. Clean, clean, check the breadfruit tree which ripens in November, check what is giving fruit. August, September, October, November: Ninon would tell when it was going to rain, and would slow down. Let the soil do its job after a job well done. She taught him beautiful gardens steaming in the reappearing sun, how to watch the growth budding in the ground, which weeds were to be ousted. He found out how to dig the canals that rerouted the waters. Beneath the big rains, Ninon stayed home to repair his tools, file his machete, whittle stakes. She would come out only to take a yam from the soft earth, a potato, a cabbage, and shove the ash-covered reserves under the bed.

September. Pick and sell. It's sugar apples, it's soursop, Spanish lime, and naseberry. November. Clean the puddles, drain the sap from the cinnamon, pick the mature coffee, take the cocoa under the shade of the big trees. In December's winds, the earth slows down, the sap spirals down. The leaves are feverish. Ninon was teaching him to live through that pause of the land by standing still in the middle of the garden or by the cliff in front of a landscape.

In January, catch up with the dry season: plant the land's vegetables. In February it's flower time. The Quarter smells like balm. Songs are heard. Smells of coffee, cocoa, cinnamon, nutmeg, annatto, rise everywhere. In the silence of the heat spells, the castor oil plants make their seeds explode.

In March you've got to water, water, water, go down to the ravine and come back up to water. Ninon linked the garden to the springs'

clear nets with a web of bamboo gutters. Vegetables only grow
where there is the right amount of water, so decide your watering
and be constant with your watering. Thus, Ninon sowed between
her hollow bamboo stems. In March, April: burn, burn the thickets,
weeding, weeding, prepare the earth for the May planting, let the cut
grass rot, and manure the garden well.

Ninon set up a rotation: manioc-cabbage-yams, then potatoes, then
cabbage and yams. When the moon rose, she planted what was to
grow tall; during the full moon she trimmed but never cut; when the
moon went down, she pulled up the weeds which would then no
longer find the strength to spread. Then she would put in the ground
the plants whose well-being fed the garden. She also planted the desired trees on hand. And it would all start over again. And it would
all start over again.

Their Quarter had grown around fifteen hutches. Each month
brought a newcomer who settled by their side or climbed higher.
Their crops in their sacks, the women took the roads to City. They
would come back at night with two-three coins' worth of oil, butter,
cocoa, a few grains of salt. My Esternome barely ever moved then.
Crazy about the garden, he spent his time there. He planted his soul
there, as the song goes. His plantings were not at all as fruitful as
Ninon's. But despite the stories about the green thumb, he planted
with perseverance: losing himself in the way of the land exonerated
him from the failures in City.

Coming back from Saint-Pierre, Ninon gave him news: the roles had
been switched. The békés had watched their plantations drown.
What had worked well with slavery worked less well without slavery. In the countryside, listlessness thickened. The canes grew less
quickly than the thorny thickets. The cane's sugar seemed less good
than the beet's. On top of it all, that business of wages to pay when
no one had any coin had stuffed the planters into unspeakable wor-

ries. The governors, one after the other, set up banks. Loans made
the wage payments possible. But it was just as difficult for planters
to recoup their wage debts. It was no blackman's ambition to sweat
in the old chains. Those who resigned themselves to it demanded a
rhythm other than slavery's. That bothered the békés' luxury. So
they sent for other models of slave.

Ninon saw them get off the boat year after year. She described them
to my Esternome. He'd nod his head with its pipe (he had begun to
smoke like most blacks in the silence of the hills). She saw Portuguese arrive from the Madeira Islands. They took small steps
under the sun. Of the people gathered in their path, they only looked
at the long shadows. Their skin knew the sun. Their bodies disappeared under a pile of dark cloth, tied in all directions like scarecrows. She saw coolies with black skin, and those from Calcutta, of
a lighter cocoa-red. They wore a blue line that went down to their
nose. These would weep at a birth and explode with joy in the cold
hours of a death. Wrapped from top to bottom, they lived gathered
up like a clump of pigeons and ate strange things. She saw the congos arrive. Calm, disciplined, they nevertheless looked like late-
blooming maroons. She saw the hour when the chinese arrived
under their pointy hats, inscrutable as cliffs and cleverer than their
torturers.

My Esternome kept blinking. All of these people, he thought, would
climb up the hills. He told Ninon: You'll see, they'll come, they'll be
here anytime now. But he saw them very late, and only the congos
took the hills very quickly, to return to the land. The Madeirans
melted. The chinese took over City with groceries, then with stores
of all kinds. The coolies were gathered by the plantations and the
peaceful market towns: they were soon becoming prosperous and re-
spectable butchers, esteemed horse masters, expert in all manner of
donkeys. Though their gods killed off the sheep in long sacrifices.

· · ·

Despite the gendarmes on horse and the military furies, everyone abandoned the cane. Ninon saw the plantations' mills slow down. She saw all the Big Hutches close down one after the other. The big békés swallowed the little ones. The banks distributed a few flawed lands to blacks touched by the grace of work. One day Ninon took my Esternome to the tip of a hill, to see the horizon. She wanted to show him the new landscape: lots of fields, few Big Hutches, and everywhere, connected by laces of train tracks, of roads and of rivers, were the powerful torches of the big sugar factories—the new queens of the country.

Lots of blacks from the Quarter were leaving their gardens. From Tuesday to Friday, they went to work at the Factory's boilers or at some other machines. They consecrated the rest of their time to their waning dreams in the hills. The Noutéka of the Hills seemed aborted. Sure, one survived, sure, one was free, but the aftertaste of misery was rising quickly. It was the bitterness of a land whose promises fly away. It was from the boredom with nature that did away with all patience before the least wish came true. It was from seeing the mulattoes ceaselessly take over, speak well, eat well, and go to school. The hills had neither schools nor lights. You just found yourself with the sky over you like a lid, getting anxious, sometimes destitute, and always without perspective. The still hills did not care for any weakness. Thus, year after year, the maroon Trail began to go down to the Factory. There was opportunity there.

In her turn, Ninon too had the urge to go down there. First she only wished to go down and cram the harvests into the little trains that smoked toward the Factory. Then she desired to know the Factory itself. She would say: They're really hiring, it's not like land work, there are machines. And my Esternome would reply: Yes, but they are békés. And he mumbled, the Factory, the Factory, the Factory. That word was the thickest word of all in those days. Every life gave it a season. The great conquest of the hills was piteously going down the Factory's heap of connecting rods, its greasy straps, its tanks and pipes.

Oh the Factory gasped like a seven-headed Beast. The Factory panted with energy. The Factory vibrated with derailments which filled the hills with fateful murmurs. Sometimes my Esternome went near a cliff's edge to watch one of those monsters. He remained stunned before such power, a bit like before the Big Hutch or the City lights. But there was something else there. The roar of steel. Decisive toothed wheels. An untamable smell. An impassive array of rust and bolts. My Esternome didn't know what to think: his Mentoh hadn't predicted this.

AN INFERNAL SERENADE

Ninon wanted to go down to work at the Factory; he, Esternome, didn't want her to. So Ninon sulked. She pouted and looked at him scornfully when his eyes met hers. At night, in bed, she lay so as to be seven hills away from him. He would then remain stiff as a honeymoon hard-on. He had to take her as you would a yam when the ground is hard. While he milled, she sang whatever lalala, to show him that he didn't have her soul. And worse than that, no matter that he brought her whatever she needed, she disdained their promises. No swelling breasts, no music in the belly. Each month she exposed her flowers, red with empty eggs, and the not-so-good mood that came with it. My Esternome waited for it to go away. Then he would put it into her. Through force, as if pulling a mussel out of its thick shell. He thought (like more than a few men wishing to hold on to a gypsy) that a child would busy her enough to pluck out her desire of flying off to the Factory. But instead of a child, came the red flux, the red death, the cotton strips to wash, to hang, to wash and to hang . . . My Esternome counted them as if they were steps to martyrdom.

. . .

Ninon seemed happy about the absence of a child. My Esternome
heard her cry, without ever knowing if that pain poured from her desire for the Factory or if she mourned the clots in her belly. And such
doubts enraged him. He doubled his assaults without the least result.
And that, despite the fact that, I'm not lying to you, my Esternome
used all of the great fucker's pharmacy: woody liquor, onion juice
cut with honey, manioc porridge, fat round peanuts, dwarf-pineap-
ple hearts, carpenter's grass . . . And of course, every morning (on an
empty stomach) he drank three soft-boiled eggs whipped with old
mabi. That he took such great care of his seeds (or his fertility) allowed him to reach an age of great peace with great vitality; oh great
age, oh incomparable old age: you can fall in love with your memories there at the mere prick of a sigh. Thus, ages afterward, he was
able to mutterputter about how he lost his Ninon, without too much
turmoil.

Fate is like that. It often comes drumming in without ringing. You
don't see it coming. So, when my Esternome saw the bastard come—
the suspenders-wearing cur, Ninon's ravisher—he didn't feel anything, he welcomed him with joy. He was the kind of blackman who
was pretty as a picture. He had delicate hands, a tralala voice, fiery
big-peanut eyes, my Esternome said, and carried a banjo or a mandolin. That hound besieged the Quarter in the middle of a full moon
night, like a toad sent bearing a curse. While the Christians were fast
asleep, the firebrand flew from hutch to hutch . . . —and doing
what? *Serenading.*

The Quarter wobbled out of its dreams a bit frightened. The less
brave ones thought it was a zombie bacchanalia on this earth. Others dug up bottles of alkali, holy water, or ether out of their rags. But
right then all concern for misfortune disappeared. They saw themselves as the addressees of music. Music's wonderful sweetness. It
charmed people. It brought them to their heart of hearts, before a
great array of feelings, of sweet languor, of childish emotions which

made them all very drunk. In each hutch the small coconut oil lamps lit up. Sleepy silhouettes emerged out of each hutch, then eyes full of clear joy, then sleepwalking bodies which bumped into the musician.[1] Everyone begged him to stay by their hutch just a tad bit longer before moving on. But the musician went from hutch to hutch. Though some brought out tafia bottles, handed him sweets, a rare jelly, benches made of precious wood, no hutch seemed to be able to keep him—except of course Esternome's once he saw his Ninon come out of a good sleep.

The musician was a fellow with shining melancholy eyes. He wore a little hat with a fringe. His voice (su-seeping in French out of his perfumed mouth) was crammed with flats and sharps. His hand bewitched the mandolin's neck, cast a spell on the mandolin's belly, and the strings lent a music, as knotted as rabbit grass, to the beauties of his song. Good God, what a tale! . . .

If my Esternome savored the music, Ninon was ripped apart. For her alone the musician opened a world onto other landscapes. She first thought she was benefitting from music's grace. The following day, through questioning the others, she realized she was the sole recipient of this inexpressible thing. Bending over her garden, she remained worried: her heart beat larger; her head sheltered unaccustomed thoughts. When that scumbag came back evening after evening, around midnight, tuning his magic to that of the night, meandering between the hutches to come to a standstill before Esternome's, Ninon must have (with no maybes) understood the truth: this musician was the source of her confusion.

My Esternome was at first proud to see him stop before his hutch (the nicest one, besides). He offered him a bench with back support, sat Ninon at his side and sat on the musician's other side. In the mid-

---

[1]My Esternome used to say: mutt-sician. But such disdain is too easy . . .

dle of the Quarter, he sipped the serenade, seeing nothing of misfortune: the musician directed his music toward Ninon; he'd open up his inspired eyes only on her; in his semi-incomprehensible glob of French, he spoke of heart-on-heart, lips-on-lips, folly and drunkenness . . . For Ninon, this was the holiest of wafers. Soon the people in the Quarter began to throw words around (. . . Well now, it seems like the musician has found his accompanist, eh? . . . Oh la la! the music fellow has found some music around here . . . Hey, Esternome, someone's shitting on your feet . . .).

My Esternome no longer appreciated the serenades. His window was imprisoned by nails. The mandolin fellow began to play before the shuttered hutch. Then the unavoidable happened: his sweet songs became more and more bitter until they were so filled with pain that they killed off the fireflies. Morning would find the poor things blinking with sadness, the left wing tied to the right in an afflicted twitching. Jesus, Mary, what a tale . . .

> People have only moaned about the insalubrity of Texaco and other such quarters. But I want to listen to what these places have to tell. I hear them spell out the other urban poem at a new, disconcerting rhythm which we must decipher and even sing along . . . To take in their poetics without fear of dirtying our hands in its mud. What barbarism, and what an unspeakable indifference it would take to raze this process.
>
> THE URBAN PLANNER'S NOTES TO THE WORD SCRATCHER.
> FILE NO. 6. SHEET XVIII.
> 1987. SCHŒLCHER LIBRARY.

The musician would disappear as soon as the sun showed up. No one knew where he was from or what he did with his days. Some said he was master sugar worker at such or such a factory. Others whispered that he had brought a science of sugar learned from the

Portuguese in England and that the factory owners paid very dearly for it. In any case he would disappear around five in the morning.

He disappeared even faster when one night Esternome, victim of his nerves, ran after him with his big machete and made him stumble down the slope on all fours, or on all paws, if you prefer. No one saw him the following night, nor the night after that, nor even when the full moon, accomplice to his hateful songs, was at its highest point in the sky.

At first my Esternome was happy about his disappearance (the people in the Quarter didn't like it as much; the serenade's absence plowed their insomnia). Then my Esternome was no longer very happy, for Ninon too had disappeared. This took place on a night of a bad sort. Some sleepwalkers heard a serenade far away. It went not from hutch to hutch but in a celestial way, from high hill to high hill as if carried by a cloud, the musician threaded in the air. People found this exploit tremendous. My Esternome did too. The only thing was that Ninon herself had taken that path.

In fact, my Esternome never admitted that his Ninon was taken away by that scumbag with the serenade. He began to make up childish yarns.

First yarn. It went like this: Ninon one day went down a ravine to wash her reddened strips. So that ravine was not a good ravine, because in it lived not one of our water sprites, one of our Water-mamas, but one of those mermaids that move the france-whites. The mermaid lived there. Whoever can describe her has seen her, yet whoever would have seen her would have seen no one again. At this point the mermaid had never caught sight of any black person on this earth. To see Ninon was finally to discover absolute true beauty. The creature hummed for herself the way mermaids far away do. Her song was like no musician could hope for. Her voice lifted an ocean of algae and fresh wind. Ninon got caught in all of that and remained under the charm. Each time her monthly dew gave her a wash to do, the dreamer went down the ravine where no one ever went. There she listened to the song only women imagine. This is not a wound which bleeds, the mermaid would sing, but the divine window that women still have on life, it bleeds not with pain but with regret for life. Man, the mermaid would sing, has lost touch with the divine power. Those invalids desired to close this portal to women. And their blind wood released not life but a kind of cement for a grave without All Saints' Day. Woman, despite everything, transcended this death to create life, in secret alchemy.

Thus, each month, Ninon celebrated her red dew with the mermaid in great ceremony. She plunged naked into the water. Her red dew spread around her. On a round stone, the mermaid sang-sang. Ninon stayed longer and longer doing this. Often the night blocked her way. My Esternome began to suspect God knows what and resolved to catch her in the act. So he followed her, opening for her, without his knowledge, a very strange grave.

As usual, when her belly's red dew came, Ninon went down the ravine. The mermaid had expected her and welcomed her warmly. Ninon took off her clothes and went in the water. My Esternome, who was walking behind, taking possum steps, came out a bit later. He saw the mermaid without hearing her songs because he instinctively covered his ears. The sight of him made the mermaid go into a not very good rage. Her tail flapped furiously. Thirteen yellow scales fell off. And her fish spines went up. My Esternome understood the danger. He stumbled screaming to Ninon to run away. Ninon didn't even have time to understand. Convinced of betrayal, the mermaid tore down on her in a shwash of foam. And the foam, which filled the ravine to the brim as if a thousand laundresses were soaping in it, was all that my Esternome saw.

. . .

When he tried to move down into the ravine, he found the foam warm, then boiling hot. He soon had to back out: his skin was blistering with many droplets. So he stayed on the edge of the ravine, watching the foam gloat, broken with fear and the papaya-hope,[1] crying out Ninon's name, thinking he'd sometimes heard her in a lost echo. The Quarter people came to get him from the edge of this mud. Broken bamboos. Naked ground. Scales and grass mingling in the wind that blew them away. Not one of Ninon's eyelashes.

Second yarn. To explain Ninon's disappearance, my Esternome also cooked up some she-devil story even more lamentable. A witch who flew while playing a pipe and who this and that . . . He told it as seriously as he had the mermaid story, which he had forgotten: lies don't become part of memory. Anyway, whether she was taken away by the musician, the mermaid, or by God knows what pipe-playing she-devil, is all the same. Whatever the case, Ninon vanished from Esternome's life, crowned by a wreath of music. A flying she-devil . . . can you believe such hogwash?

BARBECUED LOVE

One should rather think of the fellow's despair. Without Ninon, he lived for many years like flowers in a vase. His brain was clotted with sadness. His eyes became faucets and his heart was a hot iron brand lodged inside his chest. When his despair was calmed (for despair from love dies faster than a little coal oven, heh, heh), he was seen wandering from ravine to ravine, lifting each stone, diving into each waterfall looking for his Ninon. His abandoned hutch was losing its clusters of straw, his pig was chewing soil and his chickens their own feathers, and he went around looking worse than a coolie without a contract, hunted down by the gendarmes. His neighbors would go after him. The frankest ones would say to him: Hey Ester-

---

[1][The male papaya blooms without ever bearing fruit; papaya-hope is doomed hope.]

nome, Ninon's left with a musician, and you're looking in the river? And he would retort: She left with a mermaid. They thought he had gone mad. Those were my crayfish days, he said, I had fallen lower than a freshwater crawdaddy. What an imagination . . .

This crayfish period finally had to come to an end. My Esternome's memory brought him back to his hutch without noting the path. Prostrate on his bed by his tools which were of no use to him, disgusted with life. Even disgusted with everything. When a congo revealed that in the city a young banjo was flourishing, decked out with one Ninon, without really reacting my Esternome still stammered about the mermaid. He didn't see the world change. He didn't see his Quarter make new trails, submit to the great roads. He didn't see the hill people submit to the békés at harvest time, nor lose themselves in the great factories one season at a time. He didn't see the Quarters of the clouds set their compass by the lowlands. He saw no one go die in the Mexican War nor in the hole of Bazeilles. He didn't feel the turmoil everyone felt when a tall lighthouse was lit at Caravelle. He heard nothing of the arrival of old King Béhanzin who eyed our country like a huge cemetery. He knew nothing of that rebellion in the South where some blacks reminded whites that an unleashed dog is not to be lynched. A few seasons went by like that, with my Esternome dazed inside himself, not seeing his hair whiten, nor his skin shriveling, nor the yellow spots covering the white of his eyes. Nor did he see how from time to time the horizon became roaring and how ash from the mountain suddenly floured the land, more and more often, for a longer and longer time.

One morning a huge bang blogodooom shook him into consciousness. He came out of his thousand-year stupor with a ball of hope. His first word upon his return to life was: Ninon. Ninon, which he repeated in the general tumult. Manic fleeing shook the Quarter. A fragrance of sulfur, of scorched-red wood, singed life, thickened the air. Each and every one around was screaming, *Soufrière has ex-*

ploded, Soufrière has exploded . . . ! This rumbling had undone the world. The women howled, hands clutching their heads. The fellows flinched. On the horizon, a night that defied the sun was rolling down. So for the first time in a long while, my Esternome went down to City. He wanted to seek, see, save Ninon. And I would tell him: So the mermaid hadn't taken her after all? He would put an end to such talk with a swift E-e-e-enough . . .

> Urbanity is a violence. The town spreads with one vio-
> lence after another. Its equilibrium is violence. In the Cre-
> ole city, the violence hits harder than elsewhere. First,
> because around her, murder (slavery, colonialism, racism)
> prevails, but especially because this city, without the facto-
> ries, without the industries with which to absorb the new
> influx, is empty. It attracts without proposing anything be-
> sides its resistance—like Fort-de-France did after Saint-
> Pierre was wiped out. The Quarter of Texaco is born of
> violence. So why be astonished at its scars, its warpaint?
> The Creole urban planner must rise above the insalubri-
> ous, become a medium.
>
> THE URBAN PLANNER'S NOTES TO THE WORD SCRATCHER.
> FILE NO. 6. SHEET XVIII.
> 1987. SCHŒLCHER LIBRARY.

He went down. On his way he met people. They were running away without being able to explain. My Esternome felt that something extraordinary had taken place down there. And he took greater strides. His anxiety about Ninon gave him the rhythm of a seething léwoz.* He floated in smoke. He trembled in an airless smell that had spread everywhere. He flapped his wings in silver ash. He saw black stones as light as soap bubbles fly toward him. He danced in puddles of warm springs which no memory had ever mapped. My Esternome no longer recognized the landscape that he had crossed going in the other direction with Ninon in his youth. He told himself, But how fast life goes, and stumbling down he was crying *Ho Ninon ho Ninon wah wah wah* . . . He didn't know whether he sobbed over Ninon or over this world extinguished by powdered gloom. He didn't feel his age, that's the advantage of not knowing it. Those running away only saw an old man, but he, as brave as a worker walking to the factory on that lone payday, went on. He descended, courageously.

On the edge of a hill, my Esternome discovered a lump of coal instead of Saint-Pierre. Despite his barbecued heart, it stunned him. But he only imagined it to be some horrible fire or some workers' rage against the factory owners. He began to go down with the thought of returning to relive part of his story, of finding Ninon in the middle of the crowd, at the same place, Ninon who falls in his arms. Soon he couldn't take another step forward. His eyes were burning. Even his gray hair burned him. The grass, the trees had withered. He saw white-eyed people tumble down out of a steam from hell: they went by like airborne pain. When he wasn't able to move forward, he stepped back, then advanced from another direction, moved back, then advanced further, then took side steps like a blackbird moving through glue, then like a hairy bat creeping out of a nightmare. Ninon bore him along. Soon he was able to offer more resistance to the pain. He began to jump over the animals in their agony without even looking at them. Later he forgot all about crossing himself before the dead or the flailing globs of flesh. And he moved on and on and on. So that he was the first to enter Saint-Pierre.

Much has already been said about that horror. The mountain that razed Saint-Pierre. That, my Esternome did not want to describe. He covered it with the same stubborn silence he had kept his whole life concerning the old days in chains. Maybe he wanted to forget what he'd seen on entering Saint-Pierre. He must have succeeded, for even when he wished it, he was only able to murmur scattered things, without much meaning, but just as terrible as a good description.

. . .

Anyway, much has already been said about that horror. Books upon
books. He must have whitened his last black hair over it. Dug his
forehead's creases with it. The disconcerted look in his eyes, which
he covered with his hands when he suddenly broke down, must have
arisen there too. His first step into the ruins must have cut up his life
into a before and an after. Of it he kept a pain buried in his face even
when he laughed. When at night I sometimes caught him wandering
around the hut, glimpsed the hesitation in his legs which he raised
high like ducks do, his hand calming his face, his mouth open with
asthma, I felt like I was seeing him standing in the middle of that disaster. He walked on like that, not seeing anything any more, so
much had he seen. A tide of ash. A deposit of still heat. The stone's
red glow. Intact beings stuck to wall corners, going up in strings of
smoke. Some were shriveled up like dried grass dolls. Children savagely interrupted. Bodies undone, bones too clean, and oh how
many eyes without looks.

My Esternome wandered like that searching for his Ninon. It wasn't
his day: he went from cadaver to cadaver. He examined every blackish thing, waded through the pulp looking for her face, rolled
around in guts searching for the curve of her oh-so-sweet belly.
Sometimes he thought he saw her in the mounds of flesh. Other
times, he would suspect that her hair was the halo of this fried piece
of blood. He had to climb ruins, walk in circles, often redouble his
steps. He must have collapsed once or twice but gotten up urgently
off the ash which was trying to roast him little by little. He was en-
circled by cinders, he knocked against wisps of smoke. The ash dried
onto him in a cement which his gestures broke. With a halo of dust
around him, he was becoming transparent, paler than a zombie.
Stone and people had melted into each other. Frigid fingerless hands
stuck out of the walls. Skin fed the burning furniture. Soon Ninon
was everywhere. In each blown-up chest, in each puddle of flesh, on
each pyre. So my Esternome lost a quarter of his reason. He began

to scream like a madman and to run around in a charred Saint-Pierre. Blasted ordeal, Papa . . .

Oh, my Esternome. If his lips were sealed, his scars spoke for him. The skin of his feet was burnt up to his knees. The skin of his neck crumpled into scales. The skin of his belly turned transparent. Strange and multicolored skin on the back of his hands. Stiff fingers, dried nails, holes on his scalp. His face had been left without burn marks. There only the woes of life prevailed. But these devoured him more than the cauterizing flames.

Of course, he never found Ninon. At one point his heart skipped a beat. He heard her call him. A voice rising from the stones. She was there! He plunged into the burning ash, then must have given up. Helping himself with pieces of wood, he cleared the entrance, advanced in a half-subterraneous hall strangled by a rotten-egg stench. Behind a door he heard the voices. Voices of madmen. He opened the doors to them. Two half-cooked zombies ran out of the dungeon, the only survivors of this great death. My Esternome asked them where Ninon was, *Ouéti Ninon?* But they looked at him without saying anything, ejecting themselves out of this jail which had saved them from the fire and into the frying pan of a nonexistent town. They returned to hide in the skirts of their dungeon. They almost thought my Esternome responsible for what they had seen. When he repeated *Ouéti Ninon? Ouéti Ninon?*, they, just in case, screamed shaken with terror, *We didn't do it, we didn't do it, didn't touch her* . . . My Esternome looked around some more and left, which relieved the two dungeoned fellows. Outside between the tails of smoke and whirls of ash, furtive un-Catholic shadows came out. They slipped into City and rummaged through the rubble.

They were blackmen with no shame. They pillaged the houses, lifted lumps of flesh to pull out a necklace. They would break a piece of bone to scratch off the melted gold. They knew the houses of the

rich mulattoes, and they scoured them like starving dogs, bringing
back a chest from the glowing ashes and things that looked like jewelry from under the burnt lumber. Among them were a few special
ones who grunted in other tongues. Having come in canoes, they returned to their islands with enormous sacks. Soon afterward there
were soldiers to hunt them down, shooting without thinking, and
long military processions looking for the gold of an unfindable bank.
Abbots came alongshore from far away singing a Libera. In the horizon, rolls of murmur rose from the boats reaching the catastrophe.
Everywhere the wind broke ranks in the face of the heat that
smashed the city. Witches appeared. They picked up bones. Mad-
women came. They harvested heads. Some sick people raked around
for no good reason. Around my Esternome looking for his Ninon in
the play of smoky curls, there were soon more people than there
were in the City before the hour of the volcano. A truly sad carnival,
you hear me . . .

Then the mists would choke each other. There were rains and pieces
of sun. The white horror spread beneath a clear sky. Boats crowded
the harbor. Officers disembarked by thousands, opening bulging
eyes. Guards were placed in each corner to stop the pillage, but the
pillagers went on pillaging. They were becoming invisible, crawling
beneath the embers, sliding behind the skeletons of the bushes at
night. Radiant with ash, they could swell like corpses and no sharp
eye could make them out. My Esternome, who was quite visible,
was grabbed more than once. More than once did someone want to
shoot him on the spot, but hearing him under his load of despair
Ninon, Ninon, Niiinooon, the soldiers bowed out. They said he'd
been stricken like City, right in the heart.

By dint of his moping around, they made him carry bags of quicklime on his back. Barges were bringing tons upon tons of it. He was
ordered to go dump them on the swarming maggots. Before emptying his lime, he checked to see if it was Ninon. If it seemed like it

could be her, he'd spread the lime like in a funeral. To the fizzling froth, he mumbled prayers that the Sunday abbots had taught him in the time of the plantations. When the lime finished its work, he was given straw, wood, coal, and had to light big old fires. Lines of volunteers, back from the rubble, dumped unspeakable carrion into the flames. For a time, kerosene was splashed over the oozing filth. My Esternome went around without a mask in all that devastation. The only one looking for the good smell of his beloved with his nose.

On other days, he had to dig big old holes and go harvest bones which he measured against his own before throwing them in. He'd often think he recognized one of Ninon's tibias. The width of her arm. The curve of one of her ribs. Then he would set it apart, thinking of reconstructing his sweetie. When his pile became too big, he started to make a more rigorous sorting, threw away, kept, threw away. When he got all mixed up, he would just throw everything into the pit, bawling. Then, in tears, led by a torturing heart, he would look for his Ninon in that extravaganza of bones. How does one mourn, ye gods? . . .

I once took a walk around Saint-Pierre and saw the big ossuaries. There I understood my papa Esternome better. Oh, how these bones beg! How they speak and rattle on! How souls clamor when the empty heart looks for that which used to fill it. I have sometimes pondered this. But dammit, how do you mourn? . . .

Soon there were no more bones, no more flesh, no more bodies. The mountain covered the burnt-out bodies with new ashes. And all of it melted into gray stones with soft shapes. With time they turned to charcoal without rot or smell. My Esternome would sit anywhere, eyes absorbed by his loss. He still hoped to see Ninon emerge from this or that rubble, this cave being explored, some debris being sorted out. In the swarming crowd, he often thought he recognized her, but the stranger would turn around and Esternome would fall away startled. At night he still wandered there, frequenting the spirits which smelled like incense. He heard the howls that some of the dead, curled up somewhere, had not been able to scream, and which his own pain suddenly triggered. He heard children cry, felt the maternal distress as his own. Everything was converging in him. He was dying with the whole City every night.

Soon he was seen putting walls back up, harvesting stones and beginning to pile them up. A poor mason conjuring the impossible. No one said anything to him. He seemed convinced of success. So his walls rose, his cement held tight even when there were other quakes, other disruptions, other lava flows. He wanted to rebuild City, pull it out of the void, cancel the misfortune, find that serenading rat and take his Ninon back from him. In fact, he began to set the walls upright. Whoever saw that old blackman fight against calamity thought for a long time they were looking at the dregs of misery. So sad . . .

He was the first to build in Saint-Pierre. With boards, with stone, atop some ruin, he raised his cabin. Others who had washed up there did the same. A wretched life bloomed above the disaster. The whole world was getting its picture taken before such an incredible event. My Esternome looked to the sea for food with other starving people. There he would spear big sharks which were surveying the place. Impossible things fermented in their bellies, but their flesh was good. The fishermen would eat it or exchange it for good vegetables. City was not experiencing revival. The ghosts had lost half of their heads. Their presence revived nothing: City only seemed to tremble with the chemistry of sorrow. The navymen wouldn't authorize any settling in the middle of City. The cabins grew up all around: ajoupas covered to the ground with mountain palm. Esternome could have stayed there on that spot and died eating those man-eating sharks, followed the pouring of the mulattoes and békés who were building sumptuous legacies by exceeding all bounds, watched the ruins bounce beneath the mountain's hiccups. But something not too good at all happened. Ninon came back to see him—but as a zombie, to torment him.

He told me that it had been the right night for that reunion. Under the effects of the moon, all kinds of things were sprouting up everywhere, a transient swarming, blinking sprites, white oxen, featherweight hens with two beaks, floating beings looking for God knows what, utterly dazed. My Esternome was seeing all this on his left and the same thing on his right. He was scared but he went along, hoping for Ninon's ghost. When he met it things didn't go very well, at least not as sweetly as in his tired dreams. Ninon had changed. She'd ballooned up and looked like a disgrace. Her skin had withered. My Esternome even thought he saw on her the pink lips of tafia-drinking women, and around her mouth the vulgar folds of those who curse in the streets. He had kept the sweet primordial image of Ninon. Now, there was only some sort of fishwife oozing out of Saint-Pierre, undulating toward him. She called out *Esternome, Oh Esternome* . . . but he only heard bamboo creaking. She gestured sweetly. But he only saw danger beneath that trembling. So he drew back.

A-ah! . . . a music rose wrapped around Ninon's zombie. He saw the scumbag with the serenade: pretty as a picture, a pin on his tie, Italian straw hat, checkered shirt, rings with blue stones on each finger. The dog had a new mandolin. This one dispersed silver twinkles, sounded like an Angelus. My Esternome wept: for he only saw a pimp with one of his women who danced to his music. Ninon was dancing death, dancing the bitterness of the docks, the greasy taverns, the blind cargoholds where the crewmen rooted blackwomen in the darkness. When he was able to overcome his horror and pain, he advanced toward them. That would make the serenading beast back off. Ninon stood floating nearby, chided him with her puffed-up eyes, waited for God knows what, then broke into laugher like a whore in the middle of a drunken fête. And when my Esternome quickly ran into hiding, she ran after him.

. . .

He no longer went to look for her in the ruins. He stayed home filing his pikes. But the zombies stuck to him. Around his bed obsessive melodies whirled. The fellow with the serenade became a persecutor. His notes made one's hair stand on end. My Esternome couldn't control this nightmare. When Ninon would enter the hutch through one crack in the wall, he left by another, and threw himself so violently against the sea, with so much pain, that even the mad sharks dared not make a meal of him.

She and her musician tortured him like this. At certain hours of the day when the sun was raw, when life slowed down, the ruins heating up bad memories, an old music would wrap itself around his ears: he thought he saw the musician-torturer and his fallen love floating in the glassy air. The worst was that he'd seen them on the left of his skiff too, when he went fishing. The infernal music rose from the depths of the water onto the harbor's calm sea. It filled the black sharks with anxiety. They wriggled around him, jaws wide. That Esternome of mine rowed back to shore with all of his strength. The monsters chased him up to the dry sandy coast. Seeing him leap out of his boat so fast, his buddies would say to him: What's going on, Master Esternome? What's happened? Have you seen a Watermama? But he was the only one to hear that music. The only one to suffer the sharks' assaults. When Ninon floated by his shoulder, in a breath of rotten lemon grass, no one saw or felt that atrocious thing. They only saw the frantic gestures he made to get her away, his sniffling, his flinching under a frozen hand grating him with its caress, and his hair which rose under her small evil kisses. So my Esternome had to flee the one he loved—that's the kind of sorrow that no old age assuages. I mean, can you do worse? . . .

My Esternome had to flee this crazy love of his life. He had looked for her in the ruins too madly: pain had committed him to running into zombies. He picked up himself and his fishing gear. But the hills weren't what attracted him. Up there memories of happiness[1] still floated. Once again, it was City that caught him up in its arms. This time I knew which city since I was going to be born there. So I would say to him: You took the steamer that left from the lost City on every day the good Lord made.

Since he knew you, the captain refused money. I see you sitting on the edge of the bridge among the merchandise, acting like those who'd forsworn Saint-Pierre which was still entranced by its death. Including you, they created the momentum for the leap to Fort-de-France.

—Oh Esternome of mine, come now, tell your daughter how you created it.
—Sophie-Marie, God creates, I've already told you that . . .
—But you must have helped him, no?
—A l'il tid, only a l'il.
Oh dear, Esternome . . .

---

[1]Happiness, when recalled, becomes melancholia or a heavy load of regrets.

AROUND FORT-DE-FRANCE

(in which Esternome's daughter,

bearer of a secret name,

pursues the work of conquest

and imposes Texaco)

THE AGE OF CRATE WOOD
1903–1945

We had run from Saint-Pierre. Some had left it
at the first rumbling of Soufrière's enormous
stomach. Others preferred to wait till the ash
covered up their eyes. The ageless dead had
come to touch a few of us and point to the sea
as the only way. Thousands of others waited
until seized by some pre-baptismal fear.

Saint-Pierre was behind us. We had gone far.
We had taken root all along the Trail.* Popu-
lating Alma, Médaille, Fonds Boucher, Colson's
borders, Balata's slopes. From Absalon's
springs to the edge of Pont-de-Chaînes, we had
left haggard but ended up growing roots. The
town councils housed us on the Caribs' beloved
coast. Carbet, Bellefontaine, Case-Pilote became our nests. In Fond-Lahaye they erected a
camp of dry leaves and tents for us. We
slumped there for time out of mind, until we

vanished—to grow roots in that place or to chase after fate's tail. While warming up, Saint-Pierre had splashed the land with our souls.

And Fort-de-France greeted us the way one does a tidal wave.

NOTEBOOK NO. 10 OF MARIE-SOPHIE LABORIEUX.
1965. SCHŒLCHER LIBRARY.

My Esternome didn't look too good when he arrived at Fort-de-France. He looked like an old man who had just rolled down from the hills. But who saw him? No one saw him. No gendarme asked for his papers, since there were just too many of them like that, you know, who had landed on the grasslands around the Fort. My Esternome alighted in a tizzy. The people of Foyal[1] lived as if under assault. The slightest cloud was a would-be fiery plume threatening to make them expiate their sins. The country thus wriggled about like someone with his head cut off. A different kind of life must have thrived here in this soldier town, right in the middle of a mangrove swamp, a perfect nest for fires. Rebuilt more than once, her memory was made up of cinders and of feverish miasmas. But though I begged and begged my Esternome, *So tell me about this City, what did you feel when you got there?*, he looked at me with the cloudy eyes of an absent memory. Of the Fort-de-France of his arrival, he didn't know squat. Not a thing. Ninon's zombie still burned in his brain. For many months, if not years, he walked around in this new City as if beneath a moonless night.

---

[1]Because this City was once called Fort-Royal, but a slip of the tongue turned it into Foyal.

The Flying One

A figure sometimes emerged from this darkness. Her name was Adrienne Carmélite Lapidaille. My Esternome pronounced that name, as if thinking that such people should have never been born. She had touched down on the land of Fort-de-France before him, expelled from Saint-Pierre by a fireball. He met her in the sort of camp erected on the grasslands: hundreds of huts, straw sun screens, army tents, four-footed shelters. The sooty survivors were gathered there. There army medics came and went, up and down, watering anything that moved with learned marinades. These marinades neutralized the untamable yellow fevers, the sudden deaths, the onslaughts of cholera, and all kinds of filth harmful to a wise old age. The doctors took care of burns with pasty oil. When they ran out of oil, they had to go to the black medicine men who became officialized. These only used good crushed grass. Some very old mulatto women also came out of their hiding. Taken care of by some old factory owner, they had found themselves withering in perfumed powder and, surveying this disaster in their old age, now turned to God. All saw them circulate in nurse clothing, offering prayers-to-the-Virgin instead of bandages.

When my Esternome arrived, the worst had been over for a while. The wounds had dried up. The fevers too. A few imaginary epidemics, traced to those incapable of housing themselves in City, were still feared. Worn out by stupor like my dear Esternome, they thus vegetated there like sheep at the doors of a slaughterhouse. Only the military canteen, creaking behind a donkey, could reanimate them. It brought them a surplus of migan,* which the soldiers chewed in the passageways of the Fort, pretending it was food.

So thus, Adrienne Carmélite Lapidaille had found a small job in all that. The woman plunged a ladle into the big canaris and distributed the slop du jour to the survivors.

. . .

That was good, because a thick heart was needed to do that. The starving wretches filled the time with insults meant for all, especially since their bellies were never full and since, once mild pity had its fill, Fort-de-France suspected them of being vagabonds. The authorities therefore began to fret about that anthill. They chased them with big wheelbarrows anytime the shadow of a new Quarter reared its head somewhere. Even as settlement spread around, a mysterious tide brought new human wreckage. They seemed to emerge from new fiery plumes no one had heard of. So it wasn't easy to face this whole mob. Except for Adrienne Carmélite Lapidaille.

As soon as she rolled out of the Fort, that woman would sing, vibrating all her chords. A bawdy song like in the days of Saint-Pierre. She'd undulate her hips like a matadora. Roll wondrous eyes. Shiver lips under invisible tongues . . . In another words, the woman spread a joyful clamor around the canteen. Before such a carnival, even the dogs fell silent. Adrienne Carmélite Lapidaille served the food without much care. Yet each of her servings came with a few venomous words. So, you still here, my gourmet? So you all are the biggest cretins of all of Saint-Pierre's thirty thousand burnt-up cretins? . . .

Adrienne Carmélite Lapidaille was a golden chabine. Instead of eyes, the woman set two harsh lights on the world which let everyone know that nothing in her laughed. The woman went around with an overseer's stride. By nature perched atop authority, it was as if she was discovering life from these balcony heights. About her, no man and no story. They said she had escaped from Saint-Pierre, period: whoever came from Saint-Pierre had nothing to remember or even to explain. However—one mystery among many mysteries—as my Esternome got to know her, he never heard her recall City as he did out of charred dreams.

. . .

The woman seemed to live for a cock she lugged atop her shoulder. Not a reassuring kind of cock. A cold cock. Fearing nothing. He looked like a fighting cock (but Adrienne Carmélite Lapidaille never appeared in the pits betting). A multicolored thing, decked with feathers from the four corners of the earth, he reminded one of unknown birds and game. A purplish comb drooped over his eye. If that cock moved, it was just with the head and only to see better who-knows-what mystery among mysteries.

The cock's gravity contrasted sharply with Adrienne Carmélite Lapidaille's babble. Set on her shoulder like a stone guardian, he seemed to master more wisdom about life than his strange mistress, crackling like a mad flame.

When my Esternome met her, he of course saw nothing. He assaulted the canteen in the sea of wretches. He held out his mess tin with an empty look. Seeing him, Adrienne Carmélite Lapidaille would say, *Hey, what have we here?! Looks like misery itself has come to pay us a visit . . . !* The woman gave him his share, screaming, *Little man, crying over a booboo doesn't make it all better . . . !* And her body danced the bonda* of the Marianne-lapo-figue,* hips disjointed under volleys of pleasure. Everyone around them laughed. Not my Esternome. He looked at her the way mules look at some dirty puddle during a drought. So Adrienne Carmélite Lapidaille went on her way. From time to time the woman glanced at him over her shoulder: Who's this citizen, who's this citizen . . . ? The cock, of course, never bothered to look.

> That's her, the Old Woman who gave me new eyes. She spoke so much that for a moment I thought she was delirious. But then, a certain permanence appeared in her flood of words, like an invincible duration that absorbed the chaos of her poor stories. I suddenly got the feeling that Texaco came from the deepest reaches of ourselves and

that I had to learn everything. And even: to relearn
everything . . .

THE URBAN PLANNER'S NOTES TO THE WORD SCRATCHER.
FILE NO. 4. SHEET XVIII.
1987. SCHŒLCHER LIBRARY

Soon my Esternome was basically the only one still haunting the
grounds of the Savanna camp. Every day the servicemen picked up
the debris of those who had gone. Little by a little, the Savanna was
reverting to plain savanna. He began to hear, Go on, mustn't stay
here, move on, move on. The shelters were taken apart and burned.
Only a few addlebrains stuck to the roots of the old tamarinds
stayed on, and there was Adrienne Carmélite Lapidaille who came
one last time just to shout, *Band kouyon, manjé a fini,*[1] there's nothing to eat, *allé pann kô zot,* go hang yourself! . . . Leaving, the
woman had glanced at my Esternome over her shoulder, as if asking
herself, Who is this citizen? Her dog of a cock had—you all realize
that—not even turned around . . .

My Esternome was so hungry that he began to follow her. She was
his only landmark. She was the food giver. You should follow her
until she cut the leash by holding out the ladle. So he followed her.
When she noticed it, she turned around, so very tall, so very rough,
with an old pipe in her mouth and the strange cock near her forehead, Why are you hanging on my skirts? My Esternome answered
by holding out his mess tin.

He followed her along the coast where barges opened wide to blackmen unloading barrels. He followed her along huge laundry pits,
filled with stringy water, into which some numb coolies tried to stuff
themselves. He followed her down along the row of lightless workshops where some blackmen with know-how in their pockets han-

---

[1] [The food's gone, you damn fools!]

dled big tools. He followed her down the stony façades, precariously set in the mud fermenting under City. All the streets were straight, square-cut. Nothing evoked a city. Everything had been built with no regard for memory. The wood was either too new or too old. The stonework showed the work of many mason hands. The windows didn't match each other. No one was out breathing the fresh air from the thousand little balconies which imitated Saint-Pierre. And everywhere, large soulless buildings with dusty windows resounded with the echoes of barracks, smelled bad like warehouses or army stables. Nothing evoked City, nothing that I remember.

Adrienne Carmélite Lapidaille seemed to wander aimlessly. To go up and down, completely assured, on the cobblestones sucked in place by the weepy mud underneath. All around: lots of servicemen, earthworks, fermenting water, flocks of flies, and clusters of mosquitoes. Everywhere, people on bicycles kicking up dust, puttering motorcycles frightening the horses. In one street they ran into a steam machine, surrounded by blackboys, which slowly advanced as its big cylinder strengthened the mud with an overlay of shells and sea sand. He could remember other places too . . . but where was I?

Sometimes Adrienne Carmélite Lapidaille vanished inside the depths of a store, or evaporated behind a house. My Esternome would take root at the spot where the woman had dissolved. A little life would seep back into him when she happened to bring back a piece of cod, a pint of oil, a quart of scented rice. The woman was no longer astonished that he followed her. She even seemed to allow for the time he needed to do so, for my Esternome no longer had his swift legs nor his valiant stride, not because of his hunger but because of his age which had suddenly spread its wings like misfortune, making him feel its dead weight in each and every bone. Old age, Sophie-Marie, is like a slow surprise. I was still Esternome, I hadn't changed, I had felt nothing of the time going-coming, and I was the first to be startled at my deformed fingers, my stiff bones, my broken reflection in a puddle's looking-water. My lucid mind faced my flesh. And I would tell myself, still astonished, without believing a word of it, *So, here I am, already an old body*. And would forget about it. Forget about it right there and then. Until I bumped into myself trying to make a turn. So I would follow her like an ox. Tongue rolled out. I could feel her slow down for me; the canteen's noises would ring in my ears and I would take greater strides. That's how we got to her place. A canal, bigger than the other ones. A small makeshift bridge unhappy with its profession. A squabble of mud, trough water, planks used as footpaths, and hutches made of crate wood. It wasn't for nothing that this place was called Quarter of the Wretched. Looking at it, I could think of worse names for it, but my spirit no longer knew laughter.

Standing before her hutch, Adrienne Carmélite Lapidaille drew aside the piece of cloth that was her door. Then the woman turned to my Esternome to tell him an insane word: *You've followed me here like one follows one's fate*. My Esternome held out his mess tin as a reply. But she had already melted inside. He took a step behind her. And that step was just enough to tip over his life. Meaning that he walked into a new struggle which was to take up the rest of his days. In the back of the hutch (a tent lit by a candle's shivers, smelling like lost incense, smelling like mud, smelling like gasoline, full of all kinds of pieces of cloth, two mattresses, a nothing of a table, and other shapes in the shadows) stood not *one* but *two* Adrienne Carmélite Lapidailles. My Esternome thought he would go out cold.

The woman seemed to have doubled. In his heart my Esternome stuttered, *My God, what are my eyes seeing? The woman just threw a double-six*. But he remained dumbstruck. He no longer had the strength to try anything else. He was hungry. He had exhausted himself going through the city. Now he had only one wish, to rest his bones and hold out his mess tin, and after that to slip into the deep sleep of old folks. But in his black and blue flesh, his brain still ticked: he looked harder. One of the women had a cock, the other didn't. Meanness shone in the eyes of one while the other batted gentler eyes, which even so made one uncomfortable because they sent out no look. My Esternome suddenly understood: the woman had a twin sister, maybe not as old as she. That sister was blind. She seemed to live in this hutch without ever leaving it. The true Adrienne Carmélite Lapidaille introduced her double, saying, *My sister Idoménée, this is Idoménée, and sit down for some eats.* My Esternome heard this last word rather clearly. He suddenly collapsed, falling like a standard bearer with his mess tin aloft.

So my Esternome took root in this new City. He slept in the hutch without seeing the night go by and awoke the next morning amid the bland smell of mud. An awakening radiating with fatigue, which emerged intact despite this longest sleep. Idoménée looked at God with the eyes of the blind; despite this she knew the exact moment he woke up. In a kind voice she asked his name, age, origin, family. Not clumsy with words, my Esternome began to tell the tale I have just told you in all of its detail, from the plantation to the serenading dog's mandolin. The day went by like that. He narrated Saint-Pierre, narrated the Big Hutch, shed a few tears about the illusion of the hills' Noutéka, and other disappointments not called for here. He was not merely addressing the one with the eyes that had gone out, but rather himself, frantic that his life should end in muddy waters. He didn't understand his path, nor its purpose. He felt withered in one of life's corners, as if at some point he had taken off to fight not in the world but in one of its spinoffs. And eyeless Idoménée listened as only the blind know how. She touched him. She took his hands, laughed at his old man's silliness. He found a vigor, not buried youth, but a kind of surprise. He started to look at her, smell her, let her trouble and her warmth fascinate him. He started to realize that above anything else, Idoménée with the eyes that had gone out was a woman.

Adrienne Carmélite Lapidaille was out melting in the great sun. Returning at the falling day, she would find them sitting next to each other. My Esternome, having dried up his reservoir of prattle, waited for his dinner: an eternally basil-flavored soup. Sitting behind the hutch, on embers, it had simmered endlessly since time out of mind. Adrienne Carmélite Lapidaille thickened it with some vegetables, some bone marrow, some spice. She served that soup, with her cock on her left shoulder.

The woman seemed to be happy to see her sister in such good company. Life seemed to breathe in the blind one again. The evening went by without a word. Not a question. No one said anything to him and especially not Adrienne. She walked in a flight of cloth, mouth shut, cock on her shoulder, served them without a word, went to bed without a word, and fell asleep right there and then. The cock would claw the table's left side. Idoménée went behind the hutch for an evening wash in a drum full of rainwater, sleepwalked back, said goodnight to him, and blew out the candle of which she could see nothing. A certain anguish, which seemed to thicken as the night progressed, weighed on them. Despite his goose bumps, my Esternome let the century-old fatigue take him until the sun tiptoed back.

> She taught me to reread our Creole city's two spaces: the historical center living on the new demands of consumption; the suburban crowns of grassroots occupations, rich with the depth of our stories. Humanity throbs between these two places. In the center, memory subsides in the face of renovation, before the cities which the Occident inspires. Here, on the outskirts, one survives on memory. In the center, all dissolves in the modern world; but here people bring very old roots, not deep and rigid, but diffuse, profuse, spread over time with the lightness of speech. These two poles, linked by social forces, mold the faces of the city with their push-and-pull.
>
> THE URBAN PLANNER'S NOTES TO THE WORD SCRATCHER.
> FILE NO. 3. SHEET XVI.
> 1987. SCHŒLCHER LIBRARY.

As the days went by, my Esternome began to ask himself questions. What have I gotten into? Into whose hands? . . . He shut his trap and made Idoménée, with the eyes that had gone out, talk. I should have been warned: he talked of this blind chabine with a lot of sweetness. A syrupy waterfall. A naughty wink full of delicate delight. A joy to talk about some long-ago thing in its unfolding. There was nothing to say about Idoménée: barely the memory of plantation, known in the last hours of slavery. It's not a story, it's a misfortune, she said . . . Her mother had dried out beneath the canes. Her dad had neither name nor existence. She had to fight life early on and drifted onto Fort-de-France's mud. She became the gardener of some plump mulattoes living on some beautiful land in the woods of Redoute. She became a storytelling mammy, caring for the litter of a penniless béké who displayed the elegance of a Big Hutch salon in his country home. She became a cleaning lady in a workshop that smelled of the bitterness of uprooted trees. She became a market vendor when she learned to find the peasant women who sold the fruit of their gardens for almost nothing, before dawn. She became an aqueduct sweeper before the coolies (stuck in Pointe-Simon waiting to return to their distant country) began to take over that task. She also became a stone harvester, coal carter, she became this and then that. My Esternome didn't even listen to her. What he wanted to hear, he wasn't hearing: How did you lose your eyes? Where the devil does your sister come from, to whom you don't say a word? But he asked her none of these questions: Idoménée was sensitive about all that.

They were both in that overheated hutch, forgotten by the winds. Idoménée with the eyes that had gone out did not suffer at all from the heat. Used to this furnace, she consoled my Esternome. The wind's going to come, it's going to be here. Around them the Quarter of the Wretched wriggled in its bitter mud. It was all screams, rounds of Creole insults, whole swarms of women shoved around by life, herds of mad fellows. Anxious silences sometimes underlined the screeching of a group of brats: no one enrolled them in the cane work. At the end of an imaginary chain which limited their frolicking, they waited by themselves for a mother who had left early to try her luck in City.

There was a constant going and coming between the Quarter of the Wretched and City's heart. City was the open ocean. The Quarter was the port of registry. Home base of raucous blowouts, of fleeting hopes, misfortune, of memories brought from far away. One came back there in order to clean one's booboos, in order to find the strength to move toward City.

My Esternome sometimes saw things the other way around. City was exposed dry land; the Quarter was the oceanic nightmare. So the Quarter ceaselessly crashed onto City—the way the sea undermines a disdainful cliff.

But City absorbed that Quarter so compressed in the distance. Wrapped it in its noises, bent it to its rhythms, dressed it in its materials from other lands. City composed the Quarter with its mound of scraps, made-in-here, made-in-there.

The poor harvested windfalls: a box of wrapping paper to line a hutch, a pan to reinforce a shaken façade, a fork, a cracked plate, a piece of tulle, a bottle, a string, some sackcloth, a locket, an old hat, two rusty nails, a small knife blade. Everything was good, everything was good, City cast and then drew in its bamboo fish-traps, Marie-Sophie, drew them in I tell you.

Each time the land in the hills slid loose, my Esternome would see in it the beginnings of a quarter. This bubbling broth, ruled by the forces of the place, would gain some kind of equilibrium as the years went by. In those days the Quarter of the Wretched was just fighting the waters. Red soil was brought to strengthen the ground and then mold a footpath to City out of the mud. The women found themselves hired to carry sand in the cool evenings. One would bring back a nail to put here, or a picture to glue there. To raise a hutch was, as in the hills, the duty of men alone. The women had to face the rest of life, including the duty of finding food for a swarm of little ones, and all without a garden. Each mama, you hear me, had to sow in herself a small plot of cunning, and look after the harvest, ill luck or no. Perched by the window, my Esternome would shout, turning to Idoménée, The hills have come down to City, the hills have come down on City, a bloody madness . . .

That would stir up an old bitterness in him. That brought him back to his long-ago days with Ninon, his glorious rise flattened by the Factory. Their collective failure now translated into the waves descending on this city which was not City. Disdainful of Fort-de-France, he would grumble nonstop. *That, that is a City, Idoménée?* he would ask the sweet blind one. (She had a warm voice, none of her words ever rose higher than the others and her gestures were calm, and her body was calm, she crossed life like clear spring water, yes, she was unsettlingly innocent, for she touched my Esternome only to speak to him, caressed his nails without one wicked thought, but he, nasty one, began to have some.)

He grumbled, *That, that's a City?* And he kept his hands in the tenderness of hers. And she asked, *What is City, Ternome?* He, full of secular learning, exaggerated: City's a quake. A tremor. There all things are possible, and there all things are mean. City sweeps and carries you along, never lets go of you, gets you mixed up in its old secrets. In the end you take them in without ever understanding them. You tell those just-off-the-hills that that's how it is and they eat it up: but City has just gulped you in without showing you the ropes. A City is the ages all gathered in one place, not just in the names, houses, statues, but in the not-visible. A City sips the joys, the pain, the thoughts, every feeling, it makes its dew out of them, which you see without being able to point to it. That's what City is and that was Saint-Pierre. The sweet one was caressing his fingers, gently interrupting him, *That's City? Here it's just like that* . . . And my Esternome would caress her back naughtily.

Shaken with laughter, she fell into his arms without further ado. So then my macaque would make her laugh. Filled with emotion, she would snuggle up against him, shivering, lifting eyes asking to be reassured. So my sly one cultivated this emotion. To comfort him from unfortunate memories, she held him for a long time like one cradles a child. Then he, nasty old thing, suffering bone-hard from seven miseries, loaded his existence with a cart of ill luck that no pack-saddled mule could have borne.

In order to become close to her, he narrated Saint-Pierre. In Idoménée's mind that unknown City glowed like a lighthouse. Fort-de-France and Saint-Pierre were in agreement on one thing: to be the beacon in the stifling night of slavery. The bitterness of the hills (spit out once more by the Factory) flew to burn there like a moth on a garden lamp. Idoménée had right away held out her hopes for City. That surprised my Esternome: Myself, I only went because the Mentoh sent me, otherwise I would have never left the plantation. I, said Idoménée, no one told me to go there, but once I got here, I realized immediately that I had come to the end of my wandering: besides that, the only things that could change your life were taking the boat for that Guyana gold which everyone says is easy to pick or sailing toward the wealth of Panama where you become a mulatto just by digging a canal. I wouldn't have fled even if my eyes had not gone out. He, ready to bite in order to shed light on the mystery of her eyes, still did not dare to ask how it happened.

Of Fort-de-France Idoménée told him what she never got time to tell me. My Esternome, despite his ruined memory, was still able to evoke her words to me, for Idoménée's presence saturated him deeply. She became the memory of his forgetful age. What he knew of Saint-Pierre complemented what she was saying of Fort-de-France. What she knew of it came from words that she happened to hear all her life, words that had sprouted from parlors, flown out of passers-by on the Alley of Sighs, words caught from people waiting by the harbor, words that fell out of sentries who paced up and down under the Fort walls. In the heat transfixing them, with Idoménée lying in his arms, musing, they exchanged these bits of words, voices and words hushed in order not to sweat. Words already harped on but which month after month thickened with nuance. Words which curled them up right in the heart of City and tied them like a rope.

A QUICK LOOK AT IDOMÉNÉE'S MUSINGS

They say: old swamp but pretty site. They set up the Fort there. Then the Army spoke its law. A checkerboard stretch-strung from the Fort. Businesses here. Houses there. Depots here.

Wretched heat, said Esternome.

They say: Batteries were set on the hills around. Stuck in the basin, the enemy would fall beneath the infernal flood. Each hill, a battery: Desaix, Tartenson, Redoute, Balata . . . One battery, one house. Ten houses, a quarter. So each battery made its own quarter.
　　Those are memories? my Esternome would ask.
　　That's the Army, she would say.

There was the water that ran down the hills and drowned the lower lands to stop its course. What to do? . . . Big canal all around, and across, until everything flew down into the sea like off a cliff, Esternome would respond.

What is that? she would reply

A drawing is taking place: these are memories, my Esternome would declare.

Everyone had to choose their place, their land, their location on the checkerboard. No one was to step out of line or out of the plan. The houses rose according to the King's engineer and the Count of Blénac. That, is that memory?

Chance things, Esternome refuted.

They had needed a savanna so that the enemy, attacking from the rear, would stumble without cover. So they imposed a space, what space? The savanna, my Esternome would say. You have to dress it with rumors of war to truly understand it.

This City has no wind . . . heat comes down.

It depends, said Idoménée, you have to know its winds.

They say that the place resisted: fevers of all kinds tiring the conquest. They say there used to be Carib souls, emerging out of the swamp, along with other atrocities forgotten by the murderers.

What is that?

A legend, my Esternome argued. That was also City. But legends are memories greater than memories.

Clumps there, limestone here, sea flows, alluvial deposits, soil embanked against the sea . . . so? A drawing is taking place underneath, colors the soul, my Esternome accepted. But it doesn't bring cool air.

Who came to take the patchwork plots, then those of the hills? Idoménée asked. Engagés,* servicemen, fellows drifting in from France, Brazil, or elsewhere. But especially, mulattoes and free blacks, lots of mulattoes and lots of unchained blacks with a talent or a trade.

Why? the one with the eyes that had gone out would ask astonished.

Because in Saint-Pierre the békés had already taken everything, Esternome pronounced the verdict, I know, I saw it already. On the question of heat Saint-Pierre did just as well.

The fellows from France did not have wives, so they found mulattoes and blackwomen there.

No one saw that one coming, my Esternome laughed.

Saint-Pierre, the békés' city; Fort-de-France, the mulattoes' city? Idoménée would ask. City has no origin, it has memories that it stirs to death without ever getting them mixed up, said my Esternome. And it recapitulates it all. All the time. And in different ways.

The plot: 200 steps wide and 1,000 long. With taxes. Starting from the edge of the sea, going up into the center. The neighboring inland area for tobacco planting. The rest for the Army, which included 50 steps from the waves that no one could touch except for the time you first cleared that space for them. A sketch is taking shape, that's memory.

Army orders: everyone had to fill in the edge of his home, empty the swamp water, fight the ocean waves, dry the mud's tears. Like sap, my Esternome would cut in, everyone gives to City without knowing. I know that. That's memory.

· · ·

Whoever feared earthquakes, would erect a house of wood. Whoever feared hurricanes or remembered the fire, erected a house of stone. After bouncing land? City of wood, Esternome would exult. That's the memories on the face, holy sketch maker.

So Idoménée would say: But what is memory?

It's the glue, it's the spirit, it's the sap and it stays. Without memories, no City, no Quarters, no Big Hutch.

How many memories? she would ask.

All the memories, he would answer. Even those the wind and the silences carry at night. You have to talk, tell, tell the stories, live the legends. That's why.

You also make City by what you put into it, my Esternome specified.

Anything else? he would worry. So she would go on . . . And the heat would tie them together.

NOTEBOOK NO. 9 OF MARIE-SOPHIE LABORIEUX.
1965. SCHŒLCHER LIBRARY.

What was to happen happened. He, penetrating her night. She, seeing with his eyes. He, falling into the universe of the senses, filled with rigid terror. She, setting loose her memories of lights, getting drunk on color, remembering the flowers, splashing her mind with a thousand forgotten shapes. He, ears born again, feeling his fingers come to life, guessing volume, orienting himself along subtle proximities. He, embracing her. She, swallowing him. His frenzy. Her going to pieces. Then, the numb one floating, drowned in sweat. The heat thicker than ever. The happening happening.

That evening, Adrienne Carmélite Lapidaille, foot barely past the cloth door, stopped right on the smell that filled the hutch. She eyed them with horror. It just hadn't entered her mind. An old man, and a barely younger blind woman, both haloed with the strong smell of the flesh (beneath an air of innocence). You raped her . . . ! she said to Esternome. No, Idoménée cut in, I gave freely. Adrienne Carmélite Lapidaille served dinner with new silence. She went to sleep with even greater speed.

In the falling night, my Esternome felt sick. Anguish was now on the move. It no longer rested in a corner, waiting, now it was undulating toward its chosen prey. My Esternome felt that prey was he. Idoménée, still wide awake, pressed his arm. She turned her empty eyes toward the cock that was now comfortably sleeping. Her demeanor spoke of fear. What's going on? said my Esternome to his blind lover. Don't fall asleep, she breathed, don't close your eyes.

He fought his age in order to keep an open eye. The night was thickening. Around them, after having floated in the smell of fried fish, the Quarter now stood still. Only the virgin's lamps still shivered through the cracks. The little hutch seemed to have sunk in deaf marshlands. It might have even left the world. My Esternome felt butterflies. They rose in his deepest parts. Shook his hands, chilled his feet, made his eyes roam. His head pivoted to catch who knows what. From time to time, he grabbed the candle to light the erased corners of the hutch. The gleam yellowed Idoménée's innocent face now sleeping quietly. Yellowed the block that was Adrienne Carmélite Lapidaille, who was so stiff it seemed she had left her body. Then it yellowed the cock in its feathers, its usually shuttered eyes, stiffer than ever—but which this time had eyes open looking at him.

The cock was watching him. It turned its head as he dragged himself about the hutch. Its beak looked threatening. Its comb was now black, live with reddish gleams. My Esternome wanted to wake Idoménée. But she did not wake up. So he called out to Adrienne Carmélite Lapidaille. The woman moved no more than a stone would. When he tried to crawl toward her, to shake her, the cock pounced in rage and massacred him with a thousand and two blows of its beak. It stopped once my Esternome retreated far from its mistress's bed.

They watched each other silently. My Esternome half-dead from fright. He trembled even more when, at exactly midnight, the cock began to crow and walk with Adrienne Carmélite Lapidaille's step. To the left, to the right, as if following the occult requirements of a baneful liturgy. My Esternome carefully watched it without believing it. Fearing to be taken off to hell, he tried to force his eyes open. Soon, as a lost blue lightened the sky, he heard bats crash against the corrugated tin. Then a clatter of flailing wings, flying through the cloth, knocking into the partitions, appeased the cock, suddenly fallen asleep in its usual place. Suddenly revived, Adrienne Carmélite Lapidaille began to breathe peacefully.

At daylight, sleep overtook him. A pinch of heat suddenly woke him. Idoménée was holding his arm. When she felt him move, she said, *Esternome can you clearly see?* Yes I see clearly, why? No good reason, she said. They remained silent. One watching the other. The sun was slipping its rays through the cloth holes, stripping the half-light. Last night's nightmare seemed like it couldn't have happened. My Esternome wished to forget it all, but then he changed his mind. Taking a deep breath, he revealed to his Idoménée that Adrienne Carmélite Lapidaille was one of these evil ones which become flying creatures at night. That they had to leave this hutch before she sold them to Beelzebub or Lucifer. But Idoménée began to laugh. When she saw he wasn't laughing with her and wouldn't stop trembling, she told him what he wanted to know.

TEARS OF LIGHT

Her twin sister, Adrienne Carmélite Lapidaille, was born with her on the same plantation. They had suckled seven days together. Then the

Béké had carried off her Adrienne to sell her to a not-very-Catholic nobody-knows-who. Békés sometimes engaged in such commerce. Idoménée grew up with the memory of her sister whom she often forgot. At her mother's death, the end of the plantations, she had to wander to survive, cart latrines around. Idoménée soon realized that her eyes were losing some of their light, just like that, slowly, for no reason. Less light, more blur, less shape, more haze. Sometimes, under the weight of the latrines, she stood still in a dark marshland. Then a soft light would revive her eyes. Then she was able to go on, with a throbbing heart. She began to swim in the dark marshlands more and more often. They were deeper and deeper. Rushing from the back of her head, they swallowed her eyes, then her body, and then she felt herself floating like a pear leaf.

Weeks could go by without anything happening, then the shadows would surge. She was working as a cleaning lady in the home of an old mulatto woman who collected parrots, when the black waters swallowed her in one gulp. A powerful tide. She started to float, to drown, then to take flight like a flying fish over the nets. Whirls of vertigo. Sudden falling. Flocks of game would startle her heart. Idoménée cried. Idoménée wanted to die. Idoménée waited for it to pass. But it never went away.

Out of Christian kindness, the parrot lady kept her for a few months. As soon as Idoménée's light went out, the parrots had fallen silent. They would remain in their cage, stiffer than frozen birds. Their eyes would roll anxiously. Their brightest colors had nearly faded so as to hide from the eagle of misfortune. Night was most frightening of all for them. They threw themselves against the bars in a surge of folly. The small winds which had penetrated through the louvered shutters would blow their plucked feathers all over the house. So early one Saturday, the mulatto woman grabbed Idoménée and dropped her at the Bethlehem Asylum so that she might be in charge of things again. But the abandoned blind one saw no one coming and no one saw her. Not even the mulatto woman who came back for her when the parrots, deploring her departure, plucked out their eyes, wailing like children.

Idoménée had landed somewhere. She lived barely above the mud, in some isolated corner forgotten by the sun. She sensed dogs go by, then other vague things. She felt rains, winds, heat, and cold spells. Her spirit hit the bottom, then began to bounce back. One day Idoménée was able to find her feet. Then, on another day, she regained her feeling for the earth. She regained an arm, and some sort of equilibrium. Another day, she was able to distinguish lying down from standing up. So then she came out of her hole and proceeded into City's streets.

She was first offered an elbow, then a stick. On her immutable rounds, dear hearts held out bowls of creamy milk. Then she would retrace her steps and slide back into the hole which had become her nest. That's where, one day, she found Adrienne Carmélite Lapidaille, the forgotten sister. The strange woman had looked for her for a long time. Despite all the years that had gone by, despite the ash in which City was dimming, despite the smell of sulfur floating in the streets, despite the tumult of the heaving mountain, Idoménée recognized her: a familiar smell, a feeling. Taking her hands through the open pit, Adrienne said, *I'm going to give you back your eyes.* Idoménée had also sensed the rooster—let's just say that a certain stiffness had run through her.

Adrienne had found a hutch in the Quarter of the Wretched. She settled her there. During the day, she left for City. At night Idoménée would fall into a sleep unknown until then and would discover her sister at sunset when Adrienne served the soup. At first she asked: *Sésé, ki jan ou ké viré ban mwen zié mwen?*[1] Sister, how are you going to manage to give me my eyes back? *I'm going to take some-*

---

[1] [Sis, what turns will you take to give me my eyes?]

one else's, she grunted. *Lots of folks don't need them. Don't worry, I am looking, I am looking for someone. Once you have your new eyes, I'll be able to leave again.* Idoménée dropped the question right there and then. Afraid to see her return with bloody eyes in hand, she spent her days praying to the Lord. Soon she understood that Adrienne was not going to pull out anyone's eyes. She would use a power which Idoménée began to guess at as her increasingly sensitive body began to compensate for the darkness of her eyes.

She sensed that none in the Quarter of the Wretched would come near the hutch. The children would gather in a circle of unusual silence around her. When she called out to them, no one would answer, as if the partitions strangled her voice. No mosquito came near the hutch, no fly, no lizard, no roach, no spider, no blackbird made a wrong turn there. Once the soup was swallowed, a sleepiness free of fatigue overtook her and, good God, she felt like she had lost her dreams forever.

She also felt that Adrienne did not truly love her. Only the loss of her vision bothered her. They were tied up with the mystery of twins; in returning to Idoménée the light of her eyes, Adrienne would restore clarity for herself. She was there to do that and nothing else. Idoménée followed her month after month, she felt her tension when every day she brought something back to the hutch. Lots of things had been accumulated like this. There was still something missing. But what? When she saw Esternome come, she didn't make a connection between him and the terrible thing being prepared: after all, Adrienne seemed indifferent. But little by little, just before her strange slumber, she perceived the threat rising clearer and clearer.

The night before, it all came to her: *It's your eyes she's going to take, it's your eyes she's going to take.* She can take them, said my Esternome, I'm going to give them to you. The thought of having her beloved's eyes under her eyelids filled the blind one with unspeakable horror. She trembled, howled, turned her head right and left, *Keep your eyes, keep your eyes* . . . My Esternome began to figure. He had to go, leave this hutch, but go where? And on what legs? With him not being very strong and a blind one to look after? *Madness!* . . . She's never going to let us go, Idoménée. So she's the one who's got to go, my Esternome would say.

When Adrienne appeared that evening, Idoménée cried with all her strength, *I don't need your eyes, I am fine just the way I am . . . Let my Esternome be.* But the woman served the never-ending soup and went to bed without a word. The mean cock did almost the same, except that this time, sunk in its feathers, it kept its cruel eyes on Esternome, who felt anguish, etcetera etcetera . . . and the same old circus started over, word for word.

In its old heart: a clear, regulated, normalized order. Around it: a boiling, indecipherable, impossible crown, buried under misery and History's obscured burdens. If the Creole city had at its disposal only the order of the center, it would have died. It needs the chaos of its fringes. Beauty replete with horror, order set in disorder. Beauty throbbing in horror and a secret order right in the heart of disorder. Texaco is Fort-de-France's mess; think about it: the poetry of its Order. The urban planner no longer chooses between order and disorder, between beauty and ugliness; from now on he is an artist: but which one? The lady would enlighten me.

THE URBAN PLANNER'S NOTES TO THE WORD SCRATCHER.
FILE NO. 8. SHEET XIX.
1987. SCHŒLCHER LIBRARY.

How many nights like that? Full of fright and of scares? Adrienne Carmélite Lapidaille would sink into her usual stiffness. Idoménée collapsed on her straw. My Esternome, on the other hand, faced that filthy cock with its bulging eyes. Torture. At night. In order to ward off fatigue, he held his eyes open with his fingers, like his old mother, and stood stock still, facing the motionless cock. *Oh how long the nights are!* . . . At daybreak, the crashing of the big wings surrounded the roof pata pata pata, made the cloth door fly up vlaaarr, knocked the partitions down before dissolving into the sound of sand scuttling under the corrugated tin. As soon as daylight came, he fell asleep until the first rays of warmth. Then he would cry from despair in his Idoménée's arms. Where to go? Leave for what place? Who to call? How to call on neighbors who didn't even seem to see the hutch? Weeping, my Esternome looked for ways to deal with the Flying One. Unpleasant story . . .

Since his Mentoh, he had begun to believe, he said, in devilries. His life had taken shelter under all kinds of armor. Far more credulous than he, Ninon had reinforced them. All of these he had left behind in their hutch on the hills. It was with great pain that he thought of them now. He put on his shirt inside out just in case. But the threat had not wavered. He missed his bottle of clover-caterpillar which washed away all charms. He missed his green lemons with crosses on them with which he used to rub his hands. He missed his ringworm wood oil, his red vervain plants, his clumps of icy mint, his fern branch which prevented visitations, his basil which pushed all influences away, his bitter bush feared by the engagés,* his hogplum bark, his bark of red sweat pea, his incense fragrances for Fridays-the-thirteenth, his alkali, his coarse ether which the soukougnan* lament, his sea salt mixed with coal, his little silver coin behind which Ninon had noted *Aragon Tétragranmakon,* his black satin square wrapped around a reed with a pinch of salt, the ash of a young bamboo in some virgin parchment, his new glass (gotten without bargaining) where three drops of quicksilver still shivered. My Esternome wept . . .

Against flying persons, my Esternome knew what to do. The flying ones fear strong smells; he would have to burn incense throughout the hutch, splash it with alkali, sweep it with creosol. Mark the partitions with a white cross. Hang some good ringworm wood at each window. He knew that these people took their skin off in order to free their wings. That to take it off, they rubbed a special oil on themselves which Adrienne probably hid somewhere in her bedding, with the other oil which helped her to put her skin back on. He knew that in swapping these oils, in sliding three grains of salt under the skin, he would singe her powers. But how to get to the bed, with that damned cock? My Esternome wept . . .

If there were a lemon tree around, he said to his Idoménée, I would have cut half a lemon without picking it off the tree, then I would have tied a black veil to the branch, the Flying One would have hurled herself into it and would have been left torn forever. There's no lemon tree around here, said Idoménée. Oh Esternome wept . . .

Oh Ido, I would have burnt Mont-Saint-Michel incense on her, and the incense of the three gifts, sulfur, some horse's hoof, a sheaf of laurel . . . Idoménée, you hear me: on her bed I would have put a jar of quicklime, a few gully root leaves and the ache of the caca-caper . . . And he howled in a magic French *In vain are those whom God protects attacked. For the Just are always saved* . . . which did not really reassure him behind his watery eyes.

Once, when Adrienne Carmélite Lapidaille appeared, he turned around and put his head between his legs. That pose was supposed to send her off to hell. But the woman began to laugh and the cock did not move. Another time, he signed the old cross with his trembling hands. She did the same, and he (life is funny) felt a sharp pain. I haven't gone to confession so much, he admitted. With Idoménée, they spent their days reciting their Our Father, invoking Saint Peter, Saint Michael, Mèlchidael, Bareschas, the beautiful angel Gabriel, Zazel, Triel, Malcha, and others beneath them. On the left side of the entrance, he took a piece of coal and engraved + ABA + ALOY + ABAFROY + AGERA + PROCHA + . . . The woman paid it no heed.

• • •

The months went on like that. My Esternome no longer swallowed the soup. He had become thin like a Newfoundland cod. As for Idoménée, she could not help but fall asleep at sunset. One night, Adrienne Carmélite Lapidaille came in as usual and stood petrified. She touched her belly. Held on to the partitions to stop a dizzy spell. The cock pirouetted and went under the table. Adrienne Carmélite Lapidaille eyed Idoménée with some kind of terror: *What's in your belly?* she cried, *Sa ou ni an boyo'w?*[1] Despite her fright, my Esternome thought he would die of pleasure: What, what, Idoménée, what's the matter? he himself stammered. *What's in your belly?* the woman repeated; she was purging her womb, pulling her navel, seemed to want to pull out the taut knot from her gut. The agitated cock beat its wings in distress.

Adrienne fell to her bed like a picked mango. Twisted with awful seizures, she held on to her belly. The coming of night suddenly calmed her. Idoménée fell into her strange sleep. My Esternome fought with his eyes to keep them open. He thought he saw the cock fly away, but seeing better, he saw it in its place. Later, he saw it no more. He thought he heard the pata pata pata of the big wings coming, but they touched the hutch and went away into the distance. Adrienne's pallet emptied itself with a whistling. An all new silence then emerged. An innocence in which the world was being born again. My Esternome knew that they were saved. He fell asleep even faster since he knew that Idoménée was expecting a baby. This miraculous child, that was you, Marie-Sophie, little syrup of my old age, last drink of my life . . . (I pretended to be startled and kissed him for a long time.)

I was the child of an old couple. They say that such children have a round back, dismal eyes, and stiff bones. They say they're melan-

---

[1][What have you got in your gut?]

choly, that they like spoiled milk. They also say that their memories make sounds which sadden them. They say . . . They say . . . but Esternome tells me that I was really charming, with no round back, no stiff bones . . . I must say, for good measure, that never do macaques find their children ugly.

Idoménée's pregnancy acted on her like happiness. She refused to believe it. As her belly acquired its roundness, she began to cry. These long tears seemed to clean her eyes. The hutch became a migan of mud which Esternome sponged as best he could. Her tear water did not evaporate. In the sun, it broke down into seeds of dew. The wind dispersed it into the dust's flight. My Esternome would gather some in his hands, and sometimes quavered *Idoménée, it's all lit up! . . .* Then he'd fall silent . . .

Oh Mama . . .

One day she thought she saw a light. Some other time it seemed like she could make out the touch of a shade in a shadow. One day her eyelids quivered beneath the sting of a star, then beneath a scintillation. Finally, one day, she caught a sunbeam in the hutch, then she guessed at the door frame, and certain shapes in the distance. She did not regain clear sight at all, but she could give objects their volume, a bit of their color. My Esternome's face appeared very beautiful to her (here, it was love blinding her still beneath the joy of seeing).

Adrienne Carmélite Lapidaille's flight freed the Quarter. People finally saw the hutch now. The children assailed it. The men who walked in front of it raised their hats *Ladies-and-gentlemen, good day.* The women came there to hear stories from these old people. It brought gladness: these white-haired folks were expecting a child! . . . And the baby was the Quarter's. I had, before I was even born, a load of papas and just as many mamas. They took care of my Esternome, spoiled my Idoménée. A woman from Basse-Pointe (Théotine Rémicia, who once worked at the Pointe-Simon factory in a time out of mind) coaxed me into the world. My umbilical cord was buried at the entrance of the hutch and my name was recorded with the town council before an eternity went by. I was baptized at the great cathedral. And went to school at the Perrinon yard.

Having a daughter roused Esternome. He found strength to go do all kinds of odd jobs in City's windfalls. His white hair only got him charity. So he chose to give up. He applied Ninon's lessons in Balata's thickets. His garden brought him all kinds of food. With it, he could stuff us or obtain what we needed. Idoménée took care of the hutch. She did what she could, through the fog of her eyes. Poor hutch . . . my Esternome, without strength and without tools, never managed to better it. He did like everyone else, by emergency, a nail here, a piece of corrugated tin there. And in his dreams, he venerated the least crate wood plank, just like I did in my time at the beginning of Texaco.

A "war!" occurred. It strung young men along a deadly rosary: Dardanelles, Verdun, the Somme's naked horror, the foul Chemin des Dames . . . In that business with the Germans, my Esternome never understood a thing. Ever since Saint-Pierre, he lived detached from the world. Ejected from History, he lived his stories without deciphering the events which took place around him as he had in his youth. Our toes could no longer reach the bottom . . . How can I explain this to you, Marie-Sophie? Fighting the chains threw us against the world, facing freedom did too. But after that there was nothing to fight, nothing to do, except slip into City's blindness. And what was City's blindness? The mulatto way, he answered right straight.

The war (of which I remember nothing) was drums-and-fanfare departure and a tail-between-legs return. Men left singing, they came back with frozen feet. They left laughing, they came back without lungs, gangrened from mustard gas. They left with a valiant heart, they came back pelted with bits of shrapnel. They left acclaimed, they came back onto deserted quays, limping alone toward a silent house. And they would just stand there, counting their lice, bathing their scabies with vinegar, without a penny for pension, and without strength for odd jobs. *Funny war,* my Esternome who peered at all of this would say, devastated . . . Then the lines of volunteers who crowded the paths began to vanish. In the Quarter of the Wretched (where everyone gazed at the tragic ghosts), these old-dogs of young-men cooked up fevers for themselves with garlic under their armpits. Other bastards cut off their trigger finger. More than one ne'er-do-well yanked out all his teeth. Tons of troublemakers, Marie-Sophie, poisoned themselves just enough so that the rifles would fall out of their hands. A few blackmen, full of malice, set up an account of children in the area, so they could claim themselves to be indispensable papas before their adjutants. Others, truly without honor, swam without taking a breath to reach Venezuela where they had no address. My Esternome was devastated, *Ungrateful dogs . . . ! Ah, if I still had my strength! Vuve la Fouance . . . Long leeve Fwance . . .*

The war had broken out for no reason, that is for nothing to do with us and our attempts to penetrate City. We only knew one thing: Sweet France, crib of our liberty, that so-generous land of the universal, was in great danger. Everything had to be paid her back. With the countryside starving us and City rejecting us, we found in the Army the chance of becoming French, to escape the békés' clutches. Despite those who ran away, there were thousands of us stepping forward for the mobilizations. Looking upon this with more detachment, the békés shipped their merchandise to America and mobilized themselves in the land of their businesses.

Finding food was a mean matter. Lucky for us, City had not yet swallowed the countryside. We still held on to scraps of our survival instincts. In subsistence gardens around Fort-de-France, like in the

old days around the plantation, we grew things which would im-
press even ill luck. But it wasn't enough to feed all of City. The vendors, just off the hills, would spark riots. The seaside békés closed
their factories and raised the prices. Flour and bread cost as much as
a dish of chicken with rice. Coal was gold. The country békés hid
their oxen in ravines. Made rare, the price of meat went up. The factory owners, swept off their feet by the servicemen's demands, suppressed the sugar and rum meant for the country, in order to get
more money for them in France's barracks. Every morning there was
the irritation of strikes: longshoremen's strike, surveyors' strike, drydock workers' strike, shopkeepers' strike over prices, this strike, that
strike. The schoolmasters all anxious about their pay laid down their
chalk at the governor's feet. *Funny war,* my Esternome cried. *What
does Fatherland mean in all of that?* . . .

The mutual aid societies came out of their long hibernation. They
began to glean for monies for the war. There were balls and parties,
whose proceeds went to the soldiers; serbi games to help the soldiers.
Some ruined themselves playing dominoes to help the soldiers. To
survive, no need to sweat in odd jobs: bacchanalia was enough "to
help our boys." *Man is not very good* . . . my Esternome grumbled
upon seeing these aid entrepreneurs. He preferred to ignore them,
and worse: not even bother judging them. Each Saturday, clothed in
beautiful linen, Idoménée on his arm, I hanging on to his vest, with a
senator's step he would go to the Bouillé Barracks where he would
ask to be shown to the commander. He would be introduced into a
room which smelled like a stable. There, some chief with a mustache,
reddened by mosquitoes, would exclaim, Oh here comes the child of
the Fatherland . . . He took his money with an embrace. My Esternome would leave proud, duty accomplished, and saluting each soldier by clicking his heels, *Vuve la Fouance my friends!* . . .

Then the thieves flocked. The town council decided to turn off the
lights after a certain hour. This left City to an envious herd. A kind

of delirium peppered with resentment. City with no lights is like a wounded snake. Grabbed at. Walked on. Its sides are smushed. That's strange, Sophie, my sweet, City's light holds back your bitterness. If you turn out its fires, it no longer has its walls. So those in purgatory between it and the countryside start to stare at what they can't have. Or to take what they're dying to take. Groups of women, experts in contraband sugar, fought in the streets. Chickens, pigs were stolen, gardens pillaged, and houses broken into. Chairs and embroidered tablecloths were stolen. Shoes and new bikes were stolen. The békés still around lost near-ripe harvests despite the agents of the agricultural guard. Each morning revealed its procession of persons mistreated during the opportunity of the lightless night. My Esternome put a door on his hutch, sealed off a broken window, and watched the shadows machete in hand. All around, the Quarter was becoming a dog bolting toward City. My Esternome even thought he heard it bark its bitterness. *Filthy war . . . !* he would groan in my sleep and his dear Idoménée's.

> On the first day, right at the sound of the tocsin, I went, Marie-Sophie, but the servicemen wanted nothing to do with me. A dog of a warrant officer chased me away. I think I heard him curse, something about blackmen unworthy of carrying a gun or of raising their filthy selves under the flag. Mother France does not send us good people here. But I was ready to serve her, right at the sound of the first tocsin.
>
> NOTEBOOK NO. 11 OF MARIE-SOPHIE LABORIEUX.
> 1965. SCHŒLCHER LIBRARY.

During this time of war, and even afterward, I always saw people coming back from the countryside. Shelters would erupt with a helping hand beneath the light of torches. Branch and straw huts. Corrugated tin sheets. They came out at night like patches of ants, with the low look of young smugglers. The distilleries which had bloomed during the war collapsed one after the other as soon as peace came back. They spewed blackmen full of loathing for the fields, and who, more confident in their so-called knowledge, went into City like one runs to the bigger factory on hiring day. Concerned about this assault, the town council hired as many as possible. But all around City, no employment: it was already vegetating, waiting for boats from France.

LAST LOVE BITES

After the war, the town council started to get worked up about the Quarter. So much mud, so much resentment. The mayor (one named Sévère, a mulatto freemason who paraded with his brothers in the frightened streets) obtained these muddy lands from a widow's trembling hands. He crammed them as best he could, created a large square, divided them into parcels separated by streets. He sold the plots for almost nothing to whoever wanted them. My Esternome was not able to get any of them. The one in which Adrienne's hutch sat was in the path of a thoroughfare. It had to be demolished. We had to tuck ourselves away in the crate wood hutch of one named Lonyon. Professional con artist, he had received several subdivisions under cover of five or six mistresses. He rented them under the table to newcomers and those who hadn't been able to blend in properly. My Esternome paid the rent with the income from his secret gardens. My Idoménée also supplemented our resources. She had been able to find again one called Kestania, a fisherman friend of hers. He provided her with half-calabashes of titiri or turtle eggs. A coolie butcher from the canal shores put aside some ox balls for her, bled skins, blood pudding. She fried everything and leaning on my shoulder went to sell the food along the Levée, in the midst of vendors galore who sold fried stuff and cakes of all kinds.

I grew up on these fritters which perfumed the Levée. As soon as I had taken my first steps, I would be my Idoménée's eyes. I guided her into City as her work required. She honored me with a complete trust which I did not at first deserve. My childish eyes flew everywhere, rested on the crab claws standing in the scuppers, watched the coaches, stared at other children. Her light hand on my shoulder contracted a tad bit when she stepped in a puddle I had neglected, slipped on slick mud, or had to step across a gutter that I had not really gauged. So once, she fell. Her basket scattered on the Levée's mud, but she got back up without a reproach, only anxious to know if I was all right. So then, once and for all, my eyes ripened and became hers.

Idoménée pushed me away from all the frying fish. She feared that a canari of hot oil would graze my legs. Some days, however, I had to take care of it, fry and sell to whoever wished to buy, because her eyes had no consistency. They lived moments of clarity and days of obscurity. She trembled to see herself vacillate at the edges of the darkness. Only today can I truly see the predicament. Giggly little girl, I used my lightheartedness to live around my poor parents' numbness. They had to call me five times, watch me constantly, threaten me, before my stamina compensated for their old age. The selling of the fried fish took up my evenings. On the pretext of tasting them, I would swallow much more than I would sell. In the morning, before going to school where I learned nothing, I carted the water to fill the drum which was our spring. The schoolmaster was one of these iron-willed blackmen. That old cobbler had imparted reading to himself, taught himself writing, and had climbed up to the teachers' college on the back of a rage to exist. He wore hat, tie, vest, fob, handkerchiefs, walked stiffly, turned his whole body around to look over his shoulder. Speaking French was a succulence which he practiced in a mass of movements. He looked like a shepherd ceaselessly leading a herd of syllables. No word could get away from his head, he was always busy saying them, counting them, recapitulating them. The desire to say everything at the same time led him to stutter. Inexhaustible, each word vibrated inside his flowery way of sounding the tongue. We were fascinated by his art. We looked upon him as the divine keeper of the most far-flung sciences. From him I brought back a taste for the French language, that concern to have one's say in an imperial manner which I cultivated in my solitary days. For the moment I, câpresse of mud, studied that wonder: a negro blackman transfigured into a mulatto, transcended to the white through the incredible power of that beautiful language from France. Moved, my Esternome never dared speak before him: he felt like a mongrel hound.

On Saturdays I went with Esternome to sell vegetables. He stood at one end of the market, among the women, without shame. While waiting for the customers, he spoke to me, his daughter. He told me about the mistakes of his life as if teaching a lesson. It took me awhile to get interested. For me, his words were just those of the old, a babbling in which his spirit drowned but which did not fulfill my appetite for life. Only after the death of my Idoménée did I really listen to him. Oh Mama . . . losing you revealed to me how much we close ourselves to those we love, how inept we are to quench our thirst for them, their presence, their voices, what they remember, how we never kiss them enough . . . never enough. When I lost her, my mother who was almost unknown to me, I would cling to my old Esternome's crumpled flesh . . . Oh Papa . . . all he had to offer me was the last leap of his memories about the will to conquer City. Oh Oiseau de Cham, draw in excess from those you love . . .

Idoménée Eugénie Lapidaille, I think of you every first day of the year, that white day, that day of hope, that day of renewal which you would clothe in white, white tablecloths, white linen. With rum, ash, and lemon you would rub everything. You would cram the house with hibiscus flowers as if you wished to gather up the certain movement of their sap. You would unravel the money from an old praline bag. To our surprise you would unveil the whiteness of nougat. With a piece of nougat the world is wonder, life sings, happiness goes by.

A nougat . . . and your eyes of tenderness, Idoménée, are at our service much more than at your needs. I think of you, Idoménée, when I take my New Year's bath, for a fresh start, a bath of leaves, a bath for luck, and at the five o'clock mass, praying to Providence.

Idoménée, I think of you, on Easter days at the river we'd go to with the people of our Quarter. We'd catch our crabs in the holes around there. You would fricassee them with red rice. We ate them on the banks. My Esternome insisted on fishing crawdad by foraging with his hands under the stony promises. And you, Idoménée, moving little in order to avoid falling, almost absent in the middle of this joy, watching out for (who ever paid attention?) your eyes' betrayals.

Idoménée, I remember you, wrestling away your Sunday afternoons in my hair, trying to tame that impossible mass. You spoke but little (but Esternome would speak for you), silently lying in wait for the cloudy darkness which would scoff at you. It was on a day like that the misfortune knocked. *Accursed cock!* . . . My Esternome, sucking on his pipe, was telling himself dungeon stories. The dejected beating of a wing was heard. Then Adrienne Carmélite Lapidaille's cock, the existence of which I discovered that day, crashed at my Idoménée's feet. It had changed, my Esternome would say. Its feathers were burnt red now. Now transparent, its comb looked like gelatin. It wriggled about for a long time like a poisoned cat, then passed away with a woman's sigh which my Esternome warded off with a prayer. With the help of the Quarter, its body was burnt. Holy water and ether was sprinkled on its ashes. Satisfied, my Esternome went to bed pretty peppy, without even realizing that our Idoménée had not said a word, that she had sighed at the same time as the cock, that in her eyes blue with silent fright, all smiles had left, she stammered (and without any noise or fuss over putting on a madras or a scarf) an adieu to the world.

My Esternome found her dead by his side the next day. Despair did not at all swallow him as one might have expected. He went back to bed next to her, closed his eyes, and started bundling off his soul. But as a chill crept up his ankles, he remembered me. Had I cried? Had I sighed in my sleep? Whatever the case might have been, my Esternome came back into the world to take care of his daughter— just for that, completely passed away with regard to anything else.

Idoménée was buried in the Trabaut cemetery. A mutual aid society (Human Solidarity) to which my Esternome had been able to sub- scribe arranged for the coffin. Then he made it his goal to reduce my pain: a little more affection, a bit more tenderness, more words too, which inhabited my being, suddenly avid to fill myself with him. He told me everything, several times, in Creole, in French, with silences. Sometimes he found strength to laugh, other times he drew the courage to cry. I would see him limp to his little gardens hidden in the hill's hollow, from which he brought back one vegetable and two troubles. At night, I would hear him curse, from the depth of his sleep, the surveyors, all the békés, all his misfortunes and his put-out desires, all the sealed doors, all his lies, all his lost chances, and this life which he had to live and which his soul wished to leave. He would wake up absent, refusing to come back to his empty eyes until I begged him, Hey Papa, hey Papa . . . *Oh Sophie Marie, 'that you? It's really yourself there . . . ?*

I had taken up Idoménée's fish frying. My schooling forgotten, I spent the daylight preparing my ingredients and the evenings selling them. I no longer sold much. Too many expert vendors competed with me. What's more, Idoménée's old customers trembled at discov- ering that my marinades had the taste of hers, that my blood pud- ding came out the same. Imagining that one of the dead was cooking their food, they moved away from my baskets. I had to return home with my fried fish. My Esternome fed them in silence to his little pig tied behind the hutch. It became difficult to pay that fellow Lonyon. When the latter, dressed in white, would come by to collect the rent from each of his hutches, my Esternome and I would run and hide behind the Pont-de-Chaînes bridge. Lonyon was losing patience and would go off grouchy, leaving a threatening message with our nearest neighbors. One time he rushed up in the middle of the night and knocked on the door; we remained hidden, silent, not moving a hair, shaking under so many insults for the sake of two-three coins that were even impossible to promise.

He came back before dawn with two Bosses from the Sainte-Thérèse Quarter. They smashed the door, smashed the window, and began to throw our things out into the mud. My old Esternome jumped on them. He crushed the nose of the first with the pestle of his head. With his machete he tried to cut the second. The Bosses began to beat him like one tenderizes conch. I had jumped on the one called Lonyon in order to gouge his eyes out. And then I tried to bite one of his balls. I was also pelted. We would have been done for that day had the Boss of our quarter not showed up. He was one lone coolie. He lived in a crate wood hutch he had been able to buy. He didn't associate with the other City coolies regrouped inside the Béro Quarter. On his arrival among us, two-three foolhardy ones had wanted to intimidate him, *We don't want any coolie here* . . . Laughing at his stringy arms, they had stepped forward to better shove him around. When they put up their fists, the lone coolie took out a gleam of white from his pocket. He slashed the fellows with such speed, such fierceness, such meanness, such pleasure, such relentlessness, that each and every one of them put their hands to their heads screaming, *Sweet Jesus, forgive us our sins*. The fellows dashed-and-disappeared like beheaded ducks. They left congealed blood in an area the victorious coolie forbade anyone to touch, thus delimiting his territory on this earth. The mud would later swallow up that horror during an amazing flood.

Well, Lonyon's two Bosses who were murdering us saw him arrive. The sight of him calmed them. The Bosses knew each other. Each of them governed an inviolable space. One proceeded onto the other's domain only to declare war. And Bosses who faced each other went

at it, this was no joke, till the end, till death did them part. One of
Lonyon's Bosses faltered toward the lone coolie, *Silver Beak*[1] *ho!*
we're just settling some matter here and we'll be on our way. The
second one said, *Oh Silver Beak, this fight it's not for you, do for-*
give us, but we're really just passing through, no footprints even.
Lonyon expounded on a philosophy of rent due, of honor and respect; people needed to be taught how to live with others, he said,
otherwise it would be the end of delicate greens in a stew of
vagabondagerie. *Oh the coolie's eyes . . . !* I still remember them.
Two agates, blacker than a boiler bottom. They rested on no one.
He was moving forward step by step, one hand hanging, the other
resting in his back pocket. Sainte-Thérèse's Bosses dropped us in the
mud and moved away without stopping. The coolie picked up my
Esternome and picked me up too, inviting us to return to our hutch.
Which we did, dragging ourselves. Then one by one he put back our
things inside. Finally, coming near Lonyon, he declared in a voluptuous voice, '*Xcuse me Monsieur Lonyon for meddling in your busi-*
ness, but mercy is one thing and rent is another. Only dogs tear what
is already torn. But you're not a dog, Monsieur Lonyon. The dog is
good only with a leash. You're a good person in the faith of Jesus
and of Nagourmira . . . Give time to pay or time to leave . . .
Lonyon did not hesitate. Time to pay . . . he grumbled. His two
Bosses agreed right quick before retreating without exposing their
backs to the misfortunes which menace men here.

My Esternome never recovered from that treatment. He wanted to
get up but his bones betrayed him. I sat him on his bed to rub bay
rum on him. Women from the Quarter came to help me wash our
things. The coolie had gone back home without even turning
around. Once night came, my Esternome and I found ourselves in a
now unfamiliar hutch. With our things having taken a mudbath and

---

[1]Because he had gotten all of his front teeth sculpted in blessed silver. Thus, his tiniest bite
would neutralize the possible talismania of his attacker.

then being thrown about here and there, it spoiled the memories of the place for us. What's more, it finally entered our spirits that we had to leave.

Lonyon gently came to remind us of it the next morning, then at noon, then the day after that, then every time he could. He came alone, avoided a scene, darted insults at us through his teeth. I was the only one he saw; my Esternome, all disjointed, remained crucified to his bed. Only his memory functioned with despairing haste. He anchored me to his bedside to whisper his life. Terrified at feeling him go, I could hear his words knelling in my ears. I was hardly surprised to find these words intact when that madness possessed me to mark them down in notebooks a long time after. I hear. I hear. His voice was floating in that hostile hutch like the incense of benediction. The neighbors who brought us milk and broth for strength would also stay to listen. My Esternome's words took us back to a time none of us could have guessed at. That time long past vibrated over his zombified body, like a living memory. I didn't realize the reach of his words, but I foresaw their hidden importance: they would, beyond my Esternome, feed a legend that would give me momentum for my battle to found Texaco.

Then his words became incoherent. He had never told his story in a linear fashion. He proceeded by whirling paths, sort of like driftwood riding the tide of memories. But now the incoherence came from his words which no longer meant anything. They sank wandering inside slowly eroding memory, which harped on useless markers so as not to disappear altogether. He spoke of his mama. He spoke of a house frame. He spoke of Ninon. Of Idoménée's eyes beneath tears of light. Named names. Named places. Laughed to himself. He began to disremember where his body was. He sometimes thought he was in the coolness of the hills. An hour later, some sort of music would make him shudder. He would cover his head, press in his ears, hysterical at seeing himself lose it in those awful serenade days.

. . .

One day he called me by an unknown name. Then, on another day, asked who might I be.

He saw roosters flying in the house. Asked me to take off the human skins hanging on the ceiling. I began to age a little, I mean: to get used to the idea of his death. It was unbearable for me to see him dim without much elegance. My Esternome was being replaced by a shadow, disintegrating in odors, urine, bowels emptying from under him. His nails were claws, a glint of meanness shone in his eyes, his voice lost its traits and took on some hoarseness. He cried like a child and howled from centuries of anguish. On other days, reaching deep down in his spirit, he would understand what was happening to him, would be devastated at afflicting me with so much work. I would say to him, It's nothing Papa, it's nothing . . . ; but this fugitive lucidity burned like a hot iron. He would run from it into that barbaric sleep which precedes death, open-mouth sleep, foamy-lips sleep, broken-body sleep, wide-open-eyes sleep full of frantic trembling—as if life was hanging on in disbelief to something slipping away through its fingers.

I had accepted the idea, but to find him dead . . .

THE WORD SCRATCHER TO THE SOURCE

(. . .) As you asked me, I have not related the part where you spoke to me of the death of your father, Esternome Laborieux. I have only included your outpourings regarding his old age—his slow deterioration. That was useful to me in underscoring the extent to which seeing him disappear left you only the words of his memories. In any case, were you to change your mind, I would like to be able to relate that part, to consider with words this unique moment you have created in speaking about yourself, a young woman, discovering the death of your father in that Terres-Sainville hutch. Of course, I also hope you will forever refuse; writing is to be fought: in it the inexpressible becomes indecency.

647TH LETTER FROM THE WORD SCRATCHER
TO THE SOURCE.
FILE NO. 31. 1988. SCHŒLCHER LIBRARY.

My Esternome's death did not at all mollify that hound Lonyon. His shadow was not seen behind the coffin. The next day, he came to indicate that he had never had a contract of any kind with me, but only with the late Esternome, who had thus taken it to the cemetery with him. If in the days to come I refused to hightail on out of here, he would not hesitate to call the gendarmes. Tied to my solitude, I made no reply. The last shovelful of earth on my papa's coffin had dug an abyss behind me. Washed up in Fort-de-France like he had been in his Saint-Pierre long ago. It was my turn now, I had no other choice, following his failures, than to attempt to penetrate City.

MUSICIANS WITH HUNGRY EYES

My first concern was to avenge my Esternome. In my mind (ejected from carefree youth), good Sir Lonyon was the source of the world's misery. He and his two Bosses carried the death of my Esternome on their shoulders. At the hour I found my Esternome lifeless I rushed to the coolie Silver Beak to seek revenge. Collapsing in his hutch, I howled like a Christmas pig, raking my lungs. The Quarter made a circle around my misery. They eyed my pain like a bad season. A few tried to take me elsewhere. I tore away from them to implore again at that inhuman door. Coolie Silver Beak was inside, but he didn't budge. They dragged me to my hutch where they attended to the body of my dear Esternome: bathing him, clothing, covering him with the ointments which best protect the body on that unknown journey.

. . .

During that time, hatred was my life's breath. Lonyon and his two Bosses were lying in a pool of blood in my head. I had seen coolie Silver Beak at my Esternome's funeral procession, all dressed in white, inaccessible. I didn't look at him. He didn't look at me either. He probably feared to take on my pain with a mere glance. The days went by in that erased world which the death of loved ones invents. A negation of time. *Oh such hatred . . . !* One day, someone knocked on my door. I found in front of the hutch a basket wrapped in sackcloth. Imagining some devilry, I grabbed the bottle of ether which my Esternome kept under his pallet, then I changed my mind: it had mysteriously dawned on me that this was the wished-for revenge. So I was not taken aback to find in it the ears of several persons, pallid in the blood-clotted basket. The two Bosses would remember my Esternome each time their hats would droop over their eyes.

I sprang toward coolie Silver Beak's hutch. He held his door ajar, listened to my Thank you mist'r Thank you mist'r. Through my tears I saw him up close. His strange eyes no longer had any harshness; only a bottomless sadness which seemed familiar. Which he had to face every day, alone in the silences of his hutch locked on the secret of his exile.

I followed the fate of coolie Silver Beak from afar. He succeeded, they say, in leaving the Quarter and settling in Trénelle when the town decided to give him a niche there. He worked on the town council, they say, some sewage department business, then went into cock fighting, a truly lucrative business. He exhibited shiny shoes, jewelry, clean nails, a canoe, and even a car that he'd start with a cranking noise on Sundays. I got news of his death. It all started on a ferry at Lamentin which he took to get to Fort-de-France, fresh from the cockfight pit. The ferry hadn't even cast off when . . . *well looky there!* a flying fish jumped out of the canal to frisk at his feet. Silver Beak took the fish exclaiming, Here's my little broth. The captain

(Monsieur Horace Ferjule, a slanty-eyed mulatto whose father was from China) said to him with clairvoyance, Monsieur Silver Beak, please, forget about the broth, this fish has been *sent* to you. A way of saying that there was some not very Catholic devilry here. But Silver Beak, usually so prudent, paid no attention to the advice and kept the fish—as if knowingly submitting to fate.

He had the fish cooked in a saltless blaff.* He ate it, they say, in the middle of the night, alone, after a little punch. And-then he lay down to listen to the radio. And-then he got up to look at the moon. And-then he began to walk City's streets, faster and faster, turning to look behind his shoulder for an invisible presence. And-then to run after some stuff that had stumbled down his soul. They found him in the Desclieux garden in a strange form, probably not human, in such a shape that the abbot was called before any doctor. He smelled, they say, like a jellyfish in the sun or a salted white thasar fish, or like the toxic bouquet of turtle shells drying in the sun throughout the Caribbean. Oh Silver Beak, I remember your pain. On your grave each year I have, without waiting for All Saints, given thanks in etched-in-stone Latin, laid arum lilies, immortelles, three invincible candles. My homage to ward off your exile.

The severed ears of his Bosses yielded me a very sweet Lonyon. He came one morning very early, struck (as with a riding crop) by his new duty: to help me make my way in City. His solution was for me to work in his house, like a house girl, until he found me something. I wanted to kill that fellow. I looked at his round face, his light eyes which he had inherited from a Norman buccaneer, his fingers with signet rings, I smelled his perfume, his vaseline, the effluvia of his tobacco, that opulence milked from the roach holes he rented out just about everywhere. The more I looked at him, the more I wanted to kill him. That's the only reason I said yes to his offer. To bring me into his house was to introduce dirt there. Not this unfinished young lady which he looked at with appetite but a piece of filth carrying more hatred than your pen could express.

. . .

Lonyon lived in a tall-and-low house, on the left side of the Levassor Canal. He lived like a lord, with no woman, one kitchen, three swell rooms, light in the lamps, rugs, tablecloths, and a whole slew of baubles which came from France. He put me up in a room, pointed at the cleaning to be done, what was to be dusted, where to go get the vegetables every morning, where to find the fish, and at which time to set the table. All day he went up and down about different matters. He trafficked in everything. Matters involving barrels of salted meat redistributed by the strip in a bunch of stores. Involving mabi sales. Matters of cloth. Of jewelry, but he especially meddled in the incessant business of music.

He owned, I found out, some kind of dance hall on the edge of the right bank. An orchestra played Saint-Pierre beguines there, Argentinean tangos, and long Vienna waltzes. There, on Saturday evenings, clumps and clumps of people came to splash alcohol on their booboos, burn some money, dance and rub against others, breathe the music, suck bad beer and tafia. It even seemed (according to his jokes) that some big shots went there. In any case, I never saw any of them among those who came by Lonyon's and whose only religion seemed to be smuggling. I served them fritters or sumptuous madeiras while they recited inaudible prayers against the customs officers. A trail of bawds also came by to see him, bringing to his attention the case of a young girl in need of a position. He invited passing sailors, port officers, and received them with chocolate or aged whiskeys. Matadoras would also come by to be carted off to his room to spend the night panting nonstop and drinking port wine.

But the ones whose presence I enjoyed were the musicians. Lots of musicians; some from his casino. Lonyon was in love with music. This was probably a secret fever, for on my sleepless nights (I was trying to figure out a way of poisoning his blood, then to run away to the hills), I would hear beads of guitar modulations glistening from his room. The first time, I thought I was perceiving a miracle, so pure was the music, so sad was it, so much the opposite of Lonyon, this lying bastard, thief, real hound. How could he have extracted such harmony from his rottenness? People are strange. From the worst, I've seen celestial treasures flow. From the most exquisite, I've seen mud drip. The music sweetly branched off and would then slowly burn down without really stopping, as if evaporating, and the charm was broken: the magic Lonyon would vanish, leaving room for the beast I wanted to destroy. The guitar, I never saw. He must have hidden it in the West Indian cedar wardrobe which filled the room. An imposing wardrobe, giving off an imprisoned smell. Lonyon kept his life's mysteries there, his money, his papers, his tricky-dicky ledgers. Dusting the wardrobe, I felt that all of him was inside; often I would smash my fists against it in fits of useless (but satisfying) rage.

Lonyon's musicians would come to speak about money. Lonyon would answer with talk of music. Inviting them for dinner, he'd ask them to bring instruments, you the clarinet, you the banjo, you the guitar, you the trumpet, you the violin. They played at his request, timeless beguines, religious odes, mazurkas, fandangos, baroque sounds, sentimental and melancholic waves. Often they would hum hushed sighs of love which mesmerized me. They were either very somber or very happy, but always out of step with life. Their instrument carried their soul and shone like it. Never did they leave it behind; for them it was a piece of City. Far from the crate wood quarters, they knew high-class people, played at the béké baptisms, livened up political meetings, sounded madrigals for young ladies in bloom at the request of powerful freemasons. These connections allowed them to be better housed in City and to compensate for their life-weariness. They were hairdressers, cabinetmakers, watchmakers, delicate professions they held on to like one holds a note when the orchestra tunes up.

• • •

They had long fingers and long eyes. From the depths of my hatred
for that dog Lonyon, their light captivated me. Soon they had begun
to look at me: my breasts were beginning to grow, my lashes to
shiver with innocence, my well-fed flesh had found itself new shapes.
They took me for Lonyon's daughter or a relative of his, so they
didn't dare say a word to me. Some of them would try a joke. But
Lonyon would put a stop to it with one look.

I have to say that he treated me like his woman. I left the house to go
to the market for some vegetables, look for a drum of charcoal at
the other end of the canal, wait for his fisherman to entrust me with
the catch. The rest of the time, I was forbidden to go out. He also
forbade me to open the door to anyone in his absence. How many
musicians came to knock behind his back under the pretext of having forgotten something, though they could not quite recall what . . .
But I never opened. They stayed on the other side warbling or filling
their instruments with sensuous melodies, with off-beat sounds chis-
eled from a vast quiet nakedness, with layers of sounds blurred by
some siren and broken with silence. I was in a state, alright! . . .
Without the door between us, they could have picked me like a
thornless flower, pulling up something already cut.

Lonyon started taking an interest in my body's changes. He asked
me to eat with him. Sometimes after eating, knowing how receptive I
was to it, he'd speak to me of music. I, eyes down, adopted the
young woman's legs-crossed-tight pose, which seemed to amuse him,
the only pose that allowed me to suffer him without vomiting my
hatred. I'd spit in his food every day. Piss in it too. I'd grind some
flies, roaches, millipedes into it. In the meat he thought harmless I'd
hide some fish bones. I had soiled his sauces with the louvered shutters' dust, lime, chien-fers' yellow fur, mouse droppings. Each night I
went back to my room, beaming from having seen his mouth water
over this refuse.

•   •   •

Then this revenge became pathetic. So, alone in the house, I'd practice slicing his throat with a knife. But I never got the courage to do it. And if I ever did feel up to it on some nightmarish night, the guitar strains would disarm me for a long time. Lonyon was a musician: *How do you kill music?* I could have let myself be trapped in that impotent hatred, in that life apart from the world while, outside, Fort-de-France grew. But things sped up. I had to get away from Lonyon. He followed me about the house, sought my company, brushed against my hand. He wanted me to kiss him like his little girl before he left the house, kiss him when he came home, kiss him goodnight and kiss him good morning. His growing desire closed around me. It agitated me while whipping up acrid whiffs of hatred that made me sick.

One night the guitar's airs sounded less sad. Not gay, but vibrating with a new appetency. Then it stopped. I heard Lonyon's bed creak. I heard him walking. I thought I was going to die when my door opened and his cursed shadow came toward me. He was stark naked. Shivering. He covered me with his body (hot like a tin sheet in the sun), pinning down my hands. Against my belly I felt his meat throbbing. His hips wriggling. His rank winy breath, the stench of his sweat. What hard luck! . . . I never would have thought I could let forth so much strength. Enough to send him crashing against the ceiling, smash him with a chair, crush his balls, and throw him out into the hall like a bundle of dried herbs.

I spent the night hearing him curse me through the keyhole. I heard him cry, then laugh, then sweetly propose to me to be his woman. Then I heard him go nuts. His machete began to knock down the door; he would have killed me without blinking. The only words able to douse him in his fury came to me: *Silver Beak will settle things with you if you touch me* . . . He calmed down immediately. I heard nothing for a few long minutes, then his guitar began to shiver in his room. Now it was bitter. Beneath the magic, a gaping wound. I sat crying until the middle of the day.

. . .

The next day, as innocent as the dew, he was astonished that I should remain in my room. Well, my girl, you're not working today, huh? . . . I cried out to him that I wanted to go away and that I would go complain to Silver Beak if he stood in my way. All right, he said, but where are you going to go? I would reply: I don't know but I want to go . . . Three days went by like that. I felt myself dying from not drinking and not eating, but nothing could soften my resolve. He must have understood, for he found a solution: You have to come out, I got a job for you with a Madame Latisse who makes hats. She's going to teach you and you can stay with her . . . I came out of the room without thinking, ready to follow him, taking his word for it, swept by this new twist of my fate to which he himself (respectful, and thoughtful while guiding me) seemed to submit.

CITY PEOPLE

Madame Latisse was a mulatto born at Rivière-Pilote. She wore silk, poplin, and satin. I think her husband was a cabinetmaker; I never met him; long before I arrived he had fled with a bewitching Polish woman who danced naked on ocean liners. My new boss kept a store called "Stylish Fashions and Ready mades." Everything could be found there, linen lace, ribbons, veils, silver buttons, and especially hats. Apart from Madame Latisse, three more people ran that store. First, one called Sarah, a white-haired kafir woman who never left the storage room where she sewed felt all day long. Then one called Etienne, a stranger to marriage, who, despite her growing old age, still had a young girl's beauty that none dared place among the races of this earth. One of the clients' favorite distractions: to determine her origin. Kalazaza-mulatto? Three-blood-câpresse? Carib-coolie-béké?[1] Ma Etienne cultivated this mystery with puzzling

---

[1] The Source's wandering words lingered on the mystery of Ma Etienne for a long time, six times did she return to it, so much that for a long time I thought she attached some kind of importance to it, and I had to go back later and cut out 126 pages (Schœlcher Library—Notes A, XXI, 22, File no. 70). The word is strange . . .

leads: according to her, her mother used to evoke for her, during nightly chats, an Irish childhood by tall cliffs, in dark country houses; though he had been as black as a cauldron's bottom, her father was not from Africa, and the language in which he said his adieus did not have vowels. Every evening, Ma Etienne went home alone, back bowed, with small steps, standing at the street corner as if expecting something (or someone). Then, always disappointed, she nodded her head before fading into City's shadows. And finally, Madame Armand, married to Monsieur Jules Armand, a black pharmacist's assistant in the depths of a dispensary which sold an English powder against fevers. He came to pick her up every evening at six, starched in some sort of bat suit, always the same one, of which he seemed very proud. Madame Latisse ruled over these three employee-associates with authority. At first, it seemed the woman's heart was good, and it is almost certain that she at least had one. But living with her through the daily little things, you soon realized that her heart knew nothing of wonder, that her eyes never sparkled, and that her laughs (if such noises can be thus called) were brief and soulless.

I was to learn sewing there. Since Madame Latisse lived above, on two floors made of northern wood, with three of her daughters, her old parents, and a dozen proliferating Siamese cats, descendants of a pair left behind by a old sailor, I found myself playing the maid again. I spent the day with dishes, wet rags, dusting different things. I had to scour the sidewalk in front of the store, sweep the gutter along the façade, pamper the children who cried over their bewitched father. I also had to take care of the parents, who perpetually trembled in two creaky rocking chairs set next to each other by a window. They never left it except to roll out like dirty laundry onto a big stiff mattress. The old lady was narrow and dry. The old man, tall, broken, full of bones, with the lidless eyes of a wild animal. All these tasks swallowed my day, especially since Madame added, without blinking, those of peeling vegetables, scaling fish, cleaning the ox feet delivered every Saturday by some people she knew.

After the evening meal, when I had cleared the table, nibbled by myself in the kitchen, made the two old ones drink some cow's milk before putting them to bed, Madame Latisse would take me down into the universe (for me, magic) of the store. *Oh that world of velvet, straw, plush, those enchanting aigrettes and crepe-lace, those feathers, those pompons, oh the braided embroideries!* . . . The enchantment did not last long: I had to go back to work. But, this task (new for me) offered me access to the hat-making science. I did it for months before realizing that it was nocturnal slavery—and then feeling the fatigue.

The store specialized in hats for children. You had to cut them from a special cloth, adjust their shapes around wooden molds, correct their sewing, stitch the borders, daub the whole thing with gum arabic, wash them, iron them, complete them with linings, bouquets of small flowers, abundant lace feathers. City's high-class people fought over these wonders. For years, I saw these children's hats go through my fingers, then top hats with eight reflections, hats made of natural straw or of Italian straw which was the fashion for a while. They were brought to us (boater, panama, manila, or bolivar) for a shape-up, a seasonal cleaning, for an added fold on this or that side of the bow. At night, around ten, on a stool without a back, or sitting on the floor, I was sewing, tacking, oversewing, washing the hats, gumming them, completing into the night what the employees had not been able to finish. Ma Etienne, sometimes sleeping at her seat in times of emergency, could not stand the sight of me exhausted over my nocturnal travails. She would grumble to Madame Latisse who never heard, I mean I mean I mean she is a child after all . . .

I slept in the upstairs hall, on a packing-straw bed. Madame Latisse had to skip over me to enter her room and skip over me again when

some craving dragged her out of bed. I could then smell the bitter orange smell her intimate solitude exuded since her husband-turned-
pimp had left. Later, I was put into the garret. Two cloth curtains
framed the illusion of a room in that storage space which supplied
the store's shelves. Madame Latisse would wake me up at four in the
morning, or probably earlier. Hiding a lamp, she silently escorted me
along City's streets; I became the carrier of a barrel of excrement
balanced on my head scarf. It had to be emptied either in the big
canal by the Levée, or by the sea; municipal statutes prohibited such
a practice. The policemen (this assiduous task inspired their nickname of "caca-guards") would be patrolling at these hours. We
sometimes had to hide in a corner, or start running for a shadow. If
we were two fingers from getting caught, Madame Latisse would
leave me standing there and turn around home. I would then take
off as if to save my soul, putting myself (at the price of losing the
barrel) out of the reach of the police claws. When he had evoked
Saint-Pierre or his life in the hills, my Esternome had never spoken
of excrement to throw away. It seems like this problem didn't exist
then. In Fort-de-France's City, I would face it forever. The Quarter of
the Wretched was full of these smelly holes which came with each
hutch. When the hutches tangled up and the holes were nose to nose,
buckets had to be used, yes, all kinds of pots to submit to the heat
and to empty during nightly processions. Around six-seven a smell
smothered the air and spoiled the serenity. In our hutch my Esternome was the one who took care of this. At the ladies' where I was
to live, that job really became a brainteaser. City had not planned
this. To take care of this matter everyone became a night owl. No
one exposed such troubles to the daylight. I once knew a lady who
burned the whole thing in a pewter basin with cloves and spurts of
vinegar. Another one fed it to her sumptuous watercress. Another
one stirred bleach into it and emptied the new chemical mixture into
a demijohn of lime. Others paid old men who took care of "the errand" for three coins. Soon, City figured out what to do. In front of
the houses were built lean-tos which fed whatever the buckets en-

trusted them into barrels. That full barrel is what I had to empty at the end of my day, at any hour of the night, until a company took that matter into its hands in exchange for a tax. It paid hand collectors, then latrine carts that the town council soon added to the budget.

After Madame Latisse (whom I left in a rage after she insisted on making me wear white gloves to serve the food as if being blacker than her made me less clean), I did the cleaning at the home of a Madame and a Monsieur Labonne. These people fed me dwarf plantains cooked the night before or the same old leftovers but never any food cooked the same day. They made me sleep in a greasy shed behind the kitchen, on a soldier's cot wriggling with bugs. At night these people kneeled before a crucifix as if to pray to the Virgin, but they prayed to something else which drove the flame of a disturbing candle wild . . . so Jesus-Mary-and-Joseph! . . . I picked up and left.

After that I fell in with a Mademoiselle Larville, on Rue Perrinon, across from the boarding school. Some would-be innocent old spinster. Upon leaving for the five o'clock mass she'd close the windows, the shutters, lock the door click-click, and lower the meter so that I wouldn't be able to turn on the light to do my tasks. She lived with her mama (who went by the title of Ma Louise) who came from Grand-Rivière; and who also had to remain in the dark like I did. At night Mademoiselle turned off her electric bulbs and forbade the usage of the least lamp on some false pretext of the risk of fire. Fed or not, washed or not, at seven o'clock in the evening you were in pitch darkness! Ma Louise suffered from hernia, which is what we call an organ's slump. That misery caused her a big purple reddish ball between her legs which she wrapped in a cloth. This had come upon her as soon as she lifted a stone that had appeared against her hutch door (certainly "sent"). Ma Louise was overwhelmed by the scorn of her daughter who always made unpleasant remarks to her or afflicted her with shrieks for touching this or moving that. She made her eat on a separate table without tablecloth, *My, my, the shame!* I didn't hang around long at that lady's . . . ! I picked up before the end of the month (without waiting for my thirty cents), and left with disgust on my lips, my basket under my arm, along the path of my rage.

THE MADE-IN-FRANCE DRESSES AND THE FOUR BOOKS

After the Mademoiselle, I found work with a Monsieur Gros-Joseph. *There, I was queen.* I was the guardian of three children, Serge, Georges, and Guy-José. My boss's lady was named Thérésa-Marie-Rose. Monsieur Gros-Joseph had bought from a Monsieur Paul a property (called "Little France") on the heights of Balata. His sisters, Adélina and Sophélise, lived with them. They were manless women, adoring and adorable, whom I liked right away. They adopted me as a new sister. A stroke of fate: my face looked like those of the Gros-Josephs. When I rode with them (in an unforgettable American Dodge), I was taken for a family member; which granted me an agreeable existence. These people didn't have much money at first. They had gotten a bad deal when they bought this area to grow fruit trees, flowers, vegetables. Shrewdness dictated that any capital be invested in army stores, navy warehouses, struggling in City's space where hunger prowled as soon as the communists got the countryside all worked up.

The family divided its time between a small house in City and the property where the crops had to be taken care of. Everyone having to do some task or other, helped by some blackmen with machetes, they had all agreed to get a nanny. Upon my arrival, Monsieur Gros-Joseph was going through some hard times: money concerns. My coming was a blessing. During the days spent on the property, I followed the children into the furrows, watching them play, and insulted the gardening men who panted at the sight of my figure. One day one of the children got into one of those hurricane shelters like the ones they used to build in the Big Hutches of long ago to protect the family from the big winds. So the child goes in there, the others follow him, I do the same. And there comes in my head the idea to scratch the soil and wouldn't you know it, I feel shallow ground under my nails. I had heard too many treasure tales not to warn Thérèsa-Marie-Rose, Adélina, and Sophélise and show them the gaping hole. Thérèsa-Marie-Rose enjoined me to seal my lips forever and to go get Monsieur Gros-Joseph. The latter, very astute, gave the day off to the gardeners, the cook, the maid, locked the property gates, and accompanied me to the hole. We dug out a small chest heavier than a cathedral. Gros-Joseph nervously shoved it under his shirt. From then on things went better for him; in the family I was like in my own house, in the warmest spot of the nest, and I was entrusted with responsibilities.

Vegetables were to be delivered to the soldier barracks. Their number and needs had grown because of the rumors of a war that some bastard called Hitler seemed to be looking for. The family and I distributed their supplies in an old car or on a delivery tricycle. The servicemen delivered a stamped receipt with which Monsieur Gros-Joseph negotiated a payment at the Treasury clerk's. The flowers (arum lilies, tuberoses, daisies, marguerites) were delivered to the vendors as early as four in the morning on holidays. Békés and mulattoes came on the property to buy funerary wreaths, wedding bouquets, a reserve of vegetables. In the family's absence, I took care of the sales under the bitter gaze of the gardeners, the cook, and the maid (Jeannette Capron and Suzanna Pignol, good people still). All suspected me of cheating, which I did of course, not in a tizzy at all, a sou here, a franc there. These gleanings filled my insurance purse against the hazards of my wanderings in City since my Idoménée and my Esternome left me.

Gros-Joseph did business with one Monsieur Albéric. The latter stored casks of rum retrieved from obscure distilleries lost in the back of the hills. Their business consisted of retailing the alcohol to the City shopkeepers who themselves sold it by the pint and half-pint; in those days there was no bottle for the rum. Monsieur Gros-Joseph and that Sir Albéric shared work and profits. That Sir Albéric ran the rum warehouses; with an iron fist he managed the Sainte-Thérèse blackmen who had to roll the barrels, cart, deliver the rum, mind the vatfuls destined to age, and each Friday measure out the liters to the shopkeepers. The barrels also had to be brought onto ships going to France or some other faraway country. Gros-Joseph, accompanied by two Chinese (Chin and Chin-Chin), furrowed the paths in an immense cart. He visited the distilleries, negotiated the barrels, and did the smuggling for the distillers. He'd come back in the evening, dog-tired, and then, together with his wife, sisters, and myself, had to fill the property's accounting books.

It was a good time. I saw aspiring mulattoes from up close, their taste for France's tongue, their love of knowledge. They paid for the services of an old teacher for the children (Caméléon Sainte-Claire), active in his retirement. All that learning had made the big brain a little queer. Two people fought within him: a big blaring fellow, who loved vegetables stolen from the garden; and a castrated being with an exquisite knowledge carefully revealed to children who couldn't care less. With him (thank God! . . .), I learned to read and write. If the A cost me thirteen yams and the B was only a dasheen, and then from C to Z all I had to do was arouse the pleasure he took in resisting ignorance and the volcanic agony of his libido. All for a kiss on the cheek of this tormented-nasty-one-despite-his-age (to excite me, he'd whisper one of those erotic flowers by one called Baudelaire). Caméléon Sainte-Claire offered me my first book (a technical manual which must have bored him). I used it to find this or that word, to spell it, to copy it, but never read it: it offered nothing but discussions of electricity, something about screws, wire, switches, and volts and watts. It was from Monsieur Gros-Joseph himself that I would develop the taste for the books-to-read, devoid of pictures, in which writing becomes the sorcerer of the world.

• • •

He had made a library out of one of the property's rooms. He had
set up a Creole divan below a window that opened on the garden's
Surinam cherry tree. The alizés would spray the perfume of vanilla
flowers into there. Monsieur Gros-Joseph spent his Sundays reading
here, lying on the sofa, silent like the dead. When the children sometimes went to bother him, I followed after them, always puzzled by
so much immobility in that man of action. What kind of magic did
these books do, good-lord? My electrician's syllabus had never
mummified me like that. I expressed my concern to Monsieur Gros-
Joseph. He began to laugh, *Ha Ha Ha but it's because life can be
found there, my little one, it throbs there, the noblest, the highest,
the greatest in man also breathes there!* . . . He made me and the
children sit and then read us that poem which I have kept in my
memory: When with his children clothed in animal skins, Cain had
escaped from Jehovah's sight, as the night was falling, the somber
man arrived . . . *Hugo, my children . . . the greatest of all the imbecile poets!* . . .

Monsieur Gros-Joseph read Victor Hugo, Lamartine, Madame
Desbordes-Valmore, Alfred de Musset, Théodore de Banville,
François Coppée, Mallarmé, Descartes, La Fontaine, Charles
Guérin, Montesquieu, Emile Verhaeren, Jean Richepin, the Countess
of Noailles, and many others . . . Montaigne seemed to be his favorite. In the calends of March, the eve of his thirty-eighth birthday,
that old white man had left the world in order to cuddle up in the
virginal bosom of learned men up in his castle; and, rather than gobble flies, live the life of the hunter, or chase after the duchess in the
humid turrets, he had begun to read old books brought back from
his trips and to comment upon them, filling up their margins, speaking of himself, his moods, his heart, of man, death, of everything
from every angle like my papa Esternome had done with me using
his own words. Monsieur Gros-Joseph pierced Sunday's tranquil
hours with *What do I know? What do I know? Oh the goodly*

man . . . ! To speak French like Michel de Montaigne made him drunk for good. In his library with his Montaigne he (always furious, always precise, always very dry in his business) became tender, aerial, radiating virtue, piety, and grace. Sometimes, his book flat on his chest, he threw his head back with the sigh of ecstasy that I used to hear my Esternome breathe sometimes: *Aaaah, Fraaance . . . ,* he would say.

With him, I embarked upon the unknown world of books. This allowed me to dumbfound Ti-Cirique, the Haitian, when we got to know each other a long time later in Texaco. Monsieur Gros-Joseph, stunned that I knew how to read, had let me near his shelves to take a book from them, sit at the foot of the divan, silently decipher. He pretended to let me choose freely *(There breathes the universal, my girl, everything is good, everything is good . . .).* But, lifting his eyes from a chapter of Montaigne, he would guess which work I'd pulled from the shelf and pronounce his sentence: *. . . Pish, a novel . . . when it comes to novels, Cervantes is what's read and then read again, that's all . . . Ah, Diderot, what a mind, he knows how to let words fly out . . . Oh! that poor Leconte de Lisle, colder than a sword . . . Molière, lord, it holds its own, it holds . . .* After a while, I no longer listened to him. The Sunday liturgy of the book began to absorb me. I didn't read everything, and many a Sunday could go by without any possible access to the library, but when circumstances lent themselves, I skimmed many books, read lots of poems, bits of paragraphs, spellbinding moments. To Gros-Joseph's great despair, I could never tell what was by whom, nor if someone was worth more than another. For me, each book released an aroma, a voice, a time, a moment, a pain, a presence; each book cast a light or burdened me with its shadow; I was terrified feeling these souls, tied up in one hum, crackling under my fingers.

All was going well. The family was making plans for a trip to Montaigne's country. Monsieur Gros-Joseph had negotiated the adventure with a company which owned the ocean line. We had been preparing for this transatlantic odyssey for months, entranced anticipation, the trunks were finally ready, we all dreamt of ships. Excited by their father, the children declared they were going to the land of the mind. They were, they said, at every step going to meet enchanted castles, dwarfen lumberjacks, witches with mirrors, more than a few Countesses of Ségur, some Montaignes, Rabelaises, Lamartines, selling fish, some Jean-Jacques Rousseaus with bakeries, some François Villons slumped over in hovels or chased by the police. When Monsieur Gros-Joseph announced that I too was coming ... I almost went out cold ... *Oh bliss* ... *!* I jumped around his neck. I kissed him, I kissed everyone. I hopped about the garden like a sacrificial goat before a coolie priest. The cook, maid, and gardeners thought I had gone mad. Thérésa-Marie-Rose had made me three beautiful blouses of white cotton with lace for this expedition; they had bought me a pair of shoes, a hat, a big warm coat against the wind which, it seemed, blew across Montaigne's country. I had tried on these dresses over and over. I prepared myself for the trip by reading more ferociously, ingesting by dozens the descriptions of France, its seasons, stories. It seemed that nothing (not with Monsieur Gros-Joseph's business, not in the garden, not with the children's health which we all looked after) could jeopardize that trip. In the minds of all of us, and in mine most of all, it still wore the color of a chimera. What followed proved us right ...

A few days before the trip, the war was declared. Monsieur Gros-Joseph discovered this unpleasantness while delivering some vegetables. He came back to tell us the news with great despair. *France invaded by Germans!* ... France had capitulated. He locked himself up in his library and spent two days drinking his own rum and raving beneath a mound of Montaigne, Descartes, and Montesquieu ... piled on his head like the last rampart against barbarism. A doctor was called, an old-white from Carpates, a navy officer who flew from island to island like a migrating bird when the storms blew in the north. The evanescent physician diagnosed fever which he treated with nothing, saying, *It will go away . . .*

It didn't. Monsieur Gros-Joseph stayed locked up during the whole war. Our Sir Albéric came looking for his associate once or twice; noting what Monsieur Gros-Joseph had become, he would leave frightened, so much so that he later forgot the way to the Gros-Josephs. We never saw him again—not even when Thérésa-Marie-Rose sent me to bring him a few small messages demanding the payment of her husband's profits. To which Sir Albéric would retort, *What accounts, what business, we weren't associates, the money he had came from his labor and since he no longer works . . .*

In the center, an occidental urban logic, all lined up, or-dered, strong like the French language. On the other side, Creole's open profusion according to Texaco's logic. Min-gling these two tongues, dreaming of all tongues, the Cre-ole city speaks a new language in secret and no longer fears Babel. Here the well-learned, domineering, geometri-cal grid of an urban grammar; over there the crown of a mosaic culture to be unveiled, caught in the hieroglyphics of cement, crate wood, asbestos. The Creole city returns to the urban planner, who would like to ignore it, the roots of a new identity: multilingual, multiracial, multihis-torical, open, sensible to the world's diversity. Everything has changed.

THE URBAN PLANNER'S NOTES TO THE WORD SCRATCHER.
FILE NO. 17. SHEET XXV.
1987. SCHŒLCHER LIBRARY.

Soon, seeing good Sir Albéric became impossible, even when Adélina, Sophélise, and Thérésa-Marie-Rose went there in person and stood before the warehouses where huge fellows, barring their entrance, stoically bore my insults upon their mothers. The Gros-Josephs were able to more or less make it through the hard days at the beginning of the war. They concentrated on the property's market gardens, reduced the space of the flowers for the benefit of the vegetables which everyone sought. Hungry crowds piled up before the house's gate and bought the yams at golden prices. But the military authorities decided to requisition the garden's harvests. Though Thérésa-Marie-Rose spoke and argued with the commander (some blue-eyed red monkey, proud of his birth in Avignon, the city of Popes, who enforced a still-remembered asceticism in the colonies in order to forget his Quebecker wife who had died in her thirtieth childbirth called for by the Catholic Church as rampart against the Anglophone flood), the soldiers took everything. The commander not only hated Quebec, the Church, women, and successful deliveries, but also France (and thus our "Little France") on which he blamed the desertions from North America. So he didn't give a damn about the war, to use his own words, and put lives through the grinder of war orders, without ever questioning their spirit or their letter. Orders were everything. Thus, for the slight offense of an indemnity paid every six months, the military carts picked up the yam and cabbage harvests. They left almost nothing. Thérésa-Marie-Rose still decided to sell half of that in order to get more meat, oil, salt, and the rest. Things could have been settled like this, but looting brought their ruin.

What my Esternome had told me of the first war happened again, only more so. City had developed; little by little, it had loosened its ties to the land, suppressed the gardens. My Esternome's cultivations had probably been covered over by new hutches and the new inhabitants of the Quarter of the Wretched (where I sometimes went on Sundays, depending on my walks) settled without ever planting a breadfruit tree, clearing a piece of land, or throwing some watercress into the canal's clear water. Proud of their clean nails, they let City, which was swallowing everything around it, sweep them up. The

City my Esternome so admired appeared to me like a blind beast, proliferating yet incapable of surviving, following the example of the dinosaurs, too rigid for the world, about which the necktie-wearing secular few had told us. I had the feeling that all of this would collapse; the hunger born from the war and Admiral Robert reinforced that diffuse impression. For a long time I saw myself as a passer-by in this City, still thinking of starting a community in the hills . . . as soon as my pockets were full, a Noutéka of the Hills . . . that poor epic of my poor Esternome . . . I would repeat it to myself in those miserable beds where I breathed in dust, latrine odors, and clogged canals . . . the misery of the hearts anxious to rise here . . . and these respected families which I was able to stare at with intense scorn, except maybe for the Gros-Josephs—poor epic, already the accomplice of bitterness.

City modified the countryside blackmen, not one had my dear Esternome's spirit; more and more, he seemed to have come from a far-away planet; which fact, along with distance, nostalgia, and maybe that familial impulse that loneliness inspires, made him ever more appealing to me. As the years went by, he grew in stature in my spirit.

At night, during the war, the blacks invaded the gardens of the property. They carried everything away in a jealous rage. Desperate. They picked the vegetables, the fruits, the last of the flowers, as if they could eat them. They devastated the fields, scratched the soil, pissed all over, uprooted the trees out of plain old meanness. There were no more gardeners, no more maid, no more servant. Thérésa-Marie-Rose could no longer pay me but I stayed anyway. The three women, the children, and I watched the garden. When the tide of pillagers would swell, Thérésa-Marie-Rose would fire in the air, then into the crowd. The first shots frightened them, a bit less the hundredth time, then not at all, especially since Thérésa-Marie-Rose soon ran out of bullets: she screamed, *Boh! Boh! Boh! zot mô,*

You're all dead . . . , while in an inhuman voice we shrieked cannon thunders Bidam Bidam Bidam! . . . That never worried the pillagers but rather acted like a balm on our anguish.

In vain Thérésa Marie-Rose asked for assistance from the commander, the murderer of memories; then she begged for thirteen audiences with Admiral Robert (that Petainist, governor of the country, was living it up with the békés or else tracking down those crazy blackmen who each night faked their way past his armor plates to go save De Gaulle and liberate their France . . .).

Within less than a year, the estate looked like a chien-fer in the middle of a market. In the morning, disorderly mists floated above the trampled ground. The naked trees twisted in the wind like witches' fingers. This didn't help the mental stability of Monsieur Gros-Joseph, tucked away in his library which he no longer left. He pissed and shat on his own books, then ate them, and screamed bloody murder at the Surinam cherry trees whose grimace he alone perceived. I accompanied Thérésa-Marie-Rose when she brought him his milk, some boiled vegetables, which he swallowed three days later, once they had curdled and spoiled. We could hear him eat like a pig, belching Rimbaud or Lautréamont. Sometimes Thérésa-Marie-Rose sat with him in the library and ordered me to air the implacable pestilence. While I picked up the poor man's filth, she spoke to him, listened to him speak. She was trying to find her husband in a look, in a familiar gesture. Alas, screw it . . . nothing in that degenerate evoked Gros-Joseph, except maybe the authors he cited, but according to obscure laws the true Gros-Joseph would not have approved. The poems, the wretch would say, tasted better than the novels—more delicate. Rimbaud gave off a taste of silty cockle, something that choked and tortured the mouth before spreading out layers of smells, then turning into a sheaf of powder and desert sand. Lautréamont reigned in a bouquet of star-apple-green-lemon, but in large quantities would cause stomach ache. Sully Prudhomme had to be chewed like a thick cake and be very quickly forgotten. Some Lamartine left the taste of old syrup, pleasant but a bit soft. And Montaigne, alas, oh flamboyant spirit . . . his books dissipated their virtues in the mouth only to leave the taste buds the impression of stale paper . . . In listening to this vandalism Thérésa-Marie-Rose cried. She would run out of the room before I was done; and I would find myself alone with the fellow who would bite into books. Ah Jonathan Swift taste of shit, Ah Zola taste of shit, Ah Daudet taste of shit, and he would fling them across the room, pages torn by his teeth, Ah . . .

It was no longer possible for Thérésa-Marie-Rose to pay what was owed. Monsieur Gros-Joseph had not initiated that poor woman into the labyrinths of his business; she threw herself into deciphering his sibylline papers, into the vertigo of recondite accounts quilled in notebooks with ill-numbered pages. She tried to resist a number of summations and to figure out the hierarchy among a clump of creditors. Every day these mad dogs were dumping on her cartloads of debt papers signed by her husband, and would declare themselves ready to burn down the house. The bank demanded fifty payment coupons on pretty white paper, in a nice envelope. And we saw an apocalypse of officials besiege "Little France" to auction it off. Thérésa-Marie-Rose and Monsieur Gros-Joseph's sisters found themselves thrown out in the the street with the three children. On a coolie's cart, pulled by the fatigue of a viscous donkey, they took the road toward distant relatives from Gondeau-Lamentin. Gros-Joseph, after being grabbed from the library and thrown into a sack, had been deposited at the station, then taken to a special section of the prison. The boat for the insane came to pick him up at armistice time, in order to drop him in Guadeloupe's asylum where no one has seen him since, at least not I. In those days, I think mad people were locked away. Thérésa-Marie-Rose spent the remainder of her life taking that same boat to reach the asylum's gates where she flattered the guardians. She would leave them (with a thousand instructions) baskets of oranges and volumes of Montaigne which those duh-duh-um fellows probably used for toilet paper. Thérésa-Marie-Rose lived in Saint-Joseph they tell me, with Adélina and Sophélise; one of these two died soon after, the other left this world so late that no one knew who she might be. She was buried with this epitaph: *Here lies a City person* (a detail that some snoop had been able to recall about her life's prowess). Meanwhile Thérésa-Marie-Rose had passed away at the foot of the asylum's high walls. She had once more made the trip, dressed splendidly with just a lick of perfume. Once at the gate, she told the guards (new ones who didn't know her very well), *I'm here to see my husband . . .* Then, without waiting, she had sat against the left corner of their door. She was later found (a century later) stiff as a salt statue, only when an ash of perfume titillated the memory of these Cerberuses, reminding them of this woman who had spoken to them. *Mé ola Matinityèz-là pasé ô-ô?* But where could the Martinican woman have gone?

BASILE AT HEART

On eviction day, Thérésa-Marie-Rose had told me with tears in her eyes that I was on my own. She couldn't take me with her. I found myself alone in a Fort-de-France at war, rich with my dresses from France, my pair of shoes, two-three coins from my little on-the-side deals, and a bundle of four books taken from the library—before Thérésa-Marie-Rose burned it in a mad fit, hoping it would give poor Gros-Joseph his mind back. But the jackass had burst out laughing in the midst of the flames, then had fallen asleep in the shivering ashes, still mad. My books? Some Montaigne of course, whom I feel I can still hear murmuring in his freezing castle; Alice, Lewis Carroll's, wandering from wonder to wonder as in a true Creole tale; Monsieur de La Fontaine's fables, where writing looks easy; and, of course, some Rabelais, whose linguistic debauchery Monsieur Gros-Joseph abhorred. I like to read my Rabelais, I don't understand much but his bizarre language reminds me of my dear

Esternome's strange sentences stuck between his desire to speak good French and his hill Creole—a singular quality that I was never able to capture in my notebooks. Much later in Texaco, when Ti-Cirique the Haitian would quote me those writers of whom I know nothing: Cervantes, Joyce, Kafka, Faulkner, or (with great disgust) one called Céline, I would whisper to him (not very sure of myself but deeply sincere): *Rabelais first, my dear* . . .

More than ever, City, though I'd been born there, became a place of transition for me. I hung on to the memory of my dear Esternome, hoping to walk in his footsteps. I even imagined that I would find his little hutch intact in the hills, a tabernacle of his happiness with Ninon. War is what made me stay in City because City stood still on itself without the strength to reach the countryside. The countryside came to City: walking vendors and cart pushers, anxious to get some good kerosene, a bit of salt, holy water in exchange for some vegetables. So I began to wander from house to house, boss to boss. My wanderings went like this: a friend at the market (I was moaning to her about some hateful boss) would tell me about this good person there who was looking for someone. I went there and became the maid in that house. So, on my first day away from the Gros-Josephs, I was hired by Ma Mathurin: cooking and cleaning for her, her husband, her three daughters, one of whom (a tad bit loony) curled up in a ball sucking her toes. *Gone, the good life at the Gros-Josephs'!* . . . The Mathurins had less money. Ma Mathurin ran the bistro by the canal; she deposited most of her life there. Monsieur Mathurin worked at the registry of an oil plant. As soon as soap became scarce because of the war, this company had begun to produce some with potashed-up chemistry and coconut oil and did really well, all with absolutely no effect on Monsieur Mathurin's microscopic salary (weary blackman, no more words, crumpled up under some sorrow). It was at Ma Mathurin's that I met Basile.

After my work, I stood on the upstairs balcony looking at City. Basile always took the street below it to work and would call out

Psssst Pssst, Hello miss, would throw me quick glimpses and sweet words. I ignored these maneuvers, putting on my béké face. But day after day, without consulting me, my heart began to knock expecting Basile. From afar he would manage to make me laugh. He wore a boater, dressed in a white, always impeccable cotton twill. He had the hips of a little girl, the shoulders of a longshoreman, and he must have entered this world under a rising moon because he was taller than everyone. His only activity seemed to consist of combing City and of keeping up with the soccer clubs' games waged in the Savanna. When I left Ma Mathurin for Madame Thelle Alcibiade (a retired teacher and eminent member of the National Union of Elementary School Teachers) who lived with a pimply illiterate husband and a leprous sister (Julia, said not to be contagious), Basile found me with no trouble and began to frolic beneath a new balcony. His silliness simply amused me. He ended up inviting me to meet him, motioning with his hands. I didn't go down right away, but of course one night I did go down: after dinner, Madame Thelle began to tolerate my spending my twilight break standing by the street.

The first time, I came down without giving it any thought. I was choking in these days full of the stuffy heat that houses conceal. At night, I soon learned (like City folks) to sip the serenity of dusk. As soon as I got out on the doorstep, I'd see Basile appear. He said the pleasant silly things men say in such situations. I tried to look serious, not to look at him, then I began to smile, and then laugh, and even reply, revealing my name, Marie-Sophie, which he found to be the most beautiful one on earth, all of which, you get the picture, I gobbled up without hesitation. So Basile and I would have these rendezvous in the evening at Madame Thelle's. We whispered outside the door and together breathed the peace of the falling day. The winds which slipped out of City when the sun shone would return with dusk; they would pour in, loaded with sea smells, fold against the high hills which clutched Fort-de-France and meander between the houses, shaking the shutters; their salutary arrival after the asphyxiation had inspired these flowered balconies where one sat—out of dust's reach—to gather one's dreams and breathe in the night; at that time, old folks, breast-fed babies would be settled there, children would grab the wrought iron of the guardrail; City folks, wearing white blouses, tittle-tattled from one balcony to another, cared for their tuberoses and their bougainvilleas; whoever had no balcony sat on a bench at street level; though unsettled by the wind, the lingering dust did not spoil the pleasure they took in the twilight's serene hour; in the houses with huge balconies where the mulatto families gathered, the maids, glued to each other, monitored each other's lives through gossip; their presence drew predatory blackmen with an appetite for young country girls, an easy breeding ground that fed my Basile (as it did hundreds of other good-looking mastercabrones). At night Fort-de-France's streets were sown with maids drunk on these charming blackmen, great shepherds of quivers and sweet nothings, until the holler of their mistress (or master) poured a bucket of cold water on it all, sending the charmed one to a lonely slumber.

It was Madame Thelle's illiterate old man who would motion to me to go in. Taking offense at my exchanges with Basile, he sounded the alarm early on and accused me of disrespecting his house with my little talks in the street with that Ostrogoth. I would reply *I don't understand, Monsieur Thelle, so tell me why can't I be talking to someone on the doorstep* . . . But the illiterate one would give me his dull look, the same look he gave my books when he walked through my room. Madame Thelle never reproached me for anything, but he was constantly behind me, going up and down the hall, slipping in between Basile and me, and looking down at us with his pimply face before bitterly going back inside. Every five minutes, he would lean over the balcony, ask me if I had wrapped the stale bread, if I hadn't seen his screwdriver, if I had scalded out the pink mouse hole behind the vegetable garden . . . To these persecutions I would answer *Yessir, no-sir* . . . , and go on listening to Basile. In the house, the illiterate one was choking on his own impotence. One day, not being able to stand it any more, he went to the police to accuse Basile of corrupting a minor; this went nowhere; the police had their hands full with the wartime troubles. What's more, the sergeant who came at his seventh request (fat, blue, wearing a mustache, walking with feet splayed like a duck, with an icy look when it came to intimidation) knew Basile who knew everyone. So Basile, you're the one causing trouble, you bandit? . . . The sparkle in his eyes gave him away as one who also ran after young maids idling on the stoops.

> In City, Sophie-Marie, there's *Ma* and there's *Madame*. It's not the same thing. *Ma* speaks to you in Creole. *Madame* speaks to you in French. *Ma*'s nice, she's come a long way. *Madame* is severe and goes on about the Law. *Ma* remembers hills, countrysides, and fields. *Madame* only knows about City (or so she claims). What do you make of that? . . .
>
> NOTEBOOK NO. 9 OF MARIE-SOPHIE LABORIEUX.
> 1965. SCHŒLCHER LIBRARY.

Basile remained very respectful toward me until one fatal day. Monsieur Thelle had taken ill that day. He could not haunt the hall or hang over the balcony. In bed with fevers, he feared that he had caught his sister-in-law's leprosy and swallowed all kinds of teas that Madame Thelle brought back from Dillon's underwood. Basile and I had all the time in the world to talk. I knew nothing of him. Not even the rest of his name; but he made me laugh, that was the most important thing. Laughter did away with my mind. So much so that he took me in his arms while I was in the middle of one of my laughs and, laughing, we receded into the hall's darkness, both made bolder by Madame Thelle's dimmed lights. Whispering, giggling away, suffocating, I fell over in excited drunkenness. I began to shiver, to be afraid. My body gave itself to Basile's who was trembling (but a lot less). The thing happened in a convulsive silence. Pain. Vertigo. The shame. The fear. The abandonment. The detachment. The panting defeats. The glimpses of clarity during which one came out of the claws of the beast snorting through the nose. The rising pleasure. The oblivion. The drowning . . . Basile, astonished I was a virgin, sang victory. Only twenty-five years later, during my daydreaming hours between two battles for Texaco, did I notice that indelicacy, so shaken was I at that moment by what my belly had just discovered.

And each evening we talked, waiting for the moment. Less shivering accompanied it now, more desire for it to go on. We did it an etcetera of times and then I went back to my bed and my tortured dreams. Being in the hall (between the Thelle family and the deserted street full of sleepwalkers) added spice to what we did. Never since then have I found that anxious voluptuousness which comes from giving oneself and watching the world at the same time. My heart wasn't Basile's, now that I think of it. Celebrant of a low mass, he was linked to my body's pleasure and filled my thoughts. I waited for his coming with fear, shame, and an appetite which electrified the night. Our talks became almost useless, our words suffered from a drought of impatience. Everything converged toward that moment which we pretended to discover and during which (after a simper or two) I would suddenly sink as into a muddy puddle. I could see myself living with Basile; he proposed nothing. I thought I was happy with him . . . but how do you distinguish love from temporary bliss at that age and in such a tizzy?

When Monsieur Thelle's fevers were gone and he was certain he did not have leprosy, he began his watch again. We watched him too (since we were not convinced of any wrongdoing on our part), but he watched us better. He caught us off guard in the hall. He screamed *Fire! call the firemen . . . ,* and threw Basile out in the street in boxer shorts *Vade retro satanas . . . !* Basile was making to retaliate with a jab, when he remembered the fellow's age. So he chose to dust himself off while insulting fake City mulattoes who thought themselves people but were reality only rabbit shit. Monsieur Thelle ordered me to sprinkle the hall with creosol, to soap the walls, to go purify myself with raw soap, then to kneel under the little Virgin hanging in the main room. But without further ado, I ran to my pallet, picked up my suitcase, and left the house in a huff. Woken up, Madame Thelle had time to yell after me *Come back, young lady, come back, what in the name of heaven does this all mean!? . . .*

I never saw them again. People say they died of Julia's ultimately contagious leprosy. That Monsieur Thelle one day felt an itch on his back, then one between his fingers. He thought of mosquito bites, there were many mosquitoes in City, and forgot all about it. Then small dry spots covered his skin. When he scratched them, they turned into pink scales and became numb. Then oozing sores invaded him everywhere, while Madame Thelle also started scratching herself thinking about all the bugs in City. They remained together like that, scratching themselves, also chafing themselves, refusing the evidence which first reached their lips, then deformed their eyes. Soon they could no longer set foot outside. They had to be fed by Jetée's odd-jobbers who took the money they left under the door and set their food on a tablecloth on the landing. When they were found out, they were thrown to the bottom of Désirade, the terrible island of lepers, where death alone (slowed by chaulmoogra oil) fed hope.

Basile was surprised to find me on his heels with my suitcase. He wanted to bring me back to Madame Thelle's house. At that time I was already hardheaded, so he insisted in vain. He circled round me like a rabid dog. Leaning against a door, I stood still, without speaking, eyebrows all crumpled, mouth awry. When he understood that I would leave without him, to hell if that was necessary, and alone in the darkness, he consented to take me to his place. I refused of course. Exasperated, he took me in his big arms and carried me wriggling to his hutch by the Levée, by the cemetery of the rich. A hutch with two rooms separated by a curtain. An iron bed with four feet, two beautiful lamps, records, a Columbia phonograph he forbade me to touch. In the main room: an oilcloth-covered table, a small kitchen shelf with a kerosene lamp and a few pots. Doors and windows faced a muddy alley firmed up with a paving of shells. Basile ordered me not to move, not to go out, to hide myself in the bedroom if anyone came in and not to budge. That was the beginning of my tale of suffering . . .

THE MUSCLES OF CIVILIZATION

Basile left each morning. He reappeared in the evening with a piece of meat, some biscuits, and some vegetables. He obtained all that despite the war shortages, thanks to a slew of connections with Fort-de-France's upper crust. In fact, he was a member of a physical culture club called La Française and spent his days looking after ledgers and other such administrative matters. He devoted a good deal of his time to taking care of his muscles with the help of Sandow equipment, dumbbells, a chin-up bar, a trapeze . . . He even practiced fencing there under the direction of a master-at-arms with a handlebar mustache. Dressed like a pope, he very often left again in the evening for the sporting society banquets organized at the State Hall. There the party animals spent the night honoring a certain Totor Tiberge, founder of City's first athletic circle, but especially recounting the successive landmarks of La Française in its fight for existence; evoking the heroic days of outdoor workouts in the city hall yard, under the envious eyes of the town council's fifteen firemen; sighing over their emigration to the former site of the nursing home which was destroyed in the fire of 1890, on Rue Garnier-Pagès, where they had boasted something not unlike premises and somewhat more effectual equipment; then lamenting over that new emigration until the 1902 catastrophe transformed their premises into disaster shelters, and which they had to set up (the hard way, like boy scouts) on a plot of land by the sea; then rejoicing over their return to Rue Garnier-Pagès (once the stricken had dissolved somewhere) where their organization was to finally know eleven years of blissful gymnastics, until it secured its definitive seat on Fort-Saint-Louis Esplanade, by Flemish Bay, at the end of Avenue Christopher Columbus.

The huge La Française building, electrically lit, was built thanks to the generosity of all, the governor, the Colonies' general council, the town council, and the many benefactors that Basile and a few others had solicited day and night. In my day, there were about a hundred of them, including honorary members, benefactors, state employees, businessmen, workers, et cetera, civilizing themselves by developing their thighs, their pectorals, their necks, and their abdominals. The society lived on its membership dues, an annual gift from the administration, proceeds from a raffle and a huge annual ball it gave every year to which Basile never took me . . .—some men are dogs . . .

Basile lived well. While I got stale, alone in bed, he and his sport buddies would talk about Desbonnet's, Hébert's, Joinville's gymnastic methods, discuss the virtues of the Swedish walk, enumerate the virtues of physical culture endlessly . . . Oh after a hard day's work, it helps tone up the nervous system, purify the blood, fortify the organs, and put up a better resistance to life's anxieties. They would establish a seamless link between sport and intelligence, between the sporting spirit and the democratic spirit, and would demonstrate how, just as culture purifies the mind, physical culture would imbue the spirit with more elegance, more humanity, more universality. Social harmony would shine through these appeased, tamed, ennobled, *disciplined* bodies. An athletic blackman was by this fact alone no longer a blackman. It seems that Basile gave talks on sports issues before mutual aid societies, and that he contributed to the institution of the Union of Martinican Athletic Societies, a federation which paraded in great ceremony on the Fourteenth of July before the governor. It was under the auspices of highly placed people about whom I knew nothing but whom Basile mentioned with veneration, gentlemen like Louis Achille, Théodore Baude, and Henri Cadoré.

• • •

This is what I knew of Basile, but I was able to piece all of this together years later. At the time, he remained a mystery to me: living in
apparent comfort, nice clothes, and a body sculpted like a statue
which he cared for like a woman's figure, with oils and massages. I
had always seen burly blackmen around me, with big shoulders,
arms, chests, and wrists thick as electric poles, but not like Basile.
Their muscles betrayed the daily pitchfork pitcher, the longshoreman, the wheelbarrow pusher around the market. Basile's indicated
nothing, they seemed of no use, and I even suspected them to be
somewhat inflatable. That gave him the allure of an unreal blackman, a City blackman, beyond sweat and needs.

> The Creole city had not planned on the influx of people
> from the hills. It had been structured by military necessi-
> ties, shaped by the import-export business, leaving it to
> the Plantations to house the thousands of hands used in
> agricultural production. When these hands piled up in the
> city, an unproductive trading post city, they could be chan-
> neled neither into jobs nor into housing. They had to force
> themselves into the interstices. The destructuring of our
> Plantations was not followed by an economy of manufac-
> turing, factories, or industries. The Creole city did not in-
> hale the workhands useful to its expansion, it simply
> suffered (while resisting) the shockwave of an agricultural
> disaster. Faced with the Creole city, the Creole urban plan-
> ner must forget The City. When I say "Creole urban plan-
> ning," I am invoking: *a mutation of the spirit.*
>
> THE URBAN PLANNER'S NOTES TO THE WORD SCRATCHER.
> FILE NO. 13. SHEET XXIII.
> 1987. SCHŒLCHER LIBRARY.

Basile must have told me what I know of La Française: small brief
words, bored confidences, snatches of conversation caught from the

room where I lay when he talked around some punch with a secretary of the sporting society of Redoute, Entraide, or Pointe-des-Nègres. For, in fact, I spent more and more time lying in bed. Basile didn't like to see me appear in the main room, and even less at the window or at the door. Of course, I'd disobey once he turned his back.

My first surprise was learning that Basile had other mistresses. These elegant women would come by, knock, enter without waiting, to drop a piece of cake, a little folded note set in a trap of perfume. I would roll up in the depths of the bed, keeping still, just as he ordered. The elegant girlfriend would walk around a little bit in the main room, would sometimes dart a quick glimpse in the bedroom without ever seeing me in the shadow, then go away. It would never be the same person, never the same step, never the same perfume, never the same presence. When I spoke to Basile about it, he would say they were his cousins, but that it was better not to complicate things by coming out of the bedroom. Which is of course what I did during one of these puzzling visits.

Coming out of the bedroom, I fell upon a Carib-blackwoman with fiery eyes, high cheekbones, a beautiful face set in thick shining hair. I think she was the most sumptuous woman I ever saw, and I suddenly recalled my Esternome's words about the old Caribs he had known in Saint-Pierre who were melting into the population. The Carib-blackwoman almost passed out cold when she saw me at Basile's place. She had something in her hand. She threw it at me, called me *whore* and *bitch in heat*. That was a little annoying. I already had a temper then: a certain taste for bile, an appetite for scandal, a foul aptitude for meanness which could make me risk my life for the least trouble. I began by spitting up a whole lot of insults like they don't use any more. Then I dragged her around by her hair to ask her if we'd grown up together for her to know me as a bitch. I got her flying out of the hutch by going after her with a canari. Cursing her mother, father, her whole generation, I followed her down the street up to Saint-Antoine's Church built in the heart of Terres-Sainville (ex–Quarter of the Wretched), which recorded the echo of my curses.

Basile did not find out right away, but I kept coming out of the bedroom for each visit. Eyes of coolies, mulattoes, freckled chabines, thick-haired câpresses, and even the periwinkle blue eyes of a little békée, who had lost her way in City. Her father had jumped onto the urban bandwagon as soon as his distillery collapsed after the first war. He had chosen, like those of his kind, the food business and now imported salted meat into a warehouse in front of Pointe-Simon. The little one, who had only seen sweaty blackmen in the mud, discovered the elegance of City blackmen, their taste for flower talk, poems, physical culture. My Basile, people say, seduced her the same way he did me, by coming and going under her balcony with little smiles, inspired grimaces. Like other conquests, the dumb-founded little békée had seen her cunt gloried in that slaughterhouse of a sort on the street by the cemetery, until she could no longer find Basile who'd fled as he did from the others. And they would all come by at their usual hours, different hours, and rather than Basile, I was whom they met. Their eyes would fill with shock, anger, hatred, ice, smoke, pepper, all kinds of things. Some of Basile's lovers would disappear there and then, others looked down upon me, others tried spitting out *What are you doing here?* I would begin to throw up my curses, to quench my thirst for them, to run after them up to the church, gathering crowds, which Basile finally found out about. Coming out of nowhere one day, full of himself, ready to rule the world, but alas, fuck that . . . , he was forced to learn that having muscles wasn't the same as using them.

He tried his hand at authority, which I let slide off my back like the ducks do with rain. Then he raised his voice which I let rise, comfortable like an old cat in my bed. Then he raised a hand and

slapped me on the head. *O my, what trouble!* . . . I went into a fit
which he must still remember in his grave today. In no time he found
himself in the street, shredded pretty good, his record player under
his arm, and walking on all fours to pick up the records out of the
dirty water, crying over the clothes which had flown out everywhere
. . . and especially frightened by my ability to cry out loud, to cry out
for a long time, to cry out endlessly, to cry out with joy, to cry out
with faith, smashing the ears of the whole world. I mastered that art,
a panoply of Creole insults stocked up from the Quarter of the
Wretched, beyond what was necessary. And I was able to pour out
all of that in one flow without pausing for breath . . . I was no saint,
I tell you, oh no . . .

THE LONELY WATERGRASS

Basile vanished, then came back, then vanished again. We spent our
days plunged in the same sweet flesh, then other days wrestling in
the sting of salt. When he was there I ate the smuggled food; but
when he'd leave I had to learn to get along in a Fort-de-France at
war. Get in line at three in the morning to get a strip of meat. Beg the
fishermen who paraded with the chance fish. Blind the merchants
who reached City with a few vegetables, promising them a grain of
salt which I didn't have. They all spoke of De Gaulle defending
Mother France, which lots of blackmen went to support. People
spoke of Admiral Robert, who had been astonished to discover only
sugarcane and not one thing good to eat in the country because of
the American blockade. At their evening gatherings watered with
champagne, the admiral begged the békés to free up some lands (the
Germans having invaded the beetfields in the North), but they
turned a deaf ear and bet on a rise in sugarcane. Then they preferred
to wait for the good times. The admiral had to force them to con-
cede two-three hectares to grow some yam plants to feed the country. They talked about that in the ruined market. There, békés were
insulted, Germans cursed. De Gaulle, who soon began to fascinate

me though I wasn't involved in the war, was deified. The men spoke of him like a fighting cock. The women maintained that he had nothing in common with blackmen from here because each of his balls was like a locust tree pod. What a story, my dear . . .

We had to do without oil, salt, dried vegetables, rice, salted meat, soap, garlic, shoes. The poor could no longer find crate wood, corrugated tin, or nails. Coal was becoming scarce and more and more expensive. Those who lit a fire no longer had matches and did all that was possible to keep it glowing ad aeternam. The battle took place in an economy unknown to City's people but mastered by those from the Quarter. Businessmen, butchers, shopkeepers couldn't have cared less about rations and gave preference to their buddies, their families, or the chief magistrates, civil-servants-on-the-make, policemen-putting-on-stripes. To eat, you had to endear yourself to them. One day the fish vendors even refused to sell in order to put an end to threats about regulating their business. Some let the fish rot in the sun. Each and every one cherished the right to rule over the other's famine. City seemed to harden and orphan the heart.

There were people smuggling beef tails and ears. Some were selling grilled skin, eaten without salt in a Carib pimento sauce. The art of surviving, which my Esternome had transmitted to me in veiled words, allowed me to hang in there without too much damage. I drank milk, ate eggs, mashed wild arrowroot, Saint-Vincent arrowroot. I made candles with butter from the big cocoa, to trade for some soap, then I had to wash my linen with the foaming plant my droopy-eyed grandmama used. I learned to track down crayfish under the stones of the Grosse-Roche basin. To trap possum by Pont-de-Chaînes. I learned to fight in the ration lines, to keep my place by putting down a rock there and go chase some windfall to the left and a bit of luck to the right. Soon, salt from Sainte-Anne, forgotten by everyone, reappeared in the stores. Jams that more than one astute woman began to make also took their place on the shelves. Anguish also inspired orange wine, ambarella beer, and a whole army of inventions.

The navy men were everywhere. Their rations anointed them kings of those hungry days. Many were the women on the cemetery street who sucked them into their darker places and fell sick. There were fevers that doctors and pharmacists did their best to treat, but medicines no longer reached our shores and City knew nothing of the old herbal cures. In the Quarter of the Wretched where I'd still drop by, the latest newcomers had gotten rid of their science from the hills like it was some old rag. At the smallest twitch, they'd join the human piles on the hospice verandas begging for some powder or some syrup. When the powder was exhausted, they sat there, lost like fish in a bamboo trap, waiting for a miracle to fall from City.

Despite my deep misery, I managed to avoid going to the navy men like the very poor women did. First because Basile would reappear once in a while with food (he seemed to live during the war as well as a béké), also because I had something else on my mind. Basile was giving me children I did not want to keep. It was a sort of repulsion, fright, refusal, which came both from the war and from my scorn for Basile, my fear of facing City with a child on my shoulder. My first pregnancy was a shock. It took me awhile to get it, and it was Sylphénise (a poor woman who lived next door with seven children and a series of men) who gave me a hint and recommended green pineapple tea. I drank it for a whole day until I felt my whole body dripping. The second time, now more attentive, I was able to pick up on the drying up of my period and began to drink the tea, which did nothing. Sylphénise had to teach me how to handle watergrass, which could pull out the most stubborn eggs. That's how, from then on, alone, feverish, full of tears and despair, I brought myself endless bleeding, days and days of fevers in which I thought I was dying but which I always came out of. Basile often found me drained. He went looking for powders for me, through his connections. But he never found out what I had. I wasn't the only one making a hole in my belly. How much women suffer behind closed louvered shutters . . . and even today, how much harsh loneliness around the blood that flows away with some life in it . . . Oh that death faced in the heart of one's flesh . . . oh women's sorrows.

OTHER CITY PEOPLE

Toward the end of the war, Basile found me a job with a Monsieur Alcibiade, deputy secretary at the Public Works Bureau, one of his sporting friends. A game hunter, he lived for the feathers of the snipe, the wild duck, the moorhen, the plover. He'd track down the ring-dove up to the misty heights, climb cliffs looking for turtledoves. The hunter is a sportsman, Marie-Sophie, Monsieur Alcibiade explained one evening while, after I was done with the dishes, I watched him polish his gun. Going after his prey, the hunter runs, walks, climbs, crosses rivers, tumbles down ravines, long-jumps running or standing, he has to kneel before the fearful bird, crawl on his stomach or walk on his knees when the duck is tricky. In the woods, the threat of the fer-de-lance notwithstanding, he must climb trees, hug trunks, suspend himself off creepers like the most consummate horizontal bar gymnast. *It's a complete sport, worthy of a civilized metropolis!* . . . He was a greased-down blackman, a bit soft, with a big belly, who wore biking clips on his ankles and put plenty of unfamiliar words in his sentences. He never spoke in Creole to anyone and (despite his leather-bound library which I had to dust every week) really only read a hunters' newsletter from France.

His wife, Madame Eléonore (whose breasts looked like two chicken-pox bumps and who had a small hollow gap for a rear end), ran a mutual aid society called Concerned Ladies of Fort-de-France. These Ladies held meetings to which I accompanied Madame Eléonore and served madeleines and tea. They were very worthy, very that-is-to-say, very matadora. One couldn't tell who was a mulatto and who was not, so similar were they, speaking the same French, with the same words, with the same cackling of cold hens, the same bigmama jewels. They were fighting for women to get the right to vote and be elected in matters related to France. Learned, universalist, and progressive teachers came to honor them by evoking feminine figures without whom the greatest men could not have reached their potential. These learned ones stigmatized France, always in the avant-garde though it had let the Anglo-Saxons leave it behind with respect to women. History, that great schoolmistress, had nonetheless marked out a few landmarks: Maria de Medici! . . . Queen Elizabeth! . . . Queen Victoria! . . . They cited the great English writer John Ruskin: "Woman is truly the instigator of all the great and beautiful things," and even "the inspiration of the greatest literary works." They would tell of Joan of Arc (incarnation of heroism), of Madame de Sévigné, George Sand, Madame de Staël, beacons of world letters. They fawned over Madame Curie, splendor of science, benefactress of the human condition; or honored Mesdames Suzanne Grimberg and Maria Vérone, major constellations on the Parisian bar. And they pathetically concluded that woman was fit for the highest destinies, that she could climb the stairs to the seats of the administrative assemblies, general councils, parliament, and maybe even to the very heart of the State, head high. And I clapped along with these Ladies, fascinated, swept away by such loftiness. I had only known shameless survival, dark crate hutches, the quiet obstacles against penetrating City, but by the side of this Madame Eléonore, I suddenly wished to be part of such a society, and to speak of those things in that way. The Noutéka of the Hills in me was as if erased.

On the other hand, Monsieur Alcibiade militated for hunting and the mutualist movement. He participated in the hunters' banquets where everyone, drunk like an old Mexican, would sing:

O Saint Hubert
Hats in our hands
we sing your glory
to posterity
and to your health
we drink a toast . . .

With his buddies, he had created an association which he described as cynergetic. It had a moral profile, a uniform, insignia, a pennant, and paraded in the Savanna on national holidays under the sport federation banner. He was fighting to reduce the hundred-franc hunting license fee, *that awful luxury tax!* . . . He fought to obtain a permit to hunt turtledove in the national wilderness, which according to him was the best way to drive away the fer-de-lance infesting those places. He fought against the békés of the South, North, and East in order to gain access to their game-rich but tragically private lands. A true consumer cooperative, the society bought weapons, canteens, munitions, and miscellaneous equipment directly from the French manufacturers. Its members thus enjoyed the benefits of denying retailers their exorbitant profits. This activism was Sir Alcibiade's way of working toward the dissemination of the sporting spirit likely to develop in civilized countries and which our dear little Martinique should not abandon. It was necessary to aspire to the level of France and shake off the torpor of the Creole youth entranced by music, the fair sex, and the vertigo of vagabondage.

He was also a member of the Society of the Friends of Trees which worried about the disappearance of our forests, which in the long run would also mean the disappearance of our magnificent waterfalls. These Friends met behind the Palace of Justice to read Lafcadio Hearn's texts which denounced the uncontrolled deforestation that fed carpentry and coal ovens. They composed lengthy letters to the governor, the colonial ministry, expressing the idea of an immortal, glorious, universal France watching after the heavenly beauty of this piece of itself, left so far away in the Americas.

. . .

Finally, Sir Alcibiade was a member of the Mutualist Federation.
The latter fed the country's sacred flame of mutuality in the fashion
of the priestesses who in ancient Rome, he often specified, would
poke at the flame at Vesta's altar. He therefore fought for the unifica-
tion of the mutualist societies and for the cultivation of a library in
each one of them, open to Humanity. He was astonished one day to
find my four books nicely set up among my poor things. He, who
only really read that hunters' sheet, asked me if I had read them and
seemed terrified to hear me say *Oui* and to see they were blackened
by my frequent readings. For a moment I thought he would throw
me out and that I would find myself in the gloom of cemetery street.
But that same evening, during the monthly dinner with his administrative friends, he said that his house was an enlightened one because even his maid read, oh not much, Rabelais, that old drunkard,
and some story about a girl in wonderland, it's not François Coppée,
but all the same, gentlemen, all the same . . .

He carried a vision of a great Hall of Mutuality, a temple of Union,
melting pot for sentiments of love and fraternity, home of the re-
splendence of the mind, symbol of beauty and concord, which
would serve as the seat for the Federation's conferences. There he
pictured parties, banquets, scientific, artistic, literary conferences for
the benefit of the Mutual Aid members. He followed the progress of
the French with social security, that great republican conquest supported by the illustrious René Viviani, Edouard Vaillant, Léon Bourgeois, Jean Jaurès . . . He insisted that everyone mobilize to fight for
the implementation of these policies in our dear Martinique, that
little-France so far from everything. He held impassioned conferences on that subject under the honorary presidency of the chief of
public works and services and a few old doctors, Knights Templar.
With health insurance, he exclaimed, a state pension scheme and
maternity allowance, invalid pensions, aid to families with depen-
dent children, medical assistance, and so on . . . , the working class
of our dear Martinique could attain *Ci-vi-li-za-tion*, cheerful work,

far from life's ordinary casualties just like the good French of France will do! . . . All of this already existed in Germany, he fulminated, since the last century! . . . Even England, that most perfidious Albion if there ever was one, has voted for them since 1908! . . . That France of the Rights of Man thus procrastinates, gentlemen, dishonors it . . .

> While listening to the Lady, I suddenly got the feeling that in this entanglement, in this whole poetics of hutches devoted to the wish to live, nothing in Texaco was going against the grain of the city to such an extent as to make that site some sort of aberration. Beyond the peculiar trauma of partitions, cement, asbestos, corrugated tin, beyond the water tumbling down the hills, the stagnant puddles, the deviations from urban sanitary regulations, there was a coherence to decipher, which allowed these people to live there as perfectly and as harmoniously as it was possible to live in such conditions.
>
> THE URBAN PLANNER'S NOTES TO THE WORD SCRATCHER.
> FILE NO. 12. SHEET XXI.
> 1987. SCHŒLCHER LIBRARY.

It was through him that I once again heard talk of *assimilation,* during a conference conducted under the auspices of the Mutual Aid Society, "The Future of Redoute." A while back, France's bigwigs had consulted the local authorities to find out whether Martinique wished to be part of a general government that comprised the Antilles and Guyana or if it instead preferred assimilation with France. Everyone had declared themselves in favor of assimilation with France, but since the time of my Esternome and my Idoménée, and that was a long time ago, there had been discussions in all of City's parlors about the modalities of assimilation, which some mulattoes wanted to see tempered with a trace of autonomy, especially the financial kind. In the squatter districts the discussions were in full swing (assimilation here, assimilation there) but in a different way, because blackmen, always ready to say silly things, readily pronounced themselves for "ass-on-a-mule-ation" to distinguish themselves from those who strangely declared themselves "ass-on-a-goat." Monsieur Alcibiade splendidly treated the question in a prodigious flight of beautiful French. I had watched him prepare that lecture for a month, nailed to his desk, with two-three works from the library and a few colonial newsletters that the Mutualist Federation received by boat. I heard him rehearse so many beautiful sentences when I brought him his evening herbal tea (a mixture of lemon grass and chamomile) that I dared ask him to let me attend. To my great surprise, he said *Yes* full of good humor. I spent the rest of the week preparing my made-in-France dresses from the days with the Gros-Josephs, and, as if in a dream, I was able to attend that fabulous lecture.

I must say that I didn't understand much. Stiff like a Jesus-Christ-statue, "as an inevitable introduction," Monsieur Alcibiade demonstrated how something called *"Colonialism" aroused throughout the world more advantages than real problems.* How this thing had brought *"Civilization"* everywhere. *"Oh Civilization! . . . blinding light! unknown to the natives choking beneath their own shadows . . ."* It is stupid, Mr. Alcibiade exclaimed, *to be stopped by the commotions of a Jean-Jacques Rousseau, whose conception of the Good Savage opposed to the "Corrupt Civilized Man" is in fact lamentable. "That the strong dominate the weak is a natural law,"* good Sir Alcibiade cried out, startling me, *"cruel indeed, but natural." This apparently soulless natural selection, for those able to see the human future in the global perspective, is often, according to Herbert Spencer, only "the decree of benevolence and immense foresight." Definitive progress succeeds any transitional colonial sufferings. The natives get regular wages, enlightened treatment for the sick. Their humanity is elevated by being forced to live in peace, in fraternity, in universal concord . . .* The hall (and I most of all, car-

ried away by these incomprehensible words already etching themselves within me) sighed with pleasure . . .

When Monsieur Alcibiade examined what he called the fundamental
problem of the "relations between newly founded societies in the
colonies and the distant Mother-Fatherland," I began to float in
sweet vertigo. His French, his sharp accent, his flowery sentences,
worked like a little tune to which I succumbed without even trying
to understand or reflect. He said, I think, *that the same laws could
not possibly apply to all colonies, because their development, different races, geographic situation, degree of civilization were not uniform. If Réunion, the Antilles, and Guyana are now mature
societies, the work of colonization being nearly complete, New Cale-
donia, Senegal, Tonkin are barely emerging from the barbarian
straitjacket. Others like Sudan, Madagascar, or the Congo carry
barely a hint of light inside their profound night. One therefore
should take the evolution of each one into account and legislate ac-
cordingly. The colonies' progress toward the social organization of
European countries demands time, gentlemen, measure, prudence,
in a word, a colonial policy . . . !* Everyone approved, and, anxious
not to show my inability to understand these beautiful words, I approved more fervently than anyone.

Then, Monsieur Alcibiade scared me because he frowned with his
brows, thickened his voice, peering around to spit out some sort of
filth called "subjection," the goal of which was to exploit the colony
in France's interest alone. He shook his fist to better demonstrate
*how France was then forced to rule with an iron fist and kill the hen
that lays the golden eggs* . . . He twisted his face three times to better
illustrate *how France now had to warn governors who behaved like
viceroys and who treated the colonies like conquered lands. Then
the people, even more hate-filled because they were badly civilized in
general, revolted; and their legitimate rebellion aroused blind repres-
sion, as we've seen it here, at François, right in front of the factory,*

not so long ago . . . ! To subject, he roared, *is to suppress local free-dom and the inhabitants' rights, is to make deeper the natural abyss between the colonizer and the obscure native . . .* The clapping was a little softer now so that, being unsure what to do, I pretended to be suffering from the heat and used my two hands to fan my face. But a few communist teachers approved noisily, so I stopped fanning my face to move my chin in a very unclear way. *What remains,* announced Monsieur Alcibiade turning his head right to left, *is autonomy and assimilation.*

At that point, his tone became softer, which allowed me to relax in my chair a little and try to understand what he was saying. In his mouth, French seemed infinite and each word pulled forth dozens and dozens of words at the pace of a descending river. Lost in that flood, I tried to figure out nouns, pronouns, verbs, and adverbs, but I would soon give up only to try again a little later without knowing why. The goal of the thing called "autonomy," he explained, *is to found societies capable of self-rule. The Mother-Fatherland then takes on the role of a Roman tutor who must work in order to be no longer needed. But, but, but* (he let out so many buts that I thought he was stuttering, but I soon understood that it was one of his ora-torical ruses to introduce what was to follow) *when the colony becomes an autonomous State under the control of the Mother-Fatherland, the latter sees her child leave her, more and more un-grateful, which costs her nothing but which also brings her nothing!* . . . (he said that with an air of such disgust that I thought him about to throw up). *Assimilation is, however, just the opposite! The Mother-Fatherland and her children are developing themselves to-gether, erecting themselves together . . .* "France is where the flag flies," said Napoleon . . . I began to get happy because he seemed happy, satisfied, he poured his sentences like so many benedictions and I sat up in my chair so he could see me and see that I was listen-ing. *Through assimilation,* he said, going into raptures, *all of the laws of the Mainland, all of the progress of civilization and of the mind, will apply to the colonies, setting straight all those local feu-dalisms. Give it some thought, gentlemen, because the békés are watching! . . . The Mother and her children will, from now on, walk in step, in full equality. But,* he explained, *there is a But. Assimila-tion, though it be the best formula, is not conceivable in an absolute fashion.* He evoked (in the tone of a schoolmaster and peeking at some pieces of paper) *the Frankish zones of the regions of Gex and Haute-Savoie leading a distinct economic life apart from the other French départements,* he recalled that *their prefects had prerogatives in matters of expulsion which were usually those of the Minister of the Interior.* He evoked *Corsica's singular fiscal regime.* He under-lined *the specific, decentralized advantages of Alsace-Lorraine, now back in the national bosom . . .* Then he started to howl again, but this time it didn't take me by surprise and I kept listening as best I could. He said that, *without disappearing or melting, the particular-ities of our dear Martinique were to add to those of the Mother-Fatherland; that assimilation's moderation would make it richer, not with blind equalization, but rather strengthened by central authority and full of freedom and enlightened decentralizations . . . !* All hell broke loose as if there was a fire somewhere. I got up like everyone else, ready to run out, but I realized that people had stood up to bet-ter applaud Mr. Alcibiade and let him know that they approved his ardent conclusion. Each and every one added to the hubbub by tak-ing sides and arguing in a debate I would hear all my life, nonstop, again and again, like a hellish leitmotif we couldn't control and which even today, I think, agitates our people, eh, little Cham?

I learned the idea of assimilation from Monsieur Alcibiade, but Aimé Césaire, our Papa Césaire, is the one who took the project to France's parliament and obtained French département status for us, in the békés' face. I had heard Basile, Madame Thelle, and Monsieur Alcibiade speak of him as of a black blackman, blacker than my dear Esternome, so much so that he could have been taken for one of these just-off-the-boat half-dumb congos who buried themselves in the hills without having even touched City's lights. Well, that black blackman knew French better than a thick French dictionary in which he could pick out mistakes with one eye closed. People said he could speak French to you without your being able to understand even half of what was said, that he knew everything about poetry, history, Greece, Rome, Latin humanities, philosophers, to make a long story short, that he was more knowledgeable, more learned, more extraordinary than the most learned master of the Whites of France. He practiced, they say, a strange poetry without rhyme or measure, he declared himself nègre and seemed proud of it. The worst was that he was ungrateful, denouncing colonialism. He whom France had taught to read, write, called himself an African and claimed this identity as his own. That last idea contorted Monsieur Alcibiade in unspeakable horror, *Zounds! Africa!* . . . , that place of barbarism about which no civilized map goes into detail! . . . But he remained impressed by this personage because there were rumors that André Breton, pope of Surrealism, had met him and was humbled. That Césaire was *communist* also frightened Monsieur Alcibiade. That word meant nothing to me. I was only to measure its scope later, when I was fighting for Texaco, but for Monsieur Alcibiade it was a well of horrors.

But for us, caretakers of an old dream beneath City's walls, Césaire made all the difference. For a long time now, we had thought politics to be the békés' and the mulattoes' business. My Esternome had put it aside since he had gone up the hills. When he had come down to rejoin Fort-de-France, which had this mulatto mayor, Victor Sévère, very close to the poor nonetheless, he showed no interest. Only France, distant Mother-Fatherland, which he blindly honored, was on his mind. He would say to my Idoménée who used to go into raptures about Sévère's humanity, *Careful, my girl, he's a mulatto and mulattoes are like fireflies* . . . He who had witnessed their birth in Saint-Pierre had been surprised to see them rule Fort-de-France. He had also been surprised to see how blackmen, giving up the conquest of the land, had thrown themselves into the assault on schools, knowledge, the French language, and political power. He would say to his Idoménée, mulattoes have won, we're following them like sheep now, filling up their ballot boxes . . . He had never set foot in one of Sévère's meetings or in any political assembly, while the people from the old Quarters, though they felt excluded, descended upon them en masse.

But Césaire, black like the rest of us, brought politics back to us. He came to us, like Sévère, into the Quarter of the Wretched, Trénelle, Rive-Droite, Morne Abélard, Sainte-Thérèse. He wasn't afraid to step in the mud, and seeing him come elated us. We would rush to carry him above the dirty water, so he wouldn't stain his shoes. He brought us the hope of being something else. To see that little blackman, so high, so powerful, with so much knowledge, so many words, gave us an exalted image of ourselves. From then on we felt that we could make it and conquer City. When he asked us to vote for him, we voted like one man and we put him in the town council, from which nobody, and I mean this until I die and my bones hollow into trumpets, no one will ever be able to yank him out.

Yet, after my Idoménée's death, just as whispered rumors started to gather about the existence of that magic little blackman, my Esternome, leaning on my shoulder, had gone to listen to Césaire. I remember we took small steps because he had neither the eyes, nor the strength, nor even the desire to live. He went on, mumbling *It must be a Mentoh, it must be a Mentoh,* and these words would give him a surge which would melt the stiffness in his knees. Yes, now the pieces are falling back into place in my head. He had always wanted to find a Mentoh who could tell him how to go about City's conquest, the conquest to which he had devoted his life. He wanted to hear a few words about that and say something to the Mentoh too. To hear a blackman provoke such a craze, just like the mulatto politicians, probably made my Esternome take him for a Mentoh.

And there, that day, he went to see him, to hear him, to speak to him, to listen to him, find out the new orders and probably pass them on to me. But we were late. The meeting had begun already. The loudspeakers relayed Césaire's speech, French, words, voice, energy, to us from far away. My Esternome stopped, listened, then his claws dug into my shoulder: *Annou Sofi ma fi, an nou viré bo kay,* Sophie, my girl, let us go home . . . I didn't ask him why. A few steps later, he breathed something in my ear as he did into his sweet Ninon's years ago and without me understanding:

—He's a mulatto . . .

THE AGE OF ASBESTOS
1946–1960

W hen Césaire was elected to Fort-de-France's town council, Monsieur Alcibiade fell quite ill. *A blackman declaring himself African was going to administer The City . . . and a communist no less! . . .* He exhausted himself in lengthy discussions stressing that these gloomy Quarters all around City were plots of barbarism in the hands of heinous politicians; that enlightened politics should aim at reopening the fields and sending these people back to the countryside . . . ! Most of his friends thought the same (that is, they rejected Africa, the populous Quarters, the visionary poetry, the anticolonialist stance, or Césaire's other defects), but all (mulatto or not) saw themselves in the new mayor. They enjoyed his mastery of the language, his knowledge, his constant exercise of rising above the human condition. When Césaire left the Communist Party and created his own under the banner of progress, many of Monsieur Alcibiade's friends rallied round him. They then became closer to the squatter districts which supplied them with most of their militants, poster-glue-lickers, mastiffs who could keep a meeting under control. At each election (and even in '46, at the news that we were finally French, sort of) a howling flood erupted from the Quarters, in a jumble of torches, to celebrate the little blackman's coming of age, his becoming our mayor, our deputy, our mean lean poet, reelected for the whole nine yards.

• • •

Everything went downhill for me after the first vidé* with the
torches, thereby leading me to found Texaco. Those from the hills,
like myself,[1] had voted for Césaire. When the news of his election
reached City, all hell broke loose. Without asking anyone, I left
Monsieur Alcibiade's house to rejoin the people from the Quarters
of Trénelle, Terres-Sainville, Rive-Droite, Sainte-Thérèse, and even
from the distant Quarters like Coridon, et cetera. *Mi sik, mi . . . !*[2]
This was a bit of a revenge on City, the real march of our obscure
conquest. I dropped sobs, chanted, and sent my body swinging. I
was dismayed by how wrong my Esternome had been about Césaire,
and that he was not able to live through this blazing tide. Endless
torches swirled around the town council, going down the Levée, furrowing through Savanna Park, streaking City's center. Perched on
their balcony, mulatto-milatoes and milato-blacks eyed us with disbelief. We walked along the balcony where Monsieur Alcibiade,
scruffy, unshaven, hair run through with vaseline, screamed a mean
thing or two that our chanting smothered. His wife was trying to
take him away, but he, stuck to the guardrail, bellowed like an ox
being bled. Suddenly, as I approached his height, his eyes (despite the
crowd) caught mine for about half a second during which it didn't
even occur to me to stop singing. I have never since seen so much despair, hatred, and murderousness in a look. It crushed my bones, but
I went on with my vidé, carried by a mechanism without mother or
father, which, besides, threw me in the arms of Félicité Nelta, a black
longshoreman learned in politics who wouldn't let go of me and in
whose arms I wallowed after the vidé, in the shade, against a
tamarind, shaking with mischievous madness, pleasure, and a glut-
tonous heart.

---

[1] An edict by De Gaulle had finally granted women the right to vote, and Madame Eléonore
Alcibiade had mobilized the Concerned Ladies of Fort-de-France to bring their maids to the
ballot boxes, not one bit concerned about what we'd put in them.
[2] [What hip-flaunting!]

MAD SEASON

When the heat fell back again and I returned to Monsieur Alcibiade's with Nelta, then came the season of my anguish. I recalled his eyes, my taking leave without asking permission, and I got a bad feeling about it all. The door was open, so Nelta went his way. I entered the silent hall. I crossed the living room in the dark and climbed the stairs, passing the floor of the Alcibiades' room, and reached the garret where my things, my pallet, my four books were piled on each other. I went to bed, vlap, careful not to wake anyone and I sank into that kind of sleep that takes away the night. It was Monsieur Alcibiade who suddenly woke me up to bring me misery.

He was sitting by my bed. A candle lit the bumps on his face and left everything else in the dark. A rush of madness poured into his eyes. He eyed me in silence, not just without saying a thing, but in silence. I was drowning in myself like a locust tree in dead marshland. I simply opened myself on a wind of terror, then every bit of my flesh stiffened like a rock. It was no longer Monsieur Alcibiade sitting before me, but someone that I did not know, stemming in him with a deadly—fascinating—strength. Even now, when I think of it again, I don't understand the phenomenon that made me fail to react when he got on top of me, undressed me, and ruptured me with one savage thrust. His invincible body shattered me with much striving, quartered me, boned me, ran me through. He grunted with vengeful joy. I, who was just back from Nelta's arms, toppled into a ditch full of mingled pleasure, shame, pain, the desire to die, to kill and be killed, the feeling of injustice, of not existing, of being a scorned dog, the hatred of this City where I swirled about all by myself, faced seven dangers alone without ever choosing my path. Serving as Monsieur Alcibiade's flaccid toy for almost two hours—that must have been what would bring me to never let anyone order me around, to decide all by myself what was good for me and what had to be done.

. . .

Early the next day, I ran into Madame Eléonore in the kitchen. She
didn't ask me about the water flowing from my eyes and watering
the coffeepot, the table, the floor, the yard, the bowl, the dirty laundry, the gutter to scrub, the sidewalk to brush. What had occurred
had not escaped her. I saw it in the helplessness with which she
would stumble against the chairs and then pull herself together
straight like a post. Bent out of shape, I was only capable of the mechanical movements that clean houses. We spent the months that
followed caring for Monsieur Alcibiade's deliriums. He had tried
several times to grab his shotgun to go to shoot up the town council.
Madame Eléonore had (a lucky thing) hidden the bullets and, even
when he succeeded in overcoming our vigilance (when we would
find him on the balcony aiming for the night's one eye, or folded up
in a tub with the barrel in his mouth, or hanging off the drainpipe,
gun under his arm, pretending to climb toward the white wing of a
turtledove), we no longer even screamed the screams of a startled
heart. The only thing to be done was to bring him back to his bed.
At daylight he woke up alone, refused a bath, a shave, and sat on the
dining room table. With his goose feather he quilled letters of insults
to the communists, to the sportsmen who let things slide, to the mu-
tualists who watched, open-mouthed, this decline of civilization, to
the very first prefect (arrived with great ceremony) whose acceptance
of this tragedy dishonored France. He sealed all his letters and
Madame Eléonore pretended to go send them off. She hid them in
her bag as she returned home, after a stop at the market to get food.

But Monsieur Alcibiade was not all that crazy. The minute Madame
Eléonore's back was turned, he tried to grab the bowl of my tits.
Well, I can tell you that that poor dirty man paid dearly for what he
did to me, in blows to the head, flying pots, bowls, jars . . . Once I
held his two balls in my two hands and squeezed them white.
Madame Eléonore, back from the post office, found him bent in six.
She saw it as a sign of his madness and took out her rosary to sanc-

tify his meowing. When my blows had been too vigorous and left a mark, I would put it on account of him slipping in the bathtub or on some hike toward a turtledove nest. Another time, in a fit myself, I almost sent him waltzing out the window.

When I found out I was pregnant by him (who had touched me only once), and that once again I had to face the watergrass and the four days of the blood flowing with my life, I boiled some water before throwing it in his face. The water (thank God) had not really boiled. His skin suffered no damage, no trace of any kind. But he had shrieked a shriek fit for the word. I thought his scalded body would fly out of his throat. Monsieur Alcibiade galloped through the house with me following him with a burning pot, insulting him to death.

. . . that living blood which flows . . .

His friends came to see him. Madame Eléonore would invent I don't know what contagious miliaria and never let them in. They didn't insist for long. Soon they all vanished, and no mutualist gatherings, no feasting hunters, no good sporting soul remembered the spirited talker. We found ourselves isolated. Madame Eléonore no longer allowed me to go out. I could only see Félicité Nelta through the shutters. He asked me things with small signs and left discouraged. Madame Eléonore's behavior was similar to others I had associated myself with in City. Disease for her was a shame. She concealed her husband the way she would have covered up some other dishonor, a two-headed monster, or anything else returned from hell. She never called a doctor for him, not even during his fits of panic when we ran from yard to attic on his tail. The neighbors heard the circus, but, apart from some curtain shifting, they attributed the commotion to the typhoid fever going through the Quarters, and they forgot us better that way. Without knowing it, I was learning about City: that crumbled solitude, that withdrawal inside the house, these millstones of silence on the pain next door, this civilized indifference.

Everything that made the hills (the heart, the flesh, the touching, the solidarity, the gossips, the jealous butting into others' business) would fade before the coldness of City's center. Madame Eléonore still observed the twilight lull on the balcony. She would take care to lock Monsieur Alcibiade in a closet and would appear in the midst of her tuberoses, put on a happy face, in the fresh wind, with the other ladies. Her perfume. Such or such a dress. A jewel. The beauty of her flowers. Each the other's rival . . . From one balcony to another, feelings got poorer, and day after day I got the sense I was watching City build imperceptible abysses.

> The Lady taught me to see the city as an ecosystem, made up of equilibriums and interactions. With cemeteries and cribs, with tongues and languages, mummification and · throbbing flesh. And nothing which progresses or which recedes, no linear progress or Darwinian evolution. Nothing but the haphazard whirls of the living. Beyond melancholy, anxious nostalgia, or voluntary vanguards, informulable laws must be named. How then?
>
> FROM THE URBAN PLANNER'S NOTES TO THE WORD SCRATCHER.
> FILE NO. 17. SHEET XXV.
> 1987. SCHŒLCHER LIBRARY.

I ran the house the best I could, mulling over my own innumerable resolutions. I was drowning myself at the Alcibiades' without being able to react. I was numb between two parentheses, letting a few habits determine me. Staying (rather than leaving like I had decided in my heart) reassured me. Chewing over my secret bitterness, scorning the gentleman and his lady behind their back, insulting them in the bottom of my heart, envying them too, wishing to be like them and refuting them with deaf impulses—all these attitudes comforted me. I had done that all my life; it was sort of my way of surviving that disaster that lent me no horizon. I understood my Esternome better, his postures in the Big Hutch, his way of acting toward the békés, the big milatoes, that beating-round-the-bush life he led with his kind in the mud growing the timid hope of leaving the mud. I was thus foully tied to Monsieur Alcibiade. An unfortunate tie. A bad rope. For a long time I thought I was staying with him to put the finishing touches on my revenge, but I soon understood it was something else. I hated him more than I had abhorred that Lonyon, but that hatred fastened me to him with the strength of a mahoe rope. *What a foul poison hatred is!* . . . It has no limits, it mixes everything up . . . at times you feel your heart wringing, not knowing whether it's from loving, hatreding, attraction, rejection. I was bogged down in a sordid migan with that poor Monsieur Alcibiade on whom I never had (except maybe now, in my old age when I have taken the measure of my small importance) a seed of pity.

I remember my silences in that stricken house. Monsieur Alcibiade locked up somewhere. Madame Eléonore taking her siesta in her room after having locked up doors and windows. The heat leaning. The sun which wrecks the yard and bounces back in still beams that break the walls from their spell. City, all around, far away, as if erased, only a few hiccups of life, a blackman's voice, a wheelbarrow's squeaky wheel, the smell of diesel oil, the sighing of dust. And I, sitting in a rocking chair in the middle of the living room, needle in hand, a cloth to mend resting on my knees, unless I was by the table holding on to one of those congo irons with which we ironed in those days. And then nothing. Not a word in my head. Nothing but a kind of ether which filled my bones. As if, unable to pull myself out of there, I wanted to dissolve. I remember . . .

Things got worse. Madame Eléonore was neglecting herself. She was jabbering to herself, she was also writing long letters to cousins anchored in Panama (by the canal) in brutal wealth. I soon realized that she took them to the post office without putting an address on them, writing only *Panama Canal*. She was bringing fewer and fewer things that were good to eat. I started to lack soap, oil, spices, everything. I had to manage filling up the pots without leaving the house because the door was locked: she hid the key as if it were her last treasure. Soon she nailed the windows shut and forbade me to open them. When she left to mail her letters and those of her husband, I found myself in a sort of tomb and began to cry on the floor over this death in my life. Sometimes, after one of Monsieur's crises, Madame Eléonore was overtaken with religious spasms. She sang around him, whirling the Veni Creator, the Ave Maria Stella, and the Benedicitur. She recited orisons in a drone, ground out vespers and complines. Woken up, startled, all night I would hear litanies of the Virgin, the Magnificat, streaming from her room. At dawn, she hummed the psalms for the King . . .

I remember my silences when I would wake up in the dark house, in the middle of the night, half asleep, searching in my half-lucidity for a way to leave and crashing against each shutter, each window, each door. So then I would sit at the bottom of the staircase staring at the living room's angular shapes animated by the moon. In the lit varnished wood lurked an ancient presence. I would identify every piece of furniture, rug, pot, lamp, the piano nobody played, the ivory collection from Indochina that a colonist with red whiskers had lent Monsieur, before losing his mind to malaria. The night melded all of that into a different life, made of nacreous light, of more or less opaque shadows articulating shapes, of deep murmurs, of a carpenter singing, of fragrances of ancient sap under the plane's thrust, of past feelings which had bound the wood, had clogged it. I stayed there until dawn, haggard like a fallen breadfruit, and coming shy of the landed chestnut's promises.

Soon I no longer came out of my garret. Staying still in the attic's heatedness, I listened to Madame Eléonore living with her monster. Everything was dreary. The day signaled its passage with rays of light, streams of sun, bright softness, City's rumbling; then suddenly darkness came over everything. For fear of running into Madame

Eléonore, who'd molted into a graveyard bug, I did not dare use the stairs. I no longer listened to the things she addressed to Monsieur, nor her mass songs, nor her strange speeches: all of that frightened me. The words lost their meaning, the sentences were all mixed together like animal noises or I don't know what. I heard unspeakable sounds. Chaos. Sometimes, Monsieur Alcibiade brayed while the lady laughed what was not quite laughter. I heard the chirps of a bird, scraps of short speeches with which one opens banquets, loud farts, or words which seemed to float by themselves in a zombie-like echo. There were also smells of incense, of burnt candles, of fish. Stenches of boxwood, miasmas of mangrove, fumes of cut grass, perfumes of whiskey and of quicklime. Of camphor . . .

. . . I was going mad . . .

. . . one night I smelled a breath of vinegar. On another one, I got the feeling the partitions had been rubbed with garlic and soured orange. There was a whiff of white heliotrope, then gall, then nutmeg paste. The smells became tastes. Then images with reflections in the mirror. I was sometimes immensely unsettled and shivered for nothing as if my sheets were made of red satin. I felt that the Alcibiades had been transformed into I don't know what because I heard different steps, different voices, different presences. I no longer dared move for fear they should remember me and come up to my room . . .

. . . mad, I tell you . . .

. . . so, I would take refuge in City's noises. Noises of coolie brooms polishing the streets. Noises of bright and early vendors of soursops, of coconut cream by the spoon, of very hot zakari biscuits. Noises of mabi vendors escorting the sun at six in the morning. Noises of fritter and fried cod vendors invading the streets where the workers went by. Noises of washerwomen swaying toward Grosse-Roche's clear water. Noises of dogs loudmouthing the night, confused during

the day, given to whimpering between the two. Ever-growing noises
of cars, dominating the other noises a bit more every day. New
noises of the asphalt Césaire was having spread over the mud. I
would picture the snatches of slumber in the rum bars, the shock of
the day's start-up punch, the momentum of the snub-a-toe punch,
the kick of the glass of alolo in which dreams take off . . .

. . . mad for real . . .

. . . then the noises would get dim, so I would wade about in hazes
of images, no longer knowing whether they were from my life or my
Esternome's, or my Idoménée's, oh my dear ones come back to me, I
mourn that juicy leaf flattened in a book, which grows its white hair
roots, that Sunday afternoon at the park in the Alley of Sighs under
the bothered békés' unhappy eye,

over the swarm at the cathedral, people with flapping sleeves and
pinned-up dresses, over the lady Edamise giving up her rings for a
galley slave's chain her pallet for a mattress her madras for a silk
scarf her bench for a rocking chair over the lady Edamise with her
officer who sets her up in City, over July fourteenth and over
November eleventh when cannons play music and shotguns are
clarinets,

over the cemetery's three flowers of which the most wilted is an
abandoned heart, over the razzle-dazzle ball at the Select Tango beneath Saint-Hilaire's trombone, I see Régina Coco that vanilla cream
that takes the place of her father down on his luck in the games of
baccarat three-card-monte passe-passe red and black or serbi and
who herself becomes a Boss, over Dr. Pierre dying and leading his
trail of patients to the cemetery, oh oh there's trunk-jaw Eulalie,
there's Larouelle Sidonie with kilometer-tits, who drank cane juice
from a pigpen on the plantation and who now tries to put on airs
in City,

•   •   •

there's butterfly Labadie landing on a lamp and getting a burnt snout one Saturday at a gloria, here's Aristide dressed up like a hunchback to go pinch and caress his darlin' without permission from the Mrs. until City sings Hunchback-hunchback, give-the-hump-with-your-body, hump on the sides, front and back,

so he offers her something that shines, something bright, wrapped up, to make her pretty and she gives him her heart and of course something else, over the spidery morning-after with its bad promises, over the white-tailed cemetery bug reciting at your table, and I yawn, eyes fixed on three kites . . .

THE DREAM OF LEAVING

Félicité Nelta got me out of the tomb. He had roamed for months around the Alcibiades'; he had guessed that I was somewhere behind the louvered shutters, or in a glint, just to wave his hand to me like the old people do; then he had seen the door turn a stiff back, the windows get stuck to the walls; then one evening or one night he had no longer seen any lights. What we had done that night of the vidé had been good and he still remembered in each pore of his skin, *fortunately!* . . . because he probably would not have insisted so much, watched so much, nor knocked at the door, nor screamed *Are you there* . . . , asked the neighbors about the girl Marie-Sophie who works for the people next door. Fortunately . . . for he would not have (the way the neighbors had not) discovered that smell of death oozing from the door, a stench of cold zinc and silverfish.

So one night, he knocked down the door screaming *Marie-Sophie, Marie-Sophie!* He crossed the living room which seemed to gather Saint-Pierre's debris, then passed Monsieur Alcibiade on the stairs dressed in black and red, walking stiffly and singing a mazurka into a chamber pot; then he saw Madame Eléonore, or rather some person with stiff gray hair standing up on her head, unreal in her thinness, without color or life, dried skin, chapped lips, the body bruised like wet flannel, eyes bigger than a full moon, counting invisible things and singing like that dear Léona Gabriel about one called Alexander gone gone gone . . .

He took me with my meager things across sleeping City. At each step he was afraid he'd see a surge of Alcibiades, rushing like geckos at the head of a herd of rocking chairs, chairs, tables, images, and sealed letters flying all around them like a cloud of jinns.

> I understood suddenly that Texaco was not what Western-ers call a shantytown, but a mangrove swamp, *an urban mangrove swamp.* The swamp seems initially hostile to life. It's difficult to admit that this anxiety of roots, of mossy shades, of veiled waters, could be such a cradle of life for crabs, fish, crayfish, the marine ecosystem. It seems to belong to neither land nor sea, somewhat like Texaco is neither City nor country. Yet City draws strength from Texaco's urban mangroves, as it does from those of other quarters, exactly like the sea repeoples itself with that vital tongue which ties it to the mangroves' chemistry. Swamps need the regular caress of the waves; to reach its potential and its function of renaissance, Texaco needs City to ca-ress it, meaning: it needs consideration.
>
> FROM THE URBAN PLANNER'S NOTES TO THE WORD SCRATCHER.
> FILE NO. 19. SHEET XXVIII.
> 1987. SCHŒLCHER LIBRARY.

Félicité Nelta broke stones in a town quarry. He lived on Morne Abélard in a tin tent which held just a bed, his tools, two-three Sun-day garments, and a fat suitcase. I was surrounded by that solicitude which Quarters breed. I was given reinvigorating teas, hardy soups, bay rum rubs. I received nets of tenderness, cast seines full of dreams in which hands were held together. In Nelta's absence, a Ma from around there wrapped my bedside with useless words, her insults against men, her fights in City, wiped my sweat, gave me my medicine with my Idoménée's gestures. Each one of them tried to bring life back to my eyes. At night, Nelta sat by me. He spent a good part of the night entertaining me with tittle-tattles: the police had jailed the Alcibiades; an abbot had come to kneel before their house and sprinkle holy water to appease the neighbors' fear . . . Then he came along with me on my slumber's misery, by sleeping at my feet. He worked all day and reappeared at the end of the afternoon on Morne Abélard, where he was always helping someone, adjusting a tin sheet, nailing a slab of asbestos for so-and-so. But during the time I was washed out he reduced that activity (to the great despair of the others) and stayed around worried, watching me fight inside my dreamless sleep followed by foul wide-eyed musings. Then, there happened something which my old Esternome would have really liked to see.

Since I was not returning to my eyes, Nelta solicited a healer. This person lived on the other side of Schœlcher High School, in a magic Doum fed by the marshland of Bellevue, by the gasoline reservoir tanks that the békés had soldered all along the sea. The Esso gasoline béké had two tanks, a bit further down on Pointe-la-Vierge. The Shell béké also had two and had settled a bit more to the side of the lighthouse. As for the Texaco béké, he had a few at a bottom of the ledge, along the river. He had built some kind of embankment there. A little barrel boat took some fuel from the tankers and came to have it sucked by a pump on that embankment. Pipes were bringing the whole thing to the reservoirs. Year after year, cars had multiplied. They needed a whole lot of gasoline. Quick on the trigger, the békés had rushed to represent American companies. And they were competing against each other in a ferocious way without mercy or measure.

That place was a riot of mud, sand, barrels, gas bottles. Canals furrowed the half dried-up mangrove swamp of Marigot-Bellevue. Little black children came to play tag around the pipes, to follow the embankment or go straight to the technical high school. They also came to watch the boats. The Texaco béké had plopped a very conscientious black watchman onto his reservoirs. At his gate he regulated the comings and goings of the big drum trucks which distributed gasoline throughout the country. Further down, bordering the river up to the Doum, there was a magical clump of trees that the Texaco béké had left untouched, probably because of stories about the she-devils around there, or maybe because he had simply forgotten. Well, there lived Papa Totone, the healer. Nelta went to solicit him after having begged the guard to let him through.

According to Nelta, Papa Totone welcomed him as if he had been expected for a long while. He said, *What's new, Nelta?* . . . though he had never seen him and though Nelta's only known title was "Tatalité" (a twisting of his name as blackfolks like to do). But Papa Totone, springing from the Doum's trees, said to him, *What's new, Nelta?* . . . And he said (while Nelta had not yet said a word): *I'll be right there* . . . Before Papa Totone, Nelta felt very very small, . . . he had felt . . . he had felt . . . I knew what he'd felt; his words were stumbling like my old Esternome's in the same situation: in Papa Totone, Nelta had perceived *a power*—a bit like the one you feel when great storytellers tell their tale, or when the men of power appear in your life at a time of bad luck that the church can't fix.

Papa Totone came to my bedside after crossing the Abélard Quarter. Everyone was surprised to see him so far away from his waterfall. As he would do with the Christ many years later, he brushed my forehead with a casual hand, saying (he who didn't know me) *Heh-o, Marie-Sophie, hold on tight* . . . Then he disappeared like a whiff of ether. Life returned to my eyes. I began to look, to feel, to want to get up and live again . . . The people from Morne Abélard danced around me, and Nelta (mad like Saint Vitus) took out a demijohn of rum to offer the Earth the peerless fraternity of one-hundred-and-thirty proof.

• • •

I think about that time at Morne Abélard. So many women-men-children sedimented at the doors of City which opened itself on the other side of the canal. To get there, you spent time and then some on a tub that a solid blackman ferried on a rope. On that part of the right bank there grew a community of down-from-the-hill people all by themselves, right across from City's comforts. The older folks did not dare go there: life there was more brisk, pain more predatory; that solidary-solitary community used against itself (in the very heart of mutual aid) that violence born of the *impossibilities* one faces when one deals with City. Every man was armed with his pocket knife, his razor, his sea beak blade. The pocket knives so useful for survival were now preferable to the machetes of the hills which only came out of the hutches in times of danger or in efforts at firming up our foothold on some land. The women waged their war with scissors, jars of acid, but especially with their shrill voices which could break any old bum. Closer, up to Pont-de-Chaînes, hutches piled up in an un-Catholic mess but one that soon appeared to me as a subtle clump of equilibrium between the people, their pig-pens, their hen cages and rabbit boxes, their private trees accessible to everyone, their yards, their footpaths, their meeting points around some faucet donated by the town council, these aqueducts which escorted the dirty water to the river gulf, that jostling of epochs vibrant with the trace of my old Esternome, with straw, crate wood, tin sheets for the roof, and these new slabs brought here by the békés, which gave the illusion of a cement house. *Mmmmm dear Lordy . . . ! asbestos . . .* to leave the straw and the crate wood and the white tin plate, for a home in cement! That was everyone's hymn! You can't understand, Oiseau de Cham, it was a real joy. Your job's money would vanish in those fragile slabs. People would adjust them over a rotten wood partition, on the rusted misery of a flattened oil drum. Nelta knew how to nail the asbestos without shattering it. Splitting so many stones with a mallet had developed a needle's precision in each of his fingers. It was rare that he ever damaged a slab of asbestos, and when something did happen, he knew how to fix up the debris so as to decorate the house, as if it had been planned like that.

From him I learned to nail asbestos. When he came back from his job at the quarry, the afternoon's shades were no longer very distinct, but the little tin hutch was still an oven which I avoided by setting up a bench by the aqueduct's coolness. Since Nelta couldn't stand it either, he would leave to go nail up slabs, loose tin, or planks throughout Morne Abélard. When I went with him I would ask him about that Papa Totone who woke me up. His very brief attendance upon me had left a question in my head. His disappearance blip-blap, the way Nelta described him to me, all returned me to what my Esternome said about Mentohs. I was curious to see if, mad to the last drop, I was not living the silly stories of my Esternome who had faced the commandment of a supposed *Power*. Time to hold on tight? But for what and why? I questioned Nelta. He repeated the little he suspected. Despite my insistence, he had very little desire to return to the Doum behind the gasoline containers. Papa Totone does not see people like that, he said, you see him when he so wishes and no one goes very far into the Doum because it's full of she-devils. So, brooding impatiently, I helped him set his asbestos slabs, amazed like he was at the pace of progress.

Nelta's hutch was too small for us. When he and the rest of the Quarter would go across to City, leaving behind only the women suckling babes, the drooling old-timers, and the immovable Bosses, I did not know what to do and didn't feel good. What should I clean in all that mud? Put order into that poor pad made of tin sheets? I, who had known beautiful City houses, sofas, rocking chairs, soft beds which nested my wallowing once Madame's back was turned, now found myself in a hutch burning like a fire from hell. At night it was cool, the winds ran across it despite the enclosure. Under the rain it became the belly of a big fish in a mad sea, hurling us against each other even more, into each other, enlivening our shameless bodies. Nelta needed me and I no longer imagined life without him. He was from a Robert factory which had picked up and gone. He had landed in City a good while ago, to hook an opportunity. He had fallen into politics because at that time sturdy fellows were often employed to intimidate the adversaries, to beat small drums and barrels and escort the politician in his slogans of happiness through the bottom of the old Quarters. Nelta had worked with the communists, had ushered Césaire's dazzling breakthrough. He had protected him, taken a few blows for him, threatened for him. As reward, once the town council was conquered, he had obtained his position at the quarry. He remained ready-to-mobilize at any time, especially at election time or during a war against the békés, the bigtime milatoes, and the rest, plunged once more into the violence of the plantation old days.

But Nelta's dream was to get up and leave. *Partir,* that was his French word. He had checked it in the dictionary. Nelta had tried everything to leave but nothing had worked. He kept his dream intact in his fat suitcase full of pictures picked up here and there. It took a few months (once we reached the soft heart of coconut itself) for him to open that humongous suitcase for me. And there, with his neat big fingers, he showed me (on hot Sundays, after we had flattened the bed) his pictures of forests, deserts, waterfalls, cities, peoples . . . His salary was to pay for his flight to go all over the world. First to France which filled his head (like all of ours). He dreamt of a liner called *Colombia,* pictured himself setting foot in Marseilles a thousand times. Often, on Saturday afternoons, instead of going to shake at some soccer match like the fellows from around here, he would drag his big clipped wings to the port. In cahoots with the guardian, he took a thousand dreams for a stroll on the rust of the banana boat, the gleam of the still ships. When a tanker would steam into the harbor, carrying the gasoline for the oil békés, Nelta would bring me to these heights to contemplate this door open on all of the shores of the world. I don't know where his taste for departure came from, but he was the only fellow I met in that quarter who was eaten by this desire—the desire to see everything, to live through the impossible, to feel dispersed into the world's infinitude, into a thousand tongues, skins, eyes, an Earth connected.

When I complained about the hutch, he would dryly explain that it wasn't what his money was for, and that if I could keep up the position he would take me to France with him. He kept his bills in a biscuit box he buried in the hutch under a rock on which a flame flickered in some oil enhanced with three alkali drops and some amber lavender. He did not fear thieves as much as the spirits which make away with the money from the sweat of your brow without leaving you the hope of earning it back one day. I would anchor myself even more to Nelta since I felt him so far from me. His spirit flew toward the horizons, beyond pictures, which he carried within himself without becoming fanciful. He behaved like the other fellows in the Quarter, fighting life, always sweating, working, getting into disputes over soccer games at the Golden Star or the Colonial Club, into political frays. But dog dreams hide in dog hearts: no one suspected the veiled shimmers Nelta bore. When I bent over him, searching deep into his eyes to find out if I had (by dint of sweetness) built some chapel where my presence shone, I would stumble against great gusts, stunned, see lumps of warm sand, I thought I could see city façades, thirsty camels, the splendor of Indian temples, monumental igloos, reddish moons over glassy ice fields.

> The Western urban planner sees Texaco as a tumor on the urban order. Incoherent. Insalubrious. A dynamic contestation. A threat. It is denied any architectural or social value. Political discourse negates it. In other words, it is a *problem*. But to raze it is to send the problem elsewhere or worse: not to consider it. No, we must dismiss the West and re-learn to read: learn to reinvent the city. Here

the urban planner must think Creole before he even
thinks.

FROM THE NOTES OF THE URBAN PLANNER TO THE WORD SCRATCHER.
FILE NO. 36. SHEET X.
1987. SCHŒLCHER LIBRARY.

I could have kept Nelta with a child. I saw him being moved by the
children next door. He would bring them back sweet pastries, marbles, barrel hoops from City. When Nelta discharged into me, I
could sense it was like planting (or watering) with the wish for fruit.
He watched my belly which never awakened, he touched (among
other things) my breasts which never announced a season. I was
faced with the torment of wishing to give him his child, his anchor,
to get him to build us that beautiful asbestos-cement hutch with the
money meant for his dream. But nothing ever came of it. I had bled
so much, I had hurt myself so much with that watergrass (fevers and
blackish scabs had sucked on me like zombies trying to possess me)
that my belly no longer had access to the great mystery. I did not yet
know about the irremediable part. I thought that Nelta's sack was finally dried up, that my periods did not coincide with the work of the
watering. As time went by, my heart began to palpitate before this
barely imaginable horror whose true extent appeared to me only
much later.

I could only watch the paper money pile up in Nelta's box, follow
step-by-step the rise of his fever for that dream from which I was excluded. I probably spent a day (or two) full of illusions picturing myself with him—he in his syrian linen and I in my lace dress walking
down the footbridge toward the ocean liner leaving for the world. I
saw myself in a shining cabin . . . drifting coasts . . . fading shores
. . . tall cities rising crowned with mist . . . I saw myself in those
restaurants he had described to me, with chorus girls, orchestras,
whites serving you food on silver platters. Or maybe on one of those
big barges carrying sugar, leading the sailors' rootless life, living in

the ports of Saint Lucia, Dominica, or Barbados, alighting in New York, then at Le Havre, then finally in Marseilles, with Nelta, with Nelta . . . but (in the time it takes a moth to become a butterfly) this kind of vision faded only to return later, and flee again. It was then that there rose in me the Marie-Sophie Laborieux who (despite my fears, my childhood memories, my mute tenderness for my Esternome and my Idoménée) was going to fight against City with a warrior's rage.

But let me relive my Nelta, before going into my Texaco battles. *Oy Nelta* . . . I picture you getting old in Ireland by a tepid beer, telling of your islands to big red-haired whites. I see you all wrinkled up under a Masai tent, drinking burning blood or covering yourself with ox caca to ward off the mosquitoes, and unfolding your memories as a blackman from the Americas in the gatherings of these immense shepherds. Or yet again, in Harlem, Ku Klux Klan victim crossed in fire. Or again . . . oh my Nelta, I see your soul floating in that marine cemetery where the water spirals along wading roots. Or again, covered with a buffalo skin in a hole of the tundra. Even now, you season my melancholies. Tender-Nelta holding me tight. Smiling-Nelta with teeth like pearls. Nelta-of-twenty-two-dreams, sitting in his suitcase, flying on his suitcase to mosques of stone. Nelta-dripping-with-sweat who bewitched my belly and crushed me under him. Nelta-of-the-flower-days. Innocent-day-Nelta marveling at children. Carnival-Nelta, accomplice to a torrid vidé in City's streets. Nelta-of-the-Hurricanes lifting hutches to rescue children. Holy-Week-Nelta who engulfed the Quarter's lanes with Good Friday's rattling, until he disturbed the deaf. Nelta eating in the Béro Quarter just so he could travel through the coolie groceries. Nelta who'd beg the syrians to speak their tongue with him. Fritter-eating-Nelta and saki drinker. All-Saints-Nelta who whitewashed graves to fill his cashbox. Nelta who washed cars after the Sunday mass to feed his fortune. The Nelta who dashed to Robert for the nautical festival. Christmas-caroling-good-pudding-eating-and-good-shrub-drinking-before-kissing-me-Nelta . . . *Ooh Nelta . . . on the last day of the year, you read the eggwhite in a glass of water and you saw the boat of your travels appear . . .* Nelta who one day vanished from the hutch, flew away with his big suitcase without a word of good-bye, who went to his dreams the way thieves make off. Nelta who all his watery life must have been heartsick for me in his thirst for the world—a thirst still unquenched, land upon land, people upon people, tongue upon tongue later: its essence eternal as a curse.

I had prepared myself for his disappearance. The open horizons in his eyes had inspired me to steel myself. Stay-at-home cops catch no one, so I began to go back into City to earn my money. I washed the syrians' clothes, their bundles of dirty laundry. I also did washes for a bunch of milatoes. I spent days pressing with a congo iron, and evenings delivering pleated dresses. I sold sandwiches to the black-workers from the Jetée, early each morning, basket on my head. I sold buckets of titiris, airplant leaves and good-health herbs, iced mabi and sea urchin heads. I went up to Didier to sell pudding. I sold the coconuts from the tree of Pa Soltène, an old distillery-blackman who smoked away his old age under his only tree. I sold crabs which I'd dig up on Dillon's lands. I sold bottles and saucepans. I sold perfume flasks that a trinket merchant brought from Italy. These odd jobs brought me money that I (after having paid for the oil, salt, kerosene, a piece of cloth, donated a bit like all of City's good people to the mutual aid society Human Solidarity) kept like Nelta did. The rest came from barter: fish from our fishermen friends, garden vegetables for the nailing of a slab of asbestos.

Nelta's life and mine were progressing alongside each other. Our dreams no longer crossed paths. Every day brought him closer to his flight, and he'd give all of his energy to his jobs even on Saturday nights. I was preoccupied with getting my own hutch in order so as not to find myself boohoohoo in the rain. I had become one of the women in the Quarter, leaving early for City, returning to hide some windfall, and leaving for the jobs again. Anxious, irritable, frowning eyebrows, a ferocious face to tame misfortune, I was a sight to see: I walked as if hacking my way through thickets. My clothes were different: head caught in curlpapers, a madras dress, bare feet, a scarf around the waist to hold my stomach. My pace was decisive, because you had to be *decisive,* walk decisively, move forward decisively in order to leave the least hesitation in the dust. And then my personality had changed. Nelta sometimes looked at me with round eyes. I tended to take care of others, not with pity, but to tell them how to outrun distress. I added a spoonful of oil to anyone's dry flour. I lent a shoulder to the limping. Whoever was crying came to see me. Whoever had a sick child stopped by my hutch and I was the one who led the descent to the poorhouse or toward some old doctor, who'd do most anything for some fish. I organized the collections, the wakes and gatherings, ran the errands whenever trouble came. My voice could cut in like a machete blow. It was hard for anyone to look me in the eyes because war would stare back—and their eyelids would drop.

I wasn't mean, no, but I was stiff, tough as leather. Men no longer looked at the offerings of round apple-rear-end. Reassured to see me, the women would line up behind me. The Bosses saluted me wordlessly, lifting their hats. In reality, I was at war against myself, my fears, against Nelta's desertion which I saw coming. Fighting against myself brought me to the others, because I felt my fate tied to theirs. I also felt (like my Esternome must have) that we had to organize a true Quarter of the Hills against City. That determination choked me with a hoop of silence, a silence like those that take place between normal people and the ones who show up at the head of destiny.

There is a joy in being able to pay for two coins' worth of roux in a banana leaf.

NOTEBOOK NO. 16 OF MARIE-SOPHIE LABORIEUX.
1965. SCHŒLCHER LIBRARY.

MORNE ABÉLARD'S LAWS

When Nelta disappeared subito-presto with his suitcase, my spirit dressed itself in will. My eyes became marbles that only old age would soften a little. I didn't rush to the port like my heart prodded me. I simply rested my two hands on my hips, and (though derailed inside, my guardian angel broken with pain) I stood in front of the door, head high, and before those looking in on my misfortune, I howled my Creole bluster: *Nonm lan fouté li kan wi, i ké pran lan mê sèvi chimen, tyè'y an lan men dwet li, gren li an lan men góch li, bon van mon fi bon van!* . . .[1] Yes the man did leave, his heart in his right hand, his balls in his left hand, the sea will be his path, good riddance my friend! . . . Which in fact meant nothing—except to let all those who have acquired a taste for others' misfortunes and tears know that no tears would stick a frog in my throat.

To show them: I took the habit of singing each morning under the first sun, while carrying my water or putting out my laundry. Even today, I sing my most burning sorrows.

I remained stricken with grief like a conch at the bottom of a cemetery. Two wrinkles appeared early around my mouth and my eyes whose folds suffered from the sun. I began to look around me: I had enough money to buy a frame and asbestos. But not one chip of land was available on Morne Abélard. Huts were tied one to the other. In between them were the interstices for the flow of water, caca holes, gardens always under ashes, paths for people, and the snarling iron of a pigpen, a clump of hens, a rabbit cage . . . I looked for a stump of land on Rive-Droite, then at the bottom of the cliff opposite the high school . . . all in vain. I returned to Terres-Sainville which Césaire was restoring by spreading asphalt everywhere. But there too,

---

[1] [Yes, the man split, he's going to take the sea for a path, his heart in his right hand, his balls in his left hand, good riddance my dear!]

not a square to spare, all was done, all was taken. For the first time, City appeared to me like one hermetic block. So then I went back to Nelta's hutch, head high, but with nothing inside me to straighten my back.

To show them: I took the habit of speaking high and loud, with the rhythm of laughter in my voice, an appetite for life sharpening each of my gestures while I went to empty my slops in the canal's live water.

Why this obsessing about owning my own hutch? In City, to be is first and foremost to possess a roof. And I, though born there, felt like I was floating about like a country bumpkin. And then, it was to refute Nelta, to grab the country while he fled it, to take roots while he envied the clouds, to build while he dreamt. I was afraid to melt in that vagabond ambiance he had bestowed upon the partitions with his tapestry of pictures. As soon as he had vanished, I would enter his hut like it was a caravel. At night, my pallet would swim laps. I heard the knocking of peregrine rains, I breathed in smells of jungles, pagoda incense. The next morning I went to get my buckets of water with the fear that I would end up in a field of salt or a dune flat, a desert landscape of pines and snows with wolf and fox howls and a trapper's footsteps.

Looking for a hut also filled the hole of my sorrows. The things that tied me to Nelta took a strong hold of me when he left. I had always had the feeling I could live without him, besides I had prepared my-self for it with the defiance of a Creole woman. But there . . . with-out him . . . how do I say this? . . . I could count every inch of space he had taken up in me, all of which now hung like a calabash res-onating with pain. I saw how much of my morning energy came from him, the light in my eyes too, and the cool breezes in my head. I did not know how to comb my hair. I did not know what to wear. When my belly's blood would call on me, my skin would molt like a tarantula's, I felt like screaming, breaking, cursing; I wallowed in that flowing blood as if I were watching my life purge itself, watching it create a place for my pain. I piled up my bloody rags in a big bowl, added some water, some chlorine, and as it slowly filled I turned diaphanous along with them. I did not know how to get up from my pallet. Without Nelta, I was only a heavy bag of flesh to drag around, an aching spirit grouching at the world, counting its miseries, headaches, pimples, the puffed-up eyes with which I woke every morning, astonished to have cried like no one cries any more.

One day the mailman brought me a postcard from Nelta. It had been mailed from France, from an unknown province. On it there was a mill towering over a field of wheat speckled with peasant silhouettes. A cart was leaving the mill with enormous sacks. It all suggested a poem; my heart almost failed me when I pictured Nelta swimming in such poetry without me. On the back, with his thick handwriting he had scrawled some plea for forgiveness. I, in silence, inside my heart, with a bit of meanness, some naïveté, but still with some good sense in me, answered him that no "I'm sorry" could heal the bumps. The card is still somewhere in a corner with my things. It meant nothing, an obligatory card, but it was Nelta. Today, when I look at that card again, I breathe wheat which I have never smelled, I can see the inside of the mill and behold what the old Alphonse Daudet evokes in his bucolic letters. I can see the miller taking a bite of cheese with Nelta who pours him his red plonk, and it's strange, because rather than feeling my heart constrict (as I did my whole life through before this card), I feel a *contentment:* my wrinkles rise over my gums, and my belly coughs beneath the joy of an old woman, big as a universe.

The Morne Abélard people knew of my desire for a hutch. I, center of their misery, lived in a hole. More than one of them had come to fix it up for me. Carlo (a worrisome Barbadian living a few drops of sweat at a time since he had run away from a ship in drydock) had brought me a number of wooden slats which I refused. I was situated between an aqueduct which drained the dirty water from higher up and a cage of hens which fed Carlo. Carlo's hut (he lived with Adélise Canille, a false milato woman who had taken refuge under his wings since her breasts had begun to sag; she had nine children in every color except green and blue) leaned on mine and hung on to that of Paulina Masaille which bordered that of Pa Soltène, the coconut tree planter, and that of Natelle Lagrosille (a coolie who had been chased out of the Béro Quarter after a sacrifice had gone awry, I could have told you that). One should also mention the huts of Grodi, Gueule-Bec, Philène Cador, Jupiter-Gros-Graine, Péloponèse, Sertius Laidival (veteran of the First World War, secretary of veterans that every minister from France kissed when going by). All these huts formed a trapdoor spider's web in which we all lived in clusters. Before there was a community of people, there was one of huts carrying each other, tied through one another to the sliding land, each getting its bearings from the other according to laws from my poor Esternome's Noutéka. Dreams touched on each other. Sighs mingled. Miseries shouldered each other. Forces knocked each other out until you saw blood. It was a sort of rough draft of City, but warmer than City. The streets were still lanes, but each lane was more alive than a street. To walk through a lane (which would cross through lives, intimacies, dreams, fate) you had to shout *Good day everyone, Evening ladies and gentlemen,* and ask to go through, may I go through, and sometimes stop to take stock of the news of the world. If you weren't talking to so-and-so, then you had to use a distant lane. The Bosses themselves obeyed these rules.

LAW 35

Bump your feet against the ground as you approach the lane so you may be heard coming and so that none may be startled to see you all the sudden. And hail *Good day to all,* with gusto, with respect, kindness, and be obliging, with compassion and all of course in that particular octave discreet folks keep deep down inside their throats. No answer will be made to you. They'll wait to see who it is. And as for you, those you see must touch your heart, *So, such and such, I am happy to see you . . . Well, so and so, you're looking good . . .* Wish them more health than they have, more strength too, give them courage, make them feel they can count on you in solidarity, not in competition, for anyone who beams about good health is not a bad seed. And when you are in the middle of the yard, surrounded by the swarm of huts, with dozens of eyes looking at you, judging you, when you feel the misfortune of the moment on your skin, a crisp silence, an aftertaste of tears, or some sad scraps of joy, of illusory happiness, without ever resting your eyes, hail *May I pass! May I pass! . . .* And in your voice a light suspense will await the answer, the authorization, but at the same time you'll lengthen your stride so that if you're not allowed to pass through you'll be far away already. But generally they'll let you by and at your back you'll hear, *Pack your bags sir so-and-so . . .* but never turn around unless you're called. On some days, stepping forward, you'll bump (hailing *A good day to all . . .*) into a snarl, a knot that you will feel inside your stomach, a kind of stiffness, a whiff of aerial misfortune like some presentiment that you will feel flowing out of the crate wood or the asbestos slabs. If you don't hear any distress call, but only see a hostile snag, hail again *Good day to all . . . !* and following the curve of your hips, turn round and start running down another lane giving the impression that you had looked in just to say hello . . .

LETTERS FROM MORNE ABÉLARD.
MUSINGS OF A BLACKWOMAN FROM THE QUARTER.
UNNUMBERED NOTEBOOK OF MARIE-SOPHIE LABORIEUX.
1965. SCHŒLCHER LIBRARY.

I was always particularly fond of Morne Abélard's lanes, which I
had to take when responding to cries for help.[1] I've got nothing but
sensations left of them. There was the black mud lane where ducks
rested their feet. The woeful lane with its sheer gleaming clean pots.
The lane of the ox-foot soup cooking on embers. The lane of the
heart falling down the flames of memory. The 120, 110, 100-proof
lane where rum spirits bounce on pink lips. The lane of louvered
shutters smashed by feverish looks. The lane full of asbestos where
poor folks, their fates plotted by town councils, dodged ill luck. The
lane where you'll sooner see a donkey working at eleven than a
blackman without a glass at noon. The lane where hunger whittled
teeth. The calanda lane where one starts lurching, dancing the cos-
sack, the guiomba, and the bombé serré.* The pious lane from
where the white whales sparkle at night. The lane where dawn's
blackbirds learn a lot of things. The lane of forgotten mysteries
where old blackmen look like Carib warriors. The lane of black maroons twisting ferns while speaking other tongues. The cold lane of
silences. The lane of children playing in rainwater. The lane of the
syrians going through with their big bundles on Saturdays. The lane
of holy water sprinkled on each Friday the thirteenth. The lane of
drying laundry clothing the wind. The lane of slops smelling of bitter
old age. The lane of the lost chinese, drowning in big shorts, waiting
for what boat? The lane of Amélie-thimble-thumb whose sewing
machine gnawed at the fringes of her sleep. The lane of the shadow
where your foot jumps and suddenly turns around. The lane of the
insults where fifteen blackwomen peppered their talks with "Jesus!"
The lane of Adventists gathering on Saturdays on red numbered
cafeteria chairs to read the Bible's songs in some other way. The lane
where the general councilman held his meetings about the idea of
happiness . . . All of that mingled, shifted, depending on who died,
on the hours, on success, and joined us like true ox yokes. That's
why Péloponèse's misfortune brought with it, at the other end of my

---

[1]For a difficult childbirth, a disease, a sudden death, a fight that got too bloody . . .

lane, twelve misfortunes along the aqueduct. A very neat sprinkling of flames which snatched me up while going by.

SWEET PAINFUL BRIDE

When the flames surged and we had to fight them with the aqueduct water, the word would go around and around and put the pieces of the story back together. Péloponèse Marcelle, fallen from Morne Rouge on a Saturday Gloria, loved a hat-wearing blackman who lived by Pont-de-Chaînes. One Dartagnan Qualidor, watchman at Pointe-Simon's garbage dump. Dartagnan Qualidor had met Péloponèse one day when she had gone (like all of us) looking for a bit of windfall in the dump. You could find wonders that the milatoes, the békés, or French-talking blackmen of Petit-Paradis had thrown there en masse in order to keep up with the wind of fashion.[1] We went there regularly and all knew Dartagnan Qualidor, who despite his hat (the sole object of pride in his life) didn't make a fuss about letting us in. So Péloponèse went there (before I even got to Nelta's hutch) and her arrival there lights up Qualidor's eyes as he begins to follow her around. Rare phenomenon, he begins to guide her through the garbage, the old dogs, the rats, and the cats, in order to show her the day's wonders, his private findings which he probably sold dearly to those who came down the hills bright and early on Saturdays. The fellow was at home in his refuse—an incredible pile which was burned from time to time, which sweaty blackmen covered up with shovelfuls of lime or soil. That made up a lunar landscape in which Qualidor, wearing his big hat, strolled like a béké. He spoke about the garbage to our Péloponèse, almost giving away the mystery of that place to her.

---

[1]In the old days with Nelta, I myself had found a big red velvet armchair with lion legs and temple sculptures there. I also found a shimmering black casket decorated with a dragon which must have been one of those curiosities that some old person had brought here from Indochina . . .

• • •

They say City, he said, City, but that's what City is before anything else, it's like flowing daydreams, misfortune pulled apart, love withered with old bouquets, there, look at the slips of old women who never figured out what the flesh was for, there, look at the fifty thousand longings of old blackmen whose bones look like tools, and over there, moths burnt by electric bulbs, and there twelve syrian nightmares where bullets still fart, and there the pierced heart of a small syrian girl they wanted to marry off to a faraway syrian, and there Carib sea-tongues which surface from the ocean without saying why and which howl ugly screams into the conches' pink depth, and there the clotted blood of oxen escaped from Portorico which no one was able to turn into pudding, and there, fishermen's gum-tree canoes which rot away since City calls on liners, and there . . . the misery, I tell you, of the coolie souls who have not found the boat home, and there . . . the chinese sweat speedily departed, leaving us their fear, City they say, everyone wants City and starts running to it like flies to syrup, but I, posted here, I see the other side of the light, I know the wanderings which peel memories, I see the scales of the seven-headed beast, I feel its blood, its chiggers, its filth, its slops; they say City, they want City but what to do with all of this, where to throw it, City mingles its feet in City and no longer knows what to do with its own body, they say City I say the *béké's kitchen.*

Texaco was what City kept of the countryside's humanity. And humanity is the most precious thing for a city. And the most fragile thing.

From the notes of the urban planner to the Word Scratcher.
File no. 76. Sheet XXIII.
1987. Schœlcher Library.

He spoke like that, and in other ways too. Under Péloponèse's amazed eyes, the place became a shamble of dashing syrians, of dressers, windows, mirrors, royal chairs, spoons made of heavy silver, thick old books, ropes, strings, pieces of hard plastic, disheveled rugs specked with tufts of confessions, anxious tablecloths, acrid lace, cold pieces of marble impossible to lift . . . And during his speech, he must have noticed Péloponèse's impossible black eyes, her beautiful half-black-half-coolie face, the perpetual freshness emanating from her body, thrusting of round juicy flesh, rear end, breasts, sharp scents which inspired Dartagnan Qualidor and made him outdo himself. So much so that they retired to the workman's hutch which he used as an office and loved each other in the position of the pissing dog, then of the roasted game—she, drunk with the alcohol from their sweaty fermentation, and he, hat on backwards, naked like a pig-to-slaughter, wriggling under her belly, crying, vibrating, screaming out to better lose himself in her You want City?! Here! here! here! . . .

Péloponèse returned to the Quarter with the treasures of the dump. Day after day, she cluttered her hutch with extraordinary things. Assiduous, Qualidor assailed her with other wonders. Their first child brought them closer still, and (unbelievable thing) Qualidor had him registered in the town council's records. He did the same thing for the second, forgot the third . . . Beginning with the sixth, he was only seen during the rising moon, always in a hurry. I would run into him climbing when I would go empty my slops under the blanket of the shadows, and when I would go back up he would already be tumbling down. I seemed to hear Péloponèse's sighs. Her children had aged her body, but her face had retained the spell of her hybrid beauty. When her hair whitened, she radiated with a light which softened even the most hardened Bosses. So there were shouts between them. We'd hear Qualidor run away and Péloponèse go after him with scissors. We never heard insults (Péloponèse did not insult) but we felt the lane sink under cold winds, acid breath, tear flows which scalded the mud. Once, during a visit at the dump, I saw them on a mountain of garbage, with frightened white birds around them, blackmen with still shovels at the bottom of the refuse, sternly looking at them, and Qualidor backing up like Ulysses before the chimera woman with a child in each arm, three others hanging to her dress, Péloponèse was leaning toward him like a falling statue. In any case, he never moved in with her. When she would move to his place, Qualidor would vanish; discouraged, Péloponèse would return to her fairy hutch in Morne Abélard where we welcomed her with an unquestioning tenderness. But we ended up by neglecting that daily misery lying so near us. Who saw Péloponèse's pupils grow round? Who noticed the stillness of her eyes? Who worried about her children's dead silence? Who could have seen the flames coming?

It all began with the news of Dartagnan Qualidor's wedding. Announcements of this wedding at the town council caused a stir because he was marrying the Delontagne widow, a strange person of whom I have to say at least a word, what a shame. She wore no jewelry except for a ring with a black diamond which gleamed like hell itself. She was the widow of a freemason whose body had joined his brothers on Rue Lamartine and whose tomb held only the wood of a banana tree. This was revealed when the tree, fed by no-one-knows-what, smashed the coffin and shot stems through the vault, breaking the white tiles and the marble stela, and venturing three big leaves without ever promising one banana bunch (good thing, for it frightened everyone to even think about such inconceivable fruits). Bewildered, the widow didn't go to witness the phenomenon with her own eyes. Leaving their lodge called the Beehive at night, the freemasons cut down the banana tree every month, but it grew back on full moons. That mystery induced a diarrhea of gossip. The widow found herself in a solitude that no fellow dared violate except for that mongrel Qualidor. Used to City's garbage, he was able (from what I've heard, I'm not the one saying this) to approach the woman, gather nectar from her armpits' sulfurous pollen, undo her gray laces, roll down her green slip, dust her hair, and live it up with her, in a fog of incense, dishonorable candlelight humping . . . Ah, how people like to talk . . .

. . .

But the widow had money, a thing which beckons men like Qualidor to the joys of matrimony. The published announcements threw Péloponèse into algebraic despair. A silent mathematics no one counted on, not even I. When she came to ask me what to do, I told her (too easily) that, men being worth nothing, the stick of courage was the only stick that helped women stay on their feet in life. She left (too silently), locked the children in the hutch, and headed (we discovered too late) for the widow's where a wedding dress had been delivered. *Oh, my! That dress* . . . An astonishing thing, a lace monument swimming in silver buttons, veils, train, shimmering embroidery, virginal velvet, with a burst of stars swarming at the folds and arousing scattered mysteries at the fringes. That fairy dress was easier for us to imagine once we saw it on our Péloponèse. She had barged in at the widow's. Her body hauled so much sadness that the widow thought she was dealing with remnants of the nightmare that had slipped out of her sleep. So much that she closed her eyes to make it fade away like illusions do. But the vision slapped her, twice, then kicked her and took the wedding dress.

We saw her wander like that in the Morne's lanes, fabulous in that too-long dress she had put on, and which dragged in the gutter and caught on the jaggedness of asbestos. I managed to bring her home, but no one succeeded in taking off the dress. From then on she went to get her water, empty her slops, clean her hutch, light her coals, all in the wedding dress. The dress turned sour-yellow, then vomit-gray, then sigh-violet. Soon she looked like a spiderweb frayed by the wind. The police tore it from her after locking her up for two days. Péloponèse returned half-mad but completely silent and locked herself up, only to come out at night with a kerosene lamp. She hurled that lamp through the widow's window, who (asleep in Qualidor's arms) awoke all licked by flames. She owes her life only to her leathery, somewhat fireproof skin. Péloponèse returned to lock herself up in her hutch. Dartagnan Qualidor barged into our sleep without his

hat. He set fire (who, if not he?) to Péloponèse's hutch and disappeared with the widow for Guyana. At this hour they must be buried
there or wallowing in one of Cayenne's fortresses, listening to each
other's creaking bones and taking walks at night on the Palmists'
square, and then going to eat in the flying grease of a chinese restau-
rant where obscure Brazilians renounce Jorge Amado. They say that
the widow transformed herself into a Portuguese countess, that she
adopted an accent, a veil, and glasses and sold Aztec figurines that
Dartagnan brought back from a smuggling operation on the banks
of the big river. But people talk too much . . .

To set fire to a hutch was like setting fire to the whole lane. Péloponèse's hutch burned with black smoke, Pa Soltène's with a gray
smoke, Carlo's with a white smoke excited with sparks. Despite all
of my water buckets, I could only watch Nelta's tin curl up under the
heat. I had just been able to save one of Nelta's pictures, the precious
postcard, and my poor four books. I had faced the flames to save my
money and lost part of my hair for it. In the flames, I thought I could
see my Esternome reach out with his arms and my Idoménée water
the blaze with a shower of light falling from her eyes. When the firemen succeeded in pulling a hose through the maze of lanes (they
had lost their way during the night), they found us in a hullabaloo
of smoke and tears, uprooted, off-the-rails, spanked by misfortune.
Of my things, all I found was a rambling ash dissipating the traces of
my axe strokes.

Thirty-two hutches were destroyed. They were knocked back together in four nights of hand-lending. Whoever ran out of crate
wood used canvas. Coconut tree leaves, green braids of wild sage,
flattened cans, and opened barrels were used. An old congo blackman even dug up the old knowledge of the straw and put up a hutch
that looked like a big plant. Péloponèse, Carlo, Pa Soltène, Grodi,
Gueule-bec, Philène, Cador, Jupiter-Gros-Graine, Sertius Laidival,
Paulina Masaille, and Natelle Lagrosille soon had shelter. I refused

to have Nelta's hutch rebuilt. I offered the space to Carlo who was thus able to open up his. I remained lying down at Natelle Lagrosille's, in a corner with the children, where she took care of my blisters with a magical oil with useless effects. I stayed like that, without speaking, stiff like a full net, eyes empty like in my first days at Morne Abélard. When a high fever fell upon me, Carlo and Pa Soltène saw My Lady Death ready to take to the lane. She hesitated but asked if she could pass through in order to get near me. She had worn make-up so as to be unrecognizable, but Carlo and Pa Soltène saw that mud dripped from her ankles, that the sun refused to grant a shadow to her solitude, they saw that her smile was ageless, that her eyes were withered, that her jewels were made of shattered destinies. They also saw her machete, heralding the threat of hurricane, and the guano sack she carried on her shoulder from which tired screams oozed. So they got scared and carried me to the Doum of Texaco, went through the gate where the blackwatchman (called Mano Castrador, not a bad fellow really) didn't even ask them anything. They proceeded in the direction of the waterfall under cover of the old trees which seem to whisper nursery rhymes. They called out *Papa Totone, Papa Totone, are you there?!* . . . and didn't wait around for an answer—frightened, they told me, a century later, by the droves of she-devils.

THE LAST MENTOH

The gasoline smell made me open my eyes. A persistent smell going through your bones. That smell would never ever leave my life. The wind infused it with sea scents, exhalations from the big trees, the water, the shades, City's dust, the trucks' gas. Even today, once in a while I close my eyes in order to recapture that composite smell which makes me recall City: gasoline, hot cement, the old bark of a tree half-asphyxiated, heated rubber, gray iron, the façades' paint scaling off in the wind, light rain sizzling in hot steam on the noon asphalt, and still other things, escaping the nose, perennial in the memory. City has smells of oil coated onto windows, of locks and of

keys, of ink aged in paper, and of chairs. She smells of mud, tin, drying masonry, cloth, cardboard, and the smell of money rising out of
registers, she smells of solitudes and of the crazy vendors who bring
with them the fragrances of faraway worlds. She smells of coffee
water and of golden flour, of the Cinzano of the feasts and of the
morning absinthe, of life exhaling from the Saturday markets and of
the dead scales on the canal shores, she breathes in the smell of the
still aqueducts where big crabs chew on mosquito eggs, she exudes
the fear of the Portorican oxen that stumble from the port, she con-
serves the ferment of skin-tanning, the science of which is being forgotten, she sniffs the old dogs, the rats which crowd her shadow, the
dreamy tiles under the pigeon caca, the small balconies' flowers
where the butterflies sleep, and the gutters' puddle where the lady
dragonflies quench their great thirst. She smells of the bed linen
tucked under the mattress, the scourge of the bug, the DDT and the
Fly-tox that cockroaches savor. She smells of the madras cloth and
calico that the English sell us, of margarine and lard, galvanized tin
and secret liquors coming from Tenerife, she smells of Guyana wood
and of Venezuelian tobacco and all the cheap junk which rains on
the islands where blackmen speak other languages . . . I began to
feel better, especially since Papa Totone's voice reached my ear from
far away like a memory. Smell that, Marie-Sophie, smell that, City
smells like an animal, close your eyes so you can realize you're approaching a cage, smell in order to better understand, to better take
her, she throws you off by showing you her streets while in reality
she's well beyond streets, houses, people, she's all of it and takes on a
meaning only beyond all of that . . . I know, I whispered to him, my
Esternome had already told me so.

Papa Totone lived in a hutch made of crate wood. It seemed of another time. I saw no strange inscription on the partitions. It was a
blackish wood, polished by invisible time. He had laid me down on
his pallet set in the middle of strange ceramics. Thick wool covered
one partition. A candle ring hung at each corner of the hutch. He, on
the other hand, seemed to live outside, under the dome of the great

trees, at the bottom of the waterfall. He gathered crayfish and lapia fish there which he cooked over four rocks around an eternal fire. The place looked like an egg of greenery streaked with luminescent ropes. There you could see the agony of a thousand almost-falling droplets. The fern was a tree. The watergrass reinforced the shadows. The moss glistened on the shores of the river which ran clearer than a shop's window. Only City's crazy odor intruded into all of that, also the noise of nearby trucks which followed the corniche in order to get to Texaco's reservoirs.

Papa Totone seemed to have accepted that strangeness. City whirred around but he didn't seem to hear it. He only repeated *Feel it, Marie-Sophie, feel it so you can see that it is really alive . . .* The rest of the time he said nothing, fished, cared for his hens, worried about his pigs, and rolled a dry maccaboy to smoke in his pipe, looked after his canari, put medicine on me, and otherwise stayed still, eyes lost on his open-sea handline. I had a lot of questions to ask but I didn't dare too much, not that he was imposing (a small round blackman, full like a cucumber under his little wrinkles, not at all extraordinary) . . . what fascinated me was *his certitude.* It seemed that he knew something. Something uncertain always lurks between the eyelids of men his age. No such shivering in Papa Totone. His wrinkles went tranquilly on their way. His mouth did not open with hunger for impossible words or a dream language. His fingers never fretted over vain hopes. Even my presence troubled him none, seeming as natural as that of the old trees. So I stayed by him, like him, mute in his image, as light as he was on the world's surface. We lived like two plants in that semi-penumbra yet so luminous. A shiver in the leaves covered City's rumors. The waterfall chuckled before expiring in a very long sigh appeased by the rocks.

At night he lit a kerosene lamp hanging in the hutch's entrance, and spent the day repairing his fish traps, grating his manioc which he treated in a strange way, roasting coffee which he crushed in an old-fashioned mill. Sitting by him, I soon got my own tasks, my own habits, my own spots. When I was about to fall asleep in the hutch, he would disappear in a clump of tall grass, never the same one, never on the same side. He never seemed to sleep, nor suffer from insomnia. He expected nothing. He had left nothing behind somewhere. In this abandonment, far away from everything, in the company of that old man, I never felt alone, I mean I never missed anything. There was no solitude: we had fallen into the water's rhythm, the barks' texture, the movement of birds landing on the ground. The grunting of four pigs, the hens' wing-flapping seemed to rise from us. No need to turn around to look at this mango tumbling down because we fell with it, nor mind the dry wood cracking: we were just as dry. I often heard voices hailing from far *Marie-Sophie Ola ou yé, Marisofi where are you . . . ?* They seem to filter from another world without needing a reply. It was Carlo, it was Péloponèse, it was Pa Soltène, or others from Morne Abélard, left behind forever.

I never felt I could really settle by Papa Totone. There was in his demeanor the permanent decree of the temporary. He was taking me in, that was clear, and it was also clear that I had to leave. I don't know any more how I broached that question of questions with him. Maybe I told him about the man in the dungeon who I said was a Mentoh, just to test his reaction. But rounding his eyebrows, he laughed at all of that like a schoolboy, looking scared at the békés' meanness. The idea of the dungeon really made him sick at heart. He asked about that science of poisons that men of power possessed. And when I pronounced the word "Mentoh," there was in his eyes the glowing innocence that Alices in Wonderland have. Soon, he seemed to seek out these moments during which I recounted my Esternome's life. He seemed to take a mad pleasure in it, made of exaltation, fright, impatience, satisfaction. But that attitude never confused me, never did I forget the delicate aura emanating from him, that kind of confidence standing in the world which only a Mentoh could possess as my Esternome had explained to me.

• • •

One evening, under the lamp, flying ants invaded us. They smelled awful. I felt in him a slight irritation. Attracted by the lamp, the ants were covering it in waves, then falling in clusters to wander mad through the Doum. We didn't know where to hide any more nor what to do until Papa Totone in a swift gesture (that I was able to catch) seized a fist of air and threw it over his shoulder. He did that once, twice, thrice, in a gesture of authority. He had seemed to tear something from the world and throw it behind him. Two days later, it dawned on me that right after his gestures, the ants had begun to disappear.

Realizing this upon waking up one morning, I came out running through the old trees to tell him, you know (he was in the river, busy with a crab), *Ou sé an Mentô,* You're a Mentoh! . . . He looked at me like a rumbling mountain, then he gesticulated howling: taking advantage of my interruption the crab had pinched him. He must have hurt, for sure, but it seemed to me that it was his way of anes-thetizing himself from my discovery.

I would hound him every day with my question. I broke the silences which isolated him from me: *Are you a Mentoh, Papa? Are you a Mentoh?* . . . He looked at me in such a strange way, I felt I had gone mad. He never answered. His peaceful look ruined my certitudes. I wasn't going to get an answer now. So, I suddenly got the idea to get him some other way (thanks to which I heard his confidences in veiled terms, but now that I try to think of it, I get the feeling that he never spoke). So one day, I said to him: *Hey, what is City, Papa?* . . . He eyed me strangely. I felt him forced to answer . . . no silence of-fered an exit out of that . . . or else his usual silence took on a singu-lar grace. From him to me there was *a flock* of things said. But "said" how, I don't know.

I've written these words in old notebooks; at least, whatever I still remembered of them. No doubt I have articulated them according to that story of City my Esternome put in my head. Those words lived

within me without my even knowing it, and without my even understanding them. A sort of reference toward which I'd turn like one
kneels to pray. Some came back suddenly, after a stroke of effort.
Others made up an oxygen, pressed with asphyxiations when things
in my life were going wrong. A few got away from my memory, and
from my words; I barely brought back the idea of their presence. I
wrote whatever I have been able to find, as best as I could write. It's
not worth much, but you should read it one day, Oiseau de Cham,
just to touch the outline of what "I heard" during my life at the very
heart of the Doum, in the green soul of our Texaco . . .

WORDS OF THE OLD BLACKMAN OF THE DOUM

You're looking for a Mentoh. No Mentoh here.
The Word!
A word fell in your Esternome's ear. A word carried him.
It's come, *The Word.*

City? It eats time. Eats your time. It speeds your life.

Plantation Days, a broken Time.
Time of the Hills is in slow motion.
But City's time gives speed.
But it's the world which takes speed.
Hills-Time, City-Time, think of the Times.

What's a Mentoh? Nothing.

Power? What power? Killing an ox is no power.
I can kill an ox but I have no power.
No, *The Word.*

City joins and ties, each end is tied to the other, no ravine,
no cliff, no river cutting through, all is joined and tied. It

fades your life. Turning many into one, like crabs scuttling in a sack.

You say: the maroon.
You say: the hill is the maroon's wake. But don't think City to be the milatoes' wake. Whoever maroons in the hills, maroons in City. Whoever maroons in City maroons through Drifting.
It's the Drifters who walk, walk, walk . . .
Think of the Drifters who descend into City without losing *The Word*: it lives in their mad jaws like a permanent wind. The maroon does not come down without Drifting. Never ever.

What is *The Word?* If it carries you, it's *The Word*. Only if it carries you and without any illusion. Anyone who holds words-that-carry holds *The Word*. He can do everything. It's more than the Power.

Us here, on City's edges, like on the edges of plantations long ago. But there, nothing to take, you have to cross, not to come out on the other side but to throw yourself across and still stay the course.

Which course? To leave the mud, touch Man, live the whole Earth. You've got all of the roots in your heart.

But *The Word* is not words. *The Word* is more a silence than the noise of a tongue, and more like an emptiness than just silence.

What is City? you say.
It's the postures it gives you.

·   ·   ·

What is City? you say.

It's the bottleneck where all our stories come together. The Times too. The plantation used to keep us apart. The hills planted us in rooted driftings. City gets going ties moors blends and blends again at full speed.

But: Once out of the bottleneck you don't fall back in the bottle. It starts over.

How?

In another way.

What is City? you say. It's not a place of happiness. It's not a place of misfortune. It's the calabash of fate.

City is not to be taken. It's to be known. It's a place the world gives you like it gives air.

The path of this Time is through there.

And that's another kind of iron path.

There is no History of City. Rubbish. Speak of Time. It does not come like a thread but like a leashed dog that steps forward, rolls back, shivers, skids and takes a sharp right.

All the stories are here, but there's no History. Only grand Time without beginning or end, without befores or afters. Monumental Time.

Warm up your words before uttering them. Speak in your heart. To know how to speak is to know to withhold the word. To speak truly is to first polish silence. True silence is one place of *The Word*. Listen to the true Storytellers.

You'll have to let go of City. You'll have to be weary of City. The gasoline holds out its cradle to you until you take and let go of City. But that's still far away. And it's City which is going to change. It's a question of fates. It's a bottleneck but it's open. It's open, it's open . . .

Find yourself a secret name and fight with it. A name that no one knows and that in the silence of your heart you can howl for courage. It's a bit of *The Word.*

No one sees the békés in City any more. So how can we get at them? No more Big Hutches, so where are we to maroon out of? No more factory, so what blind toil to give in to? What you call the Power turns into farce: No more oxen to kill, nor treatment against snakes. So you become a magician of blunders, handle the razor against blackmen like yourself, turn into a maroon-bum that the police shoots, or you shut yourself away with France, to adore or curse her. One way or the other, it's death. *Look for The Word, my girl, look for The Word . . .*

In City one does not talk any more. Storytellers dead or turned babblers. But *The Word* is not all talk. You've got to fight here. To maroon somehow. The gasoline offers you its cradle . . .

Write *The Word?* No. But tie the knot with life again, yes.

NOTEBOOK NO. 27 OF MARIE-SOPHIE LABORIEUX.
1965. SCHŒLCHER LIBRARY.

THE SECRET NAME

Afterward, Papa Totone became a distant horizon. I felt his presence buried in a shadow, but I always hardly saw him. Evenings, under the lamp, I went through the motions of the manioc, coffee, and canari cooking alone. He would not appear to eat (if one could call his endless chewing of two bites of a vegetable eating). No hostility came from his shadow, but I felt projected out of that clearing. It's as if Papa Totone's words had prodded me away. My spirits returned. I suddenly felt his too great solitude. I began to listen to City, to better fill myself with the gasoline smell. I felt like talking to people. I walked to the edges of the Doum and looked out through the thickets. I saw how the reservoir tanks looked like red glands connecting a metallic hand. I saw the pipes rush into the sea, the trucks coming and going through the piles of barrels. I saw the barrel boat which filled the tanks. I heard workers in a tizzy on account of gas leaks or spurts of gasoline that turned the soil blue. I watched the place fall asleep under the tall cliff in its cradle of smells. On Saturdays and Sundays, the children from the squatters' Fonds would invade the place to go dive from the end of the quay, into the deep water. I saw the guard chase them by the waves. Fishermen from Rive-Droite would go through there to catch up with the lighthouse faster, bring back lobster traps, mess with an octopus. Other people came roaming around, hoping to find some odd job or inherit some empty barrels whose usefulness had no limits. Early in the morning, big fellows with mallets asked to go through to reach the Pointe-la-Vierge clearing. The béké often came by during the week with thick notebooks, red with worries, nervous with mistrust toward his employees. He squinted at the reservoir tanks as if they were going to burst open, paced up and down the pipes while looking all around with the master's eye La Fontaine speaks of. His presence provoked agitation among his blackmen: they lowered their heads. Then the oil béké rushed into his little house full of inane keys, ledgers, chabins with quills, and even a telephone.

One night, going I don't know where, I left the Doum's cocoon. I took some steps toward the barrels. Following the long pipes, I reached the quay. From there, I saw City perforated with small lights, crouching beneath its Mornes at Fort Saint-Louis's feet. Turning my head, I saw the sea, immense, spread under the starry sky. I saw the white glare of the Pointe-des-Nègres lighthouse answer to the red pulsations of Fort Saint-Louis's lights. I felt the best winds coming from afar, carrying the islands' rumors to the edge of our silence. They hemmed the gasoline exhalations and curled around these breaths sweeping Marigot-Bellevue, by picking up the scents of the soil. The place was magical.

I stood there until the sun's overture. The new day was a Sunday. Mano Castrador, the watchman, had just checked the reservoir tanks from his nightmares and had returned to his workman's hutch. He hadn't seen me.[1] So I went on my way along the other side of Texaco toward Pointe-la-Vierge and the Blanchard clearing. I discovered a gentle slope. A shower of wild sage and logwood licked the sea there. On the slope, I felt the same sweet wind, rich with the world and with the Caribbean, and I saw City's awakening from up high: the beating and blinking shutters, the morning birds fluttering the sky, the silhouettes of busy servants, civil servants going down to mass, the first dust covering the low houses. The stripped masts in the drydock made one think that boats were sinking in City's mud. I saw the trees light up in the Savanna where my Esternome settled so many years ago. I saw the sun hit the halls of the La Française athletic league where Basile was probably toning up on a bar. The rounded hills offered the Forts' opening jaws, full of rusted bombards. The sky. The sea. The land. The hills. The winds. The place was magical.

So I took a deep breath, keeping it stuck between my sides, and, bringing up one of Papa Totone's demands, *I named myself a secret name.* It came to my mind with natural simplicity. When it rang in my head, I felt my languors disappear, my hair stand on end, and

---

[1]Truth be said, as long as his little eyes did not pick up a man punching a hole in the reservoir tanks, our Mano perceived nothing else; what's more, his whole life he could never understand why anyone would ever bother piercing a bucket of gasoline—but he never opened his heart to his béké on the subject.

myself becoming a fighting cock again. At the center of a flood of
words bustling in my head, my secret name began to throb in léwoz
rhythm which shook my bones.

Repeating it ceaselessly, I returned to the Doum. Of course Papa Totone didn't seem to be there. I left with his old machete that had
been straying under a tree, borrowed his old blanket and some of his
canvas. I whittled a few very straight bamboos and dragged them
through the oil company's domain, behind Mano Castrador's back
(he was throwing stones at the dogs from the mangrove swamp so
that they wouldn't dare take the reservoir tanks for huge balls of
meat). On the slope, like my Esternome had taught me, I planted my
four bamboo sticks which I then wrapped with canvas. Then I carefully weeded my space, packed down the land within my tent, made
the logwood in the area stand aside in a four-meter radius. I found
myself surrounded with a little wall of wild sage and thorns. The
canvas was fastened to the poles on the lateral and back sides. In
front, standing still, I used it instead of a door. I crossed Texaco
again under the suspicious eye of Mano Castrador (he thought he
recognized me because of the crawling smile I gave him) and got to
Morne Abélard from where I returned with Carlo, Pa Soltène, and a
few others. They carried three rusted sheets of tin for me. We put it
over my square of canvas, against the sun. We fastened the sheets
with stones and two nails Pa Soltène had kept under his pallet for
these kinds of emergencies. And that's how I got my hutch. It was
nothing, just something against the sun, but it was my anchor in
City. I was entering myself directly into that very old struggle.

My comrades having gone their way (they did not understand my
settling alone in that logwood-hole, and so near the sea like those
worst off), I sat blissful in the center of my square, contemplating
City on the other side of the harbor. Mano Castrador had picked up
our bustling. He burst in front of me with his big shoes and his big
mustache, and the big eyes which proved to the kids that he was

mean. He told me (I remember very well) he told me, *Mustn't stay here, no, there's danger in that, the gasoline is going to explode on you, a dragon fire can start up any moment and roast the cliff, roast the rocks, roast the sea which we'll have to go buy again from Spain, you can't build no hutch here . . .* I looked at him, radiant—and disconcerted. So he was my first adversary; it was through his voice that City was addressing me directly for the first time with its millennial *no*. That scene should have been extraordinary, that voice should have been amplified by the echoing cliffs, the rumbling of centuries. But there stood only Mano Castrador, brave fellow on the leash of a landless béké.

He (imagining that his fence got low and that he could take care of it, that is frighten me) amplified his speech: *You blackpeople really are no good, the béké puts his things here, peacefully, asking nothing from no one, and here you come set your hutch right by his things! as if there was no other space left in the world! you could have gone to Balata's woods, a bit higher on the Madame River's shores, or even a bit lower, around the lighthouse, but no, it's right here in the béké's legs that you come looking for some old trouble! And after that you're going to run to the poorhouse and say how life is funny, get this out of here, get this out of here, I said! . . .* He was already beginning to take off my canvas. I rose— . . . I say "I," but in fact the being rising was no longer me, nope. It was someone else braced by her secret name, who could mangle Castrador with words but also with stones and who could crumple him like some callaloo weed. With my Esternome's pain, and my Idoménée's, with the rages, the hopes, the long trudgings, the swallowed rancors, all from the desire of City, rising in my throat, I rested my eyes on his. Already an initial shiver slid through him. I took a step toward him like that, without opening my mouth, hissing almost like a long-one, and in a French of a good sort to better sting his heart, *Well, my Monsieur Castrador, tell me one thing, where would you like me to go? When the béké came to settle here did you go up to him to tell him what you're telling me here? What is not good enough for the*

geese on good God's earth is not good enough for the ducks, dammit
. . . And then I stared wide-eyed, body thrown back, one leg set toward him, my fists drawing a strength from my sharp hips, in the
pure war pose of a Creole woman. Right away Mano was no longer
at ease. His shivers were dripping confession sweat. I wanted (he
could feel it) him to start something so I could hang myself to his
breast like legless misery, and bust his bruises. I would have (he felt
it too) unbuckled his balls and eaten his giblets, smashed his loins.
He thought a bit,[1] found nothing to say, and returned silently to his
hutch by the gate. When later he saw me crawl under the reservoir
tanks looking for empty cans useful for keeping water, he came himself and offered me already clean cans, and even an iron kettledrum,
two demijohns, and a pot. He begged me not to let myself be seen
and reminded me that if the béké found out, he'd have the whole
place flattened. *Do what you want with yourself* . . .

FOUNDATION STRICKEN[2]

At first, the béké noticed nothing. He was taken up with his problems. Weeks went by without anyone noticing my taking root in the
wild sage. From where I was, I could see the reservoir tanks. But my
eyes could not reach the Doum. I was happy. Valiance was taking me
toward City. I found myself some job with a syrian, a bit of cleaning
work, a hall to sweep. I walked in the streets looking at the ground.
From now on anything could be useful to me, a piece of string, the
grace of a nail, an abandoned crate . . . anything could turn out to
be something. My cunning bustling allowed me in the space of a few
weeks to gather three crates, two new tin sheets, five slabs of cracked
asbestos that a milato by the sea had let me have on credit. A market
odd-jobber[3] carted my harvest for me once the oil company closed

---

[1] In fact, he blinked like a cici-warbler in the rain, but I prefer to call that "thinking" . . .
[2] May that dear Asimov forgive me . . .
[3] One called Syrup, a powerhouse of a man, who seemed, along with his fellows, immortal to
me. They must have gone to France because I don't see them any more. Where can they
be? . . .

for the day. Mano Castrador would open the gate for us, gurgling all of Gros-Morne's mud in his throat, but he would open it anyway. I was piling up all these things by my hutch, waiting for a hand.

If someone gives you a hand, you have to stand ready with at least one canari of vegetables with a piece of cod, a gallon of rum, glasses, and madou. Once I was ready, I rang out the call to Morne Abélard. Five or six strong men rallied around Carlo and Pa Soltène. In blip-blap time, under Mano Castrador's desperate protestations, my tent became almost a home. A roof made of tin sheets (of which only two were rusted, the other galvanized ones were shiny), side partitions made of crate wood, and in front the extraordinary asbestos which I nailed myself without making cracks under the amazed eyes of the big-handed blackmen. Mano Castrador came and went, nervous and sweating. In front of the hutch taking shape, he'd stammer once in a while, *Come on, this can't be happening, what are you doing here, huh, no one can live here, good god . . .*

Then things went very fast. My hutch attracted other hutches. Word about the place blew about like the wind. Since every day brought with it a flood of would-be City people, it was soon known that there was room by Texaco. What's more, I went around saying it everywhere, along the warehouses where I did my odd jobs, hoping to get a few people around me so as to get a tighter hold. When the béké got wind of what was going on, he lurched, wanting to make sure if he was really seeing what he was seeing, for hanging on to mine were already two dozen hutches in different stages of development. They were built on Sundays or at night. The newcomer appeared, closed off an area, and came back with the moon to take root in the soil. Soon, there was no need to get any help from outside. The very people on the slope lent a helping hand, gave advice, helped, shouldered each other. Only experts in tin sheets, hinges, or some other craft still came around and made themselves useful. In a few months we had become autonomous.

. . .

I remember . . . The first to show up was Eugénie Labourace, a chabine from Macouba. She dragged seven children behind her, only two of whom were able to help her. She was running away from a coolie from the North, with a thirst for rum alone, though rum wasn't quite his thing, since he would then crawl toward his own daughters to touch them. So the unfortunates had to fight him off every day and every night until Eugénie Labourace decided to pick up and go on the advice of a jitney driver (known as Silver Wake, because of his way of driving). Right after she appeared in the market, people told her about Texaco. I saw her arrive one Saturday around noon, she had crossed Fonds-Populaire and followed the cliff by walking through the waves up to the mangrove swamp before the reservoir tanks. She had seen my hutch from there and approached. She was red, face scarred by her coolie's pocket knife, but I could see her mettle and so happily welcomed her. We went to get her children; they were sleeping in the hall of Madame Périne Mirza, a milato lady with old ways, a secretary at the town council relief office. Eugénie Labourace lived in my hutch two or three days, before raising her own with money earned as a laundress at the Seminary College. The coolie came to join her with good intentions, a sweet face, flag upside down. But very soon after some pretend-work at the garbage dump, he went back to drinking and jumping on his girls, a daily scandal Eugénie Labourace endured somehow or other.

The second one was Sérénus Léoza, a good woman, fat like a bucket, carrying five children and a half-useless piece of meat supposed to be a man. She worked as a servant for someone called Tarquin, assistant second-class in the tax office. Until then she had been renting part of a hutch for way too much in Terres-Sainville from a dog of the same breed as my Lonyon, but the former actually worked together with a bailiff rat, ever so ready to seize and evict. As soon as she heard of Texaco, she turned up. Rosa Labautière (called Désolée), some type of tallish câpresse, with a man's voice and the thick hands of a laundress, was the third. She brought nine children from different papas but all light-skinned, so that her litter was red-milato, banana-yellow, lemon-yellow, and passion-flower-yellow. The first man to show up was Milord Abdond, some black-fieldhand stuck in City's mud since the days of the Admiral. He lived off fighting cocks raised in a hole in Pont-de-Chaînes. The rest of the time, he hung around pits and in the shade of fatherly mistresses to whom he unfailingly entrusted a package to keep for nine months. He settled in Texaco, with asbestos cement right from the beginning. One of his mistresses, Yotte Cléostrate (called Sirodelle), barged in on him with her nine children. Milord was forced to expand by sacrificing six fighting-cock cages. That sort of thing would happen again and again . . .

There was Victor Détournel who worked at the garbage dump, Marcel Apô, assistant butcher, one called Saint-Cyr who carried that milato name on a dark-dark skin without even putting out some decent French. I remember Roseanne Honorat, Poupinet Calotte, Big Balls who carried a two-hundred-and-ten-kilo hydrocele in a special cart he pushed in front of him, Sécédias Ramnadine, Marie-Julie Capoul always pregnant and smiling, Martial Pignier and his mistress Diobine Angélique. I think of Blanchetière Carola, ball-breaker of Bib Espitalier (a rust scraper at the drydock) whom she ended up scalding to death one day. I think of Pierre Philomène Soleil (called Pipi) who marvelously handled a market cart. I think of Rossignol, of Cicéron, of Marlène-pretty-bow-back, and still many others, unlabeled in my memory but in my heart every day and night, my comrades-at-arms, my first Texaco brothers.

Well, one day the béké saw us. He climbed the slope, drawled some coarse Creole. He couldn't believe his eyes. He called on his workers to dislodge us there and then. The men rallied in great number with all kinds of implements, determined to obey. Everyone wasn't there, but the children were all there, in more or less all of the hutches, with their huge eyes, their big-buttoned bellies, their sunburnt heads, rags on their bottoms. Compassion overtook the men when they found them. Though the béké threw himself on the ground with rage, turned cocoa-red, said that the explosion of a reservoir tank would cook us good one day, his men didn't budge. Anyway, if they had so much as coughed, a whole circus would have broken out: I had stepped forward, flanked by Yotte Cléostrate and Eugénie Labourace and the rest, ready to gobble their balls without even getting up for a drop of sauce.

They left. The rest of the day, we could all see the béké peer in our direction, leave, then reappear, leave, then come back again. People saw him jump on Mano Castrador with his two feet. The latter was swearing to God that he hadn't seen anything and looked at our hutches with the astonishment of someone looking at the Red Sea parting in two before the Jews. Suddenly alarm bells went off for us. We understood that everyone shouldn't go into City at the same time. That the children should never be alone, and that each hutch should house a bunch of big-eyed blackids in order to quell the rage of any persecutor. We were ready, but all that was useless.

The béké had mobilized a police chief third-class, one called Adalgis Odéïde, only son of a poor woman from Saint-Joseph who had bled herself dry to pay for the instruction of this piece of trash. Chief-thief[1] (as Bib Espitalier, who had a quick wit when it came to nicknames, immediately called him) had dragged himself here. He had distilled forth some French, cited numbered laws, identified us, then made it clear we had two days to vanish before he turned into Attila, scourge of God. He turned on his heels and left with the béké, who had been polishing his back. But that picture show had no effect. We stayed on two more months, seeing nothing but the oil béké's rage

---

[1][The word used for "police chief" in the novel is the French *commissaire*. Bib Espitalier makes it rhyme with *comystère*, which is literally "co-mystery" and is not a French word. We have replaced a French pun with an English one.]

huffing and a-puffing at the rhythm of our partitions going up. We could have thought ourselves forgotten until all hell broke loose. Eugénie Labourace caught her coolie riding her little girl, groping at her with his dirty hands. He must have drunk a whole gutter of rum and eaten a bowl of red bees without knowing it because, caught in that position, the fellow turned to strangle Eugénie. He seized her by the neck and stumbled down our slope. The poor woman was yelping *Help Help Help . . . !* like a scalded cat. Luckily, I was there. I had already worked up a hankering for this coolie because of his twisted ways. He would go by my hutch without a hello or a good evening all the while looking me right in the eye. Running into me in the lane, he'd barely move aside to let me by. So now I let out all my anger against him. I seized him by the blue braid he tied behind his head and sent all of him into the sea. While he gulped down the waves, I screamed a load of filth at him that your pen should not be able to guess at. Eugénie Labourace dragged him out onto the rocks where his rummy vomit smote the octopuses. She properly stoned him. He bounced about everywhere, crossed the gate, rolled up on two pipes to that reservoir tank which, I guess, he must have climbed. Hands thrown up to the sky, the béké thought he was witnessing the end of the world. I don't want to say what came into Eugénie Labourace's head, probably nothing good. She returned to the hutches looking for matches, thinking of setting fire to the reservoir tank under the coolie who was praying to Mariémen in order to rejoin his native Macouba, no stopover (and at dragonfly speed).

When the béké saw Eugénie Labourace with her matches, he almost passed out cold. His men began to run to the four winds, especially toward the gate which Mano Castrador was already opening wide. The drivers abandoned their trucks, running and cursing their shortage of legs. The trucks, parking brakes loose, wandered within the gate like sleepwalkers, knocked against each other, slid back, smoked, coughed. The accounting chabins with their quills ran away haphazardly, covering their heads with open notebooks. Barrels rolled down. Abandoned gates let out gas and gasoline. Finally, an apocalypse threatened us. I latched onto Eugénie Labourace in order to take away her matches. But she dragged me behind her like a tuft of ox-eye sprouts.

The béké succeeded in taking the matches from her. With mongoose speed, he snatched away the box and took them straight toward downtown. He had, so people say, some difficulty braking and smashed into an electric pole. The firemen came to pick him up, sirens wailing. They stopped immediately when they discovered it was a béké. No line in the rulebook provided a procedure for picking up a victim when the latter was béké. So they stood there meditating over his booboos, until his family appeared and picked him up to take him straight to a béké doctor: his life made a narrow escape.

In Texaco, things soon returned to their place. The chief-thief third-class finally appeared trailed by two policemen. They handed the coolie and Eugénie Labourace over to the law at their station where they typed some things down. Eugénie Labourace returned to us. The coolie who had seen death too close returned to his Macouba. They say he became a good person (more continent than a Hindu priest before a sacrifice), that he found another chabine and that he lives off sea urchin eggs when the season is good. In his skiff he holds his head in his two hands, they say, and recites a mantra in Tamil. Clusters of urchins let go of the sea bottom to float around him and he harvests them like fallen mandarins. Good for him if it's true, too bad for us that this whole thing had put us on the map. But each day, I thank God that that coolie's name has left my head: it would have done me no good.

The incident compelled the béké to make his tales of explosions and safety heard. The C.R.S.* landed in person in our Texaco around four in the morning. You can read about that in *Justice,* the communist newspaper, sometime in November 1950. Look for that and read, you'll see . . . They fell on us at four in the morning, hurried on by one called Furret, Martinique's second prefect, (I'll have more to say about that fool, you'll have to come back and see me.) They surrounded the slope as if they were dealing with Algiers' fellaghas* or mean chinese in Vietnam's forests. They had rifles and machine guns, shields and helmets. They hid their face behind long visors and looked like two-legged machines. I thought I had lost my mind when I came out of my hutch, awakened by the third-rate chief-thief's megaphone intimating to us that we should take our things somewhere else because all of this was going to get taken apart. They were indeed flanked by sweaty blackmen carrying crowbars, clubs, nail extractors. I had no idea where these hounds came from, probably from the depths of a jail where they had set aside the last shred of their soul. In any case, they were not moved by the frightened children, they couldn't care less about our wails of distress, our tearful fits on the ground in the dust. The seyaress* (Hitler's old henchmen whom the békés had ordered into the Colonies especially for us, one rumor had it) barged into the hutches, unwedging doors and throwing out tables, sheets, bed rags, children, and all kinds of things. As soon as they emptied a hutch, the soulless-blackmen would go at it with crowbars, smashing the crate wood, splintering the asbestos. They unnailed the tin sheets, laughing like dumb beasts, and threw them down the hill. One of them, taken by a sudden whim, exhibited his thing and began to piss on what he had broken, grunting that it was a sacrilege. The worst was that they were all laughing, the chief-thief, but also the police captain and another pink piece of filth, delegated by the prefect.

It's still tricky though, despite that secret name strengthening your heart, to grab the balls of a policeman. They must hide them in a special pocket. Besides, with their canvas clothes, their big shoes, their helmets, their sticks, their rifle butts, even when we did fly onto them like wretchedness with claws, we'd get tossed into the logwood shrubs in no time, tumble down the slope, all bumps and booboos. Boots squashed my tits. A baton made my ears ring (and even nowadays it still jangles like a jack-in-a-tin-box). My nails stayed behind in someone's belt buckle. We insulted them, you hear me, without taking a break. When we'd use both of our hands to throw stones at them, they'd run us into the ocean from where we'd launch a new assault.

At first the men would stand aside, and only us ladies would face the police. When they saw our distress they jumped in too, but they soon landed face first in the mud: them the seyaress blasted like cannons. So-and-so rolled into the debris of his hutch. Another one slipped out from under the raised bludgeon every time until two-three policemen dragged him down the slope. That unspeakable circus lasted until sun-up. And without fail we returned to the assault, exhausting them to the maximum, yelling louder than fishmongers. We felt alone in the world, abandoned, run aground. We could only go back up, hang on to our so precious tin sheets, to our asbestos slabs whose every crack broke our hearts. Nothing to do besides holding tight.

In those days, the communists were, I tell you this in all truth, the only human ones. They were the first at our sides and they never ever left. Toward seven in the morning (misfortune's violins had already played, they'd herded us down the slope like cattle and the soulless-blackmen finished destroying our homes), we saw the mayor who assumed office in the absence of Césaire (the latter being God knows where). He was a communist milato, first deputy mayor, lawyer by profession. A man of decision. He ordered the chief-thief and the police captain to put a stop to the violence. I thought I was seeing the Pory-Papy that my Esternome had described to me, in the rages of Saint-Pierre, but this one's name was Gratiant, a Monsieur Georges Gratiant, handsome fellow with a beautiful voice, who spoke properly, calming the tumult.

. . .

Surrounded by aldermen, he surveyed the disaster. The chief-thief declared that he only took his orders from the prefect himself and that the expulsion would continue. Already, military trucks were coming to take away our materials. The communist milato roared that as long as he was standing there no one would touch these poor people's things and that their fate was now the town council's business. Then he went on a diatribe about the exploited working class, the impending advent of a new society, he denounced colonialism and shook everyone when he recalled the horrors of slavery which was upheld in other forms, and that all of this had to come to an end . . . The C.R.S. and the prefect's delegate felt their white skin grow heavy with the burdens of the Earth. They turned pale. The communist milato rushed into the rift and gave orders to one of the aldermen. The latter went to get other comrades who took our materials in the town council's vans. Everyone rushed to gather theirs. The communist milato comforted each of us, kissed the children, explained that the town council would house us at Trénelle, where technical services would clear a few trees and help us build our homes again.

TIME BIDING ITS TIME

I refused the honor of riding in a military truck. I picked up my clothes, my pots, my four books (they had trampled on my Rabelais), and I left in the direction of the Doum where Papa Totone welcomed me laughing. I told him what had happened . . . He reminded me that City didn't make itself as available as wild arrowroot, that it was a scuffle, that all I had to do was go down to Trénelle under the town council's wing. I am going to stay here, I told him, all the while realizing that he already knew that, as if he heard the secret name ringing in me.

My brothers and sisters were housed in Trénelle as announced. In no time, the city's services cleared the trees off a slope, a little bit below

Fort Tartenson, by a few hutches which were already sprouting there. Under the direction of militant communists like Nelzy and Sainte-Rose, they rebuilt hutches with beautiful boards and beautiful tin sheets. In a few days, everyone had housing. They're still there, I believe . . . I often think of them . . . in a tender season . . . they, turned blood siblings under the first fury of the seyaress.

Mano Castrador did not believe his own eyes when he saw me return with my four bamboo poles and my new canvas. I planted them six times, and six times some of the béké's blackmen from God knows where (his own workers refused to do it) set fire to them in my absence. I'd start all over again with mad constancy, but the béké never yielded. I ran into him once or twice. He was barely ye tall, half-bald, his skin stained with some old pox, with the ringing voice of the oldest of the old-blackmen. For a while, we exchanged millions of insults. He called me Whore, Rab-ble, Dirty-skin, Gutter-bitch, Vagabond, Cunt-ever-smelling, Cemetery-ant, Ass, Mad-woman, Zombie-tuft, Ground-mouse, Public-calamity, Harlot, Filth-capital, Hot-piss-bottle, Unswept-gutter-dirt (he knew nothing of the invincible barrier my secret name erected) . . . I would call him Pale-gecko, Sticky-nightgown, Churchless-bastard, Dirty-cock, Rotten-white-potato, Grated-manioc-skin, Duh-duh-um, Mama-yaws-sauce, Itchy-pimple, Big-belly-pig, What-an-imbecile, Child-of-all-the-Fatherland, Flour-scum . . . I had just as much to say about his mother: humpback, pussyrags, potatoes, siguine-siguine, phone-liner, cunt. And about his kin and kind. I took such pleasure in cursing him out that sometimes he could hardly believe his ears. He was often far away when I would still be insulting him without even taking a breath, to the point that, at the end of his tether, Mano Castrador would have to lock himself in his hutch and ward all this away under his pillow. And I could remain like that for hours before the setting sun, standing like a Madonna on the ashes of my hutch and howling my misfortune, mobilizing the aggressive depths of our Creole language, the only depths, so far from the plantations, that were still of any use. When my throat got tired, I would fall like an empty sack and in my head, in my heart, insult myself.

Sometimes I would manage to raise my hutch up to the point of asbestos, but it would be destroyed as soon as I'd turn my back. Alone, I couldn't organize any defense, nor prevent the henchmen from taking advantage of my absences. So I swayed between the Doum and the slope for a good number of years, enough to make a dirty novel out of if I had strength enough to tell it. But what's the use now? Lives don't make sense in reality, they come and go and often, like tsunamis, with the same crash, and they sweep away the dregs stagnating in your head like they were relics, which are treasures to you but don't stand still. What a necropolis of sensations! . . . these heart throbs of which there's nothing left . . . these smiles remembered by a simple wrinkle . . . what's the use of all these people one meets and who go by and are no more? . . . and why forget those it would be pleasant not to forget, these beings with a heart in your image, and who go away from you . . . transient zombies, how to keep you inside?

Should one count the days, describe them, keep what hope they bring . . . these moonless nights where one freezes in the anguish of one's skin? . . . and these joys spurting out from God knows where, knocking you over with happiness for a while? . . . and then, you have to put on music, songs, melodies, these balms of joy which help you go on . . . An account of the tears? when you recall them they bring back perceptible touches, numb of all pain, but which you can *feel* and which one can examine from afar as if looking at so many trails taken by our flesh in the world, such wealth gushing out from torment . . .

Can you, Oiseau de Cham, write these futile nothings which make up the ground of our living spirit . . . a smell of burnt wood in the alizé . . . that would be satisfaction . . . or else, the sun brushing the shivering skin . . . thirst stretching toward the waters of a fresh Didier . . . the shadow of an afternoon when one thinks of nothing . . . picking a flower one does not smell, does not look at, that one puts in the vase on the table in the hutch without losing one's arrogance but which dresses your heart for the whole week . . . hmm?

. . . count the days of sickness, the sweats, the fevers, the stomach aches, the heavy legs anxiously massaged, and the scurvy-grass teas, that blood from the belly which breaks up the months . . . count the illusions which make one feel like there's progress, and the cruel realization that all one has gathered could fit on one sheet . . . one sheet for my life . . . hmm?

. . . and Nelta's postcard which you peer at like that, on tearful days, joyful days, empty days? And your Esternome who comes to see you and breaks your heart because you hadn't kissed him enough . . . and your Idoménée whom you would like to welcome in your arms like your little girl and make her go to sleep on your heart like you could have done and never did? . . .

Should one speak of the time that one sees flying by and that one discovers exhausted at Christmas with the blood pudding and the pork pâté, and that one celebrates on Morne Abélard, happy at having put up some resistance to the year now gone . . . listening to the radio, cooking crab rice, talking with Papa Totone who goes about his delirium as usual but who still intoxicates me, singing, crying, thick laughing, howling my secret name in days of strength and soft days, forgetting oneself, cleaning a fish, finding a conch's pearl, touching the syrians' beautiful cloths, getting a dress made at Caroline's, the dressmaker who gives easy credit, speaking of life to someone who's not listening, gossiping to live other lives and share one's own, wishing to be something else, hating oneself, then loving oneself, learning to sit up straight in one's chair . . . what work living is . . . and all the nooks and crannies that my words can't reach . . . hmm?

• • •

I've known about loving different men in similar ways. Always with the same number of pleasures and tears, burns and mysteries . . . the illusion always brand new . . . Love dresses life, colors survival, disperses all the gathered-up grime. Love is a heart accelerated, a beating on the heart. With him, I rolled into the deep gutters inside myself, sipped some very bitter vinegar, sucked on some fierce peppers. With him, I knew pain of the dead belly, the desire for little ones which grows like mushrooms on the ruins of ovaries. I've tasted the abandonments, I made some people suffer, they made me suffer everything, I often got it wrong and took courtliness for feelings. I learned to write letters, to make myself sweet for a fellow who wasn't worth it, to make myself sweet anyway without knowing why . . . Oh, Gostor who'd always do it in the roasted fowl position . . . Oh, Nulitre, who would hang onto my back and rock me back and forth . . . Oh, Alexo who called me mama . . . hmm . . . None of them managed to get me out of the Doum and the surroundings of Texaco. Everyone thought Papa Totone was my papa and I let them think so, saving up my coins in the Doum, sleeping during the week at my mistresses' in City, and always returning, always, as often as possible toward my anchor point, my very own Texaco (on top of which they were beginning to build a high school for girls)—my life's gasoline.

CHRISTMAS DOWN HERE

The opportunity was during one December when City went up in flames. A disagreement between blackmen and france-whites following a tale of some illegally parked bike. Shots were fired. The white man's shot hit. Other Martinicans drinking by the kiosk nearly stoned the white shooter and probably other whites nearby, Hitler's seyaress mustered sloppily, and beat up on everyone as expected. Fate would have it that they beat up on black servicemen from Guadeloupe on leave in the Savanna. The servicemen retaliated with stones. More policemen appeared, more tear gas, more blazes. The seyaress were routed by crowds of blackwomen surging from Sainte-Thérèse, Morne Pichevin, Trénelle, Terres-Sainville, Morne Abélard, Rive-Droite, from places where people chewed pebbles without bread on the side. These harnessed, out-of-City quarters rode high upon this skirmish to bellow their suffering and strike down all the hard luck City had imposed on them.

The Hotel Europe where the boss had called the policemen was devastated, cars and stations set on fire. Night roadblocks were set up. Howling bands were taking the world apart, the seyaress went after them in vain. A young fellow was struck by a grenade and his heart stopped beating. So City went up in flames for two or three days. The prefect thought he was facing a revolution. He ordered in the commune gendarmes and called up the seyaress from Guadeloupe and France. This armada was stopped at Pont-Démosthène by a barrier of blackmen at war. But the seyaress went around through Ravine-Vilaine and entered City. They freed the police stations, crushed the barricades, arrested people, and smothered all life with a curfew, going even so far as to proscribe the midnight mass on Christmas Eve.

> Texaco remembers the play of forces between the hutches and the Big Hutch, between the plantation and the market town, the rural market town and the city. Fort-de-France, swept by the townhouse ideal and the infernal block-house, had forgotten a little about the original equilibriums. Texaco, like the other quarters, brought all of that back, still hot and rough. The urban planner must live its richness.
>
> NOTES OF THE URBAN PLANNER TO THE WORD SCRATCHER.
> FILE NO. 17. SHEET XXXIII.
> 1987. SCHŒLCHER LIBRARY.

Things went back to normal, but something seemed to have tipped over in the world. City was undone, its defenses against the Quarters were broken. The communists with Césaire at their head had spoken loudly, had threatened, denounced, made a terrible circus. They had changed the people from the old Quarters into a people's army. They had understood that that crate wood and asbestos misery was ready to be called upon, sensitive to the least bloodshed, avid for any dreamy flag, as long as it permitted them to enter City. The communists had understood that their old troops from the fields and from the central factories had taken the colonial roads, forgetting the Trails, to pile up here, right in City's mouth. A proletariat without factories, workshops, and work, and without bosses, in the muddle of the odd jobs, drowning in survival and leading an existence like a path through embers. So they look at the old Quarters saying *Who are these people?* and that was good for me—and saying "me" is saying "us."

The word and the incredulous interest of the communists had plowed into the Quarters being born. People still dropped by clusters from the countryside. Despite the watchful eye of the authorities, they had congregated in Volga Beach's mangrove swamps, they had finished conquering Trénelle's slopes, they had taken Pont-de-Chaînes, Pavé, Grosse-Roche, Renéville, Hermitage, Béro, everywhere, in every crack of City, every small hole, every desert of refuse, black water, or briar patch. The communists and our Césaire had helped them settle everywhere, had created roads, cemented footpaths, brought water, supported them. These people they helped equaled votes to counter the milatoes from City's center or from Clairière, the petit-bourgeois blacks from Pointe-des-Nègres or Petit-Paradis, and the clans of békés on Didier's chilly heights. Well, with their number forever increasing, these poor country folks felt strong. The town council was on their side, City had been shaken, the world had trembled, they had threatened the white order which the communists called employers, exploiters, colonialists, and other insane things. For us it was just france-whites, béké-whites, not at all our beloved France, just some damn whites! . . . fascinating and hateful in the pure blindness of which my Esternome spoke ever since those old Saint-Pierre days where inside and out got all mixed up.

The old Quarters felt strong. The countryside blacks, carried along by their stories, would show up with the authority of despair. I saw hutches bloom everywhere. Swept by this momentum, I myself returned to the assault of Texaco. Once again I was putting up my tent accompanied by dozens of people who had just left more hostile places. Very often they had been participants in that Christmas of force. The slope was covered in no time. Some hutches even appeared above the reservoir tanks. They hung on to the cliff, on the edge of the void, or a few steps away from the high school for girls. Others suddenly appeared overnight along Marigot-Bellevue's river, in the mangrove swamp right under the eyes of the oil béké. These hutches stood on mud, on long stilts holding on God only knows how. The people found their own soil, rocks, junk, to strengthen the ground and advance on it. When the sea was fat, some waves would come to lick their ankles, and their hutches maintained a shaky footing. The béké was mad, he wandered through police stations, got hearings from the town council, the prefecture, the general council. But these dear communists were with us all the way.

So, around me, they were all there, bathed in the irradiations of my secret name: Marie-Clémence and her whole fallen angel legend, Annette Bonamitan, née Sonore, Néolise Daidaine, Carolina Danta, Iphigénie the Mad, the citizen, Julot the Mangy, Boss of his state, and all the others, and all the others, our maroon gang still disorganized in the midst of battle . . .

THE AGE OF CONCRETE
1961–1980

A way from City, time didn't go by.

With City nearby, it was like having the breadfruit tree by the hutch. Getting Social Security, angling for a chance to be a civil servant, all of that school business to save the little ones, wandering through a whole bunch of counters, those keys of a life more and more complicated—all of that was more easily done there.

City (like certain rich reserves of the august water yam) was the pedestal of the rare things which bettered life, for, in truth, despite everything, life is made to be lived and so then: syrian shops, terylene cloth, the hair stylists, the lights, the clubs, the merchandise from France—that no trinket vendor could get from the islands—grabbed our attention more than the idea of a shoal of mules passing through crushed shark liver.

We shoved our way about next to City, holding on to it by its thousand survival cracks. But City ignored us. Its activity, glances, the facets of its life (from every day's morning to the beautiful night neon) ignored us. We had vied for its promises, its destiny, we were denied its promises, its destiny. Nothing was given, everything was to be wrung out. We spoke to those who looked like us. We answered their call for help and they answered ours. The old Quarters held hands, going around City, families joined them, exchanges linked them. We wandered around City, going in to draw from it, going around it to live. We saw City from above, but in reality we lived at the bottom of its indifference which was often hostile.

FREE SOIL

We from Texaco, last to join the wreath of the old Quarters, we reinvented everything: laws, urban codes, neighborhood relations, settlement and construction rules. In the beginning, around the reservoir tanks there were only logwood brush and wild sage, with (behind the logwood and wild sage) more logwood and wild sage. These plants had proliferated following a rupture in the original balance of the thickets. When we came, we brought the countryside with us: carts of lemon trees, swaying coconut trees, bunches of papaya trees, tufts of sugarcane, tatters of plantains, guavas, peppers, lichees, the blessed breadfruit, the avocado trees, and a mixture of this grass and that grass to cure the aches, the heart's sufferings, the soul's wounds, the dreamy flowerings of melancholy.

We behaved according to the Noutéka of the Hills that my Esternome had described to me in detail, in communion with the open spaces right outside the hutch, to the rhythm of the moon's seasons, the rain, and the winds. And we wished, confronted with City, to live in the spirit of the Hills, that is: with our single resource, and better: our single knowledge.

On the slope, on my side, in Upper Texaco, the rock pointed its gray head on which we'd built our hutches. Here and there layers of soil appeared; they had only known the frugalities of wild sage and logwood brush, so they were grateful for the sap of fruit trees. It wasn't necessary, like it was in Lower Texaco, to cart in good soil to put over the mangrove swampwater.

• • •

Our hutches sat on the soil, espousing its contours, without scraping any ground away, no modifications in the profile of the bank. We were a part of the cliff in Upper Texaco. Sometimes, right beside, almost like a dream, I'd hear the water infiltrate the cliff, crumbling it under the sun and threatening the hutch sitting on the rock. Those on the mangrove swamp felt in their bones marine rumors, murmurings of foam.

Even at the height of the month of June, the sun didn't strangle Upper Texaco. Around four in the afternoon, its rays shifted as they approached the cliff and left us the sweetness of an alizé tasting of algae and hibiscus. In the heat of the sun, our hutches' shadows overlapped, thickened each other, thus shielding us from scorching sun strikes. What's more, the rooms turned toward the shady cliff kept the blessed airs of a lukewarm spring. Those who had built on the slopes, opposite the sea, got the sun in front, behind the canvas windows. That solar slam could have roasted them, but the constant shower of the alizés would come to refresh them. And we had learned, donkey's years ago, to pay attention to the wind like the Caribs. I reminded (but was it really necessary?) those who came to me before settling in to plan some holes, dormer windows, grids which let in the breezes. But as more hutches piled up, we started lacking fresh wind, a little less so up here in the heights, but too much so in the mangrove swamp.

Our light house frames (tested in the Noutéka of the Hills) allowed us to hook on to the most extreme points of the cliff. We knew that this way would promise each hutch almost direct access to the wind, a panoramic opening on sky and sea; this took care of the claustrophobia which our stacked-up proximity sometimes brought on. We knew how to do things like that since a cartload of time ago.

No waste of space in Texaco. Every last centimeter was good for something. No private land, no collective land, we weren't the landowners, so no one could pride himself on anything besides the number of hours, minutes, seconds of his arrival. The moment of arrival acquired intangible preeminence around here: *I was there first. The ox at the head drinks the clear water.* But if the first one had a good spot, he could only, on that good God's land, contemplate the settlement of the other; he even had to help him, for (he who sows well, harvests well) we were, in that battle to live, worried about our harvests. Each hutch, day after day, supported the other and so on. The same went for the lives which reached out to each other over the ghost fences writhing on the ground.

In our mind, the soil under the houses remained strangely free, *definitively free.*

When a crack of the soil was exempt from what-have-you, it was in fact the outline of a path, a clearing dug with the heel in the gravel, a mysterious zone which had been able to forever dodge anyone's grip, and which, open to the sun, functioned among our piles like a lung living in the wind, oxygenating the hearts.

Upper Texaco looked as if sculpted in the cliff. Battered by the rains and winds, the crate wood and the asbestos had taken on the hue of the rocks and the opaque stillness of certain shadows. Seen from the sea, the cliff seemed to grow mineral hutches, wind sculptures, barely more accentuated than the humps of dacite. When brick and cement came, the cliff went from perpend-gray to reddish-gray. Later, the pink, white, or light green of an unfinished layer of paint (on sale by the seashore) was added. The painter would very soon realize that painting was useless in our pyramid chaos and in fact created dangerous reflections and therefore heat. The naked color of the stone, brick, cement, then later concrete, was putting out the sun rays one after the other like candles.

But who besides my Esternome and Papa Totone could have understood this? These equilibriums remain undecipherable to City people and even to Texaco's. Whoever saw us would only see tangled miseries. And those who remained were only buying time till some favor assigned them a public housing unit to go die in.

WRITING-DYING

Oh, the things we went through: the tides and the rains undermined our hutches' foundations with their humidity. On the footpaths, we could see little streams run down. In Lower Texaco, by the mangrove swamp, we saw the river expand into the marshlands as it reached for the sea. The stilts, often sick, would rot until they dropped to their knees in a sudden fit of prayer which threw us, legs flying, into the water, mud, sea, death.

Everyone cleaned his hutch and around his hutch, leaving the rest of the laundry to time's washing. Everyone thought that, just like in the countryside, nature would digest the refuse. I had to tell them again and again that around City nature lost some of its strength and watched the garbage pile up along with us. But we had many other worries besides that question of garbage (the waves tossed it about, the mangrove swamp stiffened it into sinister scarecrows). I would have liked to put together a few hands to take care of all that, but there were a thousand wars to wage merely to exist. After that, we learned, between the flies and the mosquitoes, the smells and the miasmas, about living as straight-backed as possible.

Trénelle, Volga Beach, Morne Morissot, Marie-Agnès Field, Populo Field, Coco l'Echelle, Alaric Canal, Morne Pichevin, Renéville, Pavé, Pont-de-Chaînes, Béro, the Hermitage, Logwood Court, Good-Air, Texaco . . . stoneworks of survival, Creole space of brand new solidarities. But who could understand that? It was more and more clear in my mind, a solitary lucidity, and to see Texaco grow lit up my Esternome's every word in my head, brought back the mystery of the words of the old blackman of the Doum. I could only repeat all this in my heart along with my secret name, howl it in my head along with my secret name, and invoke the strength to defeat the adversary.

. . .

The idea to write down the skeleton of this revelation came into my head. Writing meant finding my Esternome, listening once again to the echoes of his voice lost in me, building myself slowly around a memory, out of a disorder of words both obscure and strong. I first wrote the secret name I had chosen for myself on the shirt boxes from the syrian shops; beautiful boxes made of white cardboard, that I piled up like tablets of law and that I covered once in a while with a fat, not very straight, undulating handwriting. I learned to draw some straight lines in order to guide my hand. I learned to draw margins and respect them. At the least blotch of my school-girl's pen, I crumpled everything to start all over. I wanted each box to be immaculate. Then one day I salvaged an accounting ledger in which there were still some blank square-covered pages. I then gained a taste for notebooks: you could yank out stained pages, the squares would discipline my hand; what's more, it looked like a book to me; it was possible to read it again, leaf through it, smell it. A brand new notebook, woah! I got carried away, the beauty of the pages, the promise of blankness, its threat too, this fear when the first word is inscribed and calls for the rush of a world one is never sure to tame.

It's around that time, you know, that I began to write, that is: to die a little. As soon as my Esternome began to supply me the words, I felt death. Each of his sentences (salvaged in my memory, inscribed in the notebook) distanced him from me. With the notebooks piling up, I felt they were burying him once again. Each written sentence coated a little of him, his Creole tongue, his words, his intonation, his laughs, his eyes, his airs, with formaldehyde. On the other hand, I was forced to accommodate myself to my scant mastery of the tongue of France: my painstaking sentences seemed like epitaphs. Something else: writing for me was done in the French language, not in Creole. *How to bring in my so Creole Esternome?* Oh, knowing I was writing him into French would have made him proud, yes . . . but I, holding the quill, measured the abyss. Sometimes I would catch myself crying when I realized how much (finding him again so I might keep him) I was losing him and immolating him myself: the written words, my poor French words, dissipated the echo of his words forever and imposed betrayal upon my memory. That's why so many could see me talking to myself, even to my body, repeating to myself inaudible things without breathing. I was hanging on to that temple I was saving in myself and losing at the same time—and in the same place. I wanted to taste that ultimate treasure of repeating it according to the freedom of my Creole and the bouncing joys of the word.

The feeling of death became even more present when I began to write about myself, and about Texaco. It was like petrifying the tatters of my flesh. I was emptying my memory into immobile notebooks without having brought back the quivering of the living life which at each moment modifies what's just happened. Texaco was dying in my notebooks though it wasn't finished. And I myself was dying there though I felt the person I was now (pledged to what I was going to be) still elaborating. Oiseau Cham, is there such a thing as writing informed by the word, and by the silences, and which remains a living thing, moving in a circle, and wandering all the time, ceaselessly irrigating with life the things written before, and which reinvents the circle each time like a spiral which at any moment is in the future, ahead, each loop modifying the other, nonstop, without losing a unity difficult to put into words?

THE WORD SCRATCHER TO THE SOURCE

I know that fright. Edouard Glissant faces it: his books work like that, with great delight.

LETTER NO. 708 FROM THE WORD SCRATCHER TO THE SOURCE.
FILE 31.
1988. SCHŒLCHER LIBRARY.

I had good reasons to give up writing. But had I done that, I couldn't have resisted Texaco's infernos. The arrival of Ti-Cirique, the Haitian, among us validated me in that path. He showed up before me, accompanied by Marie-Clémence. She had picked him up sitting in front of the sea in his outing suit with his big suitcase. He had the head of a haggard teacher, probably because of his myopic glasses which thickened his pupils. He spoke a perfect, finicky French stuffed with words which adhered to his thoughts but which made him even more obscure to us. I showed him a place at the bottom of a slope. He knocked up a rather dismaying logwood hutch. Ti-Cirique[1] wasn't very good with his hands. We built him a hutch with the remaining boards and two-three additional ones he was able to pay for himself. As soon as he was settled (hand tied to a dictionary, a thick fountain pen pampered like a fighting cock) we drifted toward him each time there was a letter to decipher, a petition to write up. For that he asked nothing, only some beautiful paper of which he was very fond, and especially, books picked up here and there in our wanderings at the garbage dump and during the demolition of old houses in City where some mulattoes-with-learning had lived.

He had been there for a few weeks when he saw me writing in my notebooks. Curious about such things, he wanted to have a look. I gave him one of them, which he read with furrowed brows, startled at the spelling and the tangled sentences in which I chained myself. *You've got to go simple, Madame Marie-Sophie,* he said to me, *simple, the greatest writing is always the simple writing.* Before my Creole spinning, a hiccup of disgust shook his body: *My God, Madame Marie-Sophie, this tongue is dirty, it's destroying Haiti and comforting its illiteracy, and it's the ground for Duvalier and the Tontons Macoutes to build their dictatorship . . . the universal, think of the universal . . .* Then he entrusted me with his own dictionary whose

---

[1]In fact, his name was Donnadieu Moléon, but we called him Ti-Cirique [Li'l Freshwater Crab] after a while because of his sideways flight under the seyaress clubs.

pages he knew back and forth—(if anyone asked him the meaning of a word, he recited the etymology, the different possible meanings, supplied two-three literary citations, and indicated the page in his dictionary where that word could be found. That was enough to build him a reputation all the way to Pont-de-Chaînes. Each and every one, along their errand runs, would take a moment to verify the phenomenon for themselves:

—Hello, Ti-Cirique, and if I say to you: Cacao?

—Prefix, from the Greek *Kakos,* meaning something bad. He goes into the composition of a few words, such as *Cacochyme, Cacodyl, Cacography, Cacology, Cacophage, Cacophony, Cacosmie, Cacostomy. Cacochyme* is from the Greek *kakokhumos,* which means bad mood (circa 1503). But when Montherlant, that shrewd master, wrote: *He had slept in an armchair, at four o'clock in the afternoon, like a cacochyme*[1] old man, he wants to point to a state of languor, of weakness . . . Thus the term is put in perspective. Page 236 of the 1955 Edition. If you take *Cacodyl* . . .

—Hey, hey, Ti-Cirique, what I was talking about was the *Big Cacao,* the cacao for making the first communion cocoa . . .

And there again, our man would rush down the labyrinths of the word *Cocoa* from its Aztec origins to Maupassant's subtle use of the word, while from the vegetable marketplace to Rive-Droite, from Morne Abélard to Texaco, everyone felt, for no good reason, and until the next word, cacochyme).

Another day, Ti-Cirique was astonished to find my four books. He congratulated me on Montaigne, the man who learned to see beyond his own culture and relativize his thought. He fell in ecstasy before Lewis Carroll who (just like that Don Quixote and that dear Kafka about whom one should say a word, madame) taught us all the extent to which the stretching of the real was pregnant with knowledge (in this case done by a child), and how rubbing the real with the

---

[1][Doddery.]

magical (as practiced in Haiti since the moon was born) has added
to the ways of apprehending human truths. He was moved by my La
Fontaine, a sympathetic man who knew how to write and whom the
French are wrong to neglect, then he remained silent on Rabelais
whose eccentricities and immoderation (I learned this afterward) he
distrusted. *He's probably the greatest, Madame Marie-Sophie, but
he's also the worst because you've got to show respect for the language, madame, you've got to show respect . . . Language is no
longer as open as it used to be in those magmatic days of patois and
the dialects of the good abbot, now it's an adult, it has cooled down,
it's reasonable, thought through, centered, directed, and you've got
to show your respect for it. But then there's that contemporary question: Is it possible to be the worst and the greatest at the same time?
. . . I'll let you decide . . .*

He developed the habit when time allowed it of sitting by me, reading my notebooks, correcting my horrors, giving sense to my sentences. He brought me his vocabulary, awakening in me a taste for
the precise words I never mastered. Then he spoke to me of the vast
fabric that is Literature, a clamor multiple and one, resembling the
languages of the world, its peoples, lives. He explained to me how
some books shine through times, forever stirring spirits. In the culture of peoples, there is shadow and there is light, he explained to
me, responding to my desire to know France. Literature (the arts in
general) finds its culmination on the side of light, which is why it always vibrates beyond the reality of the people from which it em-
anates. How would one go about finding Michel Eyquem, Lord of
Montaigne, in the brush of Périgord? Where could one meet William
Faulkner in the Southern plantations, Madame Marie-Sophie? Alas,
France is in reality neither Marcel Proust nor Paul Claudel, it's the
obscure dross of these writers. Oh, and I shouldn't forget to say:
Aimé Césaire is not Martinique . . . And worse: light and shadow
mingle in bodies, thus Louis-Ferdinand Céline is a luminous
scoundrel, Hemingway an alcoholic fury, Miller a sexual neurotic,

Pessoa a psychotic diffraction, Rimbaud a nègre but a colonialist in his African letters, and . . . On some days he spoke of poets whose power could break stones. Sometimes he'd get talking about novels to finish with his grief over Jacques Stephen Alexis, his writer friend, his brother, his sorrow, recently killed by the claws of those Tonton Macoute curs.

> . . . alas, he was a *Master of the Dew,* madame, as our compatriot Jacques Roumain used that term in a very beautiful novel, we wanted to weed out Duvalier, and we landed armed, he, myself, with others, on Haiti's beaches, with the idea of bringing the Revolution, that of the Super-France, Liberty! but the Macoutes, madame, who rallied, such murderous madness, *disaster disaster tell me about it . . . !,* Damas, Fort-Dimanche, and I succeeding in running away, but he, the luminous one whose fate was not to run, was seized, struck, carried away by the furious beast, *Look you basilisk, the glance breaker is looking at you today,* Césaire, Alexis, oh my brother whom I hear cry out, oh torment, he was a master, madame, a dew, water brought to our thirst for all that we gave up, he who dies, I who remain and wander the Caribbean, dereliction, boat people, pirates, these American dogs who turn us back, Dominican dogs who exploit us, the most terrible errancy, which washes up here in Martinique, oh Césaire, Césaire, but my country in the heart, that memory of you, Alexis, that ignominy of not being dead, courage, madame, courage. *My kingdom for some courage,* a little Shakespeare, today's literature doesn't talk about courage any more, where are the great heroic songs? Proust has atomized everything, madeleinized everything if I may say so, while here, confronted with the Macoutes, the dogs, the blood, the rages, and the furies, one needs the crashing of words, the world's great bustle, breath, Cervantes, Cer-

vantes! . . . the Caribbean calls for a Cervantes who has
read Joyce, madame, courage, oh how I mourn Alexis . . .

TI-CIRIQUE'S DIRGES
FOR MONSIEUR JACQUES STEPHEN ALEXIS.
13 UNNUMBERED NOTEBOOKS OF MARIE-SOPHIE LABORIEUX.
1209 PAGES. 1966. SCHŒLCHER LIBRARY.

And Ti-Cirique would cry, then would recite poems from everywhere, which took him far away from our obscure sufferings in the
battle of Texaco.

THE DRIFTER

The time of Ti-Cirique's arrival was a desperate time for us all. I no
longer knew how to face City's rejection. The town council cared for
the older quarters, forgetting us. Texaco was not even a quarter, we
were on no map, no road sign. When, leaving the odd jobs, most of
us assaulted the Social Security office hoping to get the most unem-
ployment benefits possible, the mailmen who would bring the forms
sent to us from the Sanitary and Social Action Bureau would bump
into Texaco's fence, or into the high school for young girls, or else
looked for us in vain at the bottom of the lighthouse. In desperation,
they would end up stuffing it all in the béké's mailbox. The béké
would always be on the verge of a heart attack before our heap of
social mail. He would gather everything in a corner of the fence and
set fire to it himself, dancing around it.

I had wanted, oh helplessness, to tell this to De Gaulle when he came
to our country. De Gaulle himself, who had cut himself the figure of
a maroon in our head. When I found out he would come (Césaire
had prolonged the boulevard from the Levée to Pont-Démosthène
and was considering naming it after him), I put on my most beautiful dress and my two-three jewels, and I reached City to wait for
him, to see him, to tell him of our bailiff and police mishaps, of

those who destroyed our nightly constructions every day. He, De Gaulle, I felt it, had the power to solve that problem like my Esternome's France had always done with our calamities.

The blackfolks had come down in clusters from everywhere. They filled Sainte-Thérèse where De Gaulle was to go through. They covered Stalingrad Square with blue-white-red flags and banderoles naming the commune they were from. They blocked Rue de la Liberté around the prefecture, strangled city hall, and peopled the space of the Savanna beneath the tamarinds like ants. I couldn't even move forward. Only some furious elbowing got me so far as the platform of the monument to the fallen where De Gaulle was to speak. I had written him a long letter on a special paper in which I spoke of us, Texaco's damned. I kept repeating in my head what I was going to tell him, once attached to his shoulder. I knew he would come with me to the hutch up on the cliff, take a look at our battle for so little existence.

I had cooked him a red snapper blaff without putting too much hot pepper because whites don't have the mouth for it. I had borrowed a truly holy rooster from Hernancia,[1] worthy of a New Year's Day, fed with plantain, maize, soursop, perfumed herbs, and of course Host. I had let it marinate in a wine filled with a tralala of spices, and I had sauteed everything right before going down, letting out an aroma which stirred up all of the gourmets and inspired two poems by Ti-Cirique.[2] I had planned for De Gaulle a pot of green peas, a canari of yellow plantains, and a chayote squash salad, sprinkled with parsley grown in Texaco. The dessert was cytherean apple jam which Thémancia from Rue Victor Hugo made better than everyone (accord-

---

[1]A Basse-Pointe merchant who had a henhouse and raised poultry on a mixture of prayers and deformed holy wafers which she extracted from the church dump.

[2]He dispatched them right away to the *Nouvelle Revue Française*, accompanied by a very scientific theory on the literary potentials of Creole spices, but those people, who never reply to anyone, didn't reply to him . . .

ing to Ti-Cirique, it seems preferable to say *better than anyone*). A syrian had offered me infinite credit on an embroidered tablecloth, and I had set two pretty dishes on the table. I had put out the hibiscus, crystal glasses, a beautiful borrowed rug, and I had gone leaving the hutch open to be swept by light and by winds, so that it might be welcoming when I returned with Papa de Gaulle.

I would have eaten with a lot of class. I would have taken out my beautiful French and seasoned it with Ti-Cirique's words. I would have told him about my Esternome who loved France so much. I would have told him how many Martinicans had gamboled in skiffs together to go save him, and how, in our worst moments of anguish, our faith in our Motherland which was in the hands of the Krauts had never wavered. I would have also told him to watch out for the békés who were from nowhere, and to swear to me before he left that he would never sell us to the people of America where blackmen were lynched. I could already picture the faces of Mano Castrador, the oil béké, the police, Marie-Clémence, Sonore, Carolina Danta, Néolise Daidaine, Ti-Cirique (he was in on the secret and had concocted an ode of welcome) . . . when they saw that big man advance in Texaco on his great legs, eyeing the world from on high like a flowering mango tree.

I waited for almost four hours under the hot sun with thousands of people. Most of them had a plan for exposing their misfortune to him. Some had brought him the rarest of juice yams, a wonder which embellishes dreams. Others had brought rare orchids from the underbrush. Others lugged mandarins as sweet as mortal sins, and fat mild lemons. An old man carried his World War I shoes as token of his love (he had lost four of his toes in them). Another one, hauled there in a wheelbarrow, came to remind him of his legs given to the Motherland and tell De Gaulle he was ready for his next call. The fishermen, in Sunday dress, had prepared him conch pearls, iridescent shells, Watermama scales, turtle shells satiny like precious wood, seahorses soaking in formaldehyde rum, great branches of transparent coral glimmering in the sun. Some carpenters lugged around caskets of ancient West Indian cedar which was like mother-of-pearl. Three seamstresses had prepared him tablecloths stitched with silver so he could receive the other kings of the world. Healer women brought him the precious clover-caterpillar's black oil, the universal antidote. Those who had lost someone to Hitler's jaws in the war brought him rare letters still unread, so he might touch them, recognize and assuage the pain of their addressees. A woman from the Morne des Esses hauled a Carib basket braided in red and black according to an immemorial geste,* and howled about her thirty patient years working on these fibers. Others only displayed big shiny eyes beaming with pride. De Gaulle came for me, he came for them, everyone hailed this moment as the honor of a lifetime.

All of this was nothing next to my beautiful letter (reviewed by Ti-Cirique) and my good food. I was confident, ready to fly out to seize his arms. But the world suddenly tipped over. A rumbling came from City. The crowd swayed back and forth like a young girl's heart, then whirled, then crumpled. I was skidding on the grass of Savanna Park and an etcetera of feet pummeled my every bone. When I understood that De Gaulle was coming and that I was all covered with mud and my dress torn, I howled with despair, leaping like a goat, insulting, knocking, beating, jumping, landing on heads. It was impossible for me to go overhead so I began to run on four legs underneath, like a dog breaking out between clumps of legs. I ran in every direction, toward the shrillest screams, the loudest tumult. Each time I came out onto more legs, more lumps, more booboos, more rage. Once, thinking I had arrived, I fell into the sea. I backed up at full speed to go in the other direction with as much stamina.

The loudspeakers hanging in the tamarind trees began to whistle and crack. De Gaulle's voice was exclaiming "My God, My God . . ." I thought some bad murderous seed had buried a pocket knife in him.

I jumped up once more on the vaselined heads. Made hats fly off. Crushed flags. Sank into straightened hairdos. I was shoved back. Then suddenly the crowd parted. I found myself head upside down in the dusty grass, and it was Arcadius who held out a hand to me. Arcadius, the new man of my new misadventure.

He picked me back up in a gesture which delivered me completely to him. Taking me in his arms, he set me on his shoulder. He, engulfed, did not see further than the sweating napes. I, hunched like a filao tree above the uproar, could make out De Gaulle. They say he cried out that we were dark but I didn't hear that. In fact, I heard nothing, I saw him in his military linen, his arms raised, his astonishing paleness, his fabulous cap, I saw him taller than a silk-cotton tree, more admirable too . . . His voice was breaking the loudspeakers . . . that voice heard over the radio in the gravest moments . . . for so long, the unique voice of France for us . . . I took as good a look at him as I could, until Arcadius collapsed with fatigue. Lying in the dust, Arcadius and I sang "La Marseillaise," joining the immense voice falling from within City's walls.

We spent the day chasing De Gaulle through City. We went down long detours to cross his path. Once we thought we saw his black DS turn a street corner. Arcadius rushed me down a strange shortcut to rejoin him at a so-called geometric point. But each time, he was elsewhere . . . at city hall . . . at the prefecture . . . at the Didier békés' . . . at the cathedral . . . through here or there . . . We ran around everywhere, Arcadius knew nothing of fatigue, he walked like he was running a race, elated with that endless dash on the tracks of the General turned invisible.

We crossed the Savanna again which had emptied little by little. And-then we went back up the Corniche up to the Schœlcher High School, to descend again toward the center of City through Morne Abélard, Rive-Droite, and Allègre Boulevard. We turned at Croix-Mission, by the rich folks' cemetery where a rubberband girl danced Saint Vitus' dance for money. And-then we jumped over the cemetery wall to go through the graves woken up by De Gaulle, the ancient warriors exhaling misty Lorraine crosses from their tombs; some old békés were sighing below their headstones forgotten by families; and everywhere, after Arcadius touched a candle, a thousand candle stubs lit up again, giving a luminous liveliness to the cemetery. Then we tumbled down Terres-Sainville's streets, now asphalted, but with canals still open on the ancient world of mud; there we met the old mayor who had been shot, the handsome Antoine Siger, who hadn't changed except that he was paler because of the blood he'd lost, he too hoping to see De Gaulle bolt through; we saw the workers from the strike of 1934 in their City clothes, still threatening the Aubéry béké; we saw the Saint-Antoine church inhale Trénelle's lights and scatter them as crumbs of hope on those worrying about whether De Gaulle had said *God oh God how Français you are,* or cried out *God oh God how foncés*[1] *you are.* And-then we followed Avenue Jean Jaurès up to the new Boulevard du Général de Gaulle, now a party place; the countryside blacks hadn't been able to return to their communes and remained sprawled around streetlamps throwing dice. And-then we galloped around the town center's every street whose old façades were sinking into the concrete. And-then we saw below the flowered balconies the stiff shadow of General Mangin who had once come to salute our patriotism after the 1914 war, and of Victor-Hugues, and of Béhanzin, and other great visitors of whom I didn't know the first thing . . .

I was lost in the drunkenness of Arcadius. He spun like a factory turbine and from walking drew the energy to walk. He spoke without ever pausing to breathe. His flood of words captured the world without periods or commas. Then I did like him, bringing out the depths of myself, the buried word, and blowing it out through my

---

[1][Dark.]

mouth like someone kite-crazy. The word came from most far away, my Esternome went by, joined the darkness of the man in the dungeon, fled along the coast and stumbled into a boat's belly where to die was to be born. I conjured up this whirlwind along Rue Ernest Renan, Rue Perrinon, or Rue Schœlcher, under Desnambuc's hieratic statue and under that of our Empress. And the word whirled up against the secret of our beings . . . so unknown . . . vertigo of worlds . . . clamor of tongues, peoples, ways, touching each other, mingling, reflecting an intact, singular brilliance to the glimmer of others. My voice echoed Arcadius, who cried oh yes help me lord, wept, blurted out the old days, opaque questions, the look in a lonely woman's eyes, and the chaos of the islands in the offended sea . . . Arcadius who bled through his eyes and who marched, marched, marched, devoted to a cadence he didn't understand and which was slowly killing him.

We furrowed Sainte-Thérèse where some blacks were playing bel-air* on De Gaulle's shadow still stuck to the pavement; and then we went through the Entraide, Coridon, Lunette-Bouillé, Citron Quarters. We went back towards Trénelle, Hermitage. We crossed Didier by the deep tunnel where we heard horses gallop, and-then we took Balata's winds perfumed with bamboos and we went back toward Cluny, Petit-Paradis, Plateau-Fofo, Bâtelière, Bellevue, Clairière. And-then we turned around Seminary College where two Caribs were waiting for Father Pinchon, before arriving at Gueydon Fountain which my Esternome called Liberty Fountain. I gave way, empty like a calabash, muscles stiff, heart beating like a fat ka-drum, great darkness in the head, chills in the belly. Arcadius didn't stop, he went on rattling until he disappeared down the end of Rue Antoine Siger, carried by all he had been feeling since time out of mind but had not known how to put into words. A most fantastic drifter.

I left with the feeling I'd never see him again. I was especially crushed by the failure of my plan. I tore up the letter destined for De

Gaulle and threw it in the canal.[1] I went back up Rive-Droite (sleep-walking on wooden legs while counting the grains of a bowl of salt) through the festive atmosphere De Gaulle had provoked. He was there, among us, taking in the same wind I did, the same smells, hearing—maybe at this very moment—the noises of our joy, and that gave me heart and made me despondent at the same time.

ROMAN GOOSE

I found Texaco's gate ajar as usual. Mano Castrador had taken our side a long time ago. The béké had made him sign some sort of contract saying that he would be fired if the gate was ever found open or if people came through it carrying materials. This hadn't frightened Mano Castrador. As soon as the béké, the boys, and the drivers left, he closed the gate with great show, shook the chain with ceremony and clicked the lock like a Colt 45. Only he left an invisible length of chain which allowed us to spread the gates and slip inside with the materials we'd hidden during the day in the roots of these acacias the she-devils adore.

With Mano Castrador in our corner, the hutches proliferated. The canvas tents were covered with planks. Various tin sheets more or less rusty, then blinding tin sheets dressing up the roof, had been added to the planks. Slabs of asbestos soon covered entire façades. My whole slope had filled up in a few weeks, while the béké started proceedings. But the blue police had come so often, threatened so often, that they no longer bothered to come. The mangrove swamp was peopled, but also and especially the heights of the cliff hanging above the reservoir tanks. And it's because of this that the béké was heard.

---

[1]*Infamous petition of the Word Scratcher:* I would have liked to read that letter one day, if you ever wished to write it again. I don't dare ask you to do it . . . [Translators' note: The original garbled tense of this footnote has been reproduced here. It may reflect a chronological confusion obviated somewhat by the conclusion of the novel.]

. . .

These huts, he explained, in-person, to the prefect (who explained it to the seyaress) used kerosene lamps, macaque-palm tree coal and countless other junk prone to give birth to a fire. All of this could hurtle down the slope at any time and produce a catastrophe, Hiroshima-style. Such weight was given to his argument that we saw seyaress, cops wearing two-blue uniforms, unskilled convicts, and demolitionists barge in for months and months.

On my slope, around my hutch, stood Carolina Danta, Marie-Clémence the gossip carrier, Néolise Daidaine, and a few others, soldered by misfortune. Our hutches were often destroyed together. And together we often found ourselves under the whacking of the seyaress. We had met to set up some guards, but they caught us by surprise at six in the morning, then at any time of the day or night, shattering everything—heartless cannons. They carried our materials away. Everything else remained on the ground, in pieces. As soon as the following night, we rebuilt with what was left, full (Ti-Cirique would say) of the persistence of Sisyphus and the invincibility of the Phoenix. Our hutches (rebuilt thirty-twelve times) resembled insane mosaics: all kinds of bits were added to all sorts of splinters. We resorted to old barrel tin which resisted the bludgeon blows indefinitely. Sometimes, the police disappeared for whole days. That was enough for our hutches to rise to their feet again, provoking tumult in the béké, who then ran back to blow on the embers of the police.

Our soul failed us at each destruction, Ti-Cirique's mythological references notwithstanding. I felt myself crumbling inside. Month after month, I shed the flesh dressing my bones. And with me that was nothing, but those who trailed little broods behind them (finding themselves shoved against the sea and forced to hope for the gendarmes' departure to cover their small ones with a few rags, and rebuild, rebuild) were losing more than flesh. Marie-Clémence had turned the color of chicken pox. Sonore, with still pupils, said she heard fire sirens. Ti-Cirique, head bowed to the ground, recited the imaginary frights of Isidor Ducasse, Count of Lautréamont. In their eyes, I saw lunacies without remedy. We resisted at the price of intimate collapses translated in wrinkles, in stains in the pupils. Fatigue softened our bones. Our foreheads bore folds of bitterness. The people from our Texaco held on to me, attributing to me a vision of everything no one asked any questions about, but which seemed to comfort them—(without doing too much for myself).

The men treaded light on this earth. When they weren't just going through, they lived lightly in the hutch, shied away from the billy clubs and watched the partitions being smashed without skipping a heartbeat. Some disappeared when the police onslaughts became so constant that a blood red stained our eyes. Those who remained seemed to bow to fate. They felt they had no right to assert their presence and practiced a supple detachment, out of reach of daily misfortunes.

That's what I revealed one day to Marie-Clémence, Sonore, Néolise Daidaine, and all the others; with their lines of children they weren't so mobile on the good Lord's earth. We had to wage the battle alone, because the men, forgetting the Noutéka of the Hills, would not organize anything, would not plant anything; they would forever entertain a temporary contact with this earth. So we began to organize.

Crossing out Texaco as I was asked to do, would be like amputating a part of the city's future and, especially, of this irreplaceable wealth which is memory. Possessing so few monuments, the Creole city becomes a monument through the care given its places of memory. The monument, there as in all the Americas, does not erect itself as monumental: it radiates.

NOTES OF THE URBAN PLANNER TO THE WORD SCRATCHER.
FILE NO. 30. SHEET XXXIII.
1987. SCHŒLCHER LIBRARY.

We instituted watches. Each night, we used salted butter on the gate. When the police barged in, Mano Castrador would take the time to cover up his dreams with the scales of sleep, before hobbling down the hill with difficulty, because it would just so happen that rheumatism was chewing his leg at that exact moment. And then he would open the gate, bent under the spasms of a familiar epilepsy treated in vain since World War I. That would set off a special set of bells which, without being too loud, alerted our guard. What's more, Ti-Cirique, making reference to a Roman legend, had advised us to buy a goose. We tied it each night at the foot of the acacia which casts its shadow over the entrance. Our Roman goose honked like a demon at the least breath of the she-devils or the vicious sigh of the police cars.

Having no children, I was often on guard duty. Even if I wasn't, I still kept an eye open when presentiment slipped in with the night. The alarm gave us the chance to wrap our fragile things blip-blap, roll up our Sunday clothes, hide our D.D.A.S.S.* papers in our slips. Sometimes (if Mano Castrador had held up the troops by losing his key in the pouch of his dream), we'd get to take away the choicest asbestos slabs and hide them in a corner of the cliff. The alarm gave us more time to parse out the kids among the hutches. My childless hutch was always pulverized; those with kids moved the hearts of the convicts and the seyaress had to threaten them to get them to raise their clubs. After that, the sick, the elderly would move away, and we would close up the doors with coffin nails, if only to delay their obligatory visit of notification before the destruction—gain some time, swindle some time from them.

We had tried to set up barricades on the slope: broken bottles, sharpened bamboo, bundles of thorns. Ti-Cirique told us about Che's guerrillas in the pampas of America or the ingenuity of the little chinese who dug tunnels (hard to picture, he conceded, in the rock of our cliff or the mud of our mangrove swamp). He suggested we use the fer-de-lance snakes which kicked the first colonists out of the countryside (but no one dared go catch some in the woods of the Doum). He spoke to us of Indian tiger traps, flaming canals, blinding mirrors, Marco Polo firecrackers, of pitch oil flung from strongholds . . . But these stories only got us excited in spirit and we did nothing of the sort. The seyaress would pass through our not-so-historical obstacles without even noticing them.

We would find ourselves in the open sun, wiped off the slope, slumped over in the mangrove swampwater, collapsing on the reef battered by the sea. The men who had resisted were dragged to the station, the others washed away their blood in the foam of the waves. The children were crying, the elders cursing, the women were damning the whole earth. Néolise Daidaine invoked the speedy return of Jesus Christ and threatened the world with bleak apocalypse. Besides, she was the only one who worried the seyaress a little by shaking her open Bible and her rosary over their heads. She'd been born in Trinité, at a time when boats came alongside there in great number. She had spent her youth under the rule of cane, lost the use of her good hands with the pesticides which withered her fingers. Although she left the fields, she fell victim to elephant-legs that some unidentified bastard had cast on her. It was a time when elephant-legs were cast on you for nothing and couldn't be returned. So she lived like that, half-addled, living from the city council's alms, until the day she decided to sit in church and pray. That's when everything changed.

Wrapped in prayers, her withered hands and elephant-legs became so many blessings. Her pain became grace. Her loneliness opened doors on celestial virtues. Her endless misery became a well-kept ledger of her merits for the kingdom of heaven. All of this was confirmed when the Madonna came to the country to see us. Arranged by the békés, her statue descended from the sky by seaplane and took the road from town to town on a float which blacks, mulattoes, békés, coolies, syrians filled with coins, jewels, pieces of paper,

fervor, and love. People scraped their knees on the road before
her. They sang out help me sweet mother of God, shaking palm
branches. Crying saltwater, they entrusted their soul to her. After her
passage, they caught the wind she had displaced in small bottles, and
kissed the dust she'd raised before taking each grain of it for protec-
tion. All along the road, the heavenly statue spread good deeds.
Blind folks saw a comet. Yellow mama-yaw* pus turned another
color. People with headaches saw their hair grow. Lepers were able
to go home without anyone objecting. Pimples dried up, itches
snuffed out, bunions fell like grapes from all the grubby feet. Blackmen with kinky hair were seen combing it out, and cursed canal-
blue skins finally lightened up. Mulattoes were seen freeing their
black mothers from dark attics so that the Madonna could take
them away. Old coolies and haggard chinese, gone mad from the
exile, jumped on the float with their suitcases, ready to disappear to
their native country and truly vanish in the crowd's fervor. Békés
were seen receiving the discharge of a blood of absolute purity and
going home happy despite their lips collapsing from the drool of
speechlessness. Mute chabins began to babble. Gossips listened to
the silence. Musicians disappointed by Saint Cecilia offered her their
violins. Everyone, really everyone, absolutely everyone, truly everyone witnessed all kinds of things, and those who did not see heard
about it.

Néolise Daidaine, candle in hand, waited for her miracle. She followed the Madonna all along the communes, went without drinking
or eating, slept on church steps where the divine statue stopped for
the night, welcomed her at dawn with a long rosary. She allowed the
God-sent envoy neither a step forward nor a step back unattended.
The békés who piloted the Madonna float were beginning to wonder
if Néolise Daidaine wasn't a nasty one, suspecting their hoax. In
doubt, hoping to tire her out, they quickened the float's pace down
the sheer descents and the steepest hills. But Néolise Daidaine held
on until she dragged herself like a wounded worm. To bleed, piss,

drool, gambol around the whole earth, but still take yet another step. Seeing her go around like that made people cry and dogs bark.

The Madonna took pity on her, because she suddenly disappeared to prevent the poor woman from dying on the road. Néolise found herself abandoned on the edge of Fort-de-France, in the middle of a crossroads. With difficulty she gave up the conviction that this would be the spot of her divine ascension and resigned herself to choosing one of the four paths. She landed among us, in Texaco, still leading the search for the evaporated Madonna with the help of the quimboiseurs,* sleeper-women,* and children smaller than their knowledge of the mysterious. They finally found her, after many an adventure in wonderland, at a chapel in the Jossaud Quarter, behind Rivière-Pilote, dusty, drab in her plaster stripped of all magic since the pilot békés had emptied the float before taking off. But that did not alter Néolise Daidaine's fervor one bit. She became a servant at the chapel where, close to heaven, she capitalized on the misery of her hands, of her elephant-legs, and her misery in Texaco. Without her blessings, I think we would have been a lot more broken than we had been for a long time.

Myself, despite the rosary I'd say with her, I often felt an urge to cry and had found it harder and harder to fight off. I wanted to show strength, and so never, once the seyaress left and our Roman goose fell silent, would I stand around taking pity on my fate like I so often felt like doing. Mistrusting my eyes, I kept returning to the remains of my hutch, recovering my goods where I had hidden them. Under the dull eyes of the others, I lifted my poles back up, straightened my partitions, spread my oilcloths, more zombie-like than my dear Esternome in the ruins of Saint-Pierre. And my tears drowned in my sweat. The others looked at me for a long time, then, one by one, the women went back to their own wreckage. We worked together, in Upper Texaco, in Lower Texaco, until broad daylight. And by the time the oil béké arrived, he'd lost his guardian angel. Our hutches had bloomed from the rubble with more stubbornness than the tough wild grasses.

I had become something like the center of this resistance against the unrelenting béké. He took note of me himself. He came to me every day on errands of hate. The women handed me their swaddled misfortunes which I was unable to undo and which terrified me. All I had to do was look all-knowing, not wide-eyed before their fateful nonsense. And the little I would say to them would be enough to bring them back (for yet another moment) to the courage of living. That attitude gave me the grave face and intense eyes men run away from.

> Out of the urban planner, the lady made a poet. Or rather: she *called forth* the poet in the urban planner. Forever.
>
> NOTES OF THE URBAN PLANNER TO THE WORD SCRATCHER.
> FILE NO. 19. SHEET X.
> 1988. SCHŒLCHER LIBRARY.

THE LAWYERLY MULATTO

The newcomers would come to see me. I was the one who would point out where they should settle. I got the hutch-building above the reservoir tanks reduced to deprive the béké of his alarmist arguments. I developed the occupation of the slope in the direction of the Blanchard clearing (up to Bâtelière). And-then, I got the mangrove swamp occupied up to the edge of the Doum, which no one wanted to come near: the she-devils emerged out of it at night to wash their cold lace shawls in the river and sing sad songs which Ti-Cirique identified as Dutch ballads.

I am the one who contacted the Rive-Droite fishermen (Casimir, Coulirou, Cal-sûr, Light Eyes), getting them to carry our heaviest materials aboard their skiffs and lay them on the bank across the mangrove swamp for us. When enough fishermen had settled in Lower Texaco, they became the ones who carried our materials by sea. I am the one who chose the hiding places at the bottom of the Corniche where one could stash the small materials throughout the day and sneak them in at night through the gate.

I am the one who convinced Mano Castrador (but that was easy) to let us have access to the béké's faucet. One of the pipes brought water to the oil tankers in order to replenish their empty vats. Mano would let us take some of that water between five and six in the morning. The sun would rise on lines of blackwomen, enlisted children, bored young girls, thirsty elders carrying containers. All converged in the direction of the faucet under Mano Castrador's anxious exhortations *'cause the béké is going to be here anytime.* The water hour gathered us too: we had to learn not to fight, to limit our turns, to respect whoever was filling their cans. We recovered rainwater in the basins and barrels placed under our tin sheets; it was for washing dishes. The drinking water was meted out in carafes, jars, bottles, demijohns which had to be washed and filled as soon as the béké had left. So they were pure treasure, these things we hid before everything else when the alarm would jingle—(it's bliss, a carafe brought home freshly filled in the rising day).

My adversary soon changed his tactics. He rang for the Law. I saw bailiffs show up with stamped papers. Some blacks with hair straightened for a funeral, more monarchist than the monarch, and who served us judiciary threats and summons. I invited everyone to tear all of that up right in the bailiffs' faces. They would flee, with us swirling around them like the paper butterflies we'd made of their deeds. They came back, however, a few eras later, with two-three sheets called "verdicts." The oil béké really got me there. I had been condemned to a fine of an unimaginable sum, plus the pressure of a thousand francs a day until I got off the slope. Time, my old friend, went by, and I let it go on its way. The bailiffs returned, between two

rounds of seyaress. This time I found out I was sentenced to jail . . .
oh my poor heart . . . I, Marie-Sophie Laborieux who hadn't killed
anyone, robbed no one, shed no blood on that earth of the good
Lord, I was being sent to jail like a scumbag.

I seized the bailiff by the collar to shake out of him a good reason
for sending me to jail. The way I squeezed his neck sent a sweeping
graveyard chill to his head; then he stuttered that it was a suspended
term, only the ghost of a jail sentence. But I didn't buy all of that. I
sent him tumbling down the slope on all fours and I went to shut
myself in my hutch to cry fat tears (without anyone knowing) over
my lost honor. I took that one on the chin, for sure.

Another time, the chief-thief appeared with his men in blue. They
entered my hutch, threw my little radio, two-three trinkets, and a
few sheets in some plastic bags, and went away explaining that it
was an expropriation ordered by the Treasury. I confess that I was
getting beyond my depth. Everyone looked to me to figure out what
to do: the bailiffs pronounced condemnations, confiscations took
place, and Ti-Cirique would explain to us (citing seventeen codes to
back this up) that by *civil imprisonment* the French law meant *the
loss of civil rights, damages* . . . We knew how to resurrect our
hutches, how to hook our claws onto the seyaress, to sneak in our
materials right under the béké's nose, but what to do against a court,
against the judges' robes, and against justice? There again, the communists were the ones who came through for us.

The communist council member from the Rive-Droite Quarter was
closely following the massacres of our huts. He was on the scene
each time, more or less early, more or less late, but could do nothing.
He would denounce these violent colonialist acts, which could have
never taken place in France, in an article in *Justice*. Ti-Cirique would
read us the articles and I would put away in a potato crate the *Justice* issues that talked about us, to keep them in memory (not a week

went by without my buying and reading that newspaper, and until my death I shall always read it). But when our journalist-alderman found out that the court had gotten mixed up in this, and that we risked going to jail for this, he sent us another communist (or progressivist) mulatto, anyway a lawyer worshipper of an *-ist*. Someone called Darsières.

The fellow appeared one day in Lower Texaco, accompanied by a white woman. He looked up, he looked down, and asked for me and advised me to send those who had received court papers to his office. Marie-Clémence, Sonore, Néolise Daidaine, and myself had to go around to each hutch and explain, reassure, gather the papers, rouse the men living by themselves *Otherwise it's a jail guard who's going to wake you up every morning*. With Ti-Cirique's help, we created a small file with the court papers—whole or in pieces—for everyone and we went down to the lawyerly mulatto. He took the files in hand without ever asking us five coins and began to work. The name of Texaco began to resound in the halls of justice like Emile Bertin's cannons. The fellow (like a jack-in-the-box with his flapping black robe) would unleash furies numbered by articles and sections from the code, legal shivers surfacing from old verdicts. He would hit the judges with laws, decrees, and clauses, and jurisprudence handled like a switch. I never would have pictured such violence possible in such a place. When we went to such or such a hearing, trembling in the temple echoes of the court, we would feel that he was ready to fly at the white judge and cut him open like we would have done. He's the one who sent the oil béké, the bailiffs, the prefect for a slow ride through a blinding alley of procedures, postponements, suspensions, legal clarifications, deliberations, appeals, further investigations, perpetually rescheduled things, then moved things around for Marquis d'Antin Day, then back to square one where he would start the whole legal circus over again. The anxious judges saw him appear and would disappear in their armchairs when (having exhausted the judiciary mysteries) our advocate would invoke the supreme code of the Rights of Man, and would overwhelm them with his furors against colonialism, slavery, man's exploitation of man, would denounce the Amerindian genocides, the benevolent complicities the Ku Klux Klan enjoyed, the Madagascar massacre, the thousands of deaths building the Congo-Ocean Railroad, giving the shaft to the Indochinese, the Algerian tortures, their gendarmes shooting at the agricultural strikers, would hit them with Marx, frighten them with Freud, cite Césaire, Damas, Rimbaud, Baudelaire, and other poets only Ti-Cirique could identify. He fought inch for inch for us on a field unknown to us. It's as if he was covering our vulnerable flank. But the battle went on because, without slackening by a hair, the seyaress would still demolish our attempts to live in the shadow of the reservoir tanks.

THE SAILORS WITH VISIONS

Things changed with the arrival of Julot the Mangy. At that time, no one knew he was a Boss. He was not one officially. He came from God knows where, fearing only the return of his mother now trapped in a coffin. He showed up among us early one Sunday. Strange thing, he didn't come to see me, as was the custom. He chose to settle in Lower Texaco, in the middle of the mangrove swamp, in a square made of tin sheets barely raised. And he lived there just like that, immutable, going into City to the rhythm of a poem known only to him, hanging around left, eyeing about right, without looking like he sweated over any béké. When I ran into him for the first time, I saw in his eyes that certain gleam always at bay, seen once, years ago, in Silver Beak's eyes. I gathered without understanding that this Julot was no regular blackman. What happened next would confirm this for me.

The oil tankers had a crew of more or less raucous sailors. These bandits would take advantage of the boat's stopover to go down in City, to see the hookers on the edge of Bois-de-Boulogne. They would spend lots of money, speak seven languages, bear nine afflictions, drink like the Mexicans in the movies, and return to Texaco reduced to ashes by alcohol's embers. Then they would confide in everyone, would describe things encountered throughout the Caribbean. They spoke of galleons stuffed with gold, glassy like jellyfish, which crossed the bows of their tankers stirring up exhalations of bitter algae, roughneck soldier songs, laughs of ladies glimpsed in the bowsprit portholes from which escaped a music gay and sad. They spoke of sharks surging in their wake, white and pink like broken coral; their jaws would snap as they had for centuries around the slave galleys which had thrown up whole cargos for them, to such a point that, poisoned by a rumor about souls, these fish would spell anguish in thirteen African tongues. Nightmares (the drunk sailors would say) haunted this Caribbean Sea which is pensive like a cemetery; abysses latched onto the oil tanks to occupy their steel with a hosannah of millions of people dissolved into a horrible rug which remembered Africa in the submarine nights, a fabric bristling with balls and chains and joining the islands in an alliance of corpses. They spoke of Christopher Columbus at the bow of the *Santa Maria* which had turned opaline with the glint of age like very old ivory; she was the crystal formed out of the dust of Aztec peoples, Inca peoples, Arawaks, Caribs, the ashes of tongues, skins, bloods, collapsed cultures, out of the dust of that immense killing field spread out among the plantations of the world called New; since eternity, well before he arrived, ghosts were judging the Discoverer now petrified at his bow before an opaque Indies, they were judging him in vain because the Baneful One always escaped them, as if amnestied by irremediable history which he was forced to mutter endlessly . . . And all of that made the tanker sailors even more disgusted, more loony, more convulsive, and would contaminate our little nightmares in Texaco; these horrors they evoked while going through our huts, we felt, alas my dear, that they filled us too.

But the city is danger, *our* danger. The automobile conquers space, the center is vacated and the washouts settle

there; she amplifies alimentary dependence, a fascination
for the outside, and non-productive energy; open on the
world she ignores the country, and in the country, ignores
man; she sojourns in new solitudes and poverties unknown to doctors; she jerks with pollutions and insecu-
rity; she spreads everywhere, threatens cultures and
differences like a global virus. The city is danger.

NOTES OF THE URBAN PLANNER TO THE WORD SCRATCHER.
FILE NO. 14. SHEET XIV.
1988. SCHŒLCHER LIBRARY.

To return to their ship, they would climb the béké's fence and cross
Lower Texaco spewing their impossible visions in all languages.
Month after month, they got into the habit of dropping by, knocking
on doors, bothering the untaken ladies and the curious young girls
standing on their doorsteps. I say "bother," but not always since
some beautiful heart-struck tales took place, as witness the banana-
yellow cherubs among Texaco's black children (just like at Morne
Pichevin, Volga Beach, or Sainte-Thérèse). Some infatuated women
flew off on tankers, a bit like my dear Esternome's Osélia. There
were also a number of broken engagements right on the verge of the
simple wedding band (the fiancé would hear the call of the sea as
soon as he had pillaged the virginal nest), but these were moving
moments, worthy of some good Cinzano. But most of the time it
was screams, blows, nuisance, which filled our nights with chilly stupor. The monthly tankers would add their afflictions to the ordeal of
the seyaress. The men of Texaco protected their own hutches, but
the hutches without men were at the mercy of the frenzies of the
drunken sailors. They wanted to caress the woman inside at all
costs, make her sing *Adieu scarves, Adios madras,* see her eyes light
up under their wads of dollars, and feel her flesh melting in the oil of
longing. Whoever was alone in her hutch with her children had to
scald them, display scissors, her acid jar, throw the tantrums of a
chabine. I (having settled in the heights, I escaped the assault, since
alcohol denied them their footing above sea level) would have to go

down with fat logwood clubs, break the shell of a back. Once, a sailor even threw me in the sea. I got back on my feet and returned to the shore, covered with sea urchin barbs that no candlewax was able to pull out. One night, Néolise Daidaine almost endured the ultimate outrage. She owed her deliverance to her appalling elephant-legs: lifting her legs to penetrate her nether parts, the drunkards ran away when they saw her trunks of congested flesh. We were burdened with these problems for a whole lot of months now when citizen Julot revealed to the visionary sailors what a pestilence he could be.

One night, the sailors picked on Marie-Clémence. She was all the way at the bottom of the slope. They knocked down her door, singing, and began to run after her. Her dry straw hair, her mulatto skin, the aura of her former beauty had made the sailors go beyond their usual monkeyshines. Some took off their pants and stalked her with their woodies. Seizing a logwood club, I fell on them. I had the time to break a nose, sand down a few balls, and pull apart a few donkey dicks pointed in her direction. She had crippled two-three too. But they ended up overcoming us with sheer numbers: we could only bray for help like goats at the slaughterhouse about to be bled.

A few lamps lit up in the hutches, some blackwomen came out in a rage, two-three fellows pulled out a machete and began to come down. Mano Castrador, his old Colt in hand, began to shoot in the air, advancing like Pat Garrett on Billy the Kid. But the sailors were mean. Some handled their tan arms like iron clubs. So they threw off our Lower Texaco and periodically decimated the waves from Upper Texaco. I could already see myself and Marie-Clémence falling victim to their vices when Julot got involved.

The Boss is not afraid to die. Seeing him advance on you is terrifying. You get the feeling he's come looking for his death and even (if he's a great Boss) that he's just come back from his grave. To look upon a life ready to die petrifies all life. Julot then was advancing on the sailors with one hand in his back pocket, in the Bosses' ritual way. What's more, he had hidden under his shirt what we knew was a machete but which none of the sailors saw. The sailors who, magnetized by his aura of death, let him go by were ignored; but one of them, not very briefed on life, held him back by the arm, hoping of course to send him back to his hutch in shredded linen. That was to say the least *unfortunate*. He who has never seen a Boss strike should never ask for it. I, knowing what was going to happen, closed my eyes.

A silence held back the night. A very ancient silence. In spite of myself, I reopened my eyes to see what I had already once seen at Terres-Sainville and would have liked never to see again. The sailor's arm flew out of Julot's hand turned graveyard-white. Everyone could see a spurt of ink rise in the sky. By the time we'd looked up, Julot had already administered fourteen blows to the poor fellow in one direction and the same number in the other. But when I say blows, it was much more foul than that. It's really a *mangling* out of shape. Man-gling. When the Boss strikes, there is in his movements so much doom, so much decision, so much that's irremediable, that one gets a feeling of an injustice no matter what the motive for his intervention is. The other sailors beheld the feat and suddenly sobered up. They ran away on all fours in the direction of their launch, then their tanker. The place was in order in no time.

Noting their flight, Julot kept on pounding the imprudent one who was now nothing but a rag. We were petrified. Julot stopped, wiping his knife on the broken sailor, and peacefully went to sit down on a nearby stone, watching the sailor struggling like a chicken with its head cut off. All of Texaco had stepped back into the shadows for fear of meeting Julot's eye. Everything seemed to be over, but I knew good Lord that that was not at all the case.

· · ·

The Boss never stops. If the poor sailor still moved, tried to get up to go, Julot would pounce on him with just as much pugnacity. Since he didn't move, the worst came to pass. Julot began to speak in a little girl's voice. He said (and it was like a death sentence): You ask nothing of no one and yet people come looking for you, you tuck yourself away like an old blackman of the hills, and you hide your words in your heart because you're stuck in this life-here, but you would have loved to be in the ground on the other side of this life-here, but where to go, where to run, where to climb without this life-here catching up with you and then you have to deal with her? There aren't any hills for that, so you run around in circles, but that's like standing still, hooked, but it's better to stand still because the sea's in front, the sea's behind, the sea's on the side, and you don't know where to turn and on what shore you can wriggle or struggle, so you flee into your own heart, but that just makes you stand still, hooked, apart from people, without asking anyone for anything, standing still like a coffin, counting the nails, eyes wide open on misfortune, and look at him over there, he's lying but not dying, these people, no, they don't die, they've got their ways to fuck others over, they play dead but they're just playing, and if you don't know they're playing, they fuck you over just like that and then you're the one having a ball, already counting the nails in your coffin . . . And while he was talking, his machete (up to now hidden in his shirt) appeared in his hand like an apocalypse. He raised it above the sailor as if he was going to split a huge block of wood, when I took my heart in my two hands to say *No Julot!* . . . all the while knowing that it was some big mistake and that I was going to die.

I must have sounded like his mother he feared so much. That probably saved my life. For the Boss breaks whatever desires to stop him. You can only gawk at the results of his rage, unless you want to risk your life. I didn't want to risk mine, but I cried *No Julot . . .* , for fear of a bunch of things I still don't know what (maybe for Texaco: a murder would have increased City's hostility). He took one look at me with his eyes that weren't eyes. I saw my death coming to meet me. I felt my blood rush in my head. I found myself forgetting myself, my memory quickly depleted. I felt my legs shimmy-shake. I was already dead inside, my soul freezing in the marrow of my bones so stiff and my flesh melting into sauce. In that tenth of a second, I must have aged seven centuries and fifty wrinkles and an array of white hairs. But Julot who was stepping toward me stopped short—just like that without saying anything. He simply turned his back and went inside his hutch which echoed like a tomb. And there I thought I heard him speak to himself, no longer waiting for a reply, crying a river.

The sailors returned (tame like muzzled dogs) to look for their mate. They left with him; they were never seen again. They must have changed firms, or never set foot in Fort-de-France again, or maybe they were swallowed one night by these flotillas of Caribs forgotten long ago, who emerge in the world to avenge their massacres. I slowly went back up to my hutch; all of Texaco was watching me limp as if I had become the cousin of a she-devil. A new branch to my legend: I had stopped a Boss at war.

The presence of a Boss among us was a good and bad thing. There was no Quarter without a Boss, and Texaco got its birth certificate when it became Julot's territory. The only problem is that Bosses attract Bosses and aspiring Bosses. So much so that the Bosses in Rive-Droite and Morne Abélard (named Scalding Danger and Sea Beak) got together in no time when they heard of the occurrence. One Saturday evening, of course. They came together, got Mano Castrador to open (with great deference) the gate for them, and stepped into Lower Texaco, speaking to one another in loud sepulchral voices:
—So is it really so that there's a baddie around here?
—That's what people say, you know . . .
—I'm reelscared, very scared of baddies and when a baddie's around I want to see him at his baddest . . .

—Me too, reelscared, the same way, all afraid . . .
—I ask him, you-hear-my-dear, to tell me why he's such a baddie . . .
—Me too, me too, you've got to do that with the baddie . . .
—But some people claim to be baddies without it really being so . . .
—Well that, that's quite awkward, 'cause they . . .
—Could be more ugly than fierce . . .
—Quite a nuisance . . .
—More obscene than mean . . .
—That's annoying anytime . . .
—More seen than mean . . .
—Definitely a concern . . .
—More lean than mean . . .

They were thus advancing into Lower Texaco, spreading fear. They looked like they were talking to themselves but evil eyes wandered across every face, looking for the person they were after. Someone came to warn me. I came down right away. Boss warfare is a calamity of no use to anyone. Shaking all over, I came to get mixed up in all of this; when I got there they were already by Julot's hutch. The almost ritual conversation began out of a Mass-kind of silence impossible to break. Behind, the setting sun was making matters worse:

—Oh will you look at that, it seems that I am looking at the person we're all looking at . . .
—Well if it's him, he should present himself . . .

Julot came out, hand in his back pocket, very peaceful, looking annoyed but formidable. He stopped before the two Bosses and remained silent, but without looking at them.

—Is he introducing himself?
—Telling us where he's from?
—Julot's the name. Anses d'Arlets. Balata. Fort-de-France. Texaco.
—And your mother?
—Ma Victorine, called Marie-Tété-Pepper-Ass.
—And your father? . . .
—Pilote Victor, forsaken son of Gustave and Corélia.
—Pilote? So you've got Carib blood, then? . . .
—Hmm . . .

—That's good blood.

—Corélia? You said Corélia was your grandmama? Corélia Salssifoire whose mama worked in the factory and had spat three times on a béké woman at the midnight mass? Is that who you said?

—Corélia Salssifoire . . . herself.

—We know her . . .

—A good person too . . .

Now, I knew the worst could be avoided. The disclosure of family braided ties beyond the Hills that none dared sever. But it was time to conclude. And that's when Julot showed he was a real Boss, because Bosses respect Bosses above all else. He carefully paid his respects in his voice of flat-chested girl:

—I know, he said, who you all are. You are Scalding Danger. And you are Sea Beak. I even heard of you at Anses d'Arlets and even further than Petite-Anse.

—You heard of us?

—I did . . .

—So you know who you're talking to?

—Scalding Danger and Sea Beak. How could I forget?

"Knowing" a boss, to "have heard" of him, is recognizing his territory, his strength, his legitimacy. But they went on talking and Julot was clever.

—So people were talking and making you out to be a baddie, not tedious or horny, not even conspicuous, they told him . . .

—People say, people talk.

—In your opinion and careful now, what is the meanest thing of all in all the world?

—The seven-year mange[1] is not a good thing, but anything more foul than that is beyond me and I just can't say . . .

That was good. A dash of humility. Scalding Danger and Sea Beak went on their way in silence, barely saluting Mano Castrador who opened the gate as if they were visiting békés.

---

[1] His answer stuck to his name.

THE CÉSAIRE EFFECT

So that's where we stood in our misfortune when De Gaulle stormed the country and I not able to see him. I felt beat that day, I returned to my hutch, dejected, without even being able to touch the rooster and the sweetness I had prepared. Marie-Clémence, Sonore, Néolise Daidaine, Carolina Danta, Ti-Cirique, and others sang their joy at having glimpsed De Gaulle, and the others returned from City after having set their heads on fire at a string of bars. Everyone came by to tell me what of De Gaulle they'd seen, and it was never the same thing, to such a point that we ended up concluding that he probably changed faces like our improbable Mentohs . . .

Julot's presence in Texaco made us known in the Hills around. That brought us still more hutches which this time hung above the reservoir tanks without my being able to do anything about it. The béké found his rage again and rang for the seyaress. When they came out, they first fell on Julot the Mangy. He didn't take out his weapons against their rifles, but he knocked down a few onto the rubble of his house. They took him bleeding toward a small wire-grilled van and threw him directly down a cell. He came out of it six months later, after the intervention of our lawyerly mulatto, and rebuilt his hutch as if nothing had happened.

The night the seyaress returned was terrible. Enraged by Julot's resistance, they went on their destructive romp with an unusual rage. They broke the partitions with more faith, hit the women as much as or worse than the men, and sent the children out flying who'd been protecting the different hutches. The Morne Abélard Quarter's communist alderman (as part of our planned defense, Ti-Cirique slipped out to go warn him) reported the facts to Césaire himself. So, around noon, in a disaster of asbestos, tin sheets, crates, mud, tears, blood, police reports, an ocean of different police forces, we saw the elected mayor in person. His black car had driven up into Texaco in silence. He had come out of it, surrounded by his mulattoes and a communist-doctor wearing white. The mayor stepped forward, looking around him, getting briefed on God knows what, showing his indignation before the smashed huts. He walked around on the slope strewn with our intimate treasures, appalled. Not knowing what to do, the police forces eyed him silently. And-then the mayor addressed the chief-thief, the seyaress captain, and the prefecture fellow who attended the operations. His presence was impressive, but not his voice which he did not raise, nor his very calm movements, but his presence: it filled the spirits of the legends woven around him. Here was Papa Césaire, our revenge on the békés and the bigwig mulattoes. He, who I hadn't even dared solicit in my bottomless despairs . . . And-then he left, having shaken a few hands, including that of Marie-Clémence. I don't know why, but when his image comes back to me, I always get the feeling of his endless loneliness. According to Ti-Cirique, it's the price paid to the world by poets whose peoples are yet to be born.

His being seen among us fed the rumor that Césaire himself authorized our settlement. Later on, we learned he had met with the prefect, that he had asked about buying up the property, or still exhorted the béké to wait without pushing the people around till he found some other solution. He found a small one, and soon the town council proposed to house us at Morne Calebasse. A dozen of us went there, but the others (already almost a Quarter nation) crowded around me, tied to this place like brigs on reef by the sea. The failure of the Morne Calebasse solution irritated the town council people; we were pretty much left to our own devices with the oil békés. As we rebuilt, as those who had left were replaced by new persons, and as the police had to intervene once more, the *Césaire effect* wondrously took place. They paid attention, respected the hutches sheltering the children, crushing only those hutches which were empty, in construction, or those which posed a fire hazard from their perch above the reservoir tanks. And they would take the time to explain to us the thinking behind each demolition. When they left again, I felt not a tear swelling in me; our Texaco had barely budged, most of our hutches stood there, straight on their feet, staying our ground from now on.

> But the city is danger; she becomes a megalopolis and doesn't ever stop; she petrifies the countryside into silence like Empires used to smother everything around them; on the ruins of the Nation-state, she rises monstrously, multi-national, transnational, supranational, cosmopolitan—a real Creole nut-case in a way, and becomes the sole dehumanized structure of the human species.
>
> NOTES OF THE URBAN PLANNER TO THE WORD SCRATCHER.
> FILE NO. 20. SHEET XVI.
> 1988. SCHŒLCHER LIBRARY.

It was then that the concrete phenomenon began. There's no precise date. The asbestos was progressing with long strides, but cement, for real, was becoming accessible. The cemented bottoms of a few walls and a few bricks were soon seen. Obsessed by the crate wood and the asbestos, the police barely scratched the cement. But cyclones like Edith, Dorothy, or the sinister Beulah, which devastated our hutches better than all of the police put together, amplified the desire for concrete. The winds blew the tin sheets to Miquelon, unnailed the crate wood, dissipated the asbestos into angel hair. In the midst of this disaster, the concrete walls held like girders in our spirits. After all, concrete was City par excellence, the definite sign of a step forward in life. We began, everything hinging on odd jobs and various savings, to buy ourselves bricks, bags of cement, rocks. The masons became princes in the heart of our hand-giving. One first added the cement-brick-concrete behind the hutch so as not to alarm the oil béké, then one had to sneak around and cover the sides. The walls were raised from inside the wood or asbestos partitions, and one day, suddenly, shedding like a snake, quite a hutch shook off its miserable coat and rose in triumphant concrete. These dazzling achievements rubbed pride on our cheeks; everyone wanted to be next.

THE DRIFTER'S DEATH

Myself, I was living through another misfortune: Arcadius had reappeared in my life like a whistling comet. We would walk entire nights. We would meet each other in my hutch to walk otherwise in bed a thousand times. I felt my heart go voom-pow for him. When he appeared, a plainsong carried me. When he disappeared carried by his drifting, a drowsiness emptied my bones and left me all mushy in the middle of everybody giving-a-hand around the holy concrete. The drifting took him far and for a long time. To make him come back, I would enter his madness. Néolise Daidaine and Carolina Danta, thinking I had really become a drifter, had to go and light some candles for me. I would go along with Arcadius but would slowly bring him back to my hutch, and there I would offer him the world's contentments, giving myself without measure, doing the things I knew he liked and which I would discover by exploring his body. In order to cure him of his love of drifting, I would raise a song of songs from his seeds, I sowed sweetness into each of his pores, I sucked his soul, I licked his life. I forced myself to melt us into each other, to give him anchor. My papaya turned into an octopus to suck him up and hold him there. It turned into apple and pear and small gilt cage, into arroz-con-pollo, into sweet liqueur on which to suck, into 120 proof tafia, temple of still drunkenness, into white-madou to be caught drop by drop with a stretched tongue, turned dangerous like the datura flower which paralyzes the legs, became a great wound which could only be cured by grafting one's life onto it, turned into cutting pliers squeezing him just enough to finish off the pleasure, into a carousel horse which he could straddle, moving up and down around the hub, into a small game fowl fallen to fit into his hand and sleep a hundred years, it widened to become gaping, became a highway without walls or horizon where he could *go* while staying in me. But he left me every time; I remained crushed, half old, looking to see if he had made a miracle in my belly where the blood of life was beginning to dry up. I felt whiffs of hot flashes, dizziness, embers which changed my personality. My unappeased desire for a child (a secret little bell, tinkling far away like a church in the middle of the countryside) sounded its great alarm bells which, combined with the pain of not being able to bridle Arcadius, made me haggard.

I consulted Papa Totone about his drifting. The old man told me that drifters can't be stopped, to stop one is to kill one. He had to go all the way into the confines of himself, but those confines were so far away. If some did reach it, others did not. Most of them ended up at the Colson Hospital, and often one found their body in the middle of four paths: they had refused to choose, wishing to walk all four roads at the same time, everywhere forever. That would dislodge their guardian angel who would take flight, leaving the drifter's body at a crossroads, quivering with the final extinction of the charm which once possessed it. I was afraid Arcadius would die like that. I went to see some small quimboiseurs who gave me some nonsense to do and which I carefully carried out. I saw many sleeper-women whose dreams held the keys to the universe. I saw Soothwriter ladies whose hand on a feather was the voice of fifteen deadmen. I consulted an African sorcerer who had settled here with a bunch of titles. I saw a Brazilian who braided together high masses for some Mammy Erzilie. But nothing worked. Arcadius came, Arcadius left. To bring him back became utterly difficult and he would disappear sooner and sooner. And there was nothing I could do. Those concrete days became a smothering time. Texaco's cement was stiffening on my body . . .

I found out Arcadius was dead a long time after it happened. He was found drowned at the bottom of the fissure. In his last days, he had begun to follow the rivers' circuit. He would walk up to their source and then go back down with them to the rhythm of their foam. His goal was to melt into their secret in order to reach the sea. Each time my poor darlin' would reach the mouth, he would close his eyes and leap out. Each time he would awaken in a jail of waves. So he would go back up and it would start all over. How many times did he look for this path in the pathless sea? He should have, Ti-Cirique (who gave me the news) confided to me, learned poetry—she opens the paths of the mind—or thrown himself into music, looked at paintings and sculptures. He should have, Carolina Danta (who spent ten months praying over my distress) told me, lived in the extraordinariness of God who fills the only worthy path with light. He should have, said Marie-Clémence (who stood by me when I would stray like a madwoman), talked to others, talked, talked to others, and not addressed his body as if he was digging his hole of misfortune there. He should have, said Iphigénie the Mad (who was glad to come see me at the Colson Hospital), gone to see the psychiatrists, not those from here, but those from France, who without so much as an injection, point out the right path for you. He should have, said Julot the Mangy (after Colson, I ran crying around his hutch, waiting for comfort), run quickly inside himself but not outside . . . But while I nodded, I knew that Arcadius could do nothing about his drifting. The drifter's destiny is to carry us, all together, toward worlds buried in us. He assumed what we were looking for and allowed us to look for it, without our having to suffer. The drifter, he was our desire for freedom in the flesh, our way of living worlds in ourselves, our City maroon.

WRITING-TORN

Arcadius' death propelled me into my notebooks. I wrote. I wrote despair. Writing does well at the end of an edge of oneself. Ti-Cirique no longer had time to read my things. He was overwhelmed by my avalanche of words undoing the alphabet, by my sadness cut up by commas to teach silences; that despondency which inspired my words slamming into each other impaled on hyphens, or these words left unfinished that would open the pages to my Arcadius. I would let my tears dry to burden each *i* with a dot. I would string the beads of my shivers onto threads of ink and crush them waiting for them to bloom in my closed notebooks. I would tie together the memories of my Esternome and my Idoménée, two daydreams about Basile, three musings about Nelta, seven thoughts on my Arcadius, and I grated them together like manioc, making ink from the tears I cried. I wrote haikais colder than seventeen coffin nails, plowed lines bitter as toad gall. I wrote dictionary words which popped out of me like a deadman's clots and left me more anemic than a cow hanging at a slaughterhouse. I wrote feelings which mingled verbs the way sleeper-women do. I wrote colors like Rimbaud having visions. I wrote melancholy which reinforced mine. I wrote blinking howls which made my ink run by. I wrote things involuntary, coming out from God knows where like frightened she-dogs . . . I spoke of it to Ti-Cirique to tell him that writers are mad to live out such things in their heart; he would tell me that today's writers don't go through such things any more: they've lost the primal drive of writing which comes out of you like necessity, which you wrestle (forever alone), your life getting in a tangle with death, in the holy inexpressible. And out of that kind of drama, no one can make a profession. Oiseau de Cham, are you a writer?

One more misery: I began to drink alone. My soul was sliding down to the bottom of Neisson bottles. I would hide them in the hutch's holes, and drink at night, straight from the bottle, until I rolled under my bed or started to read my notebooks over in a loud and sinister voice which anguished Texaco. Deep down in my drunkenness, I found *the rum's Word* that all rummies[1] know. Like them, I began to speak of the bottle as a friend whose arrival illuminates life, I gave it thirty-two nicknames (darlin' of course, bosom friend, my host-at-120-proof, my manna, my sweet-spring, my pleasure titty,

---

[1]Rum had watered our stories; around tafia, cocomerlo, holland gin (my Esternome had told me so) we had developed the discourse of malice; on the plantation, the békés doused us with rum to drown our sufferings; after the Abolition, they had done the same to compensate for the absence of wages; in the market towns and in City, the mulattoes did politics with an open bar for partisans; loyalty to so-and-so was comforted with rum, and we would sing for him, we would fight for him in the floods of his rum; and in the bars at noon, that holy hour of punch, the circle around the rum would feed the word; the Creole tongue kept a part of that spirit which I found in myself—intact.

Painsuckingsyrup . . .), I wrote non-lost songs and low-voiced poems for it. As for the rum itself, it became my enemy-companion, my bad luck man, my sweet-faced killer, *killed my mother, killed my daddy, will kill me too, but then everybody dies* . . . How many Creole words were coming back to me like that . . . ! how many sentences, how much nonsense, how much despair stampeding . . . ! Rum philosophy lightens up the morning, makes the day take off, lets you curse God the Devil the békés misfortune. It transforms you into a ball (taking away your vertical equilibrium) so that people say that you're *Bombed*. It helped you take off, was as useful as a third leg, aroused your life by stirring it up with death, and accompanied you even beyond death: there's not one blackman who hasn't requested that his tomb be a barrel of rum and that the songs, prayers, and tears be of the same ilk. In that alcoholic fever, wrecked deep down, I was Creole—and disgusted by that because it was man's thing to think . . .

A blackwoman who drinks is a great shame: more so than a man, she abdicates before life, slumps her arms, loosens her belt, wallows in mud. A woman who drinks is a swine who flies her soul like a kite . . . She lets go . . .

> But the city is danger. When she is not kneaded like an old memory, carefully amplified, her logic is inhuman. A desert is born there beneath the mechanical joy of neon and the reign of automobiles. Once absorbed, Texaco will be ruled by order. Martinique, the island, will be quickly swallowed. The Creole urban planner must from now on restart new trails, in order to arouse *a countercity in the city*. And around the city, *reinvent the countryside*. That's why the architect must become a musician, sculptor, painter . . .—and the urban planner a poet.
>
> NOTES OF THE URBAN PLANNER TO THE WORD SCRATCHER.
> FILE NO. 14. SHEET XVIII.
> 1988. SCHŒLCHER LIBRARY.

THE BÉKÉ'S SWAN SONG

The béké moved out around that time. The concretization of Texaco, the recent hurricane which had mistreated his things, the police's exhaustion, and without a doubt, many other exigencies made the tankers come less and less into the quay, then stop coming, made Texaco's reservoir tanks rarely fill up, and soon the trucks would appear in the evening only to park there. Day after day, equipment was carted off to other sites behind Cité Dillon. Oh, the béké still protected his space with the same ferocity, but you could feel that his heart wasn't in it any more. He had cursed us out so much that he had become an old, close enemy. He himself had gotten on in years. He had lost some of his mane, his skin was stained with spots, and his brick-red hands shook a bit. I was hardly surprised to see him show up before me one day and refuse, just like all békés, to enter when he had to come near a black person's hutch; he nevertheless accepted a chair and sat with me by the door. We remained silent. The gaggle of insults I reserved for him was going through my head; I suppose, the same thing was happening with him. He ogled around him. The baffled eyes from the hutches around weighed heavily on our shoulders. He seemed flabbergasted to see the incredibly dense web of construction around my hutch. Evidently, people had settled *around me:* a living space bigger than the others made my home the nucleus of Upper Texaco. Seeing a béké from so close up was a novel thing for me. What my Esternome had told me about it plaintively went through my head, words which will always raise a cold stonework between myself and any béké.

Suddenly he began to rattle on, all to himself like an old blackman at the market. His words flew all around me like little lassoes. He did not look at me. He spoke to me of the béké hierarchy based on money, name, the date of the family's arrival. He spoke to me of the old papa-békés who led the fate of their tribes without even leaving their lands. He spoke to me of the big central factories which shattered the plantations and of the Saint-Pierre catastrophe which had razed everything. He told me how these phenomena had fattened up the guava-békés, deflated the big-time ones, and given rise to bizarre inheritances and sudden aristocracy; how the wars had made the backhanded békés rich by soaking up their rum production; how the wheel of fortune had turned to leave the great families only their disputable ancientness; henceforth, a very clear genealogy, without any dubious holes, exacted the highest respect from all, more than the rustle of money in a register, *respect,* madame. He explained to me how the rise of the mulattoes had bonded his caste by forcing it to fight on the political scene (though the whites would give the mulattoes rum, land, coins, the latter would always get greedier); then how they retreated into import-export, into the loophole subsidies and the commercial luck of our corporate welfare life. The caste was now tied through a web of companies where young békés who did not yet know their ABC's held the good jobs; it was also tied by the meticulous culture of surviving in the Negro Ocean, threatened from all sides. They kept their racial purity and led the same existence as always; by living on the inaccessible shores of the François Bay, they only left their yachts for sandbanks in the middle of the sea where they savored their shaken-up champagne on floating trays. The blackman was their brother but never their brother-in-law and God help whoever broke that rule. He would be rejected everywhere (like in the old days when the slaver captain threw a negro in the sea), and could only turn to exile to save his honor. He confided to me that today one had to know how to marry and marry off one's children, the only way of climbing up the strata of the caste, to leave behind the bottom rungs of the ladder and reach for the top ones, to get rid of pockets with holes for some full pockets, to sacrifice your youth for the magical dust of age-old families. He sang his little song for me, about the béké woman who manned the watchtower, how it was tenable for a male béké to have blackids out of wedlock, but it was an impossible crime for a béké woman to give away her belly to anything other than the construction of their fragile white skiffs in our dark ocean. The woman is the one who held everything together, ensured the passage from one shore to the other; it was more or less difficult to get her hand in marriage depending on whether her hair was fair, her skin translucent, and on whether her eyes brought the azure of nobility from afar. His own family had juggled plantains, flowers, rum, a little bit of market gardening. He had chosen oil despite the disapproving eyes, but he saw its limitless future, and he would soon get his break because he knew how to marry well and how to marry off his children well. He told me they were henceforth as powerful as in the plantation days, on the agriculture front as well as in the firms, the hotel business, and the service industry; that their children had understood they had to study as hard as these mulattoes and much better than the blacks, that they were learning economics, management, marketing, and were leaving us all the literature crap, that they were also leaving us, since you seem to care about it so much, that foul heap of City, so as snuggle up along the shores, out of reach, where the lawn stretches up against the waves . . . Then he got up. I hadn't been able to put in a word during his soliloquy. While he went away with his slouched back, I understood he had come to see up close the one who had vanquished him, and remind her that the war was much larger and that on that level he was not losing and never would. So as he was reaching his jeep parked at the bottom of the slope, I howled, laughing: *Sacré Vié-isa-lope, man ké senyen'w yon sé jou-a*[1] (Hey old bastard, I'll kill you one of these days) . . . He called out to me, *Balai-senti, sé mwen ki ké pityé'w* . . . (Smelly broom, I'll prick you first . . .) and started up his motor, looking like he was leaving for good.

MEDICINE-POEM

Texaco's hutches then bloomed in broad open concrete. That brought rapture but also spread a vague fear of the next police on-

---

[1] [Blasted ole basta'd, I'll bleed you one of these days.]

slaught. Because the concrete was more expensive, heavier, more cumbersome, once destroyed it was a disaster from which it wasn't that easy to get back on your feet. Everyone, as their hutches became more solid, began to ward off police raids with fingers crossed facing the rising sun, with drops of water splattered on the walls, three times on the right, seven times on the left, and thirty-three times in front. In the face of such turmoil, I managed to get a little chapel built out of the cliff, and I collected some coins to get us a small Virgin Mary statue which we set up with great ceremony and which deep down in myself I dedicated to my Arcadius.

My shack remained the same, with its share of asbestos, tin, and its crate wood leprosy, as if my time had stopped. Adieu, I told myself, adieu, I'm leaving, I'm leaving, as if to put out the life still rising in me. When you oppose it, you realize that life is both in us and well outside of us. Like an inaccessible light scattered in our flesh, everywhere and nowhere, a law unto itself, outside of the spirit. I would say Adieu, adieu, I'm leaving, but she wouldn't move, still as an old cat that a broom does not scare any more. So more and more I took refuge in my notebooks and my nightly rum. I no longer participated in Texaco's progress, intervening only to settle some squabbles, give out advice, and complete such or such a file still dragging in the courts.

It was around that time that the lamentations bubbled up. We still didn't exist. We had no electricity, no water, no address, we could get neither the television nor the telephone blooming in City. The luckiest ones could afford a generator, and here and there a small light shone. A nightly gathering grew up around whoever had been able to get a television. A feeling of true pain struck the women who felt the years go by without going anyplace. With our homes built in concrete we began to feel the need for certainties and for conveniences which, strangely enough, we would sorely miss all the sudden. I organized many meetings of a defense committee to which the men came, dragging a trouble or two. In vain we discussed, trying to figure out what to do. The men didn't talk, they grumbled about how life wasn't as easy as gulping down a bowl of mashed wild arrowroot. The women cursed out the universe, demanded everything for everyone, invoked De Gaulle, Bissol, Césaire and sometimes went back all the way to Lagrosillière. I, my head sunk in thoughts of Arcadius, listened to them like a sleepwalker and proposed nothing. Ti-Cirique, secretary of the defense committee, even asked me, What do I write, President? . . . And I would say: Write what you want, write what you want, I'm too tired . . .

This attitude probably prompted him to read poems to me. He came regularly to my shack to continue this literary therapy. He read me Arthur Rimbaud's *Le Bateau ivre* to awaken my freedom, read me Baudelaire to contain my pain, read me Apollinaire to dilute my distress, read me Leconte de Lisle to rouse in me exaltations he called automatic, read me Saint-John Perse to take stock of the world in the rambling seaspray, he read Faulkner to show me the dark disorders in the head-depths of men, he got me to accompany James Joyce in Dublin's City where the infinite was being envisioned, read me Kafka to throw the world off balance, then he read me Césaire, the *Notebook of a Return to the Native Land,* in order to take heart in the Beast's convulsions, the prophecies, the Major General's verbal heights and the magic of words which flew from a tomtom. A sentence suddenly took possession of me. I asked him to repeat it for me. Then I took the book from him and read by myself, without understanding a word, letting myself be carried by the invocatory words that turned my blood nègre.

At the next meeting, I had regained the matador demeanor, the straight back, the steady eyes, the clear voice and sharp movements that were mine. I proposed a plan which everyone adopted. We were to pay a visit to Césaire, not to the town council where his dogs kept watch, but at his home, on the road to Redoute. There I would speak to him about getting us water, electricity, a path over the mud,

solid steps, cement scuppers. The thing was voted through by the
women (the men thinking us basically crazy but avoiding opposing
me). The next day as soon as the sun rose, a dozen of us gathered—
four women, nine men including Ti-Cirique who was trembling and
carrying his Negritude books to get them signed. We arrived at five
in the morning before the gate of his wood house, some sort of Big
Hutch, surrounded by a garden, a little dull, bushy, full of silent
shadows and tranquillity. I pushed the gate, it was open. A yellow
light was on inside. Since there wasn't any doorbell, I stepped forward first, followed by the women. The men stood at the gate calling
after us that we were "no-good to go into someone's house like
that." Ti-Cirique refused to take another step forward and lost his
one chance to get his Negritude books signed. We advanced toward
the silent house, hearts pounding. I felt my legs turn to mush. I
didn't know what to do, nor what I had planned to ask for, but
Marie-Clémence, Sonore, Néolise Daidaine trusted me, convinced
that no matter what I would stand tall before Papa Césaire.

I cried out knock-knock, no one answered. We waited then we
began to move toward the veranda. And suddenly, good lord, we
saw Césaire, sitting there, alone, at the tail of the wee hours, looking
at a banana tree (some old pathetic hougan*) shine a violet sex from
deep down in the garden. He gave a start when his eyes fell on us. I
thought I saw a gleam of disquiet in his eyes. We stood stunned, so
did he, then I saw a quiver of irritation in his eyelids:
—What are you doing here . . . !?
I felt that he was going to chase us off. They said he was capable of
shattering the pillars of the world with his holy fury. I didn't know
what to do any more, nor what to say. I couldn't stay there, arms
heavy, mouth open, looking at him like I was some duh-duh-um in a
room at the poorhouse. I invoked my Esternome, Papa Totone, the
Mentohs. Then I remembered the sentence in the *Notebook* that Ti-
Cirique had read me many times before and which I had read again
by myself; so I recited it to him, with all the energy in the world:

— . . . and room there is for all at the rendezvous with conquest and we now know that the sun revolves around our earth, lighting the parcel that only our will has fixed and that any star shall plummet from sky to earth at our limitless command . . .

I saw him calm down. He approached, shook our hands, made us come onto the veranda, and sat with us: What do you want to ask me? So then, before my petrified comrades, I asked him for running water for our schoolchildren who have to haul buckets every morning, I asked him for electricity for our children losing their eyesight over books yellowed by kerosene lamps, I asked him for a way to come in and out of Texaco without having to beg to use the béké's gate . . . I asked him for a school, I panhandled for a bit of that City life . . . At the end of the inventory of our miseries (he probably heard the same things every day at the town council), he lifted up his hands meaning to say he couldn't do much, that Texaco was outside the city limits, that it was all very complicated but that he would see and do his best. When it was time to go, hesitating, he held me back:

—Tell me, Madame Laborieux, have you read the *Notebook* or is it just a quotation that . . .

—I read it, Monsieur Césaire . . .

He must not have believed me.

Listening to that great lady's last words, a shiver ran through me: in a few years, *more than half of humanity will face, under similar conditions, what she calls City.*

NOTES OF THE URBAN PLANNER TO THE WORD SCRATCHER.
FILE NO. 12. SHEET XXIII.
1988. SCHŒLCHER LIBRARY.

HOPING FOR THE MESSIAH

We left him at around six-thirty: we'd met with him for some ten minutes. For twenty-six weeks Ti-Cirique lamented his remaining by the gate. Thanks to our intervention we obtained running water for

Texaco. What's more, the city council services came to unload rocks onto the mud, to cement paths, set steps molded from our prints which furrowed the slopes. Sweet days . . . A trip to the city council was all we had to do to get a voucher for gravel, scrap iron, tin sheets, raw coal, a few bags of cement. The town gave us a lot and we returned the favor at each election. Texaco lifted a concrete face to City; its scrap iron pile no longer knelt to the juvenile height of our fruit trees.

But, as he climbs up the tree, the macaque is never happy with his fate: more committee sessions were demanded of me to study the question of electricity. Ti-Cirique, the secretary, had dispatched thirty-and-three missives to the director of SPEDEM,* but that personage had not even bothered to reply: Texaco did not exist for him. I went down to see him once and tried to force my way into his office. Another time, we went there at night and smeared his walls with our demands. But it was like pissing on a violin to make it play. That's where we were at when the town council assaulted one of Morne Pichevin's quarters, similar to Texaco, with a blind bulldozer. The place was wiped off the face of the earth in a few months. With great anxiety, I asked Ti-Cirique and Marie-Clémence to drop by after work to gather news so that we could draw lessons from it. But the attack had been so pitiless that I understood (without saying a word to those who looked in my eyes to size up the danger) that against City's next assault we'd have no chance. They must have sensed this from my nervous gestures, from my desire to start up the old system of watches again. They began to tremble like I did in the pit of myself. And we began, in deathly anguish, to wait our turn— having suddenly understood that despite the concrete our Texaco remained a fragile embryo.

Each of our appearances at some counter underlined our nonexistence. The social workers prodded us to move into the pigeonholes of subsidized housing (how would one raise a hen or a pig there?), but rare were those who even considered it. I felt more than anyone else the threat of Texaco getting bulldozed despite our concrete. And, without paying any heed, I began to wait, wait for what? I don't know . . . some sort of sign from the world, an unraveling of the knot in which we struggled . . . An all-powerful Mentoh . . . But I soon let go of that hope: Papa Totone, for whom I went roaming with the goal of obtaining I don't know what word, looked at me smiling like a friendly dummy. He had aged incredibly and looked more than ever like a shriveled cucumber. Only his eyes were intact but he wasn't saying anything. Néolise Daidaine and Carolina Danta then put in our heads the idea of a providential Christ who would spring in front of the bulldozers and would stop their rage. Their ardent faith sank into our helplessness like into a ladle of margarine. Every single one of us, without admitting it, counted on some flight of doves, some halo of light which would send Texaco reeling with the angels . . . I was grateful to them for bringing us that dream. Faith is wonderful because it brings a momentum from inside when everything is petrified. Only Ti-Cirique would rain on that faith parade: at the end of Néolise Daidaine's liturgies (she went around the hutches praying in a loud voice so as to speed up the messianic hour and purify our bitterness with incense), he would step forward to ask: Please free me from one doubt: what color will he be this time, chestnut-blond with blue eyes despite the Judean sun or charter-pale-pink-white like the tourist who comes ashore?

THE TOLL

But more time was passing time, and nothing came of it, nothing seemed to be coming save the police menace. Furthermore, life took a keener toll on me: my flesh was beginning to weigh down, my hands to shrivel like old parchment around nests of veins, my eyes to slowly turn glassy and to look at the world from a growing distance every day. I discovered things unknown to me: stiff bones, algesia, hot flashes. My life-giving blood (once the cause of so much bitter-

ness and which I had dreamt of getting rid of) would disappear for
several months, return flooding only to disappear again, and reappear, dismaying drop by dismaying drop; it was like facing a stubborn enemy. My memory was no longer so good as to remember
yesterday. On the other hand, she did spend her time snooping
around the attic of my life, scraping up charred bits of lost memories, scraps that would catch the eye of hungry rats. I began to *remember*, to live within recollections brought back by smells . . .
fleeting moments in the company of my Idoménée . . . the air of City
streets . . . sounds from the Quarter of the Wretched . . . sugar-apple
smells . . . a collier-chou . . . hot coffee . . . burnt wood . . . a new
shoe . . . faces . . . people . . . gestures . . . drops of water from an
eye . . . my life was but the bag of a syrian, a bag which was being
shaken out onto the sidewalk. I wandered through its contents,
choked by the dust of years. I would pull out of it (during a weak
lull) such or such dead, dull, moldy object, which brought me nothing but inexpressible melancholy—and that lightness which seeps
into your bones to get them used to leaving this world. I stroked
memories I suspected of being painful; I touched them with the in-
credulity with which one would pet a domesticated wild possum.
My nails grew yellow (not transparent) and I didn't feel like cutting
them. I just used them to claw my way through books I could no
longer read (but I had read them so much that just going over the
torn pages with my nails stirred up a myriad of feelings which, in my
poor twilight, raised a sun of pleasure beneath my eyes).

Bumps in the night: I would feel birth pangs, unknown but familiar,
seize my belly. After hours of violent contractions under my pillows,
I would give birth to humongous voids which left me crushed. I
would feel my belly bulge with unspeakable things, and let myself be
moved by it until it would collapse like a dead crab's hole and leave
me panting with bitterness. I would sweat buckets for nothing. I
would shake from being licked by chills which came from God
knows where. Sometimes it got so hot that I would have to open up

my hutch and breathe in the world. My skin began to shrink around me. My full figure collapsed. I watched my boniness take up wandering. At other times, for whole months, I would be round again, swollen everywhere, as if the little water I drank slipped right under my skin. Then I would deflate again and hug my bones. I felt my papaya curl up into itself, stiffen a little more, less vibrant, and I would have to go pee every five minutes. I had backaches, hip aches, pains in the hand. It was more and more difficult for me to do my cleaning jobs. The social worker finagled me some welfare papers in the name of God-knows-who, and so I collected some change which compensated me for my exhaustion at the jobs. Behind my hutch I had my little Creole garden, my hen cage and my two rabbits; that allowed me the sweetness of meat once in a while—but most of the time I just completely forgot about them, so they would screech-lord-help until Ti-Cirique brought them his scraps. Every day Texaco's fishermen would bring me a half-calabash of red snapper or conch flesh which I seasoned with mechanical gestures or which I forgot in the half-calabash on the table where the flies, now warned, would come for their feast. My nights would sometimes become stagnant; I would watch them without finding sleep. My head became a place of disorder. I had to hold it with my two hands until it all went away like fever shivers. My heart would jump over nothing. I had to stay in one place to hear it flailing and look for a remedy. I had the feeling I was shrinking, that I was less tall, less straight, less slender. Fatigue accompanied me on all my visits around Texaco or through City. I ate twice-nothing (no longer finding any appetite in my still blood), and drank by habit or mechanically. I was getting old.

My Esternome used to say something about a slow surprise. This was worse: a *motionless* surprise which would hit you with its beams day after day. I clearly saw time going by in a thousand ways around me: Ti-Cirique's wrinkles, his way of holding books close to his eyes, his mania of always speaking alone and repeating himself, of not listening any more, his distaste for new books and his anchor-

age in two-three books constantly reread. His silhouette became
stooping, and his voice would suddenly become so strained that he
would stop talking to listen (more surprised than all of us) to the extinction of that strange noise in the depth of his throat. It became
more and more difficult for him to attend the meetings of his Haitian brothers in Sainte-Thérèse; he stayed in Texaco, pierced by
exile, with his ear pricked up by the sea in the hope of catching a
sigh from Haiti. As for Marie-Clémence, she was losing her innocence, her tales now rang bitter and sometimes contained even doses
of tittle-tattle: old age had transformed her into a Texaco she-devil
and more than a few expected her to take off in the direction of the
Doum. From time to time, she reappeared just as she used to be, oh
my dear Marie-Clémence, then would disappear again under the rising gall of age . . . oh my dear . . . Sonore, the youngest, saw herself
submerged beneath her own children and was whitening without
even waiting her turn. Néolise Daidaine began to put on weight until
she could not walk without a sighing cane. Iphigénie the Mad left
her community clinic and cared for her madness by eating the fatty
soil.[1] The men (flighty common-law concubines, unstable fiancés),
once so evanescent, took root in the hutches where they could be ca-
joled. Julot the Mangy, he dodged time, I mean his ferocity remained
intact, only his body was drying up like a mummy around his eyes.
Valiant damsels and fellows took up the torch, peopled our meetings, and were beginning to take the Quarter. But I felt outside of all
that. At the turn of a joint, I was myself discovering the extent to
which my body had gotten used up little by little and could no
longer keep up with the chaos in my head. I was forgetting what I
had to do, I no longer kept my promises, I tended to remain sitting
by the hutch, with my twenty-six notebooks on my knees like a treasure, without even rereading them as I had so often before but just
keeping them on my knees, feeling their presence, their account of
love, pain, happiness, and life. Texaco had gotten stuck in its mo-

---

[1][An allusion to the clay addiction which afflicted many slaves.]

mentum and I was getting old despite the secret name I would howl with great silences.

THE LAST SHARK CATCHER

It's about that time that Iréné the shark catcher—my old man—appeared among us. A huge whale had just washed up before Texaco. It seemed to have lost its north, and had followed the skiff of one of our fishermen returning home. Beholding a whale chasing him broke the guardian angel of our brave fisherman. He docked sloppily and, without saying anything to anyone, went to church unseen, hoping to confess no-one-really-knows-what. Then he changed profession, became sexton somewhere. He also left Texaco for the deep pocket of Balata, behind God's back, far from all waters, with no sea, no river; he lived there for a long time with his unhappy wife and children who were forced to read him books on whales. Long after his wife was dead and his children had become people, he was found drowned in the sweat of a nightmare; with the picture of Captain Cousteau right next to Christ's; with the whale books in ashes around him.

The whale got washed up in the muddy water of the mangrove swamp, between skiffs and stilts. It remained there, puffing, shivering, fluttering, until it no longer budged when the shells that were hooked to its skin suddenly got wise and jumped off. I had been fetched, because two-three mad fellows wanted to cut it up and go sell it to the Petit-Paradis bourgeois. Others ambitioned to make an enormous blaff out of it in a manioc kettle that they were already lugging around. Only my slow-paced coming (they saw me less and less, except when there was danger, and often, in their respectful eyes, I could see the distances born of my great age) managed to stop them. I forbade them to touch the animal which was probably sick with who knows what misery, and I (reluctantly) had the police alerted. An inspector dragged himself around the animal without really knowing what to do, besides measuring it and taking pictures. The sun hit it. Its coral smell turned into a dead moon stench, then into a smell of medusa and gangrened sea urchins, then of foul farts and then of cod liver, then into a rot unknown to Christians. Before such a stench, the prefect had to mobilize the services of the Army. The Army came with chainsaws which soon got lost in the monster's tissue (Ti-Cirique had called it Globicephalus, which right away became its nickname) and lifted pissing pieces of rot for nothing. So the soldiers remained in our company, looking at Globi infecting the nose of the universe, when suddenly the deputy chief officer, somehow touched by grace, got the commando units keeping watch over Cuba to come. The commando units burst in like in a war movie. They tied a few explosives everywhere around the dreadful thing. They freed Globi from the mud of the mangrove swamp, chained it, and took it out to the middle of the harbor where without further ado they exploded it. The carrion dispersed into a multicolored bouquet which right there and then attracted two hundred and fifty sharks of all kinds, including a hateful species of black shark with eyes from hell which made us think we'd been cursed forever.

Sharks began to hunt around the harbor. They raised up their maws to watch us along Texaco's banks. No one dared come near the shores any more. Ti-Cirique and Marie-Clémence woke me up in the middle of the night: somewhere around their hutch, they had run into a shark out on a stroll asking for a light. Julot the Mangy came to speak to me of a nightmare with sixteen rows of teeth. Texaco and Rive-Droite's fishermen no longer dared bring their skiffs into the water: they had seen jaws swallow their fish traps, rip their nets, twist the propellers off of smoking motors. The gendarmes had come to kill them with machine guns, but *Zounds good god and good evening,* the corpse of each shark attracted ten more, *sonofabitch!* . . . , so much so that they abandoned that problem to us and left us with that cloud of selachians which tracked down our garbage, our dreams, and the flesh of our soul. That's when Julot the

Mangy (he had tried to frighten off these furies by standing on the edge of the sea and listing all of his attributes) called on Iréné.

He went to get him himself from Anses d'Arlets, explained to him the state we were in. We saw Iréné's skiff drift right up against Texaco. Along the way, he would bring back hooked sharks, knocking them out with a club and throwing them into his skiff. He would re-bait his coppers, row out twenty-two meters, and let his skiff drift in order to bring in his lines loaded like plum trees. When he came ashore amid a general hurrah, he'd have thirty sharks of all kinds aboard. He would go sell them at the market—except for the black sharks which no one can sell to anyone (not even to the worst athe-ists), which he would eat alone in the company of Julot who would make the cross over himself with each mouthful and spit out the thirteenth.

Iréné stayed at Julot's. Every day he would leave for the harbor, bringing back dozens of sharks and accumulating a small fortune. Soon the sharks were fewer in number. He had to go look for them further and further off. But he'd taken a liking to Texaco, to being around City, to the fame which spilled the crowd onto the shores of the canal when he brought his skiff up the steps to the fish market. So he settled among us, in the abandoned hutch of the fisherman made cuckoo by the Globicephalus. He stayed there for eight days until he came to live with me—to live in my heart.

He brought me slices of white shark every day, which he sometimes took the time to have stewed for me according to the secret gnosis of great fishermen. We would sometimes tarry together, having lunch, him telling me his memories as a fisherman at Anses d'Arlets. He fas-cinated me, reminding me of my Esternome. Seeing him allowed me to imagine my dear papa in Saint-Pierre's harbor during the time of Ninon's zombie. He probably perceived this fascination but seemed conquered by my age, my authority, my glow, my legend of ballsy woman. It somewhat astonished him that I did not fear him, since, as soon as his fishing was over, everyone avoided him. People (apart from Julot the Mangy, but the latter was as opaque as factory grease) don't get along very well with a strange fellow feared by sharks. In Ti-Cirique and myself, he found company. On the basis of his stories, Ti-Cirique would poeticize the shark species and read us his verses as they came to him. But Iréné and I often remained alone in the evenings, talking, talking, talking . . .—until one full moon night he awakens old sensations in me, and I lead him to my bed with a firm hand, while he was already sighing *Till tomorrow Marie-So . . .*

Before he became a shark catcher, Iréné was simply a fisherman, but he was bored stiff between the hooks he hauled up in Miquelon, without a single glorious catch. He was a fisherman like his father had been, but he faced the sea with a spirit looking beyond this world in which he wasn't at ease. He was the only one to hear (at certain hours of the day, when the sun smashes the waves with a scintillation of salt) the conches' unsettling song, the hiccup of corals coming up to the surface, the algae's drone, a sort of deserted uproar in the water. He would hear a throbbing rise out of the blue-black troughs, terrifying the sea hogs. He felt the furrowing currents of long green hair and sunken eyes. This wasn't an ordinary fisherman, because he soon brought back strange fish (unknown to memories), which of course he couldn't sell, because how do you stew a winged fish with scales sticking out like feathers? What else besides fritters can you do with transparent sardines with a beating hearts you can see? How can you think of making a blaff out of a fish with flesh shining like the shepherd's star? Iréné had to resign himself to bringing something else, and he found nothing else but a mystery of sharks which his small boat attracted. They threw themselves against his skiff, stretched secular echoes with their jaws, raised Masses of foam, or else swirled with cries he thought only he perceived. An old Carib fisherman revealed to him that he, Iréné, was a bit of "sea flesh," that his skin had an octopus smell, that his blood crowded his pores with the sigh of morays or of a shoal of red crabs stirred by the moon. Sharks liked that, and they came toward him (or toward whatever his hands had touched) like one comes to a feast. So he, calmly, began to fish them. He was able to live like this without too many cares and to dream tranquilly atop the wavy infinite.

Iréné's presence made me young again. I began to eat, sing gloria, and stretch in the sun. I felt my flesh regain its sweetness, my papaya awakening. My heart echoed rhythms and my eyes lit up. I perceived life's colors, and some perfumes became pleasant to me. The sale of his sharks allowed us to buy two-three bricks, a bag of cement, sand, and other materials, and we were beginning to cement the backs of the hutch. My legend grew: Texaco's matadora more than ever, I had tamed the monster-killer.

CHRIST'S ARRIVAL

Time went by like that, in the profuse anxiety over a police onslaught which seemed a long time coming. If they're so late, Ti-Cirique would say looking at how much our Texaco overran the mangrove swamp and covered the cliff, it must be that they are mustering. They will pounce like Tontons Macoutes, etcetera-thousands of them. And all we are will come to an end.

That is why we looked on with horror when the town council bulldozers entered Fond Populaire, pushed back the cliff, and filled up the shore with the debris until they built a road which passed through us in the direction of Pointe-des-Nègres, exposing us to the stares of City and its cars. Everyone huddled around me, wanting to know why, to get answers which the municipal workers could not give them ("The sign says Pénétrante West and it goes through there, that's all we can tell you" . . .). I didn't have a better answer, so I convened new meetings of the defense committee, whose fever anes-thetized anxiety.

That road, Ti-Cirique decreed at the two-hundred-twentieth gather-ing, would provide the logistics for a definitive police assault. They will come with bulldozers and it will all be over for us. They're going to rub our guts into the asphalt. Boil our livers for the paint to draw the lane markings. They're going to thinly slice our skin and put it out to dry Nazi-style and make small lamps out of it to reign over their roads. They're going to nail our teeth onto their pedes-trian crossings. The wood of our hutches will go for closing off side-walks and for making shelves at the police stations. Our eyelids will keep the glare away from their red lights, forever unblinking. He cited to us Dante in his infernos, the Egyptians' Book of the Dead, Gilgamesh's epic where Outa-Napistim describes a cataclysm, the Veda from some India of old which he read from the Sanskrit, Aeschylus' Supplicants, Roland's heroism when he was broken at Roncevaux, Rutebeuf's lament, Hugo and his nightmares, Lautréa-mont in his delirium . . . , and trembled thinking that he saw the zombies of Tontons Macoutes in green coming toward him. So there was a sort of dreadful nervousness. Fearful of attracting too much attention, no one dared question the town council. We were prepar-ing ourselves to suffer what we had known and to be reborn from the storms yet again. We were ready. My voice trembling with age, held together as best I could, I told them that the only thing to do was to wait and fight. That we had to last while waiting for some-thing to happen. But what? I didn't know: I was awaiting the event without knowing what it would be.

In that atmosphere, the fellow we would call the Christ appeared. He was hit by the stone which we thought had Julot's name written all over it. When they brought him to me, I told him of Texaco like I just told you, from my Esternome to my Iréné. He was sitting before me, finishing my aged rum, closing his eyes sometimes over scraps of pain, opening them to look at me so intensely. When I was quiet, his eyes shone a wee bit. Now that he knew the bulk of the stories, I told him he could unleash his bulldozers and raze all, and destroy all, but that he should know now that we will stand, up front, me first, as from time immemorial.

He remained silent, then went out into Texaco after having squeezed my hands. He strolled around Upper Texaco, then Lower Texaco, examining each hutch, touching the stilts, evaluating our spaces on this edge of City. Leaving, returning, staying still for whole hours like a box turtle in the hot sun. He often went to the Doum to try to talk to Papa Totone who had disappeared, stopping before each vestige of a history (our history) the inscription of which he seemed to be looking for in the world. Sometimes, I would go to my window to watch him without his knowing, and always Ti-Cirique kept an eye on him in order to establish a detailed report for me. Then, the Scourge disappeared for many months leaving our anxiety intact. But the testimonies of all the things that had happened during his coming were being tied together. Sonore finally had work. Iréné had faced a monstrous shark in the harbor which he succeeded in bringing up whole the next day and which he sold by five-kilo slices (this brought us enough to finish our house in concrete). Julot the Mangy had a dream in which his cruel mother reached out and caressed him (the only time in all his life). Néolise Daidaine sighted the Virgin Mary wrapped in madras under her lemon tree. Marie-Clémence heard celestial murmurs tell her tales from all over the Caribbean, in Creole, English, Spanish, and French, and a vigor with which to spread all these stories came over her as well . . . Ti-Cirique had Jacques Stephen Alexis come, in the midday sun, to borrow some salt and reveal to him that a lavalas[1] would wash away the filth of the Duvaliers . . . An agreement of strange little facts, sudden small

---

[1][Literally, "flood," the popular rebellion that swept the dictator "Baby Doc" Duvalier from power in Haiti.]

joys, minute happiness, of changing fortunes which made this coming the point of departure for a new era. That's why the Scourge
seemed less threatening and why we began to call him *Christ*, without giving it much thought, and hoped that he would come back
with *the Good News* of which we knew nothing.

THE SECRET NAME

The E.D.F.* appeared one day along the Pénétrante West, stuck its
poles, and plugged us some electricity. It was an unblemished joy.
Later we saw men going by who were watching, studying before disappearing, but this time we were trustful: somewhere in city council
the Christ was working for us. When he reappeared one day and
made for my hutch, I knew he was bringing me the latest news: City
from now on was taking us under its wing and admitted our existence. And indeed, he told me that City would integrate Texaco's
soul, that everything would be improved but that everything would
remain in accordance with its fundamental law, with its alleys,
places, with its so old memory which the country needed. He told
me that he would help each hutch become livable, in accordance
with the resident's wishes and working from its original structure.
He told me that Texaco would be rehabilitated where it stood and in
the minds of people, just like it happened for the impenetrable mangrove swamps. I told him that it wouldn't be easy, that there would
be gnashing, tears, refusals, that we were used to fighting, crying
out, and that we were going to fight alongside him to advance what
he was proposing for us, but that the essential thing was that we
would enter City by his side, rich with what we were and strong
with a legend that was becoming clearer and clearer for us.

While he was talking, my secret name echoed in me like a Latino
trumpet. I felt a pride rise from far away. I even got the feeling that
somewhere my Esternome was beginning to smile, that my
Idoménée was opening wide eyes full of light, and that our miseries

(blossoming with so much courage over these many years) were wilting one by one like plants without water. I thought that it was nothing but an old woman's excitement, but the Christ (to whom I couldn't help but tell it) told me he felt the same elation in each of his bones. So I was happy.

Finally, I told him that I felt old. That one day when he would return, I would no longer be there. I asked him a favor, Oiseau de Cham, a favor which I would like you to note and remind him of: in the name of my Esternome, in the name of our sufferings, in the name of our battles, let no one, across the centuries and centuries, ever remove the name of this place, TEXACO, by the intangible law of our highest memories and the more intimate law of my secret name which—you may know now—is none other than that one there.

RESURRECTION

(not in Easter's splendor

but in the shameful anxiety

of the Word Scratcher

who tries to write life)

Because historical time was stabilized in the void, the writer must contribute to restoring its tormented chronology, that is, to unveiling the fecund liveliness of a recommenced dialectic between Antillean nature and culture.

Because historical memory was too often crossed out, the Antillean writer must "dig" into that memory, beginning with the some-times latent traces he has found in the real.

EDOUARD GLISSANT

I discovered Texaco while looking for the old blackman of the Doum. All had spoken of him as if he were the last of the Mentohs. I wanted to meet him to collect his secrets (without raising my hopes too high: Mentohs don't speak, and when they do, it's in a language that is too much in the becoming to be intelligible) but I especially wanted him to help me (even with silences) come out of a predica-ment: the death of the storyteller Solibo Magnifique;[1] I was trying to reconstitute the words spoken the night of his death and stumbling into that uncrossable barrier which separates the spoken word from the writing to be done, which distinguishes the writing done from

---

[1]*Solibo Magnifique*—Gallimard Editions, 1988.

the word lost. My impoverished drafts didn't get me anywhere. Defying this poverty, I would tell myself that a Mentoh might be able to indicate to me the essentials of the work a Word Scratcher must accomplish in such circumstances.

Penetrating the Doum, I found it deserted. Abandoned. I had been in so many places of Power, that I had acquired an immediate intuition for them. In my daily life, I detected around me so many cultural ruins in our mute countryside, so many gradual mummifications in the land all around, that I could at any point, before a hutch, a spot, a landscape, a river mouth, perceive a historical presence stricken with staggering wear and tear. The Doum was dead: nothing could be done. A Mentoh of great stature, probably one of the last, had lived at the feet of the ramparts which rose between City[1] and the need for the Doum.

The Mentohs had always mustered our mosaic imaginings. They had imprinted upon them a convergence—a coherence. Out of the scattering of Carib, African, European, Chinese, Indian, Levantine . . . , they fixed the fibers for a good rope. Faced with City dreams, the maroons had molted into drifters, the storytellers had ceased their telling one by one, only the Mentohs had known how to stay around *(through the word)* probably hoping to spread it into the heart of this new venture, the urban space. But City—through the magic spreading of another imagining, through the erupting uniformization of the world into invincible images—shook them about like old water and used them to the last drop. The disappearance of our Mentohs was revealing (oh silent pain) the domination of our spirit by new means unknown to traditional resistance. The boot,

---

[1] The Creole language does not say *la ville* ["the city"], but rather, *l'En-ville* ["the In-city"]: *Man ka désann an-vil, I ka rété an-vil, Misié sé an-vil, An-vil Fodfwans* . . . [I am going down to city, He lives in city. This fellow is from City, from Fort-de-France]. City thus designates, not a clearly defined urban geography, but essentially a content and therefore a kind of enterprise. And here that enterprise was about living.

the sword, the rifle, or the banking powers of the Occidental Being were no longer a threat to the peoples; the erosion of differences was. Their difference of genius, tastes, emotions . . .—imaginings.

Coming out of the Doum, I *felt* Texaco. That heap of asbestos and concrete was developing very clear vibrations. They came from afar, from the concert of our histories. This place intrigued me. It became fascinating when I was introduced to the one who was to become my Source: an old câpresse woman, very tall, very thin, with a grave, solemn visage and still eyes. I had never felt such profound authority emanate from anyone.

She told me her stories in a persnickety way. Sometimes, though she hid it from me, she had memory gaps, repeated or contradicted herself. At first, I took down her words in one of my notebooks, then I got permission to plug in my bastard of a tape recorder. I couldn't count on that machine but (despite the pauses it added to the silences and the confusion it caused my Source) it compensated for the gaps in my attention. Each time I went to see her, I brought her books on Caribbean history. I also brought her my books which she read with interest despite Ti-Cirique's warnings. I obtained her complete trust once I narrated Solibo's death and let her in on my reconstitution work of the Master's word. This brought me closer to her who had all her life run after her father's word and the rare words of Papa Totone and the morsels of our stories which the wind was sweeping away across the land just like that. That's why she entrusted me with her innumerable notebooks, covered with an extraordinary, fine handwriting, breathing with the gestures, rages, shivering, the stains of a whole life caught in full flight. Confounded before the responsibility of such treasures, I numbered them, notebook by notebook, page by page, I taped the torn pages together, sewed back the loose sheets, and wrapped each one in a plastic cover. Then I deposited them at the Schœlcher Library. From time to time, I consulted them in order to compose what she had told me, to compare what I thought I had heard, and, if need be, correct a voluntary omission, a reflexive lie.

The Source would speak in a slow voice, or sometimes very fast. She mixed Creole and French, a vulgar word with a precious word, a forgotten word with a new word . . . , as if at any given point she were mobilizing (or summarizing) her tongues. Her voice, like that of great storytellers, dipped into *un-clarity*. In such moments, her sentences whirled at a delirious pace and I would not understand squat: the only thing left for me to do was let myself (shedding my reason) plunge into that hypnotic enchantment. Sometimes, she asked me to write a certain sentence just the way she had spoken it, but most of the time she implored me to "fix up" her speech into good French—her fetishistic passion. My literary usage of what she called "her poor epic" was never evident to her. She had a high idea of it but did not perceive the aesthetics. She thought (like Ti-Cirique) that it was to be preserved, but that the writing of stories with so little nobility was a waste of time. She, however, gracefully lent herself to the demands of my work, and even when I contacted the Christ of whom she had spoken to me (an urban planner of great civility at the Fort-de-France town council, apprehending City like a Creole visionary and sharing some precious notes with me), she still spoke to me with frankness about herself, her inmost feelings, her flesh, her body, her loves, her tears, all of that mixed with the life of her Esternome, of her Idoménée, and she would still mark out Texaco's history, her heart bared.

I noted the date of each statement. I numbered the lines to establish some useful cross-references, for my Source never narrated anything in a linear fashion. She stirred together years, men, times, she spent weeks detailing a fact or rehearsing some pathetic misery for me. And I, lost in there, charmed by her word and by her delightful person, spent hours agog at a câpresse whose wrinkles radiated power, whose soul dwelt in epic struggle. I looked at those tear-faded eyes which absorbed the light. I looked at her skin drying up with age, and her voice which came from so far away, and I felt weak, unworthy of all of it, unable to transmit so much wealth. Her memory would go with her like Solibo's, and there was nothing, nothing, nothing I could do except make her talk and put some order into what she churned out. The desire to film her came over me for a second, for it seemed more and more to me that audio-visuals offered new opportunities for oraliture and permitted me to envision a civilization articulated by writing and word. But that required considerable equipment; I feared to arouse deathly silences, frozen gestures, denaturations of her word magnetized by the camera's eye. This being the case, I could only listen, listen, listen, feeling an unsettling drunkenness upon unplugging my tape recorder to better lose myself in her and to live the songs of her word at their deepest, until that November day when I found her dead at the end of her years—her shark catcher hanging on to her. I then found myself crushed by the weight of my task. Poor Word Scratcher . . . you know nothing of what there is to know to buttress the cathedral that death has broken . . .

The wake went on in the traditional manner. Julot the Mangy got a storyteller who withheld his name to come from Anses d'Arlets; two others came on their own from Morne des Esses. I cried with joy at hearing during the night in the heart of Texaco, before a death so immense, this flood of words thrown from so far away, still untouched by City, full of the Hill spirit. I also wept from dismay upon seeing how old the storytellers were and how their voices, isolated from the world, seemed to sink into the earth like a carême rain after which I trotted in vain.

In Texaco, which was being rehabilitated day by day, a listening bureau had been opened. Each inhabitant told social workers, sociologists, architects, of his tastes, desires, needs. All of this was taken into account in the restoration of the hutches, a restoration respectful of the souls of the hutches. The town council had purchased the oil company's space and organized the hutches according to their own logic. Some lawyers reinvented property rights in order to adapt them to the urban swamp: the land belonged to none, causing all a judicial uproar which also begs chronicling. The paint jobs, the new little houses, City's progressive absorption of that magic place returned me to my poor loneliness. I felt more useless than ever, the way I had been behind the coffins of my Source and her shark catcher or before their conch-decorated grave where I still run into Julot the Mangy and Ti-Cirique. Marie-Clémence, Iphigénie the Mad, and Néolise Daidaine are dead too. Of the old guard only Sonore, who works at the town council, remains and is now Texaco's ancient one. But I know her very little.

I reorganized my Source's burgeoning word around the messianic idea of Christ; this idea respected the community's dereliction prior to the urban planner who managed to decipher it. Then I did my best to write down this mythic Texaco, realizing how much my writing betrayed the real, revealing nothing of my Source's breath, nor even the density of her legend. And I was in full agreement with Ti-Cirique's judgment, that "Dear Master," upon my general incapacity which he underlined in lengthy epistles. His sentences did, however, encourage me to continue the scribbling of that magic chronicle. I wanted it to be sung somewhere, in the ears of future generations, that we had fought with City, not to conquer it (it was City that gobbled us), but to conquer ourselves in the Creole unsaid which we had to name—in ourselves and for ourselves—until we came into our own.

MORNE ROUGE,
FORT-DE-FRANCE,
LA FAVORITE,
AUGUST 1987 / JANUARY 1992

AUTHOR'S ACKNOWLEDGMENTS

To Mr. Serge LETCHIMY, whose work in urban planning and whose thoughts have fed these stories—with all my esteem and admiration.

To the writer Dominique AURÉLIA, who allowed me to discover the notion of "l'En-ville" in one of her beautiful texts.

To Mr. Stanley SANDFORD, ex-president of the sport and sociocultural association of Texaco, who decoded for me the inexpressibility of this place—with my infinite gratitude and friendship.

To all the residents of the Texaco Quarter who endeavored to satisfy my impossible curiosities: Mrs. SICOT Mathilde Georges, Mr. RÉNE "Requin" Louison, Mrs. RENÉ Démar Germaine, Mr. LAURENCE "Mano" Emmanuel, Mr. NARDY Georges, Mr. NIRENOLD "Mèt-Wobè" Robert, Mr. ACCUS "Moreau" Guy, and all the others . . . — begging them in advance to forgive me please for not having been able to offer them better—with honor and respect.

P.C.

AFTERWORD

A WORD ABOUT BRINGING CHAMOISEAU'S WORD INTO ENGLISH

There's a well-known novelty button pin with the following gag written in tiny letters: "If you can read this . . . maybe you're standing too close." Some would say, in a similar vein, that if you can read Patrick Chamoiseau's *Texaco,* maybe we overtranslated it. Or at least that may be the feeling of those who see the original as Ti-Cirique does: "a small pea lost in the pod of the monkeying of . . . Creolity." Have we then as translators betrayed the original book by actually making it readable when it can strike so many as opaque? We of course don't think so. Not only because any translated text is already a processed text, that is, text necessarily digested by an intermediary reader who in turn becomes a writer, but also because despite the Babelian ambitions of *Texaco,* Chamoiseau meant for his book to be readable. This is why he provides contexts, explanations, definitions, and translations (especially of any passage or term in the French-based Martinican Creole) in his chronology, text, and footnotes. Though he sometimes fills in his French-speaking readers tongue-in-cheek—after all, he does include two footnotes to describe the men and women who make up the crowd that gathers around the knocked-out "Christ"—Chamoiseau is serious about being read by a broad group of people. That the basic matrix of his text is largely standard written French is the most compelling testimony to this fact.

Given that writing in Francophone Martinique, even today, still mostly means writing in French, the issue of how to translate Martinican reality into literature has its place at the heart of this latest novel by Oiseau de Cham, the character-author, ethnologist-writer, who also calls himself the Word Scratcher (le Marqueur de paroles). Oiseau de Cham distinguishes two ways of approaching this issue: the first is through something I will refer to as Mulatto French for the purpose of this discussion; the second I will call Creole French. And here the terms *mulatto* and *creole* are primarily useful in labeling two distinct relations to language in general and to French more specifically.

Though Mulatto French is, of course, the French acquired by mulattoes in order to facilitate their economic and social climbing, to make "the word" *work* for them, in *Texaco* it also points to a self-administered alienation through language and therefore to a sterile—as the etymology of *mulatto* suggests—linguistic site. Though he does not belong to the mulatto class, Ti-Cirique speaks Mulatto French, that is, a laminated language spoken by the dictionary and by books from France. "More French than that of the French," Mulatto French is one which simplifies, overlooks, disregards Martinican Creole and its reality, in order to achieve correct speech in French. The following lines are telling: "And my Esternome would sometimes cry out: Wô *Ninon tan fè tan, tan lésé tan*[1] . . . , a bit of despair which a milato with a goose quill would have thought to translate as: Oh, Ninon dear, life hasn't really changed . . ." It is this penchant to iron out, to civilize Creole language and reality, to make them fit into the straitjacket of an untouchable standard French, that makes Mulatto French unsuitable as Martinique's written language.

Creole French is the organic opposite of Mulatto French. That much is immediately made clear in *Texaco*, starting with the epigraph on page 9, which establishes the two (fictional) editors of the book—the thick-lensed Haitian Francophile intellectual Ti-Cirique whom the reader is supposed to blame for all the Latinate and

---

1[Oh Ninon, time makes time, time leaves time alone . . .]

heavy-handed editing, and Oiseau de Cham, the courageous field ethnologist who dreams of a living literature—as each other's foils. Unlike Ti-Cirique, Oiseau de Cham dares mess with standard French. He creates a text whose French matrix is scattered with Martinique's flora and fauna, with Carib, Old French, Spanish, English, East Indian, Arabic, and African words, with multiple *Weltanschauungen,* registers, meanings, and word play. Play which strikes both Ti-Cirique and the Texaco Béké as "négrerie," which is why the béké class leaves the "literature crap," as well as "that foul heap of City"—in short, Texaco (both the literary work and the actual site, property of the oil company)—to those squatting at the edge of City, at the fringes of the French language.

In objecting to a Mulatto French rendering of Martinican reality, Chamoiseau objects largely to the *omission* of Creole identities. For though Chamoiseau prefers Creole French as the written language of Martinican reality, he includes Mulatto French in his novel in addition to Creole orality and the many shadings between the two. After all, multivoicedness is at the source of *Texaco,* which is the compilation of (1) excerpts from Marie-Sophie Laborieux's notebooks, which record the words of her father, Esternome, (2) Oiseau de Cham's transcription of Marie-Sophie's reiteration of her story, Texaco's story, as told to "the Christ," the urban planner, (3) Chamoiseau's letters to Marie-Sophie, his "Source," and (4) the urban planner's notes to the Word Scratcher.

But for all its multivoicedness, collage, and foreign smatterings, Patrick Chamoiseau's *Texaco* remains grounded in French—as its 1992 Prix Goncourt attests. In truth, it is a Creole work only in spirit, in that Oiseau de Cham replaces Ti-Cirique's alienating Universality with his homemade Creolity, a literary movement which begins with the awareness of the Creole self. So with an English bursting at a few seams, but English nonetheless, our text tries to remain faithful to Chamoiseau's, to the rapport between Martinican Creole and French in a Creole text with a French matrix. Incidentally, the fact that my husband, Val Vinokurov, an American who speaks almost no French, and I, a Franco-Haitian living in the United States for the past eight years, translated Chamoiseau to-gether only helped us (we hope) rewrite the novel into an English at once supple and communicative of the spirit of Chamoiseau's com-plex literary project. And here I have to stress the words *spirit* and *project,* because, just as it is true that the relationships between French and Martinican Creole are unstranslatable, so are the partic-ulars of genius.

ROSE-MYRIAM RÉJOUIS
PRINCETON, NEW JERSEY / BALATA, MARTINIQUE, 1996

Glossary

affranchi a small special social class consisting primarily of mulattoes who, in pre-revolutionary times, had gained their liberty and developed large economic interests. Under the Code Noir (9.v.) of 1685, they were considered French citizens with all corresponding rights including the right to own slaves.

alizé French name for the Antilles trade winds.

ANPE (Agence Nationale pour l'Emploi) National Employment Agency.

békés white Creoles of Martinique, descendants of old established colonial planter families. Fluent in Creole, they speak accented French.

bel-air (*bélé* in Creole) a song and dance accompanied by Afro-Caribbean percussion.

blaff a spiced fish stew.

bombé serré an intimate slowdance popular in Martinique.

bonda butt, ass. Chamoiseau uses this word to describe a manner of dancing.

boucaut a unit of measurement used for cane on plantations; the quantity of cane needed to produce 500 kg of sugar.

This glossary could not have been of manageable size without Elodie Jourdain's invaluable *Le Vocabulaire du Parler Creole de la Martinique* (Paris: Klincksieck, 1956), which helped me translate many terms directly. Other helpful resources were Lafcadio Hearn's *Two Years in the French West Indies* (New York: Harper & Brothers Publishers, 1890), and the *Dictionary of Afro-Latin American Civilization* by Benjamin Nuñez and the African bibliographic Center (Westport, Conn.: Greenwood Press, 1986).

bwa-kabritt   (lit., wild goat) a loud, enormous cricket.

canari   (Carib word) a large, all-purpose cooking pot.

câpresse   in the French Antilles, the daughter of a mulatto man and a black woman.

carême   (French word for Lent) in the French Antilles, name for the dry season which lasts from January to June. The wet season from July through December is called *hivernage*.

chabin (masc.), **chabine** (fem.)   a light-skinned mixed-race individual, often with blond or reddish hair and black facial features. European name for a kind of sheep produced by crossbreeding a ewe with a billygoat.

chien-fer   a Mexican hairless dog with iron-gray skin, now very rare in Martinique; the most hateful dog in the Creole imagination.

cocomerlo   crude cane alcohol.

collier-chou   a necklace made of several rows of large hollow beads; a long necklace of chased gold or gilt beads wrapped several times around the neck.

commune   an administrative unit. French provinces *(départements)* are divided into communes.

C.R.S.   (Compagnie Républicaine de Sécurité) sometimes spelled phonetically as *seyaress* in the novel, a special national police force used for riot control and during civil unrest.

D.D.A.S.S.   (Direction Départementale de l'Action Sanitaire et Sociale) Department of Health and Social Services.

E.D.F.   (Electricité de France) French Electric Company.

[1]**engagé**   a person who has made a pact with a spiritual power in Afro-Caribbean belief. This pact binds him to fulfill an exacting obligation in return for a fixed reward.

²**engagé**   a bondsman. Indentured servants—sometimes shanghaied—were usually from western France and occasionally from central France, as well as other European countries.

escalin   a Trinidadian sixpence.

fellaghas   (Arab word) partisans fighting for independence during the French colonial period in Algeria. Generally pejorative in Martinique; any positive connotations arose (as with the word "maroon") from recent intellectual movements.

france-whites   recent immigrants in Martinique of European descent.

geste   the French word *geste* means both "gesture" and *geste* as in *chanson de geste,* a collection of epic poems centered around the same hero.

guava-békés   poor rural whites distinguished by rustic manners and a lack of education, speaking Creole rather than French; bumpkins.

Guinea   Creole word for Africa as a whole.

hougan   a voodoo priest.

ka-drum   a large traditional drum made of a quarter-size barrel, usually played with the hands by two drummers.

léwoz   a dynamic ka-drum rhythm; one of the seven ka-drum rhythms particular to Guadeloupe.

loas   African spirits.

mabi   (Carib word) smooth beer made from fermented bark.

madou   lemonade or orangeade made with cane syrup *(jus de batterie).*

madras calendé   a madras tied on the side of the head.

manioc   (also called cassava) a shrubby tropical American plant *(Manihot esculenta)* widely grown for its large, tuberous, starchy roots; the root of this plant, eaten as a staple food in the tropics only after leaching and dry-ing to remove cyanide. Its starch is also the source of tapioca (*American Heritage Dictionary, Standard Edition*). Grated the wrong way, manioc can be poisonous.

Marianne-lapo-figue   (lit., Marianne-banana-peel) a horned female figure dressed in dried banana leaves who often appears during Carnival and who dances in a suggestive way; also, a folktale persona.

matadora   (*matadò* in Creole) "one who triumphs, who wins approval like a matador in the arena" (Jourdain). Current usage: a strong, respected, authoritative woman. "Matadora" is our rendering of Chamoiseau's French invention *femme-matador.*

migan   an old plantation dish made with coarsely mashed breadfruit and other vegetables.

morne   a term used throughout the French West Indies to designate the hills of volcanic origin that dot the landscape. Where it is not part of a proper noun, we translate this word as such.

Oiseau de Cham   (lit., Bird of Shem; phon., Bird of the Field) the shadowy (and unacknowledged) figure of the author. Appearing in previous works of Chamoiseau, he is always cast as a marginal character struggling with a study of Martinican life (cf. Afterword). *Oiseau de Cham* is a word play on Chamoiseau *(cham-oiseau),* the author's name. The storyteller's play on his own name is a traditional motif. In one of the book's epigraphs, Edouard Glissant, author of the seminal *Caribbean Discourse,* participates in that play by calling Chamoiseau (or Oiseau de Cham) "game."

pète-bombe   (lit.: farting pot or bomb) hereafter referred to as "top hat"; a variation on the word *bizbonm,* which designates a top or opera hat; the hat would presumably make a flatulent noise when popped open (Jour-dain).

quimboiseurs   a word describing magic users, derived from the old tradi-tion of curing known as Quin/Tiens Bois. Quimboiseurs dispense ancient remedies; they are professional ritual consultants. Also, pejoratively, "evildoers."

Savanna *(la Savane)* in many urban areas in the Caribbean, an open space, sometimes grassy, a central gathering place. Used as an adjective, the word is equivalent to "unofficial."

seyaress   see **C.R.S.**

sleeper-woman   *(femme-dormeuse)* a seer who holds séances and tells the future with her eyes closed in order to receive communications from saints and spirits.

soukougnan   in West Indian folklore, a creature capable of shedding its human skin at night, flying batlike, and emitting light.

SPEDEM   a body governing artistic and industrial copyrights.

tafia   white rum.

tête calendée   a pre-tied madras calendée (cf. above).

the Trail   *(la Trace)* an overland road which goes from Morne Rouge to Fort-de-France through thick forest.

vidé   (from the expression *videz les lieux,* "vacate the premises") in the French Antilles, a noisy parade during Carnival or electoral victory celebrations.

yaws   *(pian)* a skin disease causing yellowish, swollen ulcers that afflicted black slaves brought from Africa to the New World. In the novel it also seems to be used to describe the actual sores caused by the disease. "Mama-yaws" *(mapian)* refers to the principal ulcer.

TRANSLATORS' ACKNOWLEDGMENTS

I would like to thank my undergraduate thesis adviser Andy Parker for allowing me to do an intensive reading of Patrick Chamoiseau by translating his *Solibo Magnifique* (Pantheon Books, forthcoming), a project that gave birth to this one. Many thanks to Amherst College and its Robert Frost Library for continued support (financial and otherwise) in all of our endeavors. I thank François Rigolot and Princeton University for granting me a leave of absence from my graduate program in French literature. We are most grateful to Clarence Brown and all of the generous participants in his translation seminar.

Further south along the Atlantic, I thank Mr. Chamoiseau himself for his gracious fax-to-the-rescue and for granting me an interview. My research trip to Martinique would not have been possible without the support of Ezra Suleiman and the Council on Regional Studies at Princeton University. Thanks to Raphaël and Maryse Confiant, Jacques Coursil, the Berthol-Theodoze family, and Yolande and Adams Kwateh for their hospitality and enouragement, to Manuel and Evelyne Norvat for their input, and to Lucien Taylor for being a supremely gracious host, reader, social and intellectual impresario, chauffeur, and—most important—for being a quickly made friend.

This project would not have been possible without the people at Pantheon Books and the French Publishers Agency. We thank Erroll McDonald, David Kornacker, Nara Nahm, and especially Altie Karper and David Baker for their meticulous and inspired editing.

ROSE-MYRIAM RÉJOUIS,
WITH VAL VINOKUROV. 1996